Liza Marklund is an author, publisher, journalist, columnist, and goodwill ambassador for UNICEF. Her crime novels featuring the relentless reporter Annika Bengtzon instantly became an international hit, and Marklund's books have sold 12 million copies in 30 languages to date. She has achieved the unique feat of being a number one bestseller in all five Nordic countries, and she has been awarded numerous prizes, including a nomination for the Glass Key for best Scandinavian crime novel.

The Annika Bengtzon series is currently being adapted into film.

Neil Smith studied Scandinavian Studies at University College London, and lived in Stockholm for several years. He now lives in Norfolk.

Also by Liza Marklund

RED WOLF

and published by Corgi Books

By Liza Marklund and James Patterson

POSTCARD KILLERS

EXPOSED

Liza Marklund

Translated by Neil Smith

BANTAM PRESS

LONDON · TORONTO · SYDNEY · AUCKLAND · JOHANNESBURG

TRANSWORLD PUBLISHERS
61–63 Uxbridge Road, London W5 5SA
A Random House Group Company
www.rbooks.co.uk

First published in Great Britain
in 2003 by Pocket Books
Corgi edition published 2011

First published in Australia and New Zealand
in 2011 by Bantam Press
an imprint of Transworld Publishers

A CIP catalogue record for this book
is available from the British Library.

ISBN 9780593067963

Addresses for Random House Group Ltd companies outside the UK
can be found at: www.randomhouse.co.uk
The Random House Group Ltd Reg. No. 954009

Typeset in 11/13pt Sabon by
Kestrel Data, Exeter, Devon
Printed and bound in Australia by
Griffin Press, Australia

2 4 6 8 10 9 7 5 3 1

www.randomhouse.com.au
www.randomhouse.co.nz

A Note to the Reader

The events in this book take place several years before those of my previous novel, *Red Wolf*. Chronologically, *Exposed* is the first in the series about crime reporter Annika Bengtzon.

Although the Annika Bengtzon novels form part of a series, they can just as easily be read alone.

You can read an extract from my forthcoming novel, *The Bomber*, at the end of this book.

Enjoy!

Liza Marklund
May 2011

A Note on the Currency

Calculated at a rate of 10.3 Swedish Kronor to the pound, the monetary figures in this book would convert approximately as follows:

10kr = 95p	500kr = £48.50
50kr = £4.85	1000kr = £95
100kr = £9.50	10,000kr = £950
200kr = £19.50	50,000kr = £4850

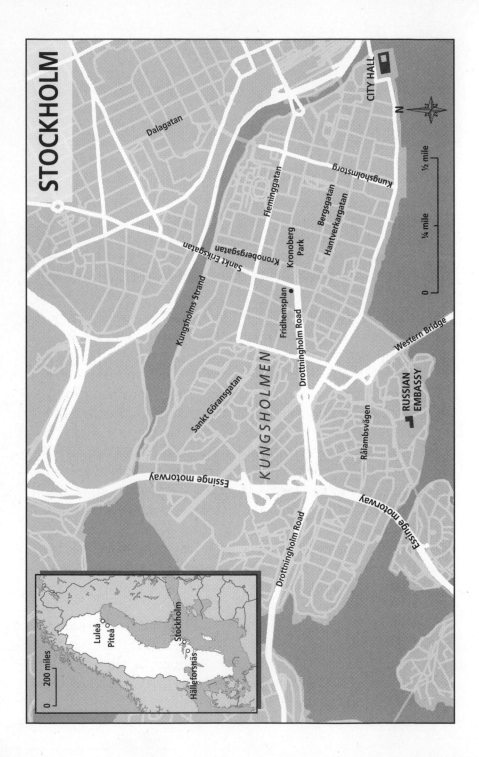

Prologue

The first thing she saw was the pair of knickers hanging from a bush. They were swaying gently, their salmon pink standing out against the lush greenery. Her immediate reaction was anger. Young people had no respect for anything! They couldn't even let the dead rest in peace.

She began to contemplate the decline of society while her dog explored further along the iron railings. She followed the animal down the south side of the cemetery, round the thin trees, and that was where she caught sight of a leg. Her fury rose: how dare they! She saw them every evening, wandering the pavements with their skimpy clothes and their loud voices, offering themselves to men. The fact that the weather was hot was no excuse.

The dog did a little sausage in the grass next to the railings. She looked away and pretended she hadn't seen. There was no one about at this time of day. Why bother putting it in a bag?

'Come on, Jesper,' she said, pulling the dog towards the eastern end of the park. 'Come on, boy.'

She glanced back over her shoulder as she walked away from the railings. The leg was no longer visible, hidden by the thick foliage.

It was going to be another hot day. She could feel beads of sweat forming on her forehead even though the sun had only just risen. She was breathing heavily as she struggled up the slope. The dog was pulling on the lead. His tongue was hanging so far out that it was touching the grass.

How on earth could you just fall asleep in a cemetery, the final resting place of the dead? Was that what feminism was all about, giving young girls a licence to behave badly and show a complete lack of respect?

She was still annoyed. The steep hill was making her mood even worse.

I ought to get rid of this dog, she thought, then felt guilty for thinking it. To make up for her uncharitable thought she bent down to let the dog off the lead, and picked him up for a cuddle. The dog struggled free and rushed off after a squirrel. She sighed. What was the point of trying to be nice?

With another deep sigh she settled onto a bench while Jesper tried to catch the squirrel. After a while the dog had worn himself out and came to a halt under the tree where the little rodent was hiding. She didn't move until the dog had finished dashing about, then she got to her feet again, her dress sticking to her back. The thought of the sweat stains down her spine made her feel embarrassed.

'Come on, Jesper darling. Over here . . .'

She waved a plastic bag full of dog treats, and the short-legged bull-terrier set off towards her. His tongue was hanging out, swinging back and forth, making it look like he was laughing.

'Is this what you want, then? Yes, I thought it might be . . .'

She fed the dog the entire contents of the bag, and took the opportunity to put him back on the lead. It was time to go home. Jesper had had his treats. Now it was her turn: coffee and a Danish pastry.

The dog showed no inclination to go back. He'd caught sight of the squirrel again, and all those dog treats had only renewed his energy for the chase. He protested noisily and furiously.

'I don't want to be out here any longer,' she complained. 'Come on, Jesper!'

They took a different path to avoid the steep slope back home. Going uphill was just about okay, but going down always made her knees ache.

She was walking down the path towards the north-eastern corner of the cemetery when she saw the body. It was lying in thick undergrowth, stretched out, with its arms up behind a broken granite headstone. A fragment of a Star of David was lying next to the head. She felt suddenly afraid. The body was naked, completely motionless and white. The dog pulled loose and rushed at the railings, the lead dancing like an angry snake behind him.

'Jesper!'

He managed to squeeze between two rails and set off towards the dead woman.

'Jesper, come here!'

She was shouting as loud as she dared, because she didn't want to wake anyone living nearby. A lot of people slept with their windows open in this heat; the stone buildings of the city centre never had time to cool down during the short summer nights. She fumbled frantically for more dog treats, but they were all gone.

The bull-terrier stopped beside the woman and eyed her curiously. Then he began to sniff, at first hesitantly, then more eagerly. When he got to her groin he could no longer contain himself.

'JESPER! Come here at once!'

The dog looked up but showed no signs of obeying. Instead he moved up to the woman's head, then started stiffing at the hands. The woman watched in horror as her dog started to chew on the corpse's fingers. Feeling sick, she grabbed at the black railings. She moved slightly to the left and bent down, peering through the headstones. She stared into the dead woman's eyes, just two metres away. They were glazed, slightly clouded, dull and cold. She had a strange sense of all sound around her vanishing; there was just a faint buzzing noise in her left ear.

I have to get the dog away from here, she thought. *I can't tell anyone that Jesper has been chewing on her.*

She got down on her knees and stuck her hand as far as she could through the railings. Her outstretched fingers were pointing right at the woman's dead eyes. Her upper arm was so plump that she almost got stuck, but she just managed to catch hold of the lead. The dog whined as she pulled on the leather strap. He was in no mood to let go of his prey. His jaw was clamped onto the body, which moved slightly.

'You stupid bloody dog!'

With a thud and a whimper he crashed against the railings. She pulled him back through with trembling hands, clutching him like never before, both hands clasped firmly round his stomach. She hurried down to the street, her heels sliding on the grass and straining her thighs.

It wasn't until she had locked the door of her flat behind her and caught sight of the pieces of flesh in the dog's mouth that she started to retch.

Part One
JULY

Seventeen years, four months and sixteen days

I thought love was just for other people, for people more assured, for people who mattered. The fact that I was wrong makes my soul sing with happiness.

I'm the one he wants.

Intoxication, the first touch, the way his fringe fell across one eye when he looked at me, nervous, not at all pushy. Crystal clear: the breeze, the light, the overwhelming sense of fulfilment, the pavement, the warmth of the wall.

I got the one I wanted.

He is my still centre. The other girls smile and flirt, but I'm not jealous. I trust him. I know he's mine. I see him across the room, fair hair shining, the way he brushes it back, his strong hand, my hand. My chest constricts with joy, I am short of breath, tears in my eyes. The light focuses on him, making him strong and complete.

He says he can't manage without me.

His vulnerability lies just beneath his skin. I am lying on his arm and he traces a finger across my face.

Don't ever leave me,
he says,
I can't live without you.

And I promise.

Saturday 28 July

1

'There's a dead girl in Kronoberg Park.'

The voice was breathless, the words slurred, suggesting drug use. Annika Bengtzon looked away from her screen and fumbled for a pen amongst the mess on her desk.

'How do you know?' she asked, sounding more sceptical than was strictly called for.

'Because I'm standing right next to it, for fuck's sake!'

The voice rose to a falsetto and Annika had to hold the phone away from her ear.

'Okay, how dead?' she said, aware that the question sounded ridiculous.

'Bloody hell, completely dead! How dead can you be?'

Annika looked around the newsroom uneasily. Spike, the head of news, was sitting over at the newsdesk, talking on the phone. Anne Snapphane was fanning herself with a pad of paper behind the desk opposite, and Picture-Pelle had just switched on his Mac over at the picture desk.

'I see,' she said, as she found a Biro in an empty coffee cup and an old printout of a news agency telegram, which she started making notes on the back of.

'In Kronoberg Park, you said. Whereabouts?'

'Behind a headstone.'

'Headstone?'

The man on the other end started to cry. Annika waited in silence for a few seconds. She didn't know what to do next. The tip-off line – officially known as the Hotline but only ever referred to in the office as Cold Calls – was almost only ever used by pranksters and nutters. This one was a strong candidate for the latter.

'Hello . . . ?' Annika said cautiously.

The man blew his nose. He took several deep breaths and started talking. Anne Snapphane was watching Annika from the other side of the desk.

'I don't know how you keep answering those calls,' she said when Annika had hung up.

Annika didn't respond, and just carried on making notes on the back of the telegram.

'I have to have another ice-cream or I'll die. Do you want anything from the canteen?' Anne Snapphane asked, standing up.

'I just need to check something first,' Annika said, picking up the phone and dialling the police emergency desk. It was true. Four minutes ago they had received a report of a dead body in the section of the park facing Kronobergsgatan.

Annika got up and went over to the newsdesk, holding the telegram in her hand. Spike was still talking on the phone, his feet up on the desk. Annika stood right in front of him, demanding his attention. The head of news looked up, annoyed.

'Suspected murder, a young girl,' Annika said, waving the printout.

Spike ended his call abruptly by simply putting the phone down, and dropped his feet to the floor.

'Is it from one of the agencies?' he wondered, turning towards his screen.

'No, Cold Calls.'

'Confirmed?'

'The emergency desk have got it, at any rate.'

Spike looked out over the newsroom.

'Okay,' he said. 'Who have we got here?'

Annika made her move. 'It's my tip-off.'

'Berit!' Spike yelled, getting up. 'This year's summer killing!'

Berit Hamrin, one of the paper's older reporters, picked up her handbag and came over to the newsdesk.

'Where's Carl Wennergren? Is he working today?'

'No, he's on holiday, sailing round Gotland,' Annika said. 'This is my tip-off; I took the call.'

'Pelle, pictures!' Spike yelled towards the picture desk.

The picture editor gave him a thumbs-up. 'Bertil Strand,' he shouted.

'Okay,' the head of news said, turning to Annika. 'So what have we got?'

Annika looked down at her scribbled notes, suddenly aware of how nervous she was.

'A dead girl, found behind a headstone in the Jewish Cemetery in Kronoberg Park on Kungsholmen.'

'So it isn't necessarily a murder, is it?'

'She's naked and was strangled.'

Spike looked at Annika intently. 'And you want to do this one yourself?'

Annika swallowed and nodded, and the head of news sat down again and pulled out a pad of paper.

'Okay,' he said. 'You can go with Berit and Bertil. Make sure we get good pictures. We can sort the rest out later, but we have to get good pictures.'

The photographer was pulling on the rucksack

17

containing his equipment as he walked past the newsdesk.

'Where is it, again?' he said, aiming his question at Spike.

'Kronoberg Prison,' Spike said, picking up the phone.

'Park,' Annika said, looking to see where her bag was. 'Kronoberg Park. The Jewish Cemetery.'

'Just make sure it isn't a domestic row,' Spike said, before dialling a London number.

Berit and Bertil Strand were already on their way to the lift down to the garage, but Annika paused.

'What do you mean by that?' she said.

'Exactly what I said. We aren't interested in domestics.'

The head of news turned his back on her demonstratively. Annika felt her anger rise through her body and hit her brain like a shot.

'That wouldn't make the girl any less dead, would it?' she said.

Spike's call was picked up at the other end and she realized the discussion was over. She looked up and saw that Berit and Bertil had already disappeared. She hurried to her desk, pulled out her bag from beneath the desk drawers and ran after her colleagues. The lift had gone, so she took the stairs. Fuck, fuck, why did she always have to argue? She was about to miss her first big story just because she wanted to put the head of news in his place.

'Idiot!' she said out loud to herself.

She caught up with the reporter and photographer at the entrance to the garage.

'Okay, we stick together until there's a good reason to split up,' Berit said, making notes in her pad as she walked. 'I'm Berit Hamrin, by the way. I don't think we've been introduced.'

18

The older woman smiled at Annika, and they shook hands as they got into Bertil Strand's Saab, Annika in the back and Berit in the front.

'There's no need to slam the door so hard,' Bertil Strand said, looking at Annika reproachfully over his shoulder. 'You'll damage the paintwork.'

Good God, Annika thought.

'Oh, sorry,' she said.

The photographers treated the newspaper's vehicles as their personal company cars. Almost all of them took their responsibilities extremely seriously. Maybe that was because the photographers, without exception, were all men, Annika thought. Even though she'd only been at the *Evening Post* for seven weeks, she was already well aware of the sanctity of the photographers' cars. She'd had to postpone several interviews because various photographers had been busy putting their cars through the carwash. And that also gave her an indication of just how important people thought her articles were.

'It's probably best to avoid Fridhemsplan and approach the park by the side streets,' Berit said as the car approached Rålambsvägen. Bertil Strand put his foot down and just made the lights, heading off down Gjörwellsgatan towards Norr Mälarstrand.

'Can you run through what the bloke on the phone told you?' Berit said, swivelling in her chair so she could look back at Annika.

Annika pulled out the crumpled telegram.

'Well, there's a young girl lying dead behind a headstone in Kronoberg Park. Naked, probably strangled.'

'Who was the caller?'

'Some junkie, from the sound of it. His mate was taking a piss against the railings and caught sight of her through the bushes.'

'Why did they think she'd been strangled?'

Annika turned the paper to read something she'd written along the edge of the sheet.

'There was no blood, her eyes were wide open and there were marks on her neck.'

'That doesn't necessarily mean she was strangled, or even murdered,' Berit said, turning to look ahead again.

Annika didn't answer. She looked out through the Saab's tinted windows at the people sunbathing in Rålambshov Park. The glittering waters of Riddarfjärden spread out ahead of them. She had to squint, in spite of the tinted glass. There were two windsurfers heading towards the island of Långholmen, but they weren't doing terribly well. There was scarcely any breeze to lift the heat today.

'What a great summer we're having,' Bertil Strand said, turning left into Polhemsgatan. 'Pretty unexpected, after all the rain we had in the spring.'

'Yes, I was lucky,' Berit said. 'I've just had my four weeks off. Sun every single day. We can leave the car just behind the fire station.'

The Saab cruised the last few blocks of Bergsgatan. Berit had undone her seatbelt before Bertil Strand even hit the brakes, and was out of the car before it stopped. Annika hurried after her, momentarily taken aback as the heat outside hit her.

Bertil Strand parked in a turning circle as Berit and Annika headed off along the side of a red-brick building from the fifties. The tarmac path was narrow, with a stone kerb along the edge of the park.

'There's a flight of steps up here,' Berit said, already out of breath.

Six steps later and they were up in the park itself. They jogged along a tarmac path that led to an elaborate playground.

To their right were several sheds; Annika read the words 'Park Games' as she ran past. There was a sandpit, benches, picnic tables, climbing frames, slides, swings and other things for kids to climb and play on. A few mothers and their children were in the playground, but it looked like they were packing up. At the far end two uniformed policemen were talking to another mother.

'I think the cemetery's a bit further down, towards Sankt Göransgatan,' Berit said.

'You certainly know your way around,' Annika said. 'Do you live near here?'

'No,' Berit said. 'This isn't the first murder in this park.'

Annika saw that the police were busy unrolling their blue and white tape to cordon off the area. So they were emptying the playground and closing it off to the public.

'It's a good job we got here quickly,' she muttered to herself.

They turned off to the right, following a path that led to the top of the hill.

'Down to the left,' Berit said.

Annika ran on ahead, crossing two more paths, and suddenly there it was. She saw a row of black Stars of David standing out against the greenery.

'I can see it,' she shouted behind her, and from the corner of her eye saw that Bertil Strand had almost caught up with Berit.

The railings were black, and attractively ornate. The iron uprights were linked by metal circles and bows. Each railing was crowned by a stylized Star of David. She was running into her own shadow and realized that she was approaching the cemetery from the south.

She stopped on the little hill overlooking the graves, where she could get a good view. The police hadn't

21

cordoned off this section of the park yet, but she could see that the northern and western approaches had already been blocked.

'Hurry up!' she called to Berit and Bertil Strand.

The railings enclosed the little Jewish cemetery and its worn granite headstones. Annika quickly counted thirty or so of them. The vegetation had almost taken over and the whole area looked overgrown and neglected. The cemetery covered an area of some thirty metres by forty. On the far side, the railings were little more than a metre and a half high. The entrance was on the western side, towards Kronobergsgatan and Fridhemsplan. She saw the team from the other evening paper stop at the cordon. A group of men, all of them in plain clothes, were inside the railings, at the east side of the cemetery. She realized why they were there: that was where the woman's body was.

Annika shivered. She mustn't mess this up, her first decent tip-off of the summer.

Berit and Bertil Strand came up behind her, and at that moment she saw a man open the gate in the railings down by Kronobergsgatan. He was carrying some grey material. Annika gasped. They hadn't covered her up yet!

'Come on, quick!' she called over her shoulder. 'We might be able to get a picture from up here.'

A policeman appeared on the crown of the hill in front of them. He was rolling out blue and white tape. Annika rushed down towards the railings, and could hear Bertil Strand behind her. Over those last metres before the railings he shrugged off his rucksack and pulled out a Canon with a telephoto lens. The grey sheet was just three metres away as Bertil Strand clicked off a whole series of shots in amongst the bushes. He moved half a metre to his left and took another sequence. The policeman holding the roll of tape shouted something, and the men inside the railings caught sight of them.

'Got it!' Bertil Strand said. 'We've got enough pictures to cover the story now.'

'Hey, what do you think you're doing?' the policeman with the tape shouted. 'We're cordoning off this area.'

A man in a Hawaiian shirt and Bermuda shorts was walking towards them inside the cemetery.

'Okay, it's time for you to leave,' he said.

Annika looked round, unsure of what to do. Bertil Strand was already heading towards the path that led to Sankt Göransgatan. The policemen in front of her and behind her both looked extremely annoyed. She realized she would have to move, otherwise the police would move her themselves. Instinctively, she shifted sideways to where Bertil Strand had taken his first pictures.

She peered through the black railings, and there was the young woman. Her eyes were staring right into Annika's from a distance of just two metres away. They were clouded and grey. Her head was tilted back, her upper arms were pointing away from her body, and her lower arms sticking up above her head. One hand seemed to have been injured. Her mouth was open in a soundless scream, the lips black-brown. Her hair was moving slightly in the imperceptible breeze. She had a large bruise on her left breast, and the lower portion of her stomach looked eerily green.

Annika absorbed the whole image, crystal clear, just for a moment. The harsh greyness of the stone in the background, the subtle green of the plants, the shadows of the leaves, the dampness and heat, the repulsive smell.

Then the sheet appeared, turning the whole scene grey. They were covering up the railings, not the body.

23

'Time to go,' the policeman with the tape said, putting a hand on her shoulder.

Such a bloody stereotype, Annika found herself thinking as she turned round.

Her mouth was completely dry, and she noticed that everything she heard seemed to come from a long way away. She moved, slightly unsteadily, towards where Berit and Bertil Strand were standing waiting behind the cordon. The photographer looked bored and unhappy, but Berit was almost smiling.

The policeman followed her, with his shoulder rubbing against her back. It had to be very hot having to wear a uniform like that on a day like this, Annika thought.

'Did you see anything?' Berit asked.

Annika nodded, and Berit jotted something down.

'Did you manage to ask the detective in the Hawaiian shirt anything?'

Annika shook her head and crept under the length of tape with the obliging help of the policeman.

'That's a shame. Did he say anything that you happened to overhear?'

'"Okay, it's time for you to leave",' Annika quoted, and Berit smiled.

'How about you, are you okay?' she asked, and Annika nodded.

'Oh, I'm fine. She might well have been strangled, her eyes were popping out. She must have been trying to scream when she died, her mouth was wide open.'

'Maybe someone heard her. We'll talk to the neighbours later. Was she Swedish?'

Annika suddenly felt that she had to sit down.

'I forgot to ask . . .'

Berit smiled again.

'Blonde, dark, young, old?'

'Twenty, tops. Long fair hair. Big breasts. Silicone, probably, or saline implants.'

Berit looked at her quizzically. She sank down into the grass with her legs crossed.

'Her tits were standing straight up, even though she was on her back. And she had a scar in her armpit.'

Annika could feel her blood pressure plummeting. She lowered her head to her knees, taking several deep breaths.

'Not a pretty sight, then?' Berit said.

'I'm okay,' Annika said.

After a minute or so she felt better. The noises around her were overwhelming: the traffic thundering along the Drottningholm road, two sirens wailing out of sync, voices shouting, the clatter of cameras, a child crying.

Bertil Strand had joined the group of reporters gathering at the entrance to the cemetery, and was chatting to the photographer from the other evening paper.

'Who's doing what?' Annika said.

Berit sat down next to Annika, looked down at her notes and started doodling.

'We can probably assume this is a murder, can't we? So to start with, we need an article about the event itself. This has happened, a young woman has been found murdered. When, where, how? We'll have to get hold of the man who found her and talk to him. You got his name, didn't you?'

'He's an addict. His friend gave a care-of address for the tip-off money.'

'Try to get hold of him. The police emergency room will have the details of the call they received,' Berit said, ticking off one of the things on her list.

'Already done.'

'Good. Then we need to get hold of a policeman who's prepared to talk. Their press spokesman never says anything off the record. Did that Hawaiian detective give his name?'

'Nope.'

'That's a shame. Try to find out. I've never seen him before; he might well be new in violent crime. Then we need to find out when she died, and why. And if they have any suspects, what's next for the investigation, the whole police angle.'

'Okay,' Annika said, making notes in her own pad.

'God, it's hot. Has it ever been this hot in Stockholm before?' Berit said, wiping the sweat from her brow.

'No idea,' Annika said. 'I only moved here seven weeks ago.'

Berit took a tissue from her bag and dabbed at her forehead.

'Right, then we've got the victim,' she said. 'Who was she? Who identified her? Presumably there's a devastated family somewhere in Sweden – we need to think about whether or not to contact them. We need pictures of the girl when she was alive. Do you think she was over eighteen?'

Annika thought for a moment, remembering the breast enlargements.

'Yes, probably.'

'So there should be pictures of her from her school graduation. All kids stay on through high school these days. And there are always pictures of them wearing their graduation caps. What do her friends have to say? Did she have a boyfriend?'

Annika made some more notes.

'Then there's the neighbours' reactions,' Berit went on. 'We're right in the middle of Stockholm – there are more than three hundred thousand women living in the vicinity. A crime like this has implications for everyone's security. What impact will it have on nightlife, on the image of the city? Well, that's probably two articles. If you take the neighbours, I'll take the rest.'

Annika nodded without looking up.

'And then there's one last aspect,' Berit said, dropping her pad to her lap. 'There was an almost identical case to this one just a hundred metres or so away, twelve or thirteen years ago.'

Annika looked up in surprise.

'If I remember rightly, a young woman was raped and murdered on some steps on the north side of the park,' Berit said thoughtfully. 'The killer was never caught.'

'Bloody hell,' Annika said. 'So it could be the same bloke?'

Berit shrugged. 'Probably not. But we'll have to mention the other murder. A lot of people are bound to remember it. The woman was raped, then strangled.'

Annika gulped. 'God, this is a terrible job really, isn't it?' she said.

'Yes, it really is,' Berit said. 'But it'll be a lot easier if you manage to get hold of our Hawaiian detective before he leaves the park.'

She pointed towards Sankt Göransgatan, where the man in the Hawaiian shirt had just left the cemetery. He was walking towards a car parked on the corner of Kronobergsgatan. Annika flew up, grabbed her bag and rushed down towards the road. She could see the reporter from the other paper trying to talk to the detective, but he simply brushed him aside.

Just then Annika stumbled on the kerb of a path and almost fell. Unable to slow down, she careered down the steep slope towards the street. There was nothing she could do to stop herself crashing into the back of the

Hawaiian detective, who was thrown onto the bonnet of his car.

'What the hell!' he yelled, grabbing Annika's arms in a vicelike grip.

'Sorry,' she squeaked. 'I couldn't help it. I lost my balance.'

'What the hell are you playing at? Are you mad?'

The man was shaken, and not a little alarmed.

'Sorry,' Annika said, feeling that she was on the verge of bursting into tears. Besides, her left wrist was aching badly.

The man pulled himself together and let go of her. He stared at her for a few seconds.

'You need to calm down. Seriously,' he said as he got into his burgundy Volvo estate and drove off with a squeal of tyres.

'Fuck,' Annika said to herself. She blinked to get rid of the tears and squinted into the sunlight to make a note of the car's police call number. She thought it said '1813' on the side. Just to be sure, she memorized the number plate as well.

Then she turned round, and saw that the whole group of reporters at the entrance was staring at her. She blushed bright red and bent over to gather together everything that had fallen out of her bag when she hit the detective: her A5 pad, a packet of chewing-gum, an almost empty bottle of Pepsi Max, and three sanitary pads in green plastic wrappers. Her pen was still in the bag. She pulled it out and quickly jotted down the car's call number and registration in her pad.

The journalists and photographers looked away and went back to chatting among themselves. Annika noted that Bertil Strand seemed to be organizing a trip to buy ice-creams.

She hoisted her bag onto her shoulder and slowly

walked over to her colleagues. They didn't appear to pay her any attention at all. Apart from the reporter from the other evening paper – a middle-aged man whose picture always appeared next to his articles – she didn't recognize any of them. There was a young woman holding recording equipment with the Radio Stockholm logo on it, two photographers from different picture agencies, the other paper's photographer, and three reporters she couldn't place. No television crew yet, there were only five minutes of local news on the main channel in the summer, and local news on the commercial channels was little more than someone just reading reports from the news agencies. Presumably the morning papers would run pictures from the agencies and base their articles on agency reports. There was no sign of the main radio news team, but she hadn't really expected to see them there. One of her former colleagues at the *Katrineholm Courier*, who had spent a summer working with radio news, had once explained the way they worked.

'We don't cover murders and that sort of thing. We leave that to the tabloids. We're not ambulance chasers.'

Annika had realized that that statement said more about her colleague than it did about radio news, but sometimes she had to wonder. Why didn't they regard a young woman's life being snuffed out as a matter of public interest? She couldn't understand that.

The other people gathered behind the cordon were curious members of the public.

She walked slowly away from the group. The police, both detectives and the forensics team, were busy inside the railings. There was no sign of an ambulance or hearse. She looked at her watch. Seventeen minutes past one. Twenty-five minutes since she got the tip-off from

29

Cold Calls. She wasn't sure what to do next. There was no point trying to talk to the police, they'd probably only get annoyed. She also guessed that they wouldn't know anything yet – not the identity of the woman, or how she had died, or who might have done it.

She headed towards the Drottningholm road. A small slice of shade had formed by the buildings on the western side of Kronobergsgatan, and she went over and leaned against one of the walls. It was rough, grey and hot. The temperature was only a degree or so cooler than out in the full sun, and the air was burning her throat. She was horribly thirsty, and fished the bottle of Pepsi from her bag. The cap had leaked, making the outside of the bottle sticky, and her fingers stuck to the label. Oh, this fucking heat!

She drank the warm, flat liquid and hid the bottle between two bundles of newspapers waiting to be picked up for recycling in the nearest doorway.

The journalists over by the cordon had moved to the other side of the street. Presumably they were waiting for Bertil Strand to turn up with their ice-creams. For some reason the situation made her feel sick. A few metres away from them there were flies buzzing round a corpse while they were looking forward to ice-cream.

She looked across at the park. Steep, grass-covered hills and a lot of big deciduous trees. From her place in the shade she could see lime trees, beech, elm, ash and birch. Some were enormous, others newly planted. In amongst the gravestones were several gigantic trees, mostly limes.

I really need something else to drink, she thought.

She sat down on the pavement and leaned her head back. Something had to happen soon. She couldn't just sit here.

2

The crowd of journalists was starting to thin out now. The girl from Radio Stockholm had left, but Bertil Strand had returned with the ice-creams. There was no sign of Berit Hamrin anywhere, and Annika wondered where she'd gone.

I'll wait another five minutes, she thought. Then I'll go and get a drink and start talking to the neighbours.

She tried to picture a map of Stockholm in her head, and work out exactly where she was. This was the very heart of Stockholm, the original city within the old tollgates. She looked towards the fire station to the south. In that direction lay Hantverkargatan, her street. She lived less than ten blocks from here, in a small building in the courtyard of a condemned property not far from Kungsholmstorg. Even so, she had never been up here before.

Beneath her was Fridhemsplan underground station. If she concentrated she could just make out the rumbling of the trains moving far below, their vibrations passing through concrete and asphalt. In front of her was a large, circular air vent from the tunnels, public toilets and a park bench. That could have been where the junkie who phoned Cold Calls was sitting in the sun while his mate went off for a piss. But why wouldn't he just have used the public toilets? Annika wondered.

She thought about this for few moments, and in the end she had to go and take a look at the toilets. As soon as she opened the door she understood why. The stench inside was quite unbearable. She backed away a couple of steps and let the door close.

A woman pushing a buggy was heading towards her from the playground. The child in the buggy was clutching a beaker containing a red liquid. The mother was staring resentfully at the blue and white tape along the edge of the park.

'What's going on?' she called.

Annika straightened up and hoisted the bag further onto her shoulder.

'The police have cordoned off the park,' she said.

'I can see that. Why?'

Annika hesitated. She glanced over her shoulder and could see that the other journalists were watching her. She took a couple of quick steps towards the woman.

'They've found a woman's body in there,' she said quietly, gesturing towards the cemetery. The mother's face went white.

'Bloody hell,' she said.

'Do you live nearby?' Annika asked.

'Yes, just round the corner. We've been down to Rålambshov Park, but it was so crowded you could hardly find space to sit down, so we decided to come up here instead. Is she still in there?'

The woman craned her neck to peer in through the lime trees. Annika nodded.

'That's terrible!' the woman burst out, staring at Annika with wide-open eyes.

'Do you often come here?' Annika asked.

'Yes, every day. My little one goes to the playgroup in the park.'

The mother couldn't tear her eyes from the cemetery. Annika looked at her for several seconds.

'Did you hear anything unusual last night or this morning? Any shouting from the park, anything like that?'

The woman bit her lip as she thought, then shook her head.

'There's always a lot of commotion around here. The first few years I was here I used to wake up every time the fire brigade set out, but not any more. Then there are the drunks down on Sankt Eriksgatan. I don't mean the ones in the hostel, they never manage to stay awake until it's dark. No, just the usual piss artists. They can keep you awake all night. But worst of all is actually the air-conditioning unit behind McDonald's. It's on twenty-four hours a day, and it's driving me round the bend. How did she die?'

'They don't know yet,' Annika said. 'So there was no shouting, no calls for help?'

'Well of course there was, there's shouting and screaming here every Friday night. Here, darling, there you are . . .'

The child had dropped the beaker and started to grizzle, and his mother picked it up. Then she nodded in the direction of Bertil Strand and the others.

'Are they the hyenas?'

'Yep. The one with the Dime ice-cream is my photographer. I'm Annika Bengtzon, I'm with the *Evening Post*.'

She held out her hand. In spite of what she had just said, the woman seemed impressed.

'Bloody hell,' she said. 'Daniella Hermansson; nice to meet you. Are you going to write about this?'

'Yes, me or someone else on the paper. Do you mind if I take some notes?'

'Sure, go ahead.'

'Can I quote you?'

'My name's got two "l"s and two "s"s, just like it sounds.'

'You were saying that it's normally quite rowdy around here?'

Daniella Hermansson stood on tiptoe and tried to look at Annika's notes.

'Yes, really rowdy,' she said. 'Especially at weekends.'

'So if anyone did call for help, people probably wouldn't react?'

Daniella Hermansson bit her lip again and shook her head.

'Mind you, that would depend on what time it was,' she said. 'By four or five in the morning things have normally calmed down. Then it's just the air-conditioning unit. I sleep with my window open, all year round, it's good for the skin. But I didn't hear anything . . .'

'Do your windows face the street or the courtyard?'

'Both. We've got a two-room flat, at the end on the right, second floor. The bedroom faces the yard.'

'And you come here every day?'

'Yes, I'm still on maternity leave with this little one. All the mums round here meet in the playground every morning. No, darling . . .'

The child had stopped drinking and had started to howl. His mother leaned over him, and with a practised hand stuck a finger in the back of his nappy and sniffed it.

'Oops,' she said. 'Time for us to go in. Nappy change and then a nap, eh, tiddler?'

The child stopped howling when he found a string on his hat to chew on.

'Could we take your picture?' Annika asked quickly.

Daniella Hermansson looked startled.

'My picture? Oh, surely you don't want . . .' She giggled and ran a hand through her hair. Annika gave her a stern look.

'The woman over in the cemetery was probably murdered,' she said. 'It's really important to give a good description of the area. I live down by Kungsholmstorg.'

Daniella Hermansson's eyes were wide open.

'Bloody hell. Murdered? Here, in our park?'

'No one knows where she died, only that she was found here.'

'But it's always so quiet round here,' Daniella Hermansson said, bending over and picking up the child.

Welcome to Cliché Central, Annika thought. A minute ago it was rowdy round here.

The boy let go of the string and started howling again. Annika took a firm grip of the strap of her bag and went over to Bertil Strand.

'Hang on,' she said to Daniella over her shoulder.

The photographer was licking the inside of his ice-cream wrapper as Annika came up to him.

'Can you come with me for a moment?' she asked quietly.

Bertil Strand crumpled the wrapper slowly in his hand, then gestured to the man beside him.

'Annika, this is Arne Påhlson, he's a reporter for our rivals. Have you met?'

Looking down, Annika held out her hand and muttered her name. Arne Påhlson's hand was hot and sweaty.

'Have you finished your ice-cream?' she asked pointedly.

Bertil Strand's suntan turned a shade darker. He didn't like the idea of being shown up by someone who was just a summer temp. Instead of answering he bent over and picked up his rucksack.

'Where are we going?'

Annika turned round and went back to Daniella Hermansson. She glanced over towards the cemetery, where the plain-clothes officers were still standing, deep in conversation.

The child was still crying, but his mother was ignoring him now. She was busy putting lipstick on, peering into the mirror on the back of a pale-green lipstick holder.

'So, how did you feel when you heard there was a woman lying dead outside your bedroom window?' Annika said, making notes.

'Awful,' Daniella Hermansson said. 'I mean, the number of times my friends and I have come back this way late from the pub. It could have been any of us . . .'

'Will this make you take more precautions in future?'

'Yes, absolutely,' Daniella Hermansson said without a moment's hesitation. 'I'm never walking through the park at night again. Oh, now come on, you're all upset, aren't you . . . ?'

Daniella bent down to pick up her son again. Annika was taking notes, and could feel the hairs on the back of her neck prickle. This was really good stuff. It might even make a headline, with a bit of editing.

'Thanks very much,' she said quickly. 'Could you look towards Bertil? What's your son's name? How old is he? And how old are you? And what title should we use? Maternity leave, okay. Maybe it would be better if you didn't look quite so cheerful . . . ?'

Daniella Hermansson's practised smile, the one that

she probably used in every holiday and Christmas photograph, faded. Now she just looked confused and lost instead. Bertil Strand took a whole series of shots, moving round the woman and child with careful little dance steps.

'Can I call you later if I need to? What's your phone number? And the code for the door? Just in case . . .'

Daniella Hermansson squeezed the shrieking toddler back in the buggy and headed off along the edge of the cordon. To her annoyance, Annika watched Arne Påhlson from the other evening paper stop her as she went past. As luck would have it, the child was screaming so hard that the young woman couldn't stop for another interview.

Annika breathed out.

'Don't try to tell me my job,' Bertil Strand said.

'Okay,' Annika said. 'So what would have happened if they'd brought the body out while you were off buying ice-cream for our rivals?'

Bertil Strand looked at her disdainfully.

'When we're out in the field we're not rivals, we're colleagues,' he said.

'I think you're wrong,' Annika said. 'We can't get good journalism if we hunt as a pack. We ought to maintain a bit more distance, all of us.'

'No one benefits from that.'

'Yes they do – our readers. And our credibility.'

Bertil Strand hoisted the bag of cameras onto his back.

'Thanks for telling me. I've only been with the paper for the past fifteen years.'

Fucking fuck, Annika thought as the photographer headed back to his 'colleagues'. Why can't I ever learn to keep my mouth shut?

She suddenly felt dizzy and weak. I have to get

something to drink, right now, she thought. To her relief she caught sight of Berit walking up from Hantverkargatan.

'Where have you been?' Annika called, walking towards her.

Berit groaned. 'I went back to the car to make some calls. I put in a request to have the cuttings of the previous murder sent up from the archive, and spoke to a few police contacts.'

She was trying in vain to cool herself by fanning one hand.

'Has anything happened?'

'I've just been speaking to one of the neighbours.'

'Have you had anything to drink? You're looking a bit pale.'

Annika wiped the sweat from her forehead and suddenly felt like she was about to cry.

'I said something really stupid to Bertil Strand just now,' she said quietly. 'About not being too chummy with our competitors when we're out at a crime scene.'

'I couldn't agree more. And I know that Bertil Strand doesn't agree,' Berit said. 'He can be a bit tricky to get on with at times, but he's a very good photographer. Go and get something to drink. I'll keep an eye on things here.'

Annika was only too happy to leave Kronobergs-gatan, and headed off along the Drottningholm road. She was standing in the queue to buy a bottle of mineral water at a kiosk on Fridhemsplan when she saw a police van turn left into Sankt Göransgatan, heading up towards Kronoberg Park.

'Shit,' she cried, running straight out into the traffic, forcing a taxi to slam on its brakes. She ran across Sankt Eriksgatan, back towards the park. She felt like she was about to faint by the time she got back.

The police van had stopped at the top of Sankt Göransgatan, and a man and a woman were just getting out.

'Why are you so out of breath?' Berit wondered.

'The van . . . the body . . .' Annika panted, resting her hands on her knees and leaning forward.

Berit sighed. 'The van will be here for a while yet. That body isn't going anywhere. Don't worry so much, we won't miss anything.'

Annika dropped her bag on the pavement and stood up.

'Sorry,' she said.

Berit smiled. 'Go and sit in the shade. I'll get you something to drink.'

Annika trudged off into the shadows. She felt like a real idiot.

'I didn't know,' she muttered. 'How could I . . . ?'

She sat down on the pavement and leaned back against the wall again. The pavement burned her backside through her thin skirt.

3

The pair who had got out of the van were standing inside the cordon next to the gate, waiting. There were still three men inside the cemetery; she guessed that two were forensics officers and the third a photographer. They were moving very carefully, leaning down to pick things up, standing up again. They were too far away for her to see exactly what they were doing. Is it always this boring at the scene of a murder? she wondered.

Berit came back a couple of minutes later. She was holding a large, chilled bottle of Coca-Cola.

'Here you go; this has got lots of sugar and minerals in it. Just what you need.'

Annika unscrewed the top and drank so quickly that the bubbles went up her nose. She coughed, spilling some of the Coke on her skirt.

Berit sat down beside her and pulled her own bottle out of her bag.

'What are they actually doing in there?' Annika asked.

'They're checking for footprints. They use as few people as possible, and they move as little as possible. Usually it's just a couple of forensics officers and maybe one of the detectives from the crime unit.'

'Do you think that was the guy in the Hawaiian shirt?'

'Maybe,' Berit said. 'If you look closely you might see one of the forensics officers holding his hand close to his mouth. He's recording the details of everything they see at the scene on a small recorder. Everything from a precise description of how the body is lying, to the way the folds of the clothing are arranged, anything like that.'

'She wasn't wearing any clothes,' Annika said.

'Maybe the clothes are nearby. They document everything. When they're done, the body will be taken to the forensics lab out in Solna.'

'For a post-mortem?'

Berit nodded. 'The forensics team will stay behind here and search the entire park. They'll go through it centimetre by centimetre, checking for any signs of blood, saliva, hair, fibres, sperm, footprints, tyre tracks, fingerprints, anything at all.'

Annika sat in silence and watched the men inside the railings for a while. They were bending down by the body; she could see their heads bobbing against the grey backcloth.

'Why have they covered the railings and not the body?' she asked.

'They don't usually cover the body at the crime scene unless there's a risk of rain,' Berit said. 'It's all about gathering evidence, and they want to cause as little disturbance as possible. They just put that cloth up to stop people looking in. Pretty smart, really . . .'

The forensics officers and photographer stood up in unison.

'Right, it's time,' Berit said.

They got up, as did the journalists a short distance away from them. They all moved closer to the cordon,

41

as if responding to an unspoken command. The photographers readied their cameras and made sure they had different lenses ready to hand. A couple more journalists had joined the group, Annika counted five photographers and six reporters. One of them, a young man, was carrying a laptop with the logo of the main Swedish news agency, and there was a woman with a notepad from *Sydsvenskan*, the regional paper in the far south of Sweden.

The man and woman from the police van opened the back doors and pulled out a collapsible trolley. They opened it out with calm, practised movements, and secured the various fastenings. Annika felt the hairs on her arms stand up. A bubble of carbon dioxide rose from her stomach, making her feel queasy. They were about to bring the body out. She was ashamed at her morbid curiosity.

'Can you move aside, please?' the woman pushing the trolley said.

Annika looked at the trolley as it rolled past. It shook as the wheels rattled over the rough pavement. On top was a neatly folded blue-stippled plastic sheet. The shroud, Annika thought, and a cold shiver went up her spine.

The pair crept under the cordon. The orange 'Keep Out' sign hanging from it carried on swinging long after they had passed.

They had reached the body. The little group stood there, discussing what to do. Annika could feel the sun on the back of her arms.

'Why is it taking so long?' she said in a stage whisper to Berit.

Berit didn't answer. Annika pulled the Coke from her bag and took a few sips.

'Isn't it awful?' the woman from *Sydsvenskan* said.

'Yes, isn't it?' Annika said.

As the plastic sheet was spread over the trolley, it fluttered behind the foliage. They lifted the young woman onto the trolley and covered her in plastic. Suddenly Annika felt tears pricking her eyes. She saw the woman's soundless scream, her clouded eyes, bruised chest.

I mustn't start crying, she thought, staring at the worn headstones. She tried to read names and dates, but the inscriptions were in Hebrew. The ornate letters had been almost completely worn away by time and weather. Suddenly everything was very quiet. Even the traffic on the Drottningholm road seemed to have stopped for a moment. The sun filtering through the heavy treetops danced over the granite.

This cemetery was here before the city, Annika thought. And these trees were already here when the dead were buried. They would have been smaller, less sturdy, but their leaves would have cast the same shadows when the graves were freshly dug.

The gates opened, the photographers got to work. One of them forced his way past Annika, elbowing her in the stomach and making her gasp. She stumbled backwards in shock, and lost sight of the trolley. She took a few quick steps back towards the van.

I wonder which end her head is, Annika thought. They'd hardly push her feet first, would they?

The photographers followed the trolley along the length of the cordon. The cameras were clicking in an uneven rhythm, and one or two flashes went off. Bertil Strand was jumping about behind his colleagues, holding his camera either above them or between them. Annika was holding tight to the door of the van, the hot metal burning her fingers. Through the flashes she watched the bundle containing the woman's body come closer. The van driver stopped just a foot or so away from her. As he fiddled with the catches on the trolley, Annika could see how sweaty and stressed he was. She looked down at the plastic.

I wonder if the sun has kept her warm, she thought.

I wonder who she is.

I wonder if she knew she was about to die.

I wonder if she had time to feel scared.

Suddenly the tears started to fall. She let go of the van door, turned and took a step back. The ground felt unsteady, and she thought she was going to be sick.

'It's the smell, and the heat,' Berit said, suddenly appearing at Annika's side. She put an arm round her shoulders and led her away from the van.

Annika wiped away her tears.

'Right, time to get back to the newsroom,' Berit said.

4

Patricia woke up feeling stifled. There was no air in the room, she couldn't breathe. Gradually she became aware of her own body on the mattress, completely naked. When she raised her left arm, sweat ran down her ribs and into her navel.

God, she thought. I have to get some air! And water!

She thought about calling for Josefin, but something made her decide not to. The flat was completely quiet, so either Josie was still asleep or she'd already gone out. Patricia groaned and rolled over, wondering what time it was. Josefin's black curtains shut out the daylight, leaving the room in gloomy darkness. It smelled of sweat and dust.

'It's a bad omen,' Patricia had said when Josefin came home with the heavy black material. 'You can't have black curtains. It means the windows are in mourning. It gets in the way of positive energy.'

Josefin had just got cross.

'That's crap,' she had said. 'Okay, go without, then. But I want my room to be dark. How the fuck are we going to work nights if we never get any sleep? Any better ideas?'

Naturally, Josefin had got her way, like she usually did.

Patricia sat up with a sigh. The bottom sheet had wound itself up into a damp umbilical cord running down the middle of the bed. Suddenly annoyed, she tried to straighten it out.

It's Josie's turn to go shopping, she thought, so there probably isn't any food in the house.

She got up and went to the bathroom. Then she put on Josie's dressing-gown and went back to her room to open the curtains. The light hit her eyes like metal spikes, and she quickly closed the curtains again. Instead she opened one of the windows wide, wedging a flowerpot to stop it from slamming shut. The air outside was hotter than indoors, but at least it didn't smell.

She wandered slowly out to the kitchen, filled a beer glass with tap water and drank greedily. She felt better straight away. At least she hadn't slept the whole day away, even though she'd been working till five that morning. She put the glass on the draining board, between an empty pizza box and three mugs containing dried-up teabags. Josie was hopeless at cleaning. Patricia sighed and started to tidy up, throwing away the rubbish and doing the washing-up without really thinking about it.

She was on her way to have a shower when the phone rang.

'Is Josie there?'

It was Joachim. Without realizing she was doing it, Patricia straightened up and made an effort to sound together.

'I'm only just up, I don't actually know. She might still be asleep.'

'Would you mind getting her? Thanks.' His tone of voice was curt but friendly.

'*En seguida*, Joachim. Hang on a moment . . .'

She padded along the hall to Josefin's room and knocked gently on the door. When there was no answer she carefully pushed it open. The bed was just as it had been before Patricia went to work. She hurried back to the phone.

'No, sorry; she must have gone out.'

'Where? Is she meeting someone?'

Patricia laughed nervously. 'No, of course not; unless she's gone to see you? I don't know. It's her turn to do the shopping . . .'

'But she definitely came home last night?'

Patricia tried to sound indignant. 'Of course she did. Where else would she sleep?'

'Exactly, Patty. Any ideas?'

He had already hung up by the time Patricia realized how annoyed she was. She hated it when he called her that. He only did it to humiliate her. He didn't like the fact that she came between him and Josefin.

Patricia went slowly back to Josefin's bedroom and peered in. The bed looked exactly as it had the previous evening, the duvet on the floor to the left of the bed, and Josefin's red bathing suit on the pillow.

Josie hadn't come home last night.

The realization made her very uneasy.

5

The air of the newspaper's lobby hit the staff like a cold, wet flannel. The moisture in the air was making the marble floor shine, as well as the bronze bust of the paper's founder. Annika shivered as her teeth began to chatter. Behind the glass of the receptionist's booth, Tore Brand, one of the caretakers, was in a bad mood.

'It's all right for you,' he called as the little group went towards the lifts. 'You can go outside and thaw every now and then. It's so cold in here that I've had to bring in one of the car-heaters to stop my feet freezing.'

Annika tried to smile, but couldn't summon up the energy. Unlike most people, Tore Brand was having to wait until August for his holiday this year, and he seemed to regard this as a personal insult.

'I have to go to the toilet,' Annika said. 'I'll catch you up.'

As she went past Tore Brand's little booth she could tell he had been smoking on duty again. After a moment's hesitation, she went into the disabled toilet rather than the ladies'. She wanted to be alone, not to have to jostle with other sweaty women at the hand-basins.

Tore Brand's complaints followed her into the toilet. She locked the door and looked at her reflection in the mirror. She really did look terrible. Her face was blotchy and her eyes red. She turned the mixer tap to cold, bent over, pulled up her hair and let the cold water run over her neck. The porcelain was ice-cold against her forehead. A trickle of water ran down her spine.

Why on earth am I doing this? she thought. Why aren't I lying in the sun by a lake up in Norrbotten reading a trashy magazine?

She pressed the red button on the dryer and held the neck of her top open, trying to dry her armpits. It didn't really work.

Anne Snapphane's chair was empty when Annika got back to the newsroom. There were two dirty mugs on her desk, but the Coca-Cola had gone. Annika assumed that Anne had been sent out on a job.

Berit was talking to Spike over by the newsdesk. Annika sank onto her chair and let her bag fall to the floor. She felt dizzy and exhausted.

'Well, how was it?' Spike called, looking at her expectantly.

Annika struggled to pull out her notepad and went over to him.

'Young, naked, plastic tits,' she said. 'A lot of make-up. She'd been crying. No signs of decomposition, so she couldn't have been there long. No clothes nearby, as far as I could tell.'

She looked up from her pad. Spike was nodding encouragingly.

'Well, well,' he said. 'Any terrified neighbours?'

'One twenty-nine-year-old mum called Daniella. She's never walking through the park at night again. She said: "It could have been me".'

Spike was making notes, nodding approvingly.

'Do they know who she is?'

49

Annika pressed her lips together and shook her head. 'Not as far as we know.'

'We'll just have to hope they release her name sometime this evening. You didn't see anything else – anything that might give an idea of where she lived, anything like that?'

'What, like the address tattooed on her forehead, you mean? Sorry . . .'

Annika smiled, but Spike didn't respond.

'Okay. Berit, you take the police hunt for the killer, who the girl was, and check out the relatives. Annika, you do the scared mum and check the cuttings about the old murder.'

'I think we'll have to do a lot of this together,' Berit said. 'Annika has information from the scene that I haven't got.'

'Do what you want. I need you to brief me on how far you've got before I go to the handover meeting at six o'clock.'

He spun round on his chair, picked up the phone and dialled a number. Berit shut her notepad and went over to her desk.

'I've got the cuttings,' she said over her shoulder. 'We can go through them together.'

Annika took a chair from the next desk. Berit pulled out a bundle of yellowing files from an envelope marked 'Eva murder'. Evidently it had happened before the paper's files were computerized.

'Anything more than ten years old only exists in hard copy,' Berit said.

Annika picked up one file. The paper felt stiff and brittle. She glanced through it. The typeface of the headline looked spiky and old-fashioned, and the print quality wasn't good. A black-and-white picture of the north side of the park stretched across four columns.

'I was right,' Berit said. 'She was on her way up that flight of steps, and halfway up she met someone on their way down. And that was as far as she got. The case was never solved.'

They sat on either side of Berit's desk, immersed in the old articles. Annika noted that Berit had written a lot of them. The murder of young Eva was very similar to the new case.

One warm summer's evening twelve years before, Eva had been on her way up the steep slope at the end of Inedalsgatan. She was found right next to the seventieth step, half naked and strangled.

There were a lot of articles right after the event, at the top of their pages, with big pictures. There were reports from the murder inquiry and the coroner's findings, interviews with neighbours and friends, one article entitled, LEAVE US ALONE. It was about Eva's parents, pleading, their arms round each other as they stared at the camera. There were articles about senseless violence, violence against women, violence against young people, a memorial ceremony in Kungsholmen Church, and the mountain of flowers left at the scene.

Why don't I remember any of this? Annika wondered. I was old enough to have been aware of what was going on.

As time passed, the number of articles dwindled. The pictures got smaller, and they slowly crept down the page. A short piece three and a half years after the murder announced that someone had been taken in for questioning, then released. After that there was nothing.

But now Eva was back in the news again, twelve years later. The similarities were striking.

'So what do we do with all this?' Annika asked.

'A short reference piece, that's all,' Berit said. 'There's

not much more we can do right now. We'll write up what we've got – you take your young mum and I'll take Eva. By the time we've done that, the crime unit ought to be up to speed and we can start phoning round.'

'So are we in a rush?' Annika asked.

'Not particularly.' Berit smiled. 'The final deadline for copy isn't until four forty-five tomorrow morning. But it would be good it we were ready before that, and we're off to a good start.'

'What will they do with these two articles in the paper?'

Berit shrugged. 'They may not even get in, you can never tell. It depends what else is happening round the world and how much space there is.'

Annika nodded. The number of pages in the paper often determined which articles got in. That was certainly the case on the *Katrineholm Courier*, where she usually worked. In the middle of summer, management often cut back on paper, partly because July was such a bad month for advertising, but also because very little ever happened then. The number of pages always rose or fell in fours, because there were four pages on each print-plate.

'I reckon this will end up quite far back in the paper,' Berit said. 'First there'll be the report of the murder, and what the police are doing. Then a spread of the girl and who she was, assuming we get a name in time. Then the reminder of the Eva murder, your scared mother, and maybe a final article about Stockholm, a city gripped by fear. That's my guess, anyway.'

Annika leafed through the cuttings. 'How long have you worked here, Berit?' she asked.

Berit sighed and smiled. 'Almost twenty-five years. I wasn't much older than you when I arrived.'

'Have you been on the crime-desk the whole time?'

'God, no. I got to write about animals and cookery to start with. Then I covered politics for a while – there was a period when it was fashionable to have a female reporter doing that. Then I was on the foreign news team for a while. And now I'm here.'

'What do you like most?' Annika asked.

'The actual writing; getting hold of facts and teasing out the story. I really like it here in crime. I get to do what I like a lot of the time, working on my own stories. Can you pass me those articles? Thanks.'

Annika got up and went over to her desk. Anne Snapphane still wasn't back. It felt empty and silent when she wasn't there.

Annika's Mac had put itself on standby, and she jumped at the shrill bleep it made as it came back to life again. She quickly wrote up what Daniella Hermansson had said, giving it an introduction, main text and a caption. Then she sent the piece to the paper's online file-store, commonly known as 'the can'. There, that was easy!

She was about to go and get some coffee when her phone rang. It was Anne Snapphane.

'I'm at Visby Airport,' she shouted. 'Has there been some sort of murder in Kronoberg Park?'

'Oh, yes,' Annika said. 'Naked and strangled. What are you doing on Gotland?'

'Forest fire,' Anne said. 'The whole island's gone up in flames.'

'The whole island or almost the whole island?' Annika said with a smile.

'Pah, that's just details,' Anne said. 'I'll be here at least until tomorrow. Can you feed my cats?'

'Haven't you taken them back to your parents yet?' Annika said.

'What, drive two cats hundreds of miles in this heat?

That would definitely be cruelty to animals! Can you change their litter as well?'

'Yeah, of course.'

They hung up.

Why can't I ever say no? Annika wondered with a sigh. She got a cup of coffee and a bottle of water from the canteen, and walked idly round the newsroom with one in each hand. The air-conditioning couldn't quite cope this far up the building, and the air was hardly any cooler than outside. Spike was on the phone, as usual, two big patches of sweat spreading from his armpits. Bertil Strand was standing at the picture desk talking to Pelle Oscarsson, the picture editor. She went over to them.

'Are these the pictures from the park?'

Pelle Oscarsson double-clicked an icon on the screen. The deep green of the park filled the screen, with patches of bright sunlight. Granite gravestones hung between the iron railings. You could just make out a woman's leg, from her hip right down to her foot, in the middle of the picture.

'That's a bloody good picture, but maybe a bit hard to stomach,' Annika said spontaneously.

'Then you should see this one,' Picture-Pelle said, clicking open the next image.

Annika shrank back as the woman's clouded eyes stared out at her.

'These were the first pictures,' Bertil Strand said. 'It's a good job I moved, don't you think?'

Annika gulped.

'Daniella Hermansson?' she asked.

Picture-Pelle clicked a third icon. The picture showed a nervous Daniella clutching her child and looking up at the park in horror.

'Brilliant,' Annika said

'"It could have been me",' Picture-Pelle said.

'How did you know that's what she said?' Annika asked in surprise.

'That's what they always say, at least in our captions,' Pelle said with a sigh.

Annika walked away.

All the doors leading to the management offices were closed. She hadn't seen the editor-in-chief today. He'd been fairly invisible all week, now she came to think about it. None of the editors had arrived yet. The men who looked after the paper's layout normally turned up after seven each evening, suntanned and drowsy after an afternoon in Rålambshov Park.

They usually started the night by each drinking a litre of black coffee, then they spent a while arguing about the mistakes they claimed to have found in that day's paper, and then they would set to work. They juggled headlines, cut texts and clattered away on their Macs until the paper was sent to press at six in the morning. Annika was slightly afraid of them. They were noisy and a bit thoughtless, they were pretty cynical, and had a tendency to put people in boxes. But their skill and professionalism were astonishing. A lot of them seemed to live for the paper, four nights on, four nights off, year after year. The rota rolled throughout the year, taking no account of Christmas, Easter or Midsummer. Four on, four off. Annika couldn't imagine how they did it.

She went over to the empty sports section. A television tuned to Eurosport was on in one corner. She stopped at the large windows at the end of the room, with her back to the newsroom, and looked out over the multi-storey car park opposite. The concrete looked as though it was steaming. When she put her nose to the glass and peered to her left, she could just make out the Russian Embassy. She rested her forehead against the glass, surprised it was so cool. Her sweat made a greasy mark on the glass, which she tried to wipe off with her hand. She drank the last of the mineral water. It tasted metallic. Slowly she walked back through the newsroom, and was gradually filled with an intense feeling of happiness.

She had made it. She was part of it. She was one of them.

This is going to work, she thought. Nothing's going to get me out of here now.

6

It was a little after three o'clock. It was time to call the police. On her way back to her desk she popped into the staff kitchen and filled the empty bottle with tap water.

'We don't know enough yet,' an officer on the duty desk said curtly. 'Call the press office.'

The press spokesman had nothing to say.

The operations room confirmed that they had sent several units to Kronoberg Park, but of course she already knew that. The emergency control room told her once again how the call had been received from a member of the public at 12.48. There was no landline connected to the caller's care-of address.

Annika sighed. She picked up her notepad and leafed through it, and her eye was taken by the call number on the Hawaiian detective's car. She thought for a few moments, then called the operations room again. The car belonged to the Norrmalm crime unit. So she called them.

'It's out on loan today,' the duty officer told her when he checked his list.

'Who to?' Annika wondered, her pulse rising.

'Violent crime. They don't have their own cars. There's been a murder on Kungsholmen today, you see.'

'Yes, I heard something about that. Do you know anything else?'

'Not my district – Kungsholmen comes under south Stockholm. But this case has probably already been passed up to the national violent crime unit.'

'The officer who was driving the car had short, fair hair and a Hawaiian shirt. Do you know who that might be?'

The duty officer laughed. 'It sounds like Q,' he said.

'Q?' Annika said.

'That's what we call the inspector of the violent crime unit. Okay, I've got another call coming in.'

Annika thanked him and hung up. She dialled the main reception desk again.

'I'd like to talk to Q in violent crime,' she said.

'Who?' the receptionist said in surprise.

'An inspector with the nickname Q who works in the violent crime unit.'

She heard the receptionist groan. It was probably just as hot there as it was here.

'One moment . . .'

There was a ringing tone as the call was put through. Annika was about to hang up when an irritated voice answered.

'Hello, is that the violent crime unit?' she said.

Another groan. 'Yes, this is violent crime. What is it?'

'I'm trying to get hold of Q,' Annika said.

'That's me.'

Bingo!

'I just wanted to apologize,' Annika said. 'My name's Annika Bengtzon; I'm the woman who ran into you up in Kronoberg Park.'

The man on the other end sighed. There was a scraping

noise in the background, it sounded like he was sitting down.

'What paper are you calling from?'

'The *Evening Post*. I'm on a placement here for the summer. I don't know what you normally do in cases like this, how you organize your dealings with the media. Back home in Katrineholm I usually call Johansson in crime at three o'clock, he always knows everything.'

'Here in Stockholm you call the press spokesman,' Q said.

'But you're leading the investigation?' Annika chanced.

'Yes, so far, anyway.'

Yes!

'Why not a public prosecutor?' she hurriedly asked.

'There's no reason for that at this point.'

'So you don't have a suspect?' Annika concluded.

The man didn't answer.

'You're not as stupid as you make out,' he said eventually. 'What are you getting at?'

'Who was she?'

He groaned again. 'Listen, I've already told you, you'll have to ask the—'

'He says he doesn't know anything.'

'Then you'll just have to make do with that for the time being!'

He was starting to get annoyed.

'Sorry,' Annika said. 'I didn't mean to pressure you into saying.'

'Of course you did. Right, I've got a lot to—'

'She'd had breast enlargements,' Annika said. 'She was wearing loads of make-up and had been crying before she died. Do you know why?'

The man on the other end didn't say anything. Annika held her breath.

'How do you know that?' he asked, and Annika could tell he was surprised.

'Let me put it like this: she hadn't been lying there for long. Her mascara was smeared, she had lipstick on her cheek. She's at the forensics lab out in Solna right now, isn't she? So when do I get to know what you know?'

'I didn't actually know about the breast enlargements,' he said.

'Normal breasts kind of hang to the side when you're lying down, whereas silicone tits stick straight up. That's not very common in young girls. Was she a prostitute?'

'No, definitely not,' the detective said, and Annika could almost hear him biting his tongue.

'So you *do* know who she is! When will you be releasing her name?'

'We're not sure yet. She hasn't been identified.'

'But she will be soon? By the way, do you know what had been chewing at her?'

'I haven't got time for this,' he said. 'Goodbye.'

And Inspector Q hung up. It was only when she heard the dialling tone again that Annika realized that she still didn't know what his real name was.

7

The minister put the car into fourth gear and accelerated into the Karlberg Tunnel. The air inside the car was oppressively hot, and he leaned across to the air-conditioning button. The cooler started up with a click, followed by a gentle hum. He sighed. The journey yawned endlessly ahead of him.

At least it'll get cooler this evening, he thought.

He emerged onto the northern bypass, then turned into the tunnel leading to the E4 motorway, heading north. Various noises echoed through the car, growing and bouncing around the windows: the tyres on the tarmac, the hum of the air-conditioning, the whistle from a window that wasn't shut properly. He switched on the car radio to drown them out. The sound of the most popular national station, P3, blared out. He looked at the digital clock on the dashboard. 17.53. Soon time for *Studio Six*, the evening news programme, with its debates and analysis of the news.

I wonder if I'll be on, he thought briefly. Of course I won't. Why would I be? They haven't interviewed me today.

He pulled into the left-hand lane and overtook two French mobile homes. The north junction for Haga flew past, and he realized he was driving too fast. I really don't want to get caught speeding right now, he thought, and pulled in again. The mobile homes filled his rear-view mirror, blowing their horns at his sudden braking.

At six o'clock he turned up the volume to hear the news. The US president was concerned about the progress of the peace process in the Middle East. He had invited the various parties to talks in Washington next week. No one knew if the Palestinian representative would accept the invitation. The minister listened attentively. This could have consequences for his own work.

That was followed by a report from Gotland, where there was a large forest fire burning. Vast areas on the east of the island were under threat. The reporter interviewed an anxious farmer. The minister noticed that his attention was divided. He was passing the Solna junction, and hadn't even noticed that he had already gone past the intersection at Järva krog.

Then the newsreader read some short items from the studio. Negotiations to avoid the threatened strike by air-traffic controllers were underway, and the union was to respond to the mediators' latest proposals by seven o'clock that evening. The body of a young woman had been found dead in Kronoberg Park in central Stockholm. The minister's ears pricked up and he turned the volume up again. The police were saying little about the case at the moment, but there were clear signs that it was murder.

Then there was a short piece about a former party secretary who had written an article about the old Information Bureau affair in one of the morning papers. The minister started to get angry. The old git! Why the hell couldn't he have kept his mouth shut, especially in the middle of an election campaign?

'We did it for democracy,' the former secretary said

through the speakers. 'Without us, the doors would have been wide open for a Marxist-Leninist paradise.'

And then the weather forecast. High pressure staying over Scandinavia for the next five days. The water table had sunk so low throughout the whole country that there was a severe risk of forest fires. A ban on outdoor fires covering the whole country had been imposed. The minister sighed.

The newsreader ended the broadcast just as he was driving past Rotebro, and he caught a glimpse of a large shopping centre down to his right. The minister waited for the shrill electric guitar that was the theme tune for *Studio Six*, but to his surprise it didn't come. Instead the announcer introduced yet another programme presented by hysterical youngsters. Shit, of course, it was Saturday. *Studio Six* was only on Monday to Friday. Annoyed, he switched the radio off. At that moment his mobile phone rang. To judge by the sound, it was somewhere at the bottom of one of the cases on the back seat. He swore loudly and stuck his right arm through the gap between the seats. As the car wove erratically along the edge of the lane, he pushed his suitcase aside and got hold of the little overnight bag. A brand-new silver Mercedes honked angrily at him as it drove past.

'Capitalist pig,' the minister muttered.

He emptied the bag onto the passenger seat and found his mobile.

'Yes?' he said.

'Hello, it's Karina.'

His press secretary.

'Where are you?' she asked.

'What do you want?' he countered.

'*Svenska Dagbladet* want to know if this latest crisis in the Middle East peace talks poses any threat to the delivery of Saab fighter planes to Israel.'

'They're just fishing,' the minister said. 'We haven't signed any contracts to deliver JAS fighters to Israel.'

'That wasn't what they meant,' his press secretary said. 'They want to know if the negotiations are under threat.'

'The government doesn't comment on any potential negotiations regarding the purchase of Swedish arms or military aircraft. There are often a number of protracted negotiations underway with a number of interested parties, and in only a relatively small number of cases do these result in substantial deals. So there is definitely no threat to any deliveries in this instance, because none were due to take place, as far as I am aware, anyway.'

The press secretary was making notes in silence.

'Okay,' she said when she was finished. 'Have I got this right: the answer is no. No deliveries are threatened, because no contract has been signed.'

The minister rubbed his tired brow.

'No, Karina,' he said, 'that's not what I said at all. I certainly didn't give no as the answer. It's unanswerable. Because no deliveries are planned, they can't be under threat. Saying no to the question means implicitly that some sort of delivery will be made.'

He could hear Karina's breathing down the phone.

'Maybe you should talk to the reporter yourself,' she said.

Bloody hell, he really ought to give this useless woman the sack! She was utterly and completely incompetent.

'No, Karina,' he said. 'It's your responsibility to formulate an answer in such a way that my point is conveyed and the statement correct. What else do you think we're paying you for?'

He ended the call before she had a chance to reply. Just to make sure, he switched the phone off and tossed it back in the bag.

The silence was deafening. Gradually those earlier noises crept back into the car, the whistling window, the hot tarmac, the air-conditioning. Annoyed, he pulled open the top two buttons of his shirt and switched on the radio again. He really didn't want to listen to fake phone-calls on P3, and clicked at random to get one of the pre-programmed stations. He got Radio Rix, where an old hit from his youth was playing. The song triggered some sort of memory, but he couldn't identify exactly what it was. Probably a girl. He resisted the urge to turn the radio off again. Anything was better than those repetitive noises.

It was going to be a long night.

8

The editorial team rolled in just before seven with the usual noise. Their boss, Jansson, had settled in opposite Spike at the newsdesk. Annika and Berit had been down to the staff canteen, known generally as 'The Seven Rats', where they had had beef stew.

The combination of the heavy food and the men's loud laughter gave her stomach cramp. She hadn't got anywhere. She hadn't got hold of the junkie informant. The press spokesman was a miracle of affability and patience, but he didn't know anything. She had spoken to him three times that afternoon. He didn't know who the woman was, or where and how she died, and he didn't know when he would find out. It was making Annika nervous and was probably contributing to her cramp.

She had to come up with a portrait of the woman; otherwise she'd lose her chance of the front cover.

'Calm down,' Berit said. 'We'll make it, just you see. And tomorrow's another day. If we don't have her name, then neither does anyone else.'

The main television news at 7.30 started with the crisis in the Middle East, and the US president's appeal for new talks. The story seemed to go on for ever, and involved a satellite discussion with their Washington correspondent. Long speeches in standard-issue official Swedish were illustrated by archive footage of the intifada.

Then the forest fires on Gotland, precisely the same order of stories as on the radio earlier. The aerial footage was undeniably striking. They spoke to the head of the team combating the fires, a fireman from Visby. Then there was some film of an improvised press conference, and Annika couldn't help smiling when she saw Anne Snapphane forcing her way through to the front, holding her recorder in front of her. The item concluded with an anxious farmer, and Annika thought she recognized his voice from the radio.

After the fire there wasn't much news to report. There was a feeble attempt at a story about the election campaign starting early. Annika had been under the impression that it had started six months ago. The Prime Minister, a Social Democrat, was shown walking hand in hand with his wife across the main square of his hometown in Södermanland, waving to the people around him. Annika smiled when she saw her old workplace flash past in the background. The Prime Minister made a brief statement about the article his former party secretary had written on the IB affair.

'I don't think this is a story we want to drag around with us,' he said tiredly. 'We need to get to the bottom of it, once and for all. If we conclude that an official inquiry is what's needed, then that's what we'll do.'

Then they played a pre-recorded piece, by Swedish Television's Russian correspondent, an extremely talented reporter. He had been to the Caucasus to report on one of those interminable bloody conflicts that had blown up in the old Soviet republics.

This is the good thing about the news drought in the

summer, Annika thought. You get to see a load of things on the news that otherwise never get covered.

There was an interview with the ageing president of the republic. To the reporter's astonishment, he spoke Swedish.

'I was posted to the Soviet Embassy in Stockholm between 1970 and 1973,' he said in a strong accent.

'Brilliant!' Annika said in amazement.

The president was extremely concerned. Russia was supplying the rebels with weapons and ammunition, while he was suffering the effects of the UN arms embargo that had been imposed on his country. He had been the subject of repeated assassination attempts, and had a serious heart condition.

'My country is suffering,' he said in Swedish, staring into the camera. 'Children are dying. This is not justice.'

God, some people have a terrible time, Annika thought as she went to get a cup of coffee. When she got back a short sequence of domestic news was running. A car accident in Enköping. The body of a young woman had been found in Kronoberg Park in Stockholm. The threat of a strike by air-traffic controllers had been averted now that the union had accepted the mediators' final offer. The stories were quickly rattled through, as a commentary to some fairly generic images. A television cameraman had evidently been out to Kungsholmen, because they showed a few seconds of blue and white tape fluttering in the breeze in front of the thick greenery of the park. And that was it.

Annika sighed. This wasn't going to be easy.

9

Patricia was freezing. She wrapped her arms around her chest and pulled her legs up onto the seat. The air-conditioning was blowing at floor level, bringing with it exhaust fumes and pollen. She sneezed.

'Are you getting a cold?' the man in the front seat asked. He was quite good-looking, but he was wearing a really hideous shirt. No style at all. But she liked older men, they weren't usually so pushy.

'No,' she said crossly, 'hay fever.'

'We're almost there,' he said.

In the driver's seat next to him sat a real bitch, one of those female police officers who thought she had to be tougher than all the men to get any respect. After greeting Patricia rather gruffly, she'd ignored her completely.

She looks down on me, Patricia thought. She thinks she's better than me.

The bitch had driven down the Karlberg road and crossed Norra Stationsgatan. Usually only buses and taxis were allowed to do that, but the bitch obviously didn't care. They passed beneath the Essinge motorway and entered the Karolinska Institute the back way. It was a whole collection of red-brick buildings in different styles, a city within a city. There was no one about: it was Saturday evening, after all. They passed the Scheele

Laboratory on the right, with the red-brick palace of the Tomteboda School up on the left. The bitch turned right and pulled up in a small car park. The man in the loud shirt got out and opened the door on her side of the car.

'Can't be opened from the inside,' he said.

Patricia couldn't move. She had her feet up on the seat, her knees pulled up to her chin, and her teeth were chattering.

This isn't happening, she thought. It's just a whole series of nasty coincidences, nothing more than that. Positive thoughts, positive thoughts . . .

The air was so heavy that she was having trouble getting it down to her lungs. It got stuck somewhere in her throat, swelling and solidifying, suffocating her.

'I can't do this,' she said. 'What if it isn't her?'

'Well, we'll soon find out,' the man said. 'I realize this must be very difficult for you. Come on, let me help you out. Do you want anything to drink?'

She shook her head and took the hand he was holding out to her. She stumbled onto the tarmac on unsteady legs. The bitch had started walking down a narrow path, her heavy shoes crunching on the gravel.

'I feel sick,' Patricia said.

'Here, have some chewing-gum,' the man said.

Without saying anything she held out her hand and took a piece from the packet.

'It's just down here,' the man said.

They passed a sign with a red arrow saying, *95:7 Forensic laboratory: mortuary.*

She chewed hard on the gum. They were walking through trees, limes and maples. A gentle breeze was rustling the leaves, maybe the heat was about to lift at last.

The first thing she caught sight of was the long canopy

roof. It stuck out from the bunker-like building like a vast peaked cap. It was yet another red-brick building, its door dark grey iron, heavy and forbidding.

STOCKHOLM MORTUARY, she read in gilded lettering under the canopy, then, in slightly smaller letters: *Entrance for next of kin. Identification deposition.*

The plastic entry phone had seen better days. The man pressed a chrome button and a low voice responded. The man said something.

Patricia turned away from the door and looked back towards the car park. She had a vague feeling that the ground was moving, like slow waves on a huge ocean. The sun had disappeared behind Tomteboda School, and beneath the canopy the daylight had almost vanished. Straight ahead of her lay the Medical School, a dull, red-brick building from the sixties. The air seemed to be getting thicker, and the chewing-gum was getting bigger and bigger in her mouth. A bird was singing somewhere in the bushes, its sound reaching her through some sort of filter. She could feel her jaw muscles clenching.

'We can go in.'

The man put his hand on her arm and she had to turn round. The door was open. Another man was standing in the doorway, smiling cautiously at her.

'This way; please come through,' he said.

The lump in her throat rose, settling at the back of her tongue, and she swallowed hard.

'I just have to get rid of my chewing-gum,' she said.

'There's a bathroom in here,' he said.

The bitch and the man in the shirt let her go in first. The room was small. It reminded her of a dentist's waiting room: the little grey sofa to the left, a birch-wood coffee table, four chrome chairs with blue-striped covers, an abstract picture on the wall, just three colours, grey, brown, blue. A mirror on the right. Cloakroom straight

71

in front, toilet. She headed in that direction with an unpleasant feeling of not quite touching the floor.

Are you here, Josefin?

Can you feel that I'm here?

Inside the toilet she locked the door and threw her chewing-gum in the bin. The woven basket was empty and the gum stuck to the plastic lining just below the rim. She tried to push it further down, but it stuck to her finger. There were no plastic cups so she drank directly from the tap. This is a mortuary, after all, she thought. They must be pretty hot on hygiene.

She took several deep breaths through her nose, then went out. They were waiting for her. They were standing next to another door, between the mirror and the exit.

'I want you to know that this will probably feel pretty tough,' the man said. 'The girl in here hasn't been washed since she was found. She's also lying in the same position we found her in.'

Patricia swallowed once more.

'How did she die?'

'She was strangled. She was found in Kronoberg Park on Kungsholmen just after lunchtime today.'

Patricia put her hand to her mouth, her eyes opened wide and filled with tears.

'We usually cut through the park on our way home from work,' she whispered.

'It's not certain that this girl is your friend,' the man said. 'I need you to be as relaxed as you can and have a good look at her. You'll be okay.'

'Is there . . . much blood?'

'No, not at all. She's in a reasonable state. The body has started to dry out, which is why the face looks a little sunken. Her skin and lips are discoloured, but not too badly. She's not going to scare you.'

The man's voice was calm and low. He took her by the hand.

'Are you ready?'

Patricia nodded. The bitch opened the door. A cool draught swept out of the room inside. She breathed in the smell, expecting it to reek of corpses and death. But there was nothing. The air was fresh and clean. She took a cautious step inside. The floor was stone, shiny, grey-brown, the walls pure white, plastered, a little uneven. Two electric radiators hung on the far wall. She lifted her eyes. An uplighter hung from the ceiling. Twelve glowing bulbs spread a smooth light over the room. It reminded her of a chapel. Two candelabra, tall, wooden. They weren't lit, but Patricia could still make out the smell of wax. Between them stood the mortuary trolley.

'I don't want to,' she said.

'You don't have to,' the man said. 'We can ask her parents to come, or her boyfriend. The only problem is that that would take time. The killer's already got a head start. Whoever did this can't be allowed to get away with it.'

She gulped. Behind the trolley hung a large blue tapestry. It covered the whole of the back entrance. She stared into the blue of it, trying to make out a pattern.

'Okay, I'll do it, then,' she said.

The man, still holding her hand, pulled her slowly over to the trolley. She was lying under a sheet. Her hands were raised above her head.

'Now Anya's going to lift the sheet slowly from her face. I'll be right beside you the whole time.'

Anya was the bitch.

She saw movement from the corner of her eye, the white cloth being pulled down, the faint movement in the air. She let go of the blue tapestry and let her eyes fall to the trolley.

73

It's true, she thought. She looks okay. She's dead, but she isn't disgusting. She just looks a bit surprised, like she didn't really know what had happened.

'Josie,' Patricia whispered.

'Is this your friend?' the man asked.

She nodded. Her tears poured out; there was nothing she could do to stop them. She reached out a hand to stroke Josefin's hair, but stopped herself.

'Josie, what have they done to you?'

'Are you quite sure?'

She closed her eyes and nodded.

'Oh, God,' she said.

She put a hand to her mouth and screwed her eyes tight shut.

'So you can confirm that this is your flatmate, Josefin Liljeberg? You're one hundred per cent sure?'

She nodded and turned away – away from Josie, away from death, away from the blueness hanging behind the trolley.

'I want to get out of here,' she said quietly. 'Get me out of here.'

The man put his arm round her shoulders and pulled her towards him, stroking her hair. She was crying helplessly now, soaking his nasty tropical shirt.

'We'd like to search the flat properly tonight,' he said. 'It would be good if you could be there.'

She wiped her nose with the back of her hand and shook her head.

'I have to go to work,' she said. 'With Josie gone I'll have even more to do. They'll be missing me already.'

He looked hard at her.

'Are you sure you'll be okay?'

She nodded.

'Okay,' he said. 'Let's go.'

10

The press release rolled out of the fax machine at 21.12. Because the press section of the Stockholm Police always sent their communiqués to the editorial secretary, Eva-Britt Qvist, who didn't work weekends, no one noticed it. It wasn't until the main news agency sent out an alert at 21.45 that Berit picked up the information.

'Press conference in Police Headquarters at ten p.m.,' she called to Annika as she hurried towards the picture desk.

Annika dropped her pen and notebook in her bag and headed for the exit. A sense of expectation was churning in her stomach: now she was about to find out. The uncertainty was making her nervous; she had never been to a press conference in Stockholm Police Headquarters before.

'We have to shift the fax machine away from Eva-Britt's desk,' Berit said in the lift.

They squeezed into Bertil Strand's Saab, just like before. Annika sat in the back again, in the same seat. She closed the door gently. As the photographer accelerated towards the Western Bridge she realized that she hadn't shut the door properly. She quickly clicked down the lock and took a firm hold of the handle, hoping the driver wouldn't notice anything.

'Where are we heading?' Bertil Strand wondered.

'Kungsholmsgatan, the Falck entrance,' Berit said.

'What do you think they're likely to say?' Annika asked.

'They've probably found out who she is and informed the relatives,' Berit said.

'Yes, but why call a press conference?'

'They haven't got a single thing to go on,' Berit said. 'They need as much coverage in the media as they can get. It's a matter of shaking a bit of life into their unpaid helpers, the general public, while the body is still fresh. And we're the alarm clock.'

Annika gulped. She switched to hold the door handle with her other hand and looked out of the window. The evening looked cloudy and grey through the tinted glass. The neon signs of Fridhemsplan shone dully in the fading evening light.

'Oh, to be sitting on a terrace with a glass of red,' Bertil Strand said.

Neither of the women responded.

As they passed the park Annika could see the police tape fluttering. The photographer headed round the park, aiming for the Falck entrance at the top of Kungsholmsgatan.

'It's almost ironic,' Berit said. 'The largest concentration of police in the whole of Scandinavia is just two hundred metres from the scene of the murder.'

The brown-panelled mass of National Crime Headquarters loomed up to Annika's right. She turned and looked at the park through the rear window. The green of the hill lay in shadow now, filling the window. All of a sudden she felt faint, caught between the building and the heavy greenery. She dug about in her bag and found a roll of strong English mints. She popped a couple in her mouth.

'We're just going to make it,' Berit said.

Bertil Strand parked a bit too close to the junction, and Annika hurried to get out. Her wrist felt stiff after holding on to the door all the way there.

'You look a bit pale,' Berit said. 'Are you okay?'

'Oh, I'm fine,' Annika said.

She hoisted her bag onto her shoulder and headed for the entrance, chewing aggressively on the mints. A guard from Falck Security was standing by the door. They showed their press cards and went into a narrow space, where most of the floor area was taken up by a photocopier. Annika looked around curiously. Long corridors stretched off to the left and right.

'Those are the departments for identification and fingerprinting,' Berit whispered.

'Straight ahead,' the guard said.

The words 'National Crime Department' were printed in reverse in blue letters on the glass doors in front of them. Berit pushed them open. They found themselves in yet another corridor with beige, panelled walls. Some ten metres along they found the room for the press conference.

Bertil Strand sighed. 'This is the worst room in the whole of Sweden for taking pictures in,' he said. 'You can't even get a decent flash reflection off the ceiling. It's all dark brown.'

'Is that why press spokesmen always have red eyes?' Annika asked with a smile.

The photographer groaned.

The room was fairly large, with an orange carpet and beige armchairs with a blue and brown pattern. A small group of journalists had gathered at the front of the room. Arne Påhlson and another reporter from the other evening paper were already there, talking to the police press spokesman. The detective in the Hawaiian shirt wasn't there. To her surprise, Annika saw that a radio news team had turned up, as well as reporters from the prestigious morning paper that shared a building with the *Evening Post*.

'Murders always get taken more seriously when there's a press conference,' Berit whispered.

The room was oppressively hot, and Annika broke into a sweat again. They sat at the front seeing as there was no one from television there. The first few rows were usually occupied by television cameras and cables. The other evening paper's reporters sat next to them, and Bertil Strand prepared his cameras. The press spokesman cleared his throat.

'Well, welcome, everyone,' he said, stepping onto the little platform at the front of the room. He sat down heavily behind a conference table, leafed through his papers and tapped the microphone in front of him.

'So, we've invited you here this evening to tell you about a body that was discovered in central Stockholm at lunchtime today,' he said, pushing his papers aside.

Annika was sitting next to Berit, and they were both taking notes. Bertil Strand was moving about somewhere to the left of them, looking for the right angles for his pictures.

'We've received a lot of requests for information about the case over the course of the day, which is why we decided to call this somewhat impromptu press conference,' he continued. 'I thought I might run through some of the facts first, then I'll be happy to talk to you individually. If that's okay with you?'

The journalists nodded. The press spokesman picked up his notes again.

'The emergency desk received notification about a

dead body at twelve forty-eight,' he said. 'The informant was a member of the public who happened to be walking past.'

Junkie, Annika wrote in her notebook.

The spokesman fell silent for a moment, before beginning again.

'The dead body is that of a young woman. She has been identified as Hanna Josefin Liljeberg, nineteen years old, and a Stockholm resident. Her relatives have been informed.'

Annika could feel her stomach lurch. Those cloudy eyes now had a name. She looked around surreptitiously to see how her colleagues were reacting. No one was showing any emotion.

'Josefin had been strangled,' the press spokesman said. 'The time of death is as yet not one hundred per cent certain, but we believe it occurred between three o'clock and seven o'clock this morning.'

He hesitated before going on.

'Examination of the body suggests that she was the victim of a sexual attack prior to death.'

The image flashed past in Annika's head, breasts, eyes, screams. The spokesman looked up from the table and his notes.

'We are going to need the public's help to catch the madman who did this,' he said tiredly. 'We don't have much to go on.'

Annika glanced at Berit; she had been right.

'Our initial investigations indicate that the site where the body was found was also the site of the murder; there's forensic evidence to support that theory. As far as we know, the last person to see Josefin alive, apart from the murderer, was her flatmate. They went their separate ways from the restaurant where they both worked shortly before five o'clock this morning, which means that we can narrow the time of death down to a two-hour period.'

A few flashes went off. Annika assumed it was Bertil Strand.

'So,' the spokesman concluded, 'between five o'clock and seven o'clock this morning Hanna Josefin Liljeberg was murdered in Kronoberg Park in Stockholm. Evidence from her body indicates that she was raped.'

He looked around his audience, his eyes settling on Annika. She gulped.

'We're interested in contacting everyone, I repeat, everyone, who was in the vicinity of Kronoberg Park, Parkgatan, Hantverkargatan or Sankt Göransgatan between five o'clock and seven o'clock this morning. We are happy to receive any information that might be of use. We have set up special phone-lines for the public to call. People can either talk to an operator or leave a message. Even if people think that their information isn't important, it could be highly relevant to the broader picture of events. Which is why we are asking everyone who saw anything at all unusual at the time in question to contact us . . .'

He fell silent. Dust was hanging in the air. The dryness was irritating Annika's throat.

The reporter from one of the morning broadsheets cleared his throat.

'Do you have a suspect?' he asked in an assured tone of voice.

Annika looked at him in surprise. Hadn't he understood a thing?

'No,' the press spokesman replied amiably. 'That's why it's so important that we hear from members of the public.'

The reporter took some notes.

'What sort of forensic evidence do you have that

indicates that the murder was committed where the body was found?' Arne Påhlson asked.

'We can't go into that at this point,' the spokesman said.

The reporters asked several more semi-idiotic questions, but the press spokesman was unwilling to say anything more. Eventually the radio reporter asked if he could ask some questions by himself. The press conference broke up. It had lasted almost twenty minutes. Bertil Strand was leaning against a large black-and-white partition at the back of the room.

'Do you want to wait until radio have finished with him, then talk to him afterwards?' Annika asked.

'I think we should split up,' Berit said. 'One of us can stay and talk to him while the other tries to find pictures of the girl.'

Annika nodded; that made sense.

'I can go round to the duty desk of the crime unit and check the passport register,' Berit said, 'if you want to stay and talk to Gösta.'

'Gösta?'

'That's his name. Are you staying, Bertil? I can get a taxi . . .'

After radio had finished Arne Påhlson took over. The second reporter from the other evening paper had vanished. Annika was willing to bet that Berit would bump into him when she was checking the passport register.

Arne Påhlson took his time, at least as much time as the press conference itself. At quarter to eleven everyone apart from Annika and Bertil had given up. The press spokesman was tired when Annika finally sat down with him in one corner of the empty room.

'Do you find this difficult?' Annika asked.

Gösta looked at her in surprise. 'How do you mean?'

'You must get to see so much crap. How do you do it?'

'It's not so bad. Did you have any questions?'

Annika leafed back a few pages in her notebook.

'I saw the girl up in the park,' she said calmly, almost in passing. 'She wasn't wearing any clothes, and I couldn't see any clothes nearby. Either she climbed into the cemetery naked or else her clothes are somewhere else. Have you found them?'

She looked directly at the press spokesman's eyes. He blinked in surprise.

'No, just her underwear,' he said. 'But you can't write that!'

'Why not?'

'It could jeopardize the investigation,' he said quickly.

'Come on!' Annika said. 'How?'

The man thought for a moment.

'Well,' he said, 'I suppose we could make that public, I don't suppose it will make much difference.'

'Where did you find her underwear? What state was it in? How do you know it was hers?'

'Her pants were hanging on a nearby bush, pink polyester. We've had them identified.'

'Ah, yes,' Annika said. 'You managed to get the body identified pretty quickly. How did you manage that?'

The press spokesman sighed. 'Yes, well . . . She was identified by her flatmate, like I said.'

'Man or woman?'

'A young woman, just like her.'

'Had Josefin been reported missing?'

The press spokesman nodded. 'Yes, by her flatmate.'

'When?'

'She didn't come home last night, and when she didn't show up at work her friend called the police, at half past six.'

'So the girls lived and worked together?'

'Looks like it.'

Annika made some notes, and thought for a moment.

'What about the rest of her clothes?' she said.

'We haven't found them. They aren't within a five-block radius of the scene of the murder. Unfortunately the rubbish bins around Fridhemsplan were emptied this morning, but we've got people searching the tip at the moment.'

'How was she dressed?'

The press spokesman put his hand in his right jacket pocket and took out a small notebook.

'Little black dress,' he read, 'white trainers and a blue denim jacket. And probably a Rocco Barocco hand-bag.'

'I don't suppose you've got a picture of her? From her school graduation, maybe?' Annika said.

The spokesman ran his hand over his hair.

'Yes, it's important that people know what she looked like,' he said. 'Do you need it tonight?'

Annika nodded.

'A graduation picture . . . I'll see what I can do,' he said. 'Anything else?'

She bit her lip.

'Something had been chewing at her body,' she said finally. 'On one of her hands.'

The press spokesman looked surprised. 'Well, you know more than I do, in that case.'

Annika put her notebook on her lap.

'Who was she?' she asked quietly.

Gösta sighed. 'We don't know,' he said. 'We don't know anything, except that she's dead.'

'What sort of life did she lead? What restaurant did she work at? Did she have a boyfriend?'

The press spokesman put his notepad in his pocket again.

'I'll try to get that picture sorted,' he said as he got up.

11

Berit was busy writing when Annika and Bertil Strand
got back to the newsroom.

'She was a real looker,' Berit said, pointing towards
Pelle at the picture desk.

Annika went straight over and looked at the little
black-and-white picture from the passport register.
Hanna Josefin Liljeberg was laughing into the camera.
The radiant eyes and blinding smile could only have
belonged to a teenager full of self-confidence.

'Nineteen years old,' Annika said, suddenly feeling a
weight on her chest.

'It would be better if we had a proper picture,' Pelle
Oscarsson said. 'This one's going to look all blurred and
grey if we try to blow it up to more than one column-
width.'

'I think we're getting that sorted,' Annika said, with a
silent prayer to Gösta, then went over to Berit.

'Are you any good with the National Population
Address Register?' Berit wondered.

Annika shook her head.

'Okay, let's go and see Eva-Britt,' Berit said.

Berit switched on the editorial secretary's computer
and logged into the network. Via the Infotorg site she

clicked through to the National Population Address Register.

'This database contains the details of everyone currently registered as living in Sweden,' she explained. 'Their home addresses, previous addresses, maiden names, ID numbers, place of birth, all that sort of thing.'

'That's amazing,' Annika said, astounded. 'I had no idea it even existed.'

'It's a really useful tool for us. If you get time, look up some people you know to see how it works.'

Berit searched for the name 'Liljeberg, Hanna Josefin'. They got two results, an eighty-five-year-old woman in Malmö, and a nineteen-year-old girl from Dalagatan in Stockholm.

'There she is,' Berit said, and bookmarked the record.

Liljeberg, Hanna Josefin, born in Täby, just outside Stockholm; single. The most recent amendment to her records was dated just two months ago.

'Let's see where she used to live,' Berit said, and clicked to bring up the girl's history.

After a few seconds the computer flashed up a different address.

'Runslingan, in Täby kyrkby,' Berit read. 'That's a smart residential area.'

'Where does it say that?' Annika said, her eyes flickering across the screen.

Berit smiled. 'There are some things that are only on this hard-drive,' she said, tapping her head. 'I live in Täby. This must be her parents' address.'

She printed out the details, then performed another search. Liljeberg Hed, Siv Barbro, Runslingan in Täby kyrkby, born forty-seven years ago, married.

'Josefin's mother,' Annika said. 'How did you find her?'

'By searching for women with the same surname and the same postcode,' Berit said, printing the details and running the same search for men.

The database produced two results, Hans Gunnar, fifty-one, and Carl Niklas, nineteen. Both listed as living on Runslingan.

'Look at the boy's date of birth,' Berit said.

'Josefin had a twin brother,' Annika said.

Berit printed this last page and logged out. She switched off the computer and went over to the printer.

'Take these,' she said, giving Annika the printouts. 'See if you can talk to anyone who knew her.'

Annika went back to her desk. The editorial team were immersed in their work; Jansson was shouting down the telephone.

The flickering light from all the computer screens on it made the newsdesk look like a blue island floating in the sea of the newsroom. The sight made her aware of the darkness outside. Night had fallen. She didn't have much time.

As she sat down the tip-off hotline rang. She picked up the receiver without thinking.

It was a group of drunk youngsters who wanted to know if Selma Lagerlöf was lesbian.

'Call the Centre for Sexual Equality,' Annika said, and hung up.

She pulled out the stack of phone books with a sigh, looking at the various titles. Back home in Katrineholm they had just one phone book for the whole county; but here there were four covering the Stockholm code alone.

She looked up Liljeberg, Hans, Runslingan in Täby kyrkby. He was listed as 'Revd'. She wrote down the number, then sat staring at it.

No, she eventually thought. There must be another way of getting information.

She looked up the details of high schools in Täby. There were two of them: Tibble and Åva. She called both main numbers, but they redirected her to a central council exchange.

After a bit of thought, she tried to get round the main school numbers: instead of dialling 00 at the end, she tried 01, then 02, 03. On 05 she struck lucky: the voicemail of a headmaster, a Martin Larsson-Berg, which announced that he was on holiday until 7 August. In the phone book he was listed as living in Viggbyholm, and when she called he was both at home and still awake.

'I'm sorry to call so late on a Saturday evening,' Annika said. 'I'm afraid there's a rather serious reason.'

'Is it my wife?' Larsson-Berg asked anxiously.

'Your wife?'

'She's out sailing this weekend.'

'No, it's not about your wife. A girl who might have been a former pupil of yours was found dead in Stockholm today,' Annika said, closing her eyes.

'Oh.' The man sounded relieved. 'I thought something had happened to her. What was the student's name?'

'A girl called Josefin Liljeberg; she grew up in Täby kyrkby.'

'What course did she take?'

'I don't even know if she went to Tibble High School, but that seems most likely. You don't remember her? Nineteen years old, pretty, long fair hair, big breasts—'

At that the headmaster interrupted. 'Ah, Josefin Liljeberg,' he said. 'Yes, you're right. She graduated from our Media Studies course this spring.'

Annika breathed out and opened her eyes.

'You remember her?'

'Dead, you say? That's awful. Where?'

'The Jewish cemetery in Kronoberg Park. She was murdered.'

'That's just terrible. Do they know who did it?'

'Not yet. Is there anything you'd like to say about her, something about what she was like? Any sort of response, really.'

Martin Larsson-Berg sighed. 'Ah, well,' he said. 'What can I say? She was like most girls that age. Giggly and vain. They're all pretty much the same, they sort of blur together.'

Annika was astonished. The headmaster paused to think.

'I think she wanted to be a journalist – preferably on television. She wasn't the brightest of kids, if I'm honest. Murdered, you say? How?'

'Strangled. She graduated, then?'

'Oh yes, she passed all her subjects.'

Annika leafed through the printouts.

'Her father's a priest,' she said. 'Did that affect her in any particular way, do you think?'

'Is he? I didn't know that . . .'

'She had a twin brother, Carl Niklas. Did he go to Tibble High School as well?'

'Niklas . . . ? Yes, I think he was on the Science course last spring. Wanted to go on and study in the States.'

Annika was taking notes.

'Is there anything else you remember?'

Jansson came over and stood waiting impatiently beside her. She waved him away.

'No,' the headmaster said. 'There are so many of them.'

'Did she have many friends?'

'Yes, I think so. She wasn't particularly popular, but she certainly had a few girls that she hung around with. She wasn't bullied or anything like that.'

'I don't suppose you happen to have a list of students in her year?' she wondered.

'What, Josefin's class?' He grunted. 'Yes, I've got the school yearbook. Do you want me to send it to you?'

'Have you got a fax machine?'

He had. Annika gave him the number of the crime-desk's fax and he promised to send the class photograph straight away.

She hung up, and was on her way over to Eva-Britt Qvist's desk when the tip-off hotline rang again. She hesitated, but stopped to answer it.

'I know who shot Olof Palme,' a voice slurred on the other end.

'I see,' Annika said. 'So who was it?'

'What's the reward?'

'We pay a maximum of five thousand kronor for a tip-off.'

'Only five? That's crap. I want to talk to one of the editors.'

Annika could hear the man drinking.

'I'm one of the editors. We pay five thousand, no matter who you talk to.'

'That's not enough. I want more.'

'Call the police. They'll give you fifty million,' Annika said, and hung up.

What if the drunk was actually right? she thought as she headed towards the fax machine. What if he really did know? What if the other evening paper had Palme's killer on the front page tomorrow? She would forever be known as the person who ignored the tip-off of the century, just like the publishers who rejected Astrid

Lindgren, or the record company that turned down the Beatles on the grounds that 'guitar music is on the way out'.

The quality of the fax was hopeless: Josefin and her classmates were nothing but black blobs on a stripy grey background. But beneath the picture were the names of all the pupils, twenty-nine young people who had all known Josefin. On her way back to her desk she underlined all the unusual names, the ones she stood a chance of finding in the phone book. The kids presumably didn't have their own lines, so she'd have to look for their parents.

'You've got a parcel,' Peter Brand, the caretaker, said. He was Tore's son, and was doing some nightshifts in July.

Annika looked up in surprise and took the stiff white envelope. It was marked, *Do not fold*. She quickly pulled it open and emptied the contents onto her desk.

There were three photographs of Josefin. In the top one she was smiling straight at the camera. It was a fairly informal studio shot, taken for her graduation, to judge by the student's cap she was wearing. Annika felt the hairs on her arms stand up. The picture was so sharp it could easily be blown up to cover ten columns if need be. The other two were decent amateur pictures. One showed the young woman holding a cat, and the other had her sitting on a sofa.

Beneath the pictures was a note from Gösta, the press spokesman.

I've promised the parents that the pictures will be circulated to any media outlets that want them, he wrote. *So please can you send them over to your competitors when you've finished with them.*

Annika hurried over to Jansson and put the pictures down in front of him.

91

'Daughter of a priest, dreamed of becoming a journalist,' she said.

Jansson picked up the pictures and studied them carefully.

'Fantastic,' he said.

'We have to let our beloved competitors have them when we're done with them,' Annika said.

'Of course,' Jansson said. 'And we'll courier them over to them, just as soon as their final edition has gone to press tomorrow. Good work!'

Annika went back to her desk. She sat down and stared at the telephone. There wasn't much to think over, really. It was half past two. If she was going to get hold of any of Josefin's friends, she had to start now. It was only going to get even later if she put it off.

She started with two foreign names, but got no answer. Then she tried a Silferbiörck, and a young woman answered. Annika's pulse started to race, she shut her eyes and put her right hand over them.

'I'm very sorry to call in the middle of the night,' Annika said, slowly and quietly. 'My name is Annika Bengtzon, and I'm calling from the *Evening Post*. I'm calling because one of your classmates, Josefin Liljeberg, has—' Her voice cracked and she cleared her throat hard.

'Yes, I know.' The girl, whose name was Charlotta according to the photograph, sniffed. 'It's so awful. We're all so sad. The rest of us will just have to help each other through this somehow.'

Annika opened her eyes, grabbed her pen and made notes. This was much simpler than she had anticipated.

'This is what we fear most,' Charlotta said. 'This is what young girls like us fear most of all. And now it's happened to one of our friends, one of us. We have to do something about it.'

92

She had stopped sniffing and sounded pretty perky. Annika carried on taking notes.

'Is this something you and your friends have talked about?'

'Yes, of course it is. But no one actually thought it would happen to one of us. You never think that's going to happen,' she said.

'Did you know Josefin well?'

Charlotta sniffed again, a dry, deep sigh.

'She was my best friend,' she said.

Annika could tell she was lying.

'What was Josefin like?'

Charlotta had her answer ready.

'Always happy, always kind,' she said. 'Helpful, fair, good at school. Liked going to parties. Yes, I think you could say that . . .'

Annika listened in silence.

'Do you want a picture of me?' Charlotta asked.

Annika looked at the time. Out to Täby and back, then tidying up the picture – no, it would be too tight.

'Not tonight,' Annika said. 'The paper's going to press soon. Can I call you again tomorrow?'

'Of course, or you can call my mobile.'

Annika jotted down the number. She leaned her head on her hand and thought. Josefin still felt unfocused, distant. She had no real idea of what the dead woman was actually like.

'What did Josefin want to do with her life?' she asked.

'What do you mean, do? She wanted, well, you know, to have a family, a job, and all that,' Charlotta said.

'Where did she work?'

'Work?'

'Yes, which restaurant?'

'Oh, yes, um, I don't know.'

93

'She'd moved to Stockholm, to Dalagatan. Did you ever visit her there?'

'On Dalagatan? No . . .'

'Do you know why she moved?'

'I suppose she must have wanted to live in the city . . .'

'Did she have a boyfriend?'

Charlotta didn't answer. Annika understood. The girl didn't actually know Josefin well at all.

'Well, thanks for letting me bother you in the middle of the night,' Annika said.

After that there was just one more call she had to make. She looked up 'Liljeberg' in the phone book, but there was no Josefin listed at Dalagatan. She didn't have time to get into the phone book, Annika thought, and dialled Directory Inquiries.

'No, I haven't got a Liljeberg at Dalagatan sixty-four,' the woman said.

'It might be a completely new listing,' Annika said.

'I can see all the lines that were connected up to yesterday.'

'Is it possible that she was ex-directory?'

'No,' the Telia woman said. 'I'd still have been able to see the information. Could the account have been under a different name?'

Annika leafed helplessly through the printouts. She found Josefin's mother. 'Liljeberg Hed, Siv Barbro.'

'Hed,' she said. 'Can you check if there's anyone called Hed listed at Dalagatan sixty-four?'

The woman looked.

'Yes, a Barbro Hed. Could that be the one?'

'Yes, that's it,' Annika said.

She dialled the number without pausing to think. At the fourth ring a man answered.

'Is this Josefin's number?' Annika wondered.

'Who is it?' the man asked.

'My name's Annika Bengtzon, and I'm calling from—'

'Bloody hell, you keep popping up all over the place,' the man said, and now Annika recognized the voice.

'Q!' she said. 'What are you doing there?'

'What the hell do you think I'm doing? And how did you get hold of this number? Even we haven't got it!'

'It took a lot of work,' Annika said. 'I called Directory Inquiries. What have you found out?'

The man gave a tired sigh. 'Look, I haven't got time for this right now,' he said, and hung up.

Annika smiled. At least she had the right number. And now she could say that the police had been searching Josefin's flat during the night.

'Okay, I need to know what you've got,' Jansson said, sitting down on her desk.

'This is what I'm working on,' she said, and did a rough outline in her notebook.

Jansson nodded, pleased, and jogged back to his own desk.

Then she wrote her article about who Josefin was, the ambitious vicar's daughter who dreamed of becoming a journalist. She wrote another piece about her death, her eyes, her screams, her chewed hand, how upset her friend was. She left out the silicone breasts. She wrote about the police hunt, the missing clothes, her last hours, the distraught man who had made the call, local resident Daniella Hermansson's worries, and the press spokesman's plea: 'We have to stop this madman.'

'This is really good,' Jansson said. 'Great style, full of concrete facts. God, you're good!'

Annika had to get away from him quickly. She was no good at taking criticism, and even worse at accepting praise. She was superstitious about the magic that seemed to be responsible for forming her articles. If she started to believe in praise, maybe the bubble would burst.

'Come on, let's go and have some hot chocolate before you go home,' Berit said.

12

The minister was crossing the Bergnäs Bridge in Luleå. An old American car was cruising towards him, top folded down, with some ageing drunks hanging over the car doors. Apart from them he couldn't see a single person.

Once he had turned into the narrow streets behind the green-plated bulk of the social services building he breathed out. The noise and whining had followed him for almost a thousand kilometres. Now it was almost over.

He parked the car outside the rental office and sat and enjoyed the silence for a moment. He could still hear whistling in his left ear. He was so tired he thought he was going to be sick. But he had no option. He sighed and climbed out of the car on stiff legs. He glanced quickly around him, then urinated behind the car.

The bags were heavier than he had expected. I'm not going to manage this, he thought. He walked up the main street, passing the police station, until he reached the old residential district of Östermalm. He could just make out his own house behind the birch trees, the hand-blown glass of the windows sparkling. The children's bicycles lay abandoned by the veranda. The bedroom window was open; he smiled as he saw the curtain sway in the breeze.

'Christer . . . ?'

His wife looked up at him, startled, as he crept into the bedroom. He hurried over to the bed and sat down beside her, stroking her hair and giving her a kiss.

'Sleep a bit longer, darling,' he whispered.

'What time is it?'

'Quarter past four.'

'Was the drive okay?'

'Yes, fine. Get some more sleep.'

'And the trip went well?'

He hesitated.

'I brought back some Azerbaijani cognac,' he said. 'I don't think we've tried that before, have we?'

She didn't answer, just pulled him to her and unbuttoned his trousers.

The sun had risen, hanging like an overripe orange just above the horizon, shining right in her face. It was already hot, at half past four in the morning. Annika was giddy with tiredness. Gjörwellsgatan was completely empty, and she followed the central traffic markings towards the bus-stop. She slumped down on the bench, her legs quite exhausted.

She'd seen the draft of the front page on Jansson's computer before she left. It was dominated by Josefin's graduation picture and the headline: SEX KILLING IN CEMETERY. She had written the front-page blurb with Jansson. Her articles were spread across pages six, seven, eight, nine and twelve. She had filled more columns tonight than in the whole of her first seven weeks on the paper put together.

Well, that worked, she thought. I managed to do it.

She leaned her head back against the Plexiglas of

the bus-stop and closed her eyes, breathing deeply and concentrating on the sounds of traffic. There wasn't much, and it was far off in the distance. She was on the point of nodding off when she was woken up by a hysterical bird calling from inside the embassy compound.

Some time passed before she realized that she had no idea if a bus was coming. She got stiffly to her feet and checked the timetable. The first number 56 wasn't due until 07.13 on Sunday mornings, and that was two and a half hours away. She let out a loud groan. There was nothing for it, she'd just have to walk.

After a few minutes she'd built up a bit of speed. It didn't actually feel too bad. Her legs were moving automatically, making waves in the air around her. She followed the ramp from the Western Bridge towards Fridhemsplan. As she reached the Drottningholm road the vegetation loomed up ahead of her. Kronoberg Park was backlit, and looked oppressively dark. She knew she had no choice: she had to go up there again.

The cordons had been removed. Only the railings themselves still had plastic tape on them. She walked up to the iron gate, her fingers tracing the metallic curve of the padlock. The sun had reached the crowns of the lime trees, making the leaves glow.

She must have got here at about this time of day, Annika thought. She would have seen the same sun making the same patterns in the leaves. How fragile everything is. How quickly it can all change.

Annika walked round the cemetery and emerged on the eastern side, her hand dancing along the curves and bows of the railings. Her legs gave way and she slumped softly onto the grass. Without her consciously realizing it, she was in tears. They ran silently down her cheeks and fell onto her crumpled skirt. She leaned her forehead against the railings, sobbing gently and quietly.

'How did you know her?'

Annika flew up. Her arms flailing, she slipped on the grass and landed hard on the base of her spine.

'Sorry, I didn't mean to startle you.'

The young woman talking to her was red-eyed and messy from crying. She spoke with a faint but noticeable accent. Annika stared at her.

'I . . . Not at all. I never met her. But I saw her when she was lying here. She was dead.'

'Where?' the young woman said, taking a step closer.

Annika pointed. The woman went over and looked down in silence for a minute or so. Then she sat down on the grass next to Annika, facing away from the cemetery, her back against the railings.

'I saw her too,' she said, fiddling with the hem of her blouse.

Annika looked for something to blow her nose on in her bag.

'I saw her at the mortuary. It was her. She looked okay, fine really.'

Annika gulped and stared at the woman once more. Good grief! This was Josefin's flatmate, the girl who had identified her. They must have been really good friends.

She found herself thinking of tomorrow's front page of the *Evening Post* and suddenly felt ashamed. It made her start crying again.

The woman beside her started to sniff as well.

'She was lovely, wasn't she?' the woman said. 'She could be really lazy, but she never meant anyone any harm.'

'I never knew her,' Annika said, blowing her nose on a page torn from a pad of paper. 'I work for a newspaper, I've written about Josefin.'

The woman looked at Annika.

'Josie wanted to be a journalist,' she said. 'She wanted to write about children in trouble.'

'She could have ended up working at the *Evening Post*,' Annika said.

'What have you written?'

Annika took a deep breath, hesitating for a moment. Every trace of satisfaction she had felt about her articles had vanished. She wanted the ground to open up and swallow her.

'That she was killed in a sex attack in the cemetery,' she said quickly.

The woman nodded and looked away.

'I warned her about this,' she said.

Annika, busy screwing the paper into a little ball, stiffened.

'What do you mean?'

The woman wiped her face with the back of her hand.

'Joachim was no good for her,' she said. 'He was always hitting her. She could never do anything right in his eyes. She always had bruises. It sometimes caused trouble at work. I kept saying she ought to leave him, but she never did.'

Annika was listening wide-eyed.

'Bloody hell!' she said. 'Have you told the police?'

The woman nodded, pulling a handkerchief from her pocket and blowing her nose.

'I get awful hay fever,' she said. 'I don't suppose you've got any antihistamines?'

Annika shook her head apologetically.

'I should go home,' the young woman said, standing

up. 'I'm working again tonight, so I'd better get some sleep.'

Annika stood up as well, brushing the grass from her skirt.

'Do you really think it could have been her boyfriend?' she said.

'He used to tell Josie he'd end up killing her one day,' the young woman said, as she set off along Parkgatan.

Annika stared towards the graves with an entirely new feeling in her gut. Her boyfriend? Then the case ought to be solved pretty quickly.

Suddenly she realized that she didn't know the young woman's name.

'Sorry, but what's your name?' she called across the park.

The young woman stopped and called back: 'Patricia!'

Then she turned and disappeared towards Fleming-gatan.

13

Annika had already reached her front door when she remembered that she had promised to feed Anne Snapphane's cats. She groaned, then made a snap decision. The cats would probably survive, and the issue was really whether or not she would if she didn't get some sleep soon. On the other hand, it wasn't more than a couple of hundred metres away, and she had promised, after all. She hunted through her bag and found Anne's keys at the bottom, stuck to a piece of old chewing-gum.

I'm just too damn nice, she thought.

As she went up the steps from Pipersgatan to Kungsklippan she could feel her legs getting weaker and weaker. And the bottom of her spine ached from the fall in the park.

Anne Snapphane's little apartment was on the sixth floor, with a balcony and a wonderful view. The cats started to miaow as soon as she put the key in the lock. When she opened the door the pair of them were fighting to look through the gap.

'Oh, sweethearts, did you wonder where I was?'

She shepherded the cats back inside with her foot, pulled the door shut behind her and sank to the hall floor. The two animals jumped up into her arms and started rubbing their noses against her chin.

'So we're doing kissing now, are we?' Annika laughed.

She played with them for a couple of minutes, then got up and went into the tiny kitchen. The cats' bowls stood on a bit of spare cork mat by the cooker. The milk had gone off and smelled terrible. And the food and water bowls were empty.

'Okay, you'll soon have some more . . .'

She poured the sour milk away and rinsed the dish under the tap, then found some more milk in the fridge. The little cats were winding round her legs and miaowing like mad.

'Okay, okay, calm down!'

They were so eager they almost upset the dish before she had time to put it down. While the cats were busy with that she filled the water dish and looked around for cat food. She found three tins of Whiskas in one of the cupboards. She suddenly felt on the verge of tears again. Her own cat back home in Hälleforsnäs was called Whiskas. He was staying with Annika's grandmother in Lyckebo for the summer.

'I'm getting way too sentimental,' she said out loud.

She opened one of the tins, wrinkling her nose at the smell, and emptied the gloop into the third bowl. She looked in the bedroom to check their litter-tray, but that would have to wait until tomorrow.

'Well, bye for now, little ones,' she said.

The cats ignored her.

She left the apartment quickly and went back down to Kungsholmstorg. It was almost daylight. All the birds had started up. She felt groggy and her walking was erratic; she was having trouble judging distances.

I can't go on like this, she thought.

*   *   *

Her apartment was oppressively hot. It was at the top of a building in a courtyard from the 1880s, and had no bathroom and no hot water. But it did have three rooms and a large kitchen. Annika couldn't believe her luck when she got hold of it.

'No one wants to live in such primitive conditions these days,' the woman in the estate agents had said when Annika filled in her form, saying that she was prepared to live without a lift, hot water, a bathroom, and even electricity if need be.

Annika had held her ground.

'All right. No one wants this one,' the woman had said, giving her a printout. Hantverkargatan 32, the fourth floor out in the courtyard.

Annika took it without even going to see it. She had thanked her lucky stars every day since then, but she knew her happiness could end up being short-lived. She had agreed to being evicted with just one week's notice if the owner got the money he needed to renovate the building.

She dropped her bag on the floor and went into the bedroom. She had left the window open while she was at work, but it had blown shut. With a sigh she pushed it open once more and headed towards the living room to try to get a bit of a through-draught.

'Where've you been?'

She was so shocked that she screamed and jumped clean off the floor.

The voice was low, and came from the shadows over by her bed.

'Bloody hell, you can't be that much of a scaredy-cat?'

It was Sven, her fiancé.

'When did you get here?' she said, her heart still pounding in her chest.

'Yesterday evening. I was going to take you to the cinema. Where've you been?'

'At work,' she said, going into the living room.

He got out of bed and followed her.

'No you haven't,' he said. 'I called an hour ago, and they said you'd already left.'

'I had to feed Anne's cats,' she said, opening the living-room window.

'That's a fucking useless excuse,' he said.

Seventeen years, six months and twenty-one days

There's a dimension where the boundaries between human bodies blur. We live with each other, in each other, spiritually, physically. Days become moments; I drown in his eyes. Our bodies dissolve, enter another time. Love is gold and crystals. We can go wherever we please in the universe, together, two, but also one.

A soulmate is someone who has the locks that our keys fit into, and who has the keys that fit our locks. We feel secure with people like this, in our own private paradise. I read that somewhere, and it's true of us as well.

I long for him every moment we're apart. I didn't know love could be so obvious, so total, so all-consuming. I can't eat, can't sleep. Only with him am I whole, a real person. He provides the reason for my life, my sense of meaning. I know I mean the same for him. We have been granted the greatest gift of all.

Never leave me,
he says,
I can't live without you.

And I promise.

Sunday 29 July

14

Patricia put her hand on the door to Josefin's room. She hesitated. The bedroom was Josefin's domain. She wasn't allowed in there. Josie had been very strict about that.

'You can live here, but the bedroom is mine.'

The handle was loose. Patricia had wanted to tighten it, but they had no screwdriver. She carefully pushed down on it. The door creaked. A smell of dust hit her; the heat was stagnant and dense. Josie insisted on cleaning her room herself, which meant that it never got done. The police had stirred up two months' worth of dirt and dust when they searched the room last night.

The room was bathed in harsh sunlight. The police had opened the curtains. It struck Patricia that she had never actually seen the room like that before. The daylight showed up the dust and how dirty the wallpaper was. Patricia felt suddenly ashamed when she thought of the police being in there. They must have thought she and Josie lived like pigs.

Slowly she walked over and sat down on the bed. It was actually just a mattress from IKEA that they'd put straight on the floor, but, unlike Patricia's own foam mattress, at least this one had a bit of height to it.

Patricia was tired. She had slept badly because of

the heat, waking up, sweating and crying. She slowly lay down on top of the duvet. When she got home this morning she had been struck by how lonely she felt the moment she walked into the silent apartment. They really had turned the whole place upside down, but they hadn't taken very much.

She was on the verge of falling asleep among the pillows, feeling her limbs start to twitch the way they did before she dozed off. She hurriedly sat up again. She mustn't sleep in Josie's room.

There was a bundle of magazines beside the bed, and Patricia leaned over and leafed through the top one. *Weekly Review*, Josie's favourite. Patricia didn't think much of it, there was too much about diets and make-up and sex. She always felt ugly and clumsy after reading it, like she wasn't good enough. She realized that that was the whole point. Under the pretence of helping young girls become more confident, it actually made them feel worse.

She picked up the next magazine on the pile. It was much smaller; Patricia had never seen it before. The paper was cheap and the print quality was pretty poor. She opened it in the middle. Two men had their penises inside a woman, one in her anus, the other in her vagina. You could just make out the woman's face in the background. She looked like she was screaming, as if she were in pain. Patricia felt a physical response to the picture in her groin. She jerked back, disgusted, partly by the picture, and partly by her own reaction. She threw the magazine on the floor, as if it had burned her. Josefin didn't read that sort of thing. She knew it had to be Joachim's.

She lay down again, staring up at the ceiling and trying to stop the shameful feeling of horniness. It slowly subsided. She ought to be used to this by now.

She looked round the room. The wardrobe door was open. Josefin's clothes hung haphazardly from their hangers. Patricia knew the police must have left them like that. Josie was careful with her clothes.

I wonder what's going to happen to them now, she thought. Maybe I could take some of them.

She got up and went over to the wardrobe, her hand stroking the clothes. Expensive outfits, Joachim had bought most of them. Patricia wouldn't be able to wear the dresses: they were too big across the bust. But maybe the skirts and a few of the outfits?

The sound of keys in the front door made her heart skip a beat. She quickly shut the wardrobe, her bare feet flying over the wooden floor.

She just managed to close Josefin's bedroom door behind her when Joachim stepped into the hall.

'What are you doing?' he said.

He looked sweaty, and had dark rings under his arms.

Patricia just looked at him, her pulse racing, her mouth completely dry. She tried to smile.

'Nothing,' she said nervously.

'Haven't we told you to stay the fuck away from Josefin's room?'

He pulled the front door shut with a bang.

'It's the police,' she said. 'The pigs have been here snooping. Everything looks a right mess, in there too.'

He walked into the trap.

'Pigs?' he said, and Patricia could hear the fear in his voice. 'Did they take anything?'

He walked towards Patricia and the bedroom door.

'I don't know,' she said. 'Nothing of mine, anyway.'

He pushed the bedroom door open and walked over to the bed, and lifted the duvet.

'The sheets,' he said. 'They've taken the sheets.'

Patricia watched cautiously from the doorway. He walked round the room, checking things as he went, but evidently couldn't see anything else missing. He sat down heavily on the bed with his back to the door and put his head in his hands.

Patricia inhaled the dancing dust, unable to move. She looked at the man's broad shoulders and muscular arms. The light from the window made his blond hair glow. He really was very good-looking. Josefin had been so happy when they got together. Patricia remembered her crying with joy, and telling her how wonderful he was.

Joachim turned round and looked at her.

'Who do you think did it?' he said in a low voice.

Patricia kept her face neutral.

'Some madman,' she said, calmly and decisively. 'Some drunk on his way home from the pub. She was in the wrong place at the wrong time.'

He turned away again.

'Do you think it could have been one of the clients?' he said without looking up.

Patricia weighed her answer.

'One of last night's crop, you mean? I don't know, what do you think?'

'It would ruin the club,' he said.

She looked down at her hands, fiddling with the bottom of her T-shirt.

'I miss her,' she said.

Joachim got up and went over to her, put his hand on her shoulder and gently stroked her arm.

'Patricia,' he said quietly, 'I understand how upset you are. I'm just as upset myself.'

She shivered uncomfortably and had to make a real effort not to pull away.

'I hope the police catch him,' she said.

114

Joachim pulled her to him, a sob racking his muscular frame.

'Fuck, fuck,' he said through gritted teeth. 'Fuck. Why's she dead?'

He started to cry. Patricia put her arms round his back carefully, gently rocking him.

'My Josie, my angel . . .'

He went on crying, great snorting sobs. Patricia shut her eyes and forced herself not to pull away.

'Poor Joachim,' she whispered. 'You poor thing . . .'

He let go of her and went into the bathroom, where he blew his nose, then peed. She waited helplessly in the hall, listening to the splash of urine and then the flush.

'Have the police spoken to you?' he asked as he came out.

She gulped. 'A bit, yesterday. They want to talk more today.'

He looked intently at her.

'Good,' he said. 'They've got to catch the bastard who did this. What are you going to say?'

She turned away and went into the kitchen, and poured a glass of water.

'Depends what they ask. I don't know anything, anyway,' she said, then drank.

He had followed her, and was leaning against the door frame.

'They'll want to know what Josie was like and all that. What her life was like . . .'

Patricia put the glass down noisily on the draining board and looked Joachim in the eye.

'I'd never say anything that showed Josie in a bad light,' she said firmly.

The man looked content at this.

'Come here,' he said, putting an arm round her

shoulders. He guided her through the hall and over to Josie's wardrobe.

'Look,' he said, his free hand running over Josefin's expensive outfits. 'Is there anything you'd like? What about this one?'

He pulled out a bright pink, figure-hugging silk and wool dress with big gold buttons. Josefin had loved that one. She thought it made her look like Princess Diana.

Patricia felt her eyes start to water. She swallowed.

'But, Joachim, I can't—'

'Take it. It's yours.'

She started to cry. He let go of her and held the dress up in front of her.

'Your tits are too small, but we can probably fix that,' he said, smiling at her.

Patricia stopped crying, looked down and took the hanger.

'Thanks,' she whispered.

'Wear it for the funeral,' he said.

She heard him go out into the kitchen, where he took something out of the fridge, then he left the flat.

Patricia stayed where she was, in Josefin's room, frozen to the spot even though it was so hot.

15

The other evening paper had spoken to the father. He had nothing interesting to say, just that he couldn't believe she was gone, but even so . . . At least they had some quotes.

'You never know which way the wind's going to blow,' Berit said. 'If they're unlucky they'll end up the focus of a big debate about media ethics.'

'For talking to the relatives?' Annika wondered, scanning the rest of the article.

Berit nodded and took a sip from her bottle of lemon-flavoured mineral water.

'You have to be really careful when you do that,' she said. 'Some want to talk, but a lot don't. You must never trick anyone into talking. Did you call the parents?'

Annika folded the paper and shook her head. 'I couldn't bring myself to do it. It felt too awkward.'

'That's not a good way to judge things like this,' Berit said seriously. 'Just because it feels awkward to you doesn't mean the relatives will feel the same. Some of them find it a comfort to know that the papers are interested.'

'So you think everyone in the media should call a family when their child dies?'

Annika could hear how aggressive she sounded.

Berit took another sip of water and thought for a moment.

'Well, no two cases are the same. All you can know for certain is that people react differently. There's no definitive right or wrong way to handle it. You just have to be very, very careful, to make sure you don't hurt anyone.'

'Well, I'm glad I didn't call,' Annika said, getting up to fetch some coffee.

When she got back with her steaming plastic cup Berit had gone back to her own desk.

I wonder if I've upset her, Annika thought. She could see Berit leaning over another paper on the far side of the newsroom. She quickly picked up the phone and dialled Berit's internal number.

'Are you annoyed with me?' she said, meeting Berit's gaze from across the room.

'Not at all. You've got to work out what's right for you.'

The Cold Calls phone rang, and Annika switched phones.

'How much do I get for a really good tip-off?' an agitated male voice asked.

Annika groaned silently and told him.

'Okay,' the man said. 'Listen to this. Are you taking notes?'

'Yep,' Annika said. 'So what is it?'

'I know all about a television personality who dresses up in women's clothes and goes to dirty sex clubs,' the man said, sounding ready to burst.

He mentioned the name of one of Sweden's most popular and admired TV presenters. Annika could feel her anger radiating, right to her toes.

'Bollocks,' she said. 'What makes you think that the

Evening Post would be interested in publishing malicious crap like that?'

The man at the other end lost his confidence.

'But it's a huge scandal,' he said.

'For fuck's sake,' Annika said. 'People can do whatever the hell they like. And whatever makes you think this is true?'

'I got it from a reliable source,' the man said.

'Sure you did,' Annika said. 'Well, thanks for calling.'

She hung up.

The other evening paper had pretty much the same articles and picture about the murder as the *Evening Post*, but Annika thought that the *Post* had done a better job all the way through.

The other paper didn't have the graduation photograph of Josefin, for instance. Their pictures of the crime scene were tamer, their texts flatter, they had interviewed more boring neighbours and they hadn't made the link to the old Eva murder. They had no teacher, and no friends. The *Evening Post* had short interviews with both Josefin's friend Charlotta and the headmaster, Martin Larsson-Berg.

'Good work,' Spike said above her. She looked up and saw her boss looking at her.

'Thanks,' she said.

He sat down on the edge of her desk.

'So what are we doing today?'

A strange warmth ran through her. She was one of them now. He had come to her to find out.

'I thought I might go and see her flatmate, the girl who identified her.'

'Do you think she'll talk?'

'Maybe. I've tried to establish contact with her,' she said.

Instinctively she knew that she shouldn't mention her encounter with Patricia in the park. If she did, Spike would only be cross with her for not coming back and writing an article about it straight away.

'Okay,' the head of news said. 'Who's covering the police?'

'We're sharing that between us,' she said.

'Good. What else? Do you think the mum and dad are ready to shed a few tears?'

Annika squirmed on her chair.

'I don't think it's the right moment to intrude on them,' she said.

'He's already spoken to the press,' Spike said. 'What did he say when you called?'

Annika could feel herself blushing.

'He . . . I . . . didn't think I could disturb them so soon after—'

Spike stood up and walked off without a word.

Annika wanted to call him back, to explain how wrong it had felt, that you couldn't behave like that. Her mouth was open but no sound came out, and her raised arm did no good. She just had to get on with it; it wasn't her decision to make.

Spike's broad shoulders glided away, and he slumped onto his chair over at the newsdesk. Annika could almost feel his weight hit the chair even from a distance.

She quickly put her pen, notepad and tape-recorder in her bag and headed over to the picture desk. There were no photographers there, which meant no cars. She called for a taxi.

'To Vasastan. Dalagatan.'

She wanted to know how the dead woman had lived.

* * *

He woke up with a start to find his wife gently shaking his shoulder.

'Christer,' she whispered. 'It's the Prime Minister.'

He sat up with a general feeling of disorientation. The bed seemed to be rocking, and his whole body felt exhausted. With a groan he stood up and headed towards his office.

'I'll take it in here,' he said.

The Prime Minister's voice sounded calm and neutral. He'd evidently been up for hours.

'Well, Christer, did you get home okay?'

The Minister for Foreign Trade sank into the chair next to the desk and ran a hand through his hair.

'Yes, fine,' he said. 'It took quite a while to drive up here, that's all. How's everything with you?'

'Fine, just fine. I'm out at Harpsund with the family. So how did it go?'

Christer Lundgren cleared his throat.

'As expected, really. They're not exactly delicate when it comes to negotiating.'

'Well, I don't suppose it's the sort of situation where you'd expect delicacy,' the Prime Minister said. 'So where do we go from here?'

The Minister for Foreign Trade quickly arranged his thoughts in his foggy brain. When he spoke he sounded more or less organized and focused. He had had several hours to think on the drive up to Luleå.

After the call ended he stayed where he was, his head hanging over the desk. It was covered with a map of the world before the fall of the Iron Curtain. He let his eyes roam across the various republics, anonymous yellow areas without cities or boundaries.

His wife peered anxiously round the door.

'Would you like some coffee?'

He turned and smiled at her.

121

'Yes, that would be good,' he said, smiling even more. 'But first of all I'd like you.'

She took him by the hand and led him back to the bedroom.

16

Patricia jumped at the sound of the doorbell. The police weren't due for several more hours. Her mouth went dry. What if it was Josie's parents?

She padded quickly out into the hall and peered through the spyhole in the door. She recognized the figure outside: it was the woman from the park earlier that morning. She opened the door at once.

'Hello,' Patricia said. 'How did you know where to find me?'

The journalist smiled. She looked tired.

'Computers,' she said. 'There are registers for everything these days. Can I come in?'

Patricia hesitated. 'It's a bit of a mess,' she said. 'The police were here, and they turned everything upside down.'

'I promise not to start cleaning,' Annika said.

Patricia hesitated for a few more seconds.

'Okay,' she said finally, throwing the door open. 'But it isn't always like this. What did you say your name was?'

'Annika. Annika Bengtzon.'

They shook hands.

'Come in.'

The journalist stepped into the dark hallway and took off her shoes.

'God, it's so hot,' Annika said.

'I know,' Patricia said. 'I hardly slept a wink.'

'Because of Josefin?'

Patricia nodded.

'Nice dress,' Annika said, gesturing with her head. Patricia blushed, running her hand over the shiny, bright pink dress.

'It was Josefin's. I was given it,' she said.

'It makes you look like Princess Diana,' Annika said.

'Not really,' Patricia said. 'I'm too dark. I'll take it off. Hang on . . .'

She disappeared into her room, the living room, and hung the dress on its hanger again. She looked around for a hook to hang it on, then gave up and hung it on one of the door-hinges.

She quickly pulled on some shorts and a vest.

The journalist was standing in the kitchen when she emerged.

'It was pretty mean of them not to tidy up after themselves,' Annika said, nodding towards the stacks of plates on the table.

'It's going to take me all day to sort it out,' Patricia said. 'Would you like some tea?'

'Please,' Annika said, settling onto a chair.

Patricia lit the gas stove, filled an aluminium pan and quickly put the contents of the kitchen cupboards back in their place.

'Josie had the stars against her,' Patricia said. 'The signs weren't good. Saturn has been in her sign for almost a year now; she's been having a really tough time.'

She fell quiet, blinking back tears. The journalist looked at her in surprise.

'Do you believe in all that?' she said.

124

'I don't believe, I *know*,' Patricia said. 'We've got Lipton or Earl Grey.'

Annika chose Lipton.

'I brought a copy of the paper,' she said, laying the first edition of the *Evening Post* on the table. Patricia's expression didn't change.

'You can't write about anything I tell you,' she said.

'Okay,' Annika said.

'You can't write that you've been here.'

'Whatever you want,' Annika said.

Patricia studied the reporter in silence. Annika looked young, hardly any older than her. She dunked her teabag a few times, then pressed it with a teaspoon and squeezed the last drops out of it.

'So what are you doing here, then?' Patricia asked.

'I want to understand,' Annika said quietly. 'I want to know who Josefin was, how she lived, what she thought, what she felt. And you know all that. Then I'll be able to ask other people the right questions, without letting on what you've told me. Anything you say to me is protected by law. No one in any position of authority is entitled even to ask who I've spoken to.'

Patricia considered this for a moment as she sipped her tea.

'What do you want to know?' she asked.

'Well, you know best,' Annika said. 'What was she like?'

Patricia sighed. 'Sometimes she could be really childish. I used to get cross with her. She'd forget that we'd arranged to meet up, things like that. So I'd be left standing there like an idiot. And afterwards she was never even sorry. She'd just say, "Oh, I forgot."'

Patricia fell silent.

'But I'm really going to miss her,' she added.

'Where did she work?' Annika asked.

125

She had taken out her pen and notepad. Patricia noticed and straightened up.

'You're not going to write any of this, are you?'

Annika smiled. 'Sometimes my memory's as bad as Josefin's,' she said. 'I'm only making notes to remind myself of what we've talked about.'

Patricia relaxed.

'At a club called Studio Six. On Hantverkargatan,' she said.

'Really?' Annika said, astonished. 'I live there! Where on Hantverkargatan?'

'On the slope. There's no flashing neon sign or anything like that. It's pretty discreet, just a small sign in the window.'

Annika was thinking.

'Isn't there a radio programme called *Studio Six*?' she said, suddenly unsure.

Patricia giggled.

'Yes,' she said. 'But Joachim – he owns the club – found out that Swedish Radio hadn't registered the name. So he used the same name for the club, mainly to annoy the people at Swedish Radio. Besides, it's a great name. It sounds close enough to "Studio Sex" for people to realize what it's all about. Who knows, maybe they'll all end up in court.'

'Joachim,' Annika said. 'Was he Josie's boyfriend?'

Patricia grew serious.

'That stuff I told you in the park, you mustn't tell anyone about that. Ever,' she said.

'But you said you'd told the police?'

Patricia's eyes opened wide.

'That's true,' she said, sounding horrified, 'I did.'

'That's nothing to worry about,' Annika said. 'It's really important that they get to know things like that.'

'But Joachim's so upset. He was here this morning, in floods of tears.'

Annika looked down at her notes and decided to drop the subject for the time being.

'So what was Josie's job?'

'She was a waitress and dancer.'

'Dancer?'

'On stage. Not naked, that's not allowed. Joachim sticks to the law. She wore a thong.'

Patricia could see that the reporter was easily shocked.

'So she was a . . . stripper?'

'I guess you could say that,' Patricia said.

'And you, you're a . . . dancer too?'

Patricia laughed. 'No, Joachim says my tits are too small. I work in the bar, and I'm learning how to run the roulette table. Well, I'm supposed to be learning. I'm no good at maths.'

Her laughter died away and she sniffed a few times. Annika waited in silence until Patricia had composed herself.

'Did you go to the same school, you and Josefin?' she asked.

Patricia blew her nose on a piece of kitchen roll and shook her head.

'No, not at all,' she said. 'We met at the gym, the Sports Club on Sankt Eriksgatan. We used to go at the same times and always used lockers next to each other. Josefin was the one who got us talking; she had no trouble talking to anyone. She'd just got together with Joachim and was so in love. She used to talk about him for hours. How handsome he was, how much money he had . . .' She fell quiet, lost in her memories.

'How did they meet?' Annika asked after a few seconds.

Patricia shrugged. 'Joachim grew up in Täby, like her. I first got to know Josie the Christmas before last, a year and a half ago. Joachim had only just opened the club. It was a success right from the start. Josie sometimes worked there at weekends, and she got me the job in the bar. I've got a catering qualification and everything.'

The phone rang out in the hall, and Patricia jumped up to answer it.

'Of course, no problem,' she said. 'In half an hour.'

When she came back into the kitchen Annika was putting the tea things on the draining board and had put her things away in her bag.

'The police will be here in a little while,' Patricia said.

'Well, I won't disturb you any longer,' Annika said. 'Thanks very much for talking to me.'

'Well, feel free to call again,' Patricia said.

Annika went out into the hall and pulled on her sandals.

'How long are you going to stay here?' she wondered.

Patricia bit her lip.

'I don't know,' she said. 'It's Josie's flat. Her mum pulled a few strings and got hold of it to save Josie having to commute from Täby kyrkby when she got into the school of journalism at Stockholm University.'

'Did Josefin get in there? Were her grades good enough?'

Patricia gave Annika a sidelong glance.

'Josie's really smart,' she said. 'She gets As in practically every subject. Swedish is her best subject, she writes really well. You think she's stupid just because she's done a bit of exotic dancing, don't you?'

In spite of the gloom in the hall, she could see the journalist blushing.

'I spoke to her headmaster. He didn't seem to think her grades were that good,' she said by way of explanation.

'So? He's probably just a bigot,' Patricia said.

'Did she have many friends?'

'At school, you mean? Hardly any. She was a bit of a swot.'

They shook hands and Annika opened the door. She paused in the doorway.

'Why did you move in here?' she asked.

Patricia looked at the floor.

'Josie wanted me to,' she said.

'Why?'

'Because she was scared.'

'What of?'

'I can't tell you.'

Patricia could see from the reporter's eyes that she understood anyway.

17

Annika emerged into the sunshine on Dalagatan, blinking against the light. It was a relief to get out of the dark, dirty flat. Black curtains, it was all a bit macabre. She didn't like the sound of what she'd heard. She didn't like the place Josie had lived in. And she couldn't help being deeply sceptical of her choice of career. How could anyone become a stripper of their own free will?

If it was of her own free will, she reflected.

There was an underground station right on the corner, so she travelled the two stops to Fridhemsplan. She came out of the exit on Sankt Eriksgatan, close to the gym where Josefin and Patricia had first met. She turned right, up towards the scene of the murder. There were two small bunches of flowers by the entrance, and Annika guessed that there would soon be many more. She stood by the railings for a while. It was at least as hot as yesterday, and she soon felt thirsty. Just as she had decided to leave, two young women, one fair, one dark-haired, approached on foot from the Drottningholm road. Annika made up her mind to wait. They were both wearing short skirts and high heels, chewing gum and clutching cans of Pepsi Max.

'A girl died in there yesterday,' the fair one said, pointing at the cemetery as they went past Annika.

'No!' the dark-haired one said, eyes opening wide.

The first girl nodded vigorously, waving her hand.

'They found her lying in there, all split open. She was raped after she was killed.'

'That's really horrible,' the dark-haired girl said. Annika could see that her eyes were starting to water.

They stopped a couple of metres away, staring devoutly at the dark green shadows. Within a minute or so they were both in tears.

'We ought to leave a message,' the fair-haired girl said.

They dug out an old receipt from one girl's bag and found a pen in the other. The fair-haired girl wrote the message leaning on her friend's back. Then they wiped their tears and headed off towards the underground. When they had disappeared round the corner Annika went over and read the note.

It said: *We miss you.*

At that moment she caught sight of a team of reporters from the other evening paper getting out of a car over by the children's playground on Kronobergsgatan. She turned on her heel and quickly walked off towards Sankt Göransgatan. She had no desire to engage in small talk with Arne Påhlson.

On her way to the number 56 bus-stop she realized she would be going right past Daniella Hermansson's door, the young mother who always slept with her windows open. She pulled out her notepad and checked; yes, she had the code for the front door written down next to Daniella's address. Without thinking any more about it, she tapped in the code and went in.

The air inside was so cool that it made her shiver. She stopped as the door slammed shut behind her. The hallway was decorated with murals from the 1940s, all depicting the park, probably dating from when the block was built.

Daniella lived two floors up. Annika took the lift. No one answered her knock. Annika looked at the time, ten past three. Daniella was probably down in the park.

She sighed. She hadn't really got much so far today. She looked round the stairwell. There were doors everywhere; the flats must be really small. The names on the letterboxes were spelt out with yellow plastic lettering. She glanced at the closest name: Svensson. There wasn't really much to think about. She may as well get a few reaction quotes now that she was here.

The narrow gap of Svensson's open door let out a sour smell of body odour, making Annika take a step back. A shapeless female figure in a purple and turquoise polyester dress filled the gap. She was squinting short-sightedly, and her grey hair shone with grease and setting lotion. She was clutching a small dog, although Annika couldn't make out what sort.

'I'm sorry to disturb you,' Annika said, 'but I'm from the *Evening Post*.'

'We haven't done anything,' the woman said.

She looked at Annika through the gap, terrified.

'No, of course not,' Annika said politely. 'I was just wondering if you had any reaction to the crime that was committed nearby.'

The woman started to close the door.

'I don't know anything,' she said.

Annika was starting to think that this was a bad idea.

'Perhaps you haven't heard. A young woman was murdered in the park up the road,' she said calmly. 'The police may have been here and—'

'They were here yesterday.'

'Oh, then they probably asked—'

'It wasn't Jesper!' the woman shouted, out of nowhere. Annika dropped her notepad and took two steps back.

'There was nothing I could do to stop him! And I really don't think the minister's got anything to do with it!'

With a slam the woman shut the door, the noise echoing through the stairwell. Annika stared at the door in amazement. What on earth had just happened?

A door at the far end of the landing opened up a crack.

'What's all this commotion?' an elderly male voice said, clearly irritated.

Annika picked up her notepad and went down the two flights of steps. Out in the street again she turned right and hurried off, without looking back at the park.

18

'Thanks for cat-sitting!'

Anne Snapphane was back, and now she was sitting with her feet up on her desk.

'How was Gotland?' Annika asked, dropping her bag on the floor.

'Like an oven. Huge fire, but under control now. So what the hell have you been up to?'

'What do you mean?' Annika said, not understanding.

'You've got a nasty cut above your eye!'

Annika's hand flew up to her left eyebrow.

'Oh, that,' she said. 'I hit my head on the bathroom cabinet this morning. Guess where I've been?'

'In the murder victim's flat?'

Annika grinned and sat down.

'Well, well . . .' Anne said.

'Have you had lunch?'

They went down to the cafeteria.

'So, what was it like?' Anne Snapphane asked curiously, shovelling another spoonful of pasta into her mouth.

Annika thought for a moment.

'I like Patricia, her flatmate. She's an immigrant, or first-generation Swede. From somewhere in South

America, I'd guess. A bit crazy, believes in astrology.'

'So what was Josefin like?'

Annika put her fork down.

'I don't know,' she said. 'I haven't really got a grip on her yet. Patricia says she was really intelligent, her headmaster says she was a dumb blonde. Her classmate Charlotta doesn't seem to know the first thing about her. She wanted to be a journalist, and she wanted to help children in need, but she was working as a stripper.'

'A stripper?' Anne Snapphane said.

'Her boyfriend owns some sort of porn club. Studio Six.'

'That's a radio programme. Pretentious debate on P3.'

Annika nodded. 'Yep. Joachim, the boyfriend, evidently thought that was a good joke. You're right, though: *Studio Six* is about as pretentious as you can get.'

'If he was keen to annoy pretentious bastards, that suggests a certain level of intelligence,' Anne Snapphane said.

Annika smiled and took a large mouthful.

'So tell me more, what did it look like?'

Annika thought as she chewed.

'Bare,' she said. 'Not properly furnished or decorated. Mattresses on the floor. As if she hadn't really moved in properly.'

'How the hell did she get a flat on Dalagatan?'

'Her mum pulled some strings and paid handsomely for it. The phone's listed under the mother's name.'

Anne Snapphane leaned back in her chair.

'So why did she die?'

Annika shrugged. 'Don't know.'

'What are the cops saying?'

135

'Haven't called them yet.'

They bought bottles of water and went back to the newsroom. Spike was on the phone; and no one else was there.

'What are you doing today?' Annika asked.

'There've been several more forest fires around the country. I'm putting them all out, personally.'

Annika laughed.

Back at her desk she turned on her computer, and quickly typed up the notes from her meeting with Patricia, then saved them to a memory stick and deleted the document from the hard-drive. She put the memory stick in her bottom desk drawer.

Annika's phone rang, the ring indicating it was an internal call.

'You've got a visitor,' Tore Brand said.

'Who is it?' Annika asked.

Tore Brand disappeared from the line, she could hear him shouting in the background.

'Hey, wait! You can't go through there . . .'

Then steps returning to the phone.

'He's gone up already. I don't think you need to worry. It was just some bloke.'

Annika felt herself getting annoyed. Tore Brand was supposed to stop this sort of thing happening. Stupid old fool!

'What does he want?'

'He wanted to talk about something in today's paper. We're supposed to listen to our readers,' Tore Brand said.

At that moment Annika caught sight of the man out of the corner of her eye. He was storming towards her, his eyes blazing.

'Are you Annika Bengtzon?' he snarled.

Annika nodded.

The man slammed a copy of that day's *Evening Post* down on her desk from a great height.

'Why didn't you call?' His voice broke in a spasm that seemed to come from deep in his guts.

Annika stared at the man. She had no idea who he was.

'Why didn't you tell us what you were going to write? Her mother had no idea this was how she died. And as for the fact that something had taken a bite out of her . . . Good God!'

The man turned away and sat down on her desk, putting his hands to his face and crying. Annika picked up the paper he had slammed down in front of her. It was the article about what Josefin had looked like when she was found, her soundless scream and bruised breasts, with the picture of her naked leg poking out of the grass. Annika shut her eyes and ran a hand over her forehead.

This can't be happening, she thought. Bloody hell, what have I done? She felt shame washing over her like a hot wave, and the floor began to sway. Good grief, what on earth had she done?

'Sorry,' she said. 'I didn't want to intrude—'

'Intrude?' the man screamed. 'How could anything be more intrusive than this? Did you imagine we wouldn't see the shit you decided to write? Maybe you hoped we'd die too and never find out? Huh?'

Annika was on the verge of tears. The angry man was completely red in the face, his mouth dribbling saliva. The few people in the newsroom had noticed what was happening. Spike had turned round and was staring at them. Picture-Pelle was craning his neck to see what was going on.

'I really am very sorry,' she said.

Suddenly, out of nowhere, Berit appeared. Without

a word she put her arm round the man and led him off to the cafeteria. He went with her without a word of protest, racked with sobs.

Annika picked up her bag and hurried towards the rear exit. She was panting for breath and had to make a real effort to walk normally.

'Where are you going, Bengtzon?' Spike yelled.

'Out,' she called back, far too shrilly.

She ran the last steps and threw herself at the back door. Two flights down, on the stairs outside the newspaper's archive, she sat down.

I'm a terrible person, she thought. This is never going to work.

She sat there for a while, then left the building through the print-shop, and went and bought an ice-cream.

She walked slowly down to the water through Mariaberg Park. Across the water she could hear children shouting at Smedsudden beach. She sat down on a bench to eat her ice-cream, throwing the wrapper into an overflowing bin beside the path.

This is what it means to be alive, she thought. You hear sounds, you feel the wind and heat, you fail, and you feel ashamed. This is what it's all about. Living and learning.

From now on I shall never hesitate to make a call, or establish new contacts. I shall stand for what I write. I shall never feel ashamed of my work, or my words.

She walked slowly along the shore towards the beach, then turned up the hill and went back towards the office.

'You're supposed to tell me when you leave the building,' Tore Brand said crossly as she passed the reception desk.

She didn't bother to respond, just took the lift up, praying silently that the furious vicar had disappeared.

138

He had. And so had everyone else, she noticed. Spike and Jansson would be at the handover meeting, the editors hadn't yet arrived, and Berit wasn't there.

She sat heavily on her chair. She hadn't managed to achieve anything worthwhile today. The only thing left to do was to call the police.

The press spokesman told her that work on the investigation was proceeding. The crime unit didn't answer her call. The operations centre hadn't been involved in the case at all today.

She hesitated, then decided to call the head of the investigation anyway. He'd just have to get angry if he wanted to.

He picked up her call to the duty desk in the violent crime unit. Her pulse started to race.

'Hello, this is Annika Bengtzon from the—'

'I know.'

A faint groan.

'Don't you ever rest?' she asked.

'No, I'm like you, evidently.' His tone was cold and abrupt.

'I've just got a few quick questions—'

'I can't talk to every single journalist; I'd have no time left to do my job.' Angry, irritated.

'You don't have to talk to everyone; you just have to talk to me.'

'Yes, you would say that.' Tired.

Annika thought for a few seconds.

'This is wasting time,' she said. 'It would be much quicker if you just answered my questions.'

'And it would be quickest of all if I just hung up.'

'So why don't you?'

She could hear him breathing, as if he was wondering the same thing.

'What do you want?' he said eventually.

'I want to know what you've been doing today.'

'Routine stuff. Questions and interviews.'

'Patricia? Joachim? The others at the club? Maybe a few clients? Her parents? The twin brother? The neighbours? The fat old woman with the dog? Who's Jesper? And who's the minister?'

She could sense his surprise down the line.

'You've done your homework,' he said.

'No, just standard research.'

'We've found her clothes,' he said.

Annika felt the hairs on her arms stand up. This hadn't been made public yet. He was giving her an exclusive.

'Where?'

'At the incinerator out in Högdalen.'

'The dump?'

'No, in a compressor together with a load of other rubbish. They must have been dumped in a bin somewhere on Kungsholmen. The bins are emptied onto open trucks each day, then compressed with all the other rubbish picked up off the streets. You can imagine . . .'

'Can you still use them as evidence?'

'So far our experts have found part of a television, some stuffing from a sofa, pieces of banana skin, and traces of baby faeces in the fibres.'

He sighed.

'So no use at all?' Annika said.

'Not yet, at least.'

'Were they torn?'

'Ripped to shreds. By the compressor.'

'So any fingerprints, hairs, small tears – anything that could tell you something – have been destroyed?'

'Exactly.'

'Can I write that?'

'Do you think it adds anything?'

She thought for a moment.

'The clothes must have been thrown away by the killer. Someone may have seen him.'

'Where? How many people do you think throw rubbish into the bins on Kungsholmen every day? Take a guess!'

She thought back to the ice-cream wrapper down in the park.

'Well . . . everyone?'

'Quite! And it might not even have been the killer. The clothes may have been found somewhere else and put in the bin by some civic-minded citizen.'

She waited in silence.

'At least it would show that the police are doing something,' she said.

He laughed. 'Well, that would be something.'

'We wouldn't have to say how badly the clothes have been damaged,' Annika said. 'There's no need to let the killer know that.'

He laughed again, but didn't say anything.

'The interviews, then?'

He clammed up again. 'I can't say anything about that. It's ongoing.'

'With the people I mentioned earlier?'

'That's just the start.'

'What about the post-mortem? Has that come up with anything?'

'They keep office hours. Tomorrow, in other words.'

'What sort of place is Studio Six, exactly?'

'Why don't you go and take a look?'

'Do you know what sort of minister the old woman was going on about?'

'What a relief that there are still some things for you to find out,' he said. 'I have to go. Goodbye.'

19

Annika sat thinking for a while. The business with the clothes was new; they could make something of that. It was a shame the police didn't think the find more valuable, but at least they knew that the murderer hadn't kept hold of the clothes.

Spike, Jansson and Picture-Pelle had emerged from the handover. They were sitting talking over at the newsdesk.

'I've got an exclusive. Well, so far, anyway,' she said.

The men looked up at her with the same astonished and slightly annoyed expression.

'They've found her clothes.'

The men straightened up and reached for their pens.

'Fuck. Can we get a picture of them?' the picture editor said.

'No, but we can get one of the place they were found. The incinerator out in Högdalen.'

'And are they any use?'

Annika considered her answer.

'Not really, but the police don't want to reveal that,' she said.

The men nodded.

'This could be really good,' Jansson said. 'Together

with everything else we've got a good mixture. Look at this.'

He held his notebook out to Annika.

'I think we'll kick off with your piece, "new line of inquiry for police". A picture of Josefin; a picture of the tip. It'll soon be time to get you a picture byline, Bengtzon!'

The men laughed, friendly laughter. Annika looked down and blushed.

'Then there's the father,' Jansson went on. 'Berit did a fantastic interview with him.'

Annika was astonished. 'Did she?'

'Yep, he turned up here shouting about something, so Berit sorted him out. He wanted to talk, he said. She's working on her piece with the parents as we speak. They wanted to see it first.'

'Unbelievable,' Annika muttered.

'Then we need something about the crime-scene. Are there any flowers there yet?'

'There were very few this afternoon.'

'Go and see if there are any more now. Can you do that? Maybe talk to someone bringing flowers, writing a note or lighting a candle?'

Annika sighed and nodded.

'How did you get on with her classmates?' she wondered.

'Berit couldn't find anyone, apart from your Charlotta. We've got a picture of her at home in her bedroom. Some of the others will probably be coming home this evening, now that the main holiday month is almost over, but we can't worry about that. We've got enough for today. And we've got the fires, and the Middle East as well. Looks like we'll get a war down there again . . .'

The editors rolled in, keen to get working. Annika

went back to her desk and wrote her piece about the police's new line of inquiry, then packed her bag ready to head back to the scene of the murder again.

Bertil Strand wasn't in, so she turned on the television hanging from the ceiling. There wasn't even a mention of Josefin on the local news.

The main evening news devoted half its programme to the Middle East. Seven Israelis and fifteen Palestinians had been killed in fighting today. Three of them were young children. Annika shuddered.

Then came the spokesperson of the Green Party, demanding an official inquiry into the registration of political interests and the Information Bureau debacle. Annika yawned.

At the end of the programme came the second part of the Russian correspondent's report on the conflict in the Caucasus. They had carried an interview with the Swedish-speaking president yesterday, and today the reporter was with the alarmingly well-equipped guerrillas.

'We're fighting for our freedom,' their leader said, holding a Kalashnikov in each hand. 'The President is a hypocrite and a traitor.'

The guerrillas' base contained women and children. The kids were laughing and playing, dusty and barefoot. The women pulled shawls over their heads and disappeared into the dark doorways of their homes. The guerrilla leader opened the door to an underground cellar and the reporter followed him into the earth. The harsh light of the camera lit up row after row of Russian weapons, boxes of mines, anti-aircraft guns, automatic rifles, hand grenades, shells and bazookas.

Annika suddenly felt very low. She was tired and hungry. What did it matter what she wrote about a dead Swedish girl when people in other parts of the world did nothing but kill each other?

She went to the cafeteria and bought a bag of sweets. She ate the whole lot on her way back to her desk and immediately felt sick.

'How's it going, Annika?'

It was Berit.

'Oh, okay,' Annika said. 'The world just looks a bit bleak, that's all. How did you get on with the parents?'

'Fine,' Berit said. 'They had a few comments about some of it, but we agreed on most things. I got a picture of them, sitting on the bed in Josefin's old room.'

'They haven't changed anything?' Annika wondered.

'It looks completely untouched.'

Berit went over towards the newsdesk to tell them how she had got on. At that moment Bertil Strand appeared.

'Have you got time to take a trip down to the murder-scene?' Annika asked, grabbing her bag.

'I've only just put the car away in the garage. Couldn't you have mentioned it earlier?'

Patricia was lying on the mattress behind her black curtains, sweating in the dark. Her legs ached, and she was so tired she felt sick. She didn't have the energy to spy on Joachim. They couldn't ask her to do that. Even the thought of it gave her goosebumps.

She closed her eyes and tried to shut out the sounds of the city. It was evening outside now; people were on their way to restaurants and out on dates, all short skirts and wine, beer and sweat. She focused inwards, trying to find the truth inside herself, listening to the sound of her own breathing, and sank into a state of gentle self-hypnosis.

She conjured up Josefin's voice from the darkness, from deep within herself. To start with the voice was bubbly and happy, rising and falling. Patricia smiled. Josie

145

hummed and sang, light and clear. When the screams came Patricia was ready for them. She listened patiently to the thuds and blows, at Joachim's bellowing. She hid in the shadows until he fell silent and disappeared, waiting for the crying and despair from Josie's room. She had no feelings of guilt; there was nothing she could have done to stop it. She didn't even feel horrified, and she wasn't frightened. He couldn't do any more damage now. Not to Josie.

She took a deep breath and forced herself up to the surface. Reality came back, dull and hot.

I must consult the cards, she thought.

Slowly she got up, but her blood pressure didn't keep up and she felt giddy. From her sports bag over in the corner she took out a small balsa-wood box. She opened the lid and ran her fingers over the black velvet. This was where her cards lived.

She sat on the floor in the lotus position and shuffled the cards reverently. Then she cut them three times. She repeated this procedure twice more, just as the energies demanded. After the final cut she didn't put the cards back together, but chose one half, picking it up with her left hand and then shuffling the cards one more time.

Finally she laid out a Celtic cross on the wooden floor, ten cards symbolizing the qualities of the moment from different perspectives. The Celtic cross was the most perfect layout when you were faced with great changes, and she was aware that this applied to her right now.

She held back from studying and analysing the cards until the cross was complete. Then she carefully considered her situation. Her central card was the three of swords, which stood for Saturn in Libra. She nodded, it was actually fairly obvious. The three of swords stood for sorrow, and tension in a triangular relationship. She

146

was being encouraged to make clear and unambiguous decisions.

The card crossing the central card, representing the obstacle, was naturally the fifteenth card of the Major Arcana, the Devil, the male gender. It could hardly be any clearer.

The third and fourth cards showed her conscious and unconscious thoughts about her situation. Nothing odd there, either: the nine of swords and the ten of wands. Cruelty and oppression.

The seventh and eighth cards, on the other hand, made a deep impression on her. The seventh symbolized Patricia herself, and it was the eighteenth card of the Major Arcana, the Moon. That wasn't good. It meant she would soon face a decisive and very difficult test, and this was somehow linked to the female gender.

The eighth card made her very thoughtful. It stood for external energies that would influence her situation.

The Magician, the first card, symbolizing an unscrupulous communicator, a brilliant wordsmith hovering around the margins of the truth. She already had an idea of who this might be.

The tenth card, the outcome, calmed her down again. The six of wands. Jupiter in Leo. Clarity. Breakthrough. Victory.

Now she knew she was going to make it.

Seventeen years, nine months and three days

Our happiness is so strong. He holds me, always. He's so incredibly committed, sometimes I have trouble living up to it. He gets disappointed if I don't tell him, I have to get better at that. Our travels in time and space are endless, I love him so.

I've tried to explain, it isn't his fault. It's me; I'm the one who can't appreciate him the way he deserves. He's bought me clothes that I've hardly worn, symbols of love and devotion. My ingratitude is based on egotism and immaturity, and his disappointment is deep, harsh. There are no excuses; we each have our responsibilities in this universal pairing.

I cry when I realize how inadequate I am. He forgives me. Then we make love.

Never leave me,
he says,
I can't live without you.

And I promise.

Monday 30 July

20

Spike was waiting at her desk, even though she wasn't due to start work for another hour and a half.

'Berit's just got a brilliant tip-off about another story,' he said. 'You'll have to cover the murder today with Carl Wennergren.'

Annika dropped her bag on the floor and wiped the sweat from her brow.

'It just keeps getting hotter,' she said.

'Carl's on his way up from Nynäshamn,' Spike said. 'Did you hear that he won the Round Gotland Race?'

Annika sat down and switched on her computer.

'No, but that's great.'

Spike perched on her desk and opened the other evening paper.

'Well, we win today,' he said. 'They haven't got the parents, or the recovered clothes. You did a good job yesterday, you and Berit.'

Annika bowed her head.

'So how do we follow that today?' she wondered.

'You won't get the front page,' Spike said. 'Sales always slip on the third day. And it would have to be something pretty huge to knock Berit's story off the front. Try to get some sort of theory out of the police; they ought to have come up with something by now. Do you know if they're working on a particular theory?'

Annika hesitated, thinking of Joachim, and she remembered Spike's dislike of 'domestic rows'.

'Maybe,' she said simply.

'If the police don't come up with something soon, this story will be running on empty,' Spike continued. 'We'll have to keep an eye on the murder-scene – today may be the day when the crying friends show up.'

'How about a graphic, with a map of her final hours?' Annika suggested.

Spike lit up. 'You're right, we haven't done that yet. Check what we've got for that, then have a word with the designers.'

Annika made some notes.

'Is anything else happening?' she asked.

'We're being blessed with a new editor-in-chief. Anders Schyman starts work today. We'll see how that goes . . .'

Annika was cautious in her response. She'd heard the gossip about the new editor-in-chief, a former presenter of a series of documentaries for Swedish Television. She'd never met him, just seen him on television. He was tall and blond. She thought he seemed rather boorish and unpleasant.

'What do you think of him?' Annika asked warily.

'That we're in for a rough ride,' Spike said. 'How the fuck does some television star think he can waltz in here and teach us how to do our jobs?'

He seemed to be expressing the general attitude in the newsroom.

Annika dropped the subject.

'Is Anne Snapphane doing anything special today, or can she help with the murder?'

Spike got to his feet.

'Miss Snapphane is suffering from a brain tumour again, and is having yet another MRI scan. Ah, Carl, bloody well done!'

Carl Wennergren was strolling into the newsroom, clutching his trophy. Spike hurried over to him and slapped him on the back. Annika stayed where she was, dumbfounded. Good grief, poor Anne, a brain tumour!

Her hands were shaking as she lifted the receiver and dialled Anne's number. She answered on the first ring.

'How on earth are you?' Annika said, her voice cracking.

'I'm so fucking worried,' Anne Snapphane said. 'I feel so giddy, so weak. I keep seeing flashes when I close my eyes.'

'Spike told me. Bloody hell – why didn't you tell me?'

Anne lost her train of thought. 'What?'

'That you've got a brain tumour!'

'But I've never had a brain tumour.' Anne Snapphane sounded confused. 'I've had loads of check-ups, but they've never found anything.'

Annika didn't get it.

'But Spike said . . . So there's nothing wrong with your brain?'

'Look, it's like this,' Anne Snapphane said. 'I suppose you could say that I have a fairly lively imagination when it comes to illness. I'm perfectly aware that this is the case, but it still doesn't stop me being absolutely convinced that I'm dying at least twice a year. Last winter I nagged my doctors so much that I actually got an MRI scan. Spike thought that was hilarious.'

Annika leaned back in her chair.

'So you're a hypochondriac . . .' she said.

Anne Snapphane gave a sad little laugh.

'Yes, I suppose that's the word for it. Well, I've still

153

got a doctor's appointment at half past three this afternoon. You never know . . .'

'So how are you going to spend your days off?'

'If they don't think I need to stay in hospital, I'll be going up to Piteå with the cats. I'm booked on the night train.'

'Okay,' Annika said. 'See you when you get back.'

They ended the call and Annika sat thinking about her own time off work. Today was the last of a five-day shift for her, followed by four days off. She was planning to go home to Hälleforsnäs, meet up with Sven, go and see Whiskas. She sighed. She would soon have to make a decision. Either hang around in Stockholm and try to find another job or give up the flat and move home again.

She looked around the newsroom. Because it was Monday there were people everywhere. It made her feel clumsy and insecure. She didn't know the names of half of them. The warm sense of belonging she had felt over the weekend had vanished. Somehow it seemed to be connected to the night-time atmosphere: strip-lights, dark windows, empty corridors and the gentle hum of the air-conditioning.

During the day it was a completely different place, full of light and noise and confident people. She didn't feel in control, and she didn't feel she belonged.

'Well, things have certainly been happening here while I've been away,' Carl Wennergren said, sitting down rather presumptuously on Annika's desk. Annika demonstratively pulled out a computer printout that he was sitting on.

'It's such a tragic story,' she said.

Carl Wennergren put the trophy down on the printout.

'It's a challenge cup,' he said. 'Not bad, eh?'

'It's lovely,' Annika said.

'The boat's owner gets the trophy, and the others get some sort of diploma. IOR Class One, the big boats, that's my arena.'

'There are a lot of different classes, aren't there?' Annika said as she opened one of the news agencies' website.

Carl Wennergren looked at her for a few seconds without saying anything.

'You're not really that keen on boats, are you?' he said.

'Oh, I am,' Annika said. 'I often take Grandma's rowing-boat out on the lake. I love doing that, it's all so beautiful.'

She didn't look up as he got up and walked away, forcing herself to shut him and the rest of the newsroom out. She reached for a copy of the other paper. They hadn't come up with much about the murder. She saw that they had made a fuss about a note left at the scene of the crime: *We miss you*. Annika shook her head and leafed through the rest of the paper, until she came to an article about what happens to relationships when the holidays are over. The number of divorces always goes up dramatically in the autumn, she read, once any hopes of keeping the marriage alive over the winter have been crushed during summer holidays. She thought of herself and her own relationship and sighed.

'Goodness, you look miserable. Time for a coffee?'

Berit was grinning at her, and Annika tried to smile back.

'I hear you've got a scoop,' Annika said, fishing in her bag for her purse.

'Yep, a really good one,' Berit said. 'You know about the Information Bureau scandal, the IB affair?'

Annika was counting her change, and making a

mental note to get some more cash out today.

'Sort of,' she said. 'That Jan Guillou and Peter Bratt found out that the government was keeping an illegal register of political affiliations during the seventies?'

They headed towards the cafeteria.

'Exactly,' Berit said. 'The Social Democrats panicked. They arrested the journalists and basically behaved completely irrationally. And they destroyed their archives, both the domestic one and the one covering other countries. Coffee please, and a Danish.'

They sat by one of the windows, not for the view, but to be close to the air-conditioning.

'So there's no way of finding out what really happened at IB?' Annika said.

'Quite,' Berit said. 'The fact that the archives were missing put a stop to any thorough investigation. The Social Democrats have been sitting pretty. Until now.'

Annika stopped chewing.

'Why?' she said.

Berit lowered her voice subconsciously. 'I got a tip-off yesterday, in the middle of the night. The foreign archive has turned up.'

Annika's jaw dropped.

'Really?' she said.

Berit sighed. 'Well, sort of,' she said. 'Suddenly a copy of the archive has been found in the Defence Ministry. There are no sources, and the original documentation is missing, but even so . . .'

'That doesn't necessarily mean that the originals still exist,' Annika said, blowing on her coffee.

'No, it doesn't, but it does make it more likely. Until last night there was no proof that anything remained of the archive. These copies cover a lot of the material, so obviously they're extremely valuable.'

'Have you had a look yet?' Annika asked.

156

'Yes, I went over there first thing this morning. It's all in the public domain, after all.'

Annika nodded thoughtfully.

'This is big,' she said. 'And right in the middle of the election campaign.'

'You'll never guess where it turned up,' Berit said.

'In the Gents?' Annika said.

'Nope. Incoming post,' Berit said.

21

The minister pulled the swing back as far as he could.

'Are you ready?' he cried.

'Yes!' his daughter squeaked.

'Are you ready?' he yelled again.

'Yeeees!' the child shouted.

With the sound of his daughter's cry ringing in his ears, he pushed the wooden seat in front of him, then dodged underneath it as it sailed up into the air.

'Aaaaaah!' the child cried.

'Me too, Daddy, me too!'

He smiled at his son and wiped the sweat from his brow.

'Okay, cowboy,' he said. 'But this is the last time.'

He went round the tree, tickling his daughter on the stomach in passing, grabbed hold of his son's swing and went through his 'are you ready?' routine again. Then he gave a decent push, but not as hard as he had pushed his daughter: the boy was smaller and not as fearless as his twin sister.

'Daddy, push me again!' his daughter cried.

'I don't think I've got any energy left,' he said. 'When you've stopped swinging, come and sit with me on the bench.'

'But Daddy, Daddy . . .'

He walked over to where his wife was sitting under the big parasol. The blue-stained garden furniture was made of sustainably grown pine. Sometimes he felt unbearably predictable.

'When do you have to go?' she said.

He kissed her hair and settled onto the bench beside her.

'I don't know.' He sighed. 'With a bit of luck I'll be able to stay for the rest of the week.'

The phone rang, and he started to get up.

'No, you stay here, I'll get it . . .'

She got up and ran lightly over to the veranda, where the cordless phone was ringing. Her skirt flapped around her legs, her hair dancing over her suntanned shoulders. He felt a sudden wave of tenderness towards her. He could see her talking, then she turned and looked at him, a look of surprise on her face.

'Of course,' she said, loud enough for him to hear. 'He'll take the call in the office.'

She put the phone down and went over to him.

'Christer,' she said. 'It's the police.'

She couldn't get hold of Q. He was conducting interviews. She tried all the other numbers. Central control had nothing new, the crime unit were annoyed, and the press spokesman was busy. And there was no answer when she called Patricia.

She found a number for Studio Six in the phone book, but got nothing but an answering machine. A young girl's voice, trying to sound sensual, explained the opening hours, from 1 p.m. to 5 a.m. You could meet nice young ladies, offer them champagne, watch a show or a private viewing, or watch and buy erotic films. Anyone curious and adventurous was very welcome to visit Stockholm's hottest club.

It made Annika feel a bit sick.

She called once more and recorded the message on her tape-recorder. Then she tried the police press spokesman again. This time she got him.

'A magistrate has been appointed to the case, pretrial,' he said.

Annika's pulse quickened.

'Who?'

'Chief Prosecutor Kjell Lindström.'

'Why now?' she said, although she had an idea.

The press spokesman dragged it out.

'Well,' he said, 'we've made progress with the investigation, and the crime team thought it was time to bring in a prosecutor.'

'You've got a suspect,' Annika said.

The press spokesman cleared his throat. 'Like I said, we've made progress with the investigation—'

'Is it Joachim, the boyfriend?'

The press spokesman sighed. 'I can't comment on that,' he said. 'We aren't in a position to make any statements on the matter at this point.'

'But it is him?' Annika persisted.

'We've conducted a fair number of interviews now, and there are certainly indications that point in that direction. But please, don't make this public yet. It would harm the investigation.'

A feeling of triumph bubbled up inside her. Yes! It was him! The slimy bastard, the porn-club owner, the wife-beater!

'So what can I write?' Annika wondered. 'Surely I can say that the police are following one particular line of inquiry, and have a suspect in mind. And that you've conducted a number of interviews . . . Did she ever report him?'

'Who?'

'Josefin. Did she ever report him for threatening or beating her?'

'No, not as far as we know.'

'What makes you think it's him?'

'I don't want to go into that.'

'So it's something someone said in an interview? Was it Patricia?'

The press spokesman hesitated. 'Look, you're going to have to take my word for it,' he said finally. 'I can't give you any details. We haven't reached that point yet. No one is as yet formally suspected of having committed the crime. The police are still following a number of leads in their work to solve Josefin's murder.'

Annika realized she wasn't going to get any further. She thanked him and hung up, then called Chief Prosecutor Kjell Lindström. He was in court all day. She sighed. She may as well go down to the canteen and get something to eat.

22

'There's a message for you,' the caretaker said sourly, handing her a note as she walked through reception on her way back upstairs.

The headmaster of Josefin's old school, Martin Larsson-Berg, had tried to get hold of her. The number wasn't his home number, it seemed like it went through an exchange.

'Thanks for calling back,' he said enthusiastically. 'We've opened Täby youth centre a week earlier than planned.'

'I see,' Annika said. 'Why?'

'All the grief at Josefin's death had to be dealt with somehow,' he said. 'We've got a crisis management team in place to look after anyone who's upset. Counsellors, psychologists, priests, youth-club leaders, teachers . . . The whole school is mobilized to deal with all the difficult issues raised.'

Annika paused.

'Did Josefin really have that many friends?'

Martin Larsson-Berg sounded deadly serious when he replied. 'A crime like this shakes up a whole generation. For our part, we at the school feel that we have to be there for our pupils, to support them through their trauma. Collective pain of this sort can't just be ignored.'

'And you want us to write about it?' Annika wondered.

'It feels important for us here in Täby that we set an example to others in the same situation,' he said. 'To show that life goes on. It takes a lot of commitment, and a lot of resources, and we've got both of those here.'

'Can you hold on a moment?' she said, and stood up and walked over to Spike.

The news editor was on the phone, of course.

'Do we want an orgy of grief out in Täby?' she asked, without waiting for him to get off the phone.

'What?' Spike said, putting the receiver to his stomach.

'The headmaster has opened a crisis centre in the youth club. Do we want to cover it?'

'Off you go,' Spike said, and returned to his call.

Annika walked back to her desk.

'So how do I find you, then?'

She drove out with one of the other summer temps, a photographer called Pettersson. He had a clapped-out old Golf that stalled at every other junction.

I'll never complain about Bertil Strand again, she thought.

The youth club was based in a bright red seventies building, and consisted of a kitchen and a billiard room with big sofas. Most of the space was taken up by boys, of course.

The girls were huddled in a corner. Several of them were in tears. Annika and the photographer did a quick circuit before Martin Larsson-Berg came up to them.

'It's vital that we take these young people's feelings seriously,' he said with a concerned look. 'We're going to be here twenty-four hours a day for the rest of the week.'

Annika took some notes, as an uncomfortable feeling grew in her stomach.

There was a lot of noise. The youngsters were upset and shouting at each other, all of them very emotional. Two boys were trying to pull a girl's T-shirt off in the billiard room, and only stopped when the headmaster told them to.

'Lotta's a bit of a slapper,' Martin Larsson-Berg said apologetically.

Annika stared at him in disbelief.

'You're defending the boys' behaviour,' she said.

'They're having a tough time at the moment. They didn't get much sleep last night. This is Lisbeth, our counsellor.'

Annika and Pettersson said hello.

'It feels very important to be able to work through all this properly,' the counsellor said. 'To really listen to them.'

'Is that actually possible under these conditions?' Annika wondered cautiously.

'The kids have to share their pain,' the counsellor said. 'They're helping each other to deal with their grief. We're here for all of Josefin's friends.'

'Even the ones from other school districts?' Annika asked.

'Everyone's welcome,' Martin Larsson-Berg said emphatically. 'We've got the capacity to help anyone who needs support.'

Three boys started fighting over a billiard cue in the next room, and Martin Larsson-Berg disappeared to sort them out.

'Do you go out to find people who might need help?' Annika asked.

The counsellor smiled uncertainly. 'How do you mean?'

'Josefin's best friend is a girl called Patricia. Have you been in touch with her?'

'Has she been here?' the counsellor asked curiously.

Annika looked around. Four girls were sitting next to a crackly stereo, sniffling and playing Eric Clapton's 'Tears In Heaven' very loud. Three others were writing poems for Josefin with lit candles and the graduation picture from the *Evening Post* in front of them. Six boys were playing cards. She couldn't imagine that Patricia would set foot in here voluntarily.

'I doubt it,' Annika said.

'But she's very welcome, everyone's welcome,' the counsellor said.

'And you're open all night?'

'We can't let our support flag. I've interrupted my holiday so that I can be here.'

The counsellor smiled. There was a sort of glow, something almost unearthly in her eyes. Annika put down her notepad. This didn't feel right. This woman wasn't here for Josefin or her friends. She was here for her own sake.

'Perhaps I could talk to some of her friends?' Annika said.

'Whose?' the counsellor said.

'Josefin's,' Annika said.

'Oh yes, of course. Anyone in particular?'

Annika thought for a moment.

'Charlotta? They were in the same class.'

'Of course, Charlotta. I think she's organizing a procession to the scene of the murder. There's so much to sort out, hiring coaches and so on. This way . . .'

They went into an office behind the billiard room. A young woman with a short page-boy cut and a serious suntan was discussing something on the phone. She looked up with a glare at the interruption, but lit up

165

as soon as Annika mouthed, *Evening Post*. She quickly ended the call.

'Charlotta, Josefin's best friend,' she said, with a sufficiently distressed smile.

Annika looked down and muttered her own name.

'We've already spoken,' she said, and Charlotta nodded in agreement.

'I'm still in shock,' Charlotta said, with a dry sniff. 'It's been so hard.'

The counsellor gave her a sympathetic hug.

'But together we're strong,' Charlotta went on. 'We have to do something about meaningless violence like this. Josefin won't have died in vain; we're going to see to that.'

Her voice was firm and determined. She'd be perfect for television, Annika thought.

'How do you mean?' Annika wondered gently.

Charlotta glanced uncertainly at the counsellor.

'Well, we've got to come together. Protest. Show that we're not backing down. That feels so important right now. Supporting each other in our grief. Sharing our feelings and helping each other through this difficult time.'

She smiled weakly.

'And you're organizing a procession?' Annika said.

'Yes, more than a hundred young people have already signed up. We're going to need at least two coaches.'

Charlotta walked round the table to pick up a list of names.

'Of course, we're meeting the costs involved,' the counsellor interjected.

Pettersson, the photographer, appeared in the doorway.

'Can I take a couple of pictures?' he asked.

The two women stood up straight next to each other.

'Do you think you could look a bit sad?' the photographer asked.

Annika groaned to herself, shut her eyes and turned away. She was blushing with shame. To please the photographer, the women hugged each other and started to sniff a bit.

'Well, we mustn't disturb you any longer,' Annika said, heading for the door.

'There are lots more sitting crying out there,' Pettersson said.

Annika paused.

'Okay,' she said. 'We'll ask if they'd like to have their picture taken.'

They wanted to. The girls cried buckets, the candles flickered, Josefin's picture hovered behind them, blown up almost beyond recognition on a photocopier. Pettersson photographed the girls' poems and pictures, and as he worked the sound level increased even further. The youngsters had clearly been disturbed by the presence of the two journalists, and the level of hysteria was gradually growing.

'Hey, we want to be photographed too,' two boys brandishing billiard cues shouted.

'I think it's time to go,' Annika whispered.

'Why?' Pettersson said in surprise.

'We're leaving,' Annika snarled. 'Now!'

She walked off to find Martin Larsson-Berg as the photographer reluctantly packed up his equipment. They thanked the headmaster and left the building.

'Why were you in such a bloody hurry?' Pettersson said angrily on the way to the car.

He was walking a couple of metres behind Annika, his camera bag bumping on his left hip. Annika replied without turning round.

'That's not healthy,' she said. 'It could spill over at any moment.'

She got in the car and turned on the radio.

They didn't say another word all the way back into Stockholm.

23

Annika had just dropped her bag on the floor when she saw the man on the far side of the newsroom. He was big and blond, and the light from the windows on the other side of the sports desk was falling on him. She watched him out of curiosity. He stopped every couple of metres, shaking people's hands and saying hello. Only when he reached the newsdesk did she realize the editor-in-chief was walking alongside him. The thin little man, upper-class and reserved, was almost invisible alongside him.

'Well, perhaps if I could just have your attention,' the editor-in-chief said in his nasal voice from the news-desk.

Spike was on the phone, feet on his desk, and didn't even look up. Picture-Pelle glanced over at the men, then went back to his screen. Some of the others had stopped what they were doing and were looking at the men suspiciously. No one had asked to have a television star as their editor.

'If you could just listen,' the editor-in-chief said.

Everyone's faces were completely blank. Spike was still ignoring everything. Annika didn't move. Suddenly the blond man took a great leap up onto the newsdesk. He stretched to his full height up on Spike's desk, walk-ing among the telephones and coffee cups and looking round. Then he put his hands on his hips and looked straight ahead of him. The light was still falling on him, and Annika realized that she had got up and was walking over to the little group. His feet ended up right in front of Spike, who looked up, said 'I'll call you back', and hung up. Picture-Pelle left his computer and headed for the newsdesk. The noise level sank to a gentle buzz, as everyone drifted towards the newsdesk in the centre of the room.

'My name is Anders Schyman,' the man said. 'At the moment I'm in charge of a team of investigative reporters at Swedish Television. But from Wednesday, August first, I shall be your new head editor.'

He stopped, and the silence in the room was deafening. His voice had the strength and depth of someone used to providing voiceovers for imported documentaries. Annika stared, fascinated.

The man took a step and looked across a different section of the newsroom.

'I don't know your jobs,' he said. 'You do. I'm not going to teach you what to do. You know that best yourselves.'

More silence. Annika could hear the sound of traffic outside, and the air-conditioning.

'What I am going to do,' the man said, and Annika thought he was looking right at her, 'what I am going to do is make our path smoother. I'm not going to drive the engine. I'll be planning and laying new tracks. I can't do that alone, so we'll have to work together. You're the train drivers, the stokers, the conductors. You're the ones who talk to the passengers; you're the ones who wave us off on time so that the train keeps to its time-table. I'll be planning our departures, making sure that we stop at the right stations, and that there are rails all the way there. I'm not a mechanic. But I'd like to

170

be, eventually, once you've taught me everything I don't know. For now I'm just one thing: a publicist.'

He turned to look out over the sports desk, and now Annika could only see his back. But she could still hear him, almost as well as before.

'I'm deeply committed to journalism,' he said. 'The man in the street is my employer. I've fought against corruption and the abuse of power all of my professional life. That's the very core of journalism. The truth is my guiding light, not influence, and not power.'

He turned ninety degrees, and Annika could see him in profile.

'These are big words. I'm not trying to be pretentious, just ambitious. I haven't taken this job because it will give me a good salary and a prestigious title, even though it will do both of those things. No, I'm here today for one single reason: to work with you.'

You could hear a pin drop. Spike's phone rang, and he quickly took it off the hook.

'Together we can make this newspaper the biggest in Scandinavia,' Anders Schyman said. 'We've already got all the qualities we need, principally in the form of each and every one of you. The employees. The journalists. You're the brains, the heart of this paper. Eventually we may get all those hearts to beat in time, and the thunderous roar we create will be strong enough to tear down walls. You'll see that I'm right about that.'

Without another word he stepped off the desk and landed neatly on the floor, and noise returned to the room.

'Remarkable,' Carl Wennergren said, suddenly standing next to her.

'Yes, really,' Annika said, still affected by the charisma of the man.

'I haven't heard such a load of pompous crap since my

father's speech at my graduation. Well, what have you come up with?'

Annika turned round and walked back to her desk.

'The police have a suspect,' she said.

'How do you know that?' Carl Wennergren wondered sceptically behind her.

Annika sat down and looked him in the eye.

'It's pretty straightforward. It's her boyfriend. It almost always is.'

'Has he been arrested?'

'No, he's not even been identified as an official suspect.'

'So we can't publish anything,' Carl said.

'That all depends on how you phrase it,' Annika said. 'What have you got?'

'I've been writing up my sailing journal. Sport wanted it. Do you want to read it?'

Annika gave a wry smile. 'Not right now.'

Carl Wennergren sat down on her desk again.

'This murder's given you a real break, hasn't it?' he said.

Annika was sorting through some old news agency printouts.

'I wouldn't put it quite like that,' she said.

'You got the front page two days in a row, no other temp has managed that this summer,' Carl Wennergren said.

'Apart from you, of course,' Annika said, smiling sweetly.

'Well, yes, but I come from a different starting point. I did my training here.'

And your dad's on the board, Annika thought, but said nothing. Carl stood up.

'I'm heading down to the crime-scene to catch a few of the mourners,' he said over his shoulder.

Annika nodded and turned to her computer. She opened a new document and began in a dramatic tone: *The police have made a breakthrough in their hunt for Josefin Liljeberg's killer—*

She got no further before the tip-off hotline rang. She groaned out loud and grabbed the receiver.

'That's enough now,' a woman's voice said.

'I quite agree,' Annika said.

'We can't put up with the diktats of the patriarchy any longer.'

'Fine by me,' Annika said.

'We're going to get our revenge, and we're going to do it with blood and fire.'

'You must be a pretty cool bunch of girls,' Annika said.

The voice grew annoyed.

'Listen to what I say. We're the Ninja Barbies, a group of amazons who have declared war on oppression and violence against women. We aren't putting up with it any more. The woman in the park was the last straw. We women aren't the only ones who should be scared to go out at night. Men must suffer violence too. You'll see. We're going to start with the police, the hypocrites of the power structure.'

Annika was paying attention now, this one sounded like a serious nutter.

'Why have you called this number?' she asked.

'We want to spread our message through the media. We want maximum publicity. We're offering the *Evening Post* the chance to join us on our first raid.'

Annika's mouth went dry. What if the young woman was serious? She looked round the newsroom, trying to get eye contact with someone she could beckon over.

'What . . . what do you mean?' she asked, uncertain.

'We're starting tomorrow,' the woman said. 'Do you want to come?'

Annika looked around desperately. No one was paying her any attention.

'Are you serious?' she wondered weakly.

'These are our conditions,' the young woman said. 'We want full control over text and headlines. We want a guarantee of complete anonymity and control of all pictures. And we want fifty thousand kronor in advance. In cash.'

Annika took several deep breaths.

'That's impossible,' she said. 'Out of the question.'

'Are you sure?' the young woman said.

'I've never been more sure,' Annika said.

'Then we'll call your rivals,' the woman said.

'Okay, good luck. You'll get the same answer there, I can guarantee that.'

There was a click and the line went dead. Annika put the receiver back, shut her eyes and buried her head in her hands. Bloody hell, what was she supposed to do now? Call the police? Tell Spike? Pretend nothing happened? She had a feeling she was going to get told off whatever she did.

24

'And here are our evening reporters,' she heard the editor-in-chief say. She looked up and saw the editorial board heading towards her from the picture desk. Apart from the editor-in-chief it consisted of the new head editor, Anders Schyman, and the heads of sport, entertainment, pictures and culture, as well as one of the leader-writers. They were all men, and apart from Schyman they were all wearing similar dark blue sports jackets, jeans and shiny shoes. She suddenly remembered what Anne Snapphane called them and burst out laughing. The blue cock parade.

The group stopped at her desk.

'The evening reporters start at noon and work through to eleven p.m.,' the editor-in-chief said with his back to Annika. 'They work a shift system, and a lot of them are on temporary contracts. We regard the evening shift as something of a training ground . . .'

He started to move on when Anders Schyman broke away from the group and came over to her.

'I'm Anders Schyman,' he said, holding out his hand.

Annika looked cautiously up at him.

'Yes, I realized that,' she said with a smile, and shook his hand. 'Annika Bengtzon.'

He smiled back.

'You're the one who's been writing about the murder of Josefin Liljeberg,' he said.

She blushed.

'Well spotted,' she said.

'Are you permanent?'

Annika shook her head. 'No, just a summer temp. My contract ends in a couple of weeks.'

'I'm sure we'll get the chance to talk later,' Anders Schyman said, and turned back to join the cock parade again. All the eyes that had been fixed on Annika lifted and drifted away across the newsroom. She watched the group go, feeling strangely uneasy.

When the group had vanished behind the sports desk she made her decision. She was no snitch. She wasn't going to call the police about the Ninja Barbies. And she wasn't going to say anything to Spike either. So many idiots called every day. She couldn't go running to the head of news about each and every one of them.

She carried on with her article about the police's breakthrough in the hunt for Josefin's killer, managing to sound authoritative without quoting Patricia, writing about the suspect without exposing the press spokesman, and implying that Josefin's boyfriend was a bastard without actually saying so. Her piece about the orgy of grief out in Täby was short and restrained.

She swung by the cafeteria and bought a can of Coke, and listened to the headlines of *Studio Six*, the radio discussion programme. It was about the role of journalists in the election campaign. She switched it off and drew a graph of Josefin's last hours. The only thing she left out was the name of the sex club where Josefin worked, deciding to call it simply 'the club'. Then she went over to the graphics team, so that they could superimpose the details on a map or aerial photograph of Kungsholmen.

By the time she was finished it was almost seven o'clock. She was hot and tired and didn't feel like doing anything else. So she sat down and had a quick surreptitious read of the morning papers. At half past seven she turned up the volume on the television and watched the main evening news. They had nothing about Josefin or the IB affair. The only interesting item was from their Russian reporter. He was rounding off his series of reports from the Caucasus with an interview with an expert in Moscow.

'The President needs weapons,' the expert summarized. 'The country is completely out of ammunition, grenades, rifles, machine guns, everything. This is the President's over-riding problem. Because the UN has imposed a weapons embargo, it's extremely difficult for him to get hold of new supplies. The only alternative is the black market, and he can't afford to buy anything that way.'

'How come the guerrillas have so many weapons?' the reporter asked.

The expert smiled sheepishly. 'The guerrillas are actually very weak, poorly educated, and badly led. But they have open access to Russian weapons. My country has serious political interests in the Caucasus. Unfortunately, the truth is that Russia is providing the guerrillas with material support . . .'

Annika recalled the old man who could speak Swedish, the president whose people were the victims of the guerrillas' attacks. The international community was being utterly pathetic! Why wasn't anyone criticizing Russia for its involvement in the civil war?

By the time the news was over, calm had descended on the newsroom. Spike had gone home and Jansson was at the editor's desk. Annika glanced through the latest reports from the news agencies, read the articles in the shared file-store, and finally checked the news on the other main television channel. Then she went over to Jansson.

'Nice map,' the night-editor said. 'And a good piece about her boyfriend being the suspect. We could all have guessed though, couldn't we?'

'Is there anything else I can do?' she wondered.

Jansson's phone rang.

'I think you should go home,' he said. 'You spent practically all weekend here.'

Annika hesitated. 'Are you sure?'

Jansson didn't answer. Annika went back to her desk and gathered her things together. She cleared her desk – she was going to be away for four days and another reporter would be using her space.

She bumped into Berit on her way out.

'Do you fancy a beer at the pizza place on the corner?' her colleague wondered.

Annika was taken by surprise, but answered at once. 'Thanks; that would great. I haven't had anything to eat yet.'

They took the stairs. The evening was still muggy and warm. The air above the concrete car park still seemed to be vibrating.

'I've never known a summer like this one,' Berit said.

The women walked slowly towards the pizzeria on Rålambsvägen. It was shabby but it was licensed to sell beer and wine, which might explain how it had survived for so long.

'Do you have family here?' Berit asked as they stood waiting to cross the road.

'My boyfriend's down in Hälleforsnäs,' Annika said. 'You?'

'A husband in Täby, a son studying in Lund, and a

daughter working as an au pair in Los Angeles. Are you hoping to stay on at the paper in the autumn?'

Annika laughed nervously. 'Well,' she said, 'I'd like to stay on, so I'm doing my best.'

'Good, that's the most important thing,' Berit said. 'Look and learn, and make your own decision about whether or not you want to stay.'

'It's pretty tough,' Annika said. 'I think the temps get exploited. The company seems to take in loads of people and lets them fight for jobs, instead of actually appointing people to vacancies.'

'True enough,' Berit said. 'But that does at least mean that a lot of people get a chance to go for it.'

The pizzeria was almost empty. They sat down at a table a little way inside the restaurant. Annika ordered a pizza, and they asked for two beers.

'I read your piece about IB in the file-store,' Annika said. 'Here's to the scoop!'

They touched glasses and drank.

'That whole IB business never seems to end,' Berit said, putting her dripping glass down on the wax cloth. 'As long as the Social Democrats carry on wriggling and lying there'll be plenty more articles to write.'

'Mind you, perhaps it's understandable,' Annika said. 'After all, it was in the middle of the Cold War.'

'Not then, it wasn't,' Berit said. 'The first memorandum about the register of political affiliations was sent out from party headquarters on the twenty-first of September, 1945. And the accompanying letter was written by the secretary of the party himself, Sven Andersson, who went on to become Minister of Defence.'

Annika blinked in surprise.

'As early as that?' she said incredulously. 'Are you sure?'

Berit smiled. 'I've got a copy of the accompanying letter in my own archive,' she said.

They looked at the other customers in silence for a while – a few local drifters and five giggly youngsters who didn't look old enough to drink.

'So,' Annika said, 'why would they want to identify Communists if it wasn't because of the Cold War?'

'Power,' Berit said. 'The Communists were pretty strong, especially up in Norrbotten, and in Stockholm and Gothenburg. The Social Democrats were scared of losing control of the unions.'

'But why did that matter?' Annika said, feeling a bit foolish.

'Money and influence,' Berit said. 'The Social Democrats believed very strongly that the workers should be collectively tied into the party. The Metallettan union in Stockholm was run by Communists from 1943. When they broke the union's links with the Social Democrats, it cost the party thirty thousand kronor in membership fees per year. And that was a hell of a lot of money for the party in those days.'

Annika's pizza arrived. It was small, and the base was tough.

'I don't really see how this all fits together,' Annika said after a few greedy mouthfuls. 'How would the register of political affiliations help the Social Democrats to keep control of the unions?'

'Can I have a piece? Thanks. Well, some of the party's ombudsmen manipulated the votes and nominations to party congresses. All party members were ordered to vote for certain selected candidates in order to wipe out the Communists,' Berit said.

Annika chewed and looked sceptically at her colleague.

'Come on,' she said. 'My dad was a union rep in

Hälleforsnäs. Do you mean to say that people like him ignored local democracy just to obey the party line from Stockholm?'

Berit nodded and sighed. 'Not all of them, but far too many did precisely that. It didn't matter who was most suitable, or who had the confidence of the members.'

'And the Social Democrats kept a long list of all the names in their party headquarters?'

'Not to begin with,' Berit said. 'At the end of the fifties the information was still kept locally. When it was at its height, there were more than ten thousand people reporting – or spying, if you like – on their colleagues' political views in workplaces the length and breadth of Sweden.'

Annika cut a slice of pizza and ate it with her hands. She chewed in silence for a while, licking her fingers thoughtfully.

'I don't want to be difficult,' she said. 'But don't you think you're making more out of this than it actually merits?'

Berit folded her arms and leaned back.

'Of course there are some people who think that,' she said. 'We're becoming very ignorant of our own history. We're only talking about the fifties here. As far as today's generation is concerned, that might as well be the Stone Age.'

Annika pushed her plate away and wiped her mouth on her napkin.

'So what happened after the fifties?' she said.

'IB,' Berit said. 'It was set up in 1957.'

'The Information Bureau,' Annika said.

'Also known as "Information for Birger",' Berit said. 'He was the head of the domestic division, Birger Elmér. The section for foreign espionage was called the "T Office" for a while, after the boss there, Thede Palm.'

181

Annika shook her head.

'God, what a muddle,' she said. 'How do you keep all this clear in your head?'

Berit smiled and relaxed.

'I was a subscriber to *People in Focus* when the revelations came out. I've written a fair bit about IB since then. Nothing revolutionary, but I've kept up with it.'

The waiter took away what was left of Annika's pizza, the crusts and a few tough lumps of what was meant to be pork.

'My dad used to talk about IB,' Annika said. 'He thought the whole thing had been blown way out of proportion. He used to say it was all about the country's security, and that the Social Democrats really ought to be thanked for taking responsibility for defending our way of life.'

Berit put her glass down heavily on the table.

'The Social Democrats kept a register of people's political affiliations for their own purposes. They broke their own laws, they lied, they manipulated the system. And they're still lying. I talked to their spokesman today. He refuses point-blank to admit that he ever knew Birger Elmér, or had anything at all to do with the Information Bureau.'

'Maybe he's telling the truth,' Annika said.

Berit gave her a sympathetic look.

'Believe me,' she said, 'IB is the Social Democrats' Achilles heel, their biggest, most monumental mistake, even though it was also the way they were able to hold on to power. They'll do anything to cover up their abuse of power. They managed to create a map of the whole population of Sweden. They persecuted people because of their political views; they got people fired from their jobs. They're going to lie until there's categorical proof of what they did. And when that happens, they'll start coming up with excuses instead.'

'So how did they go about it, then? Some sort of Social Democratic security police?'

'No, they used the organization of Social Democratic workplace ombudsmen. There's nothing wrong with the organization on the surface – it was set up to relay party messages to people at work.'

'So why was it so secretive then?'

'The ombudsmen did all the groundwork for the Information Bureau. Everything they reported was passed to Elmér and the government. And they're the proof that IB and the Social Democrats were basically the same organization.'

Annika looked through the window at the summer evening. Three dusty plastic plants obstructed the view. Behind them the filthy window formed a grey barrier against the traffic outside.

'So what was kept in the foreign archive?' she asked.

Berit sighed. 'The names of a whole load of agents, journalists, sailors, aid workers: basically, anyone who travelled a lot. They wrote reports, and they were supposed to predict impending crises. For instance, they had agents in Vietnam reporting back to Sweden, and that information was passed on to the Americans, as well as to the British. The reports may have looked like travel diaries, but they were actually full of intelligence information. They covered things like the Vietnamese infrastructure, how people lived, what they thought about current events, what morale was like.'

'But Sweden was neutral!' Annika said, shocked.

'Oh yes,' Berit said bitterly. 'Birger Elmér used to meet the US Ambassador and Head of Intelligence for lunch at an out-of-town restaurant. And Elmér used to talk to Olof Palme a lot. Palme used to say that he would deal with the politics, as long as Elmér kept the Americans happy. And so Palme would go and shout at all the demos, while Elmér did his best to keep the Yanks on side.'

'And now a copy of their archive has suddenly popped up?' Annika said.

'I'm convinced the original archive is still out there somewhere,' Berit said. 'The question is: where?'

'What about the domestic archive, then?'

'That was completely illegal. It contained detailed personal information about people who were thought to be enemies of the Social Democratic Party, probably around twenty thousand names in total. Everyone on the list would have been interned if war had broken out. But even in peacetime they had trouble getting work. They were excluded from involvement in the unions, for instance. And you didn't have to be a Communist to end up on the list. Just reading the wrong newspaper was enough, or having the wrong friends, or being in the wrong place at the wrong time.'

They sat for a few minutes without speaking. Annika cleared her throat.

'But this is still about things that happened forty years ago,' she said. 'Back then people were still being sterilized against their will, and DDT was being sprayed all over the place. Why do these documents matter so much today?'

Berit thought for a moment.

'They probably contain a lot of pretty bad stuff, information about break-ins and bugging, and so on. But the really sensitive stuff is missing: the big picture.'

'Which means what, exactly?' Annika asked.

Berit closed her eyes. 'When it comes down to it, the Social Democrats were spying for America. Any deviation from neutrality that can be proved with these documents is, by today's standards, even worse than keeping a register of people's political affiliations. The government not only lied to the country, but were cosying up to one of the superpowers. Not that this was without risk, of course. The Soviets knew what the Swedish position was, largely from what Stig Wennerström told them before he was caught and found guilty of treason. The Russians built that into their military planning. Sweden would probably have been one of the first targets in any new war, because of the government's duplicity.'

Annika looked wide-eyed at Berit.

'Bloody hell,' she said. 'Do you really think things were as bad as that?'

Berit finished the last of her beer.

'If all the grubby details of what the Information Bureau actually did were revealed, it would ruin the Social Democrats. People would lose whatever faith they have left in them. The archive is the key. They'd have a hard time trying to form a government any time in the foreseeable future if the archive reappeared.'

The teenagers at the next table got up and left, with a great deal of noise. They tumbled out into the warm evening, leaving behind them an abstract pattern of peanuts and spilled shandy on the table. Annika and Berit watched them go through the window, as they crossed the road to the bus-stop. A number 62 pulled up and they disappeared onto it.

Should I say something about the Ninja Barbies? Annika wondered.

Berit looked at her watch.

'Well, I guess it's time,' she said. 'My last train goes soon.'

Annika hesitated, as Berit waved to the waiter.

Oh, I can't be bothered, Annika thought. No one's ever going to find out.

'Thank goodness I'm off tomorrow,' she said. 'I can't wait.'

Berit sighed, then smiled. 'I've got a couple more days' work ahead of me with IB,' she said. 'But it'll be worth it.'

Annika smiled back. 'Yes, I can see why you'd think that. Are you a Communist yourself?'

Berit laughed. 'And I suppose you're spying for IB?'

Annika started laughing as well.

They paid and headed out into the summer evening as it gradually changed colour and texture, from evening to night.

Seventeen years, eleven months and eight days

Time collapses, leaving deep tracks. Reality crushes love with its meagreness, its boredom. Our desire to find the truth is just as strong. He's right; we have to take responsibility together. I'm not focused enough, I lack concentration. It takes a long time for me to reach orgasm. We have to get closer, devote ourselves to each other, not let anything disturb us. I know he's right. If you have the right sort of love in your consciousness, nothing can stop you.

I know what the problem is: I have to learn to handle my longing. It gets in the way of our experience, of our excursions out into the cosmos. Love can take you anywhere, but only if your devotion is absolute.

He loves me more than words can say. All the wonderful details, his passion for everything about me. His choice of books, clothes, records, food and drink for me is at one with our breathing, our heartbeat. I have to let go of my egotistical desires.

Never leave me,
he says;
I can't live without you.

And I promise, over and over again.

Tuesday 31 July

25

She was woken by the draught. She stayed in bed and shut her eyes. Through her eyelids she could just make out the sharpness of the light through the open window. It was morning. Not late enough to make her feel bad about wasting the day, but late enough for her to feel properly rested.

Annika pulled on her dressing-gown and went out into the stairwell. The cracked mosaic on the floor was pleasantly cool under her feet. The toilet was one flight down; she shared it with the tenants on the upper floors.

The curtains flapped like great sails in the draught when she came back into the flat. She had bought thirty metres of light linen material and draped it over the old curtain rails, and the effect was striking. The flat was painted white throughout. The previous tenant had painted everything with undercoat and then given up. The flat walls reflected and absorbed light, making the rooms translucent.

She slowly wandered through the living room and into the kitchen. The floor space was uncluttered, she had almost no furniture. The tiles were different shades of grey, from decades of cleaning and lime-wash. The ceiling hovered like a white sky high above her, clean and soft. She set some water to boil on the gas stove, measured three spoonfuls of coffee into her Bodum cafetière, poured on the water and pushed the plunger down. The fridge was empty. She would have to get a sandwich on the train.

The morning paper lay in shreds on the hall floor: the letterbox was too small. She picked it up and sat down on the floor with her back against the pantry door.

The usual stuff: the Middle East, the election campaign, the heatwave. Not a single line about Josefin. She was already history, just another statistic. Yet another article about the Information Bureau. This time she actually read it. It was by a professor in Gothenburg who was demanding an independent inquiry. Right on, Annika thought.

She couldn't be bothered to go and shower in the next building, so just splashed herself with water from the tap in the sink. The water was no longer ice-cold, so there was no need to heat it up.

The evening papers had just been delivered, so she bought both of them from the newsagent on Scheele-gatan. The *Evening Post* was leading with IB, of course.

Annika smiled. Berit really was one of the best. Her own articles were well-placed, on pages eight, nine, ten and the centrefold. She read through her piece on the police suspect, and thought it was pretty good. She had written that the police were following a line of inquiry concerning a person close to Josefin. Josefin had felt threatened and scared before. There were indications that she had been abused previously. She smiled again. Without mentioning Joachim, she had made it very clear what the police were thinking. Then there was the orgy of grief out in Täby. She was pleased that she had managed to keep strictly to the facts. The picture had

192

turned out fine; they had used one of some girls next to the candles. They weren't crying in the picture, which was a relief.

The other evening paper didn't have anything special, apart from the next instalment of their series about 'life after your holiday'. She thought she might read that on the train.

The wind had got up, blowing the hot air around. She bought an ice-cream for breakfast on Bergsgatan, then walked down Kaplansbacken towards the Central Station. She was in luck: the Intercity train to Malmö was due to leave in five minutes. She settled down in the buffet car, and was first in line for a sandwich when they started serving. She had not had time to get a ticket, and bought one from the conductor.

Apart from her, only three Middle Eastern-looking men got off at Flen. The bus to Hälleforsnäs left in fifteen minutes, so she sat on a bench in front of the town hall, staring at a sculpture entitled *Vertical Longing*. It was spectacularly awful. She ate a bag of sweets on the bus, before getting off outside the supermarket.

'Congratulations,' Ulla, one of her mother's friends, said. She was standing smoking next to a flowerbed, wearing a bright green coat.

'What for?' Annika wondered with a smile.

'On all your success! Front pages and everything! Everyone here in Hälleforsnäs is so proud of you!' Ulla shouted.

Annika laughed and waved off the praise. She walked up past the church, heading for home. It all seemed dead and abandoned. The red-painted blocks of flats were steaming in the heat.

I hope Sven isn't there, she thought.

The flat was empty. All the houseplants were dead. An overfull bag of rubbish was stinking out the kitchen.

She took it out to the garbage chute, then opened all the windows. The plants would have to wait. She didn't have the energy to deal with them right now.

Her mother seemed genuinely pleased to see her. She hugged Annika with clumsy hands, cool but slightly sweaty.

'Are you hungry? I've got some elk stew on the stove.'

Her mother's latest boyfriend was a hunter.

They sat down at the kitchen table, and her mother lit a cigarette. The window was open, and Annika could hear some kids arguing about a bicycle outside. She looked down the hill towards the ironworks, its rough tin roofs stretching as far as the eye could see.

'So tell me, how did you do it?'

Her mother smiled expectantly.

'What do you mean?' Annika said, smiling back.

'Making such a success of things, of course! Everyone's noticed! They keep coming up and congratulating me when I'm at the till. Such wonderful articles! The front page and everything.'

Annika lowered her head.

'Oh, it wasn't so hard,' she said. 'I got a good tip-off. So how are you?'

Her mother's face lit up. 'Wait till you see this,' she said, getting up. The smoke from her cigarette formed swirling dragons in the air as she drifted over to her worktable. Annika was staring at the smoke as her mother came back. She spread out a pile of photocopies in front of Annika.

'I like this one best,' she said, tapping the table and sitting down, then taking a deep drag on the cigarette.

Annika looked at the sheets of paper with a gentle sigh. They were the details of different houses in Eskilstuna.

The top one, the one her mother liked, came from the Association of Estate Agents. She read:

Exclusive luxury villa. Maintained to a very high standard, this property takes full advantage of a sloping site. Features include a fully tiled bathroom w. sunken bathtub, an L-shaped living room and a recreation room w. open fireplace.

'Why do they shorten "with"?' Annika asked.

'What?' her mother said.

'They shorten the shortest word in the sentence,' Annika said. 'It doesn't make any sense.'

Her mother wafted away the smoke between them, irritated.

'So what do you think?' she said.

Annika hesitated. 'It's rather expensive, isn't it?'

'Expensive?' her mother said, grabbing the sheet. 'Marble-floored hall, clinker tiles in the kitchen, and there's a bar in the cellar. It's perfect!'

Annika sighed quietly. 'Of course it is. I suppose I was just wondering if you can afford it. That's a lot of money.'

'Look at the others,' her mother said.

Annika leafed through the other details. They were all luxury villas close to Eskilstuna. And they all had more than six rooms, and large gardens.

'But you don't like gardening,' Annika said.

'Leif's an outdoor person,' her mother said, putting out the half-smoked cigarette. 'We're thinking of buying a place together.'

Annika pretended not to hear.

'How's Birgitta?' she asked instead.

'Oh, fine,' her mother said. 'She gets on well with Leif. You'd like him too, if you ever get to meet him.'

Her voice carried a hint of accusation and annoyance.

'Is she going to stay on at Right Price?'

'Don't change the subject,' her mother said, straightening up. 'Why don't you want to get to know Leif?'

Annika stood up and went over to the fridge. The inside was sparking clean, but fairly empty.

'Of course I'd be happy to meet him, if it would make you happy. But this summer's been a bit busy, as I'm sure you can understand.'

She didn't care if she sounded sarcastic.

Her mother stood up as well.

'Don't go digging around in the fridge,' she said. 'We'll be eating soon. You can set the table.'

Annika took a small pot of yogurt and closed the fridge door.

'I haven't got time,' she said. 'I'm going out to Lyckebo.'

Her mother's lips thinned and went white.

'It'll be ready in a few minutes. Surely you can wait that long?'

'See you in a bit,' Annika said.

She hoisted her bag onto her shoulders and hurried out of the apartment. Her bicycle was still there, but the air had gone out of the back tyre. She pumped it up, squashed her bag onto the parcel rack and cycled off in the direction of Granhed.

•

26

The ironworks glided past on her right, and she glanced at it from the corner of her eye. That bloody factory, the once-beating heart of the little town. Forty thousand square metres of abandoned industrial premises. Sometimes she hated it, for what it had done to her youth. Twelve hundred people had worked there when she was born. When she left school that number was down to a couple of hundred. Her father lost his job when the workforce was cut back to just 120. Now there were only eight. She cycled past the car park: three cars, five bikes.

Her father couldn't handle being unemployed. He had lived for that shitty job. He never got another job, and Annika could guess why. Bitterness is hard to hide, and not very pleasant to employ.

She passed the entrance to the canoe club, and sped up unconsciously. That was where he was found, half an hour too late. His body was too cold. He lived for another twenty-four hours in the Mälar Valley Hospital in Eskilstuna, but the alcohol had already done its job.

When things were at their worst, she thought it was probably just as well. If she thought about it, which she rarely did, she realized that she had never really allowed herself to mourn his death.

Even so, she thought, he's the one I take after. She brushed the thought away.

After the turning to the lake, the road got narrower and bumpier as it wound through the trees. She never liked the colour of the forest in late summer. The dense vegetation was so full of chlorophyll that it was all exactly the same shade of green.

Paths led off into the forest to left and right. Those off to the left were all blocked off: that was the boundary of the Harpsund estate.

The road went up a hill, and she had to stand up and pedal, breathing hard. Her armpits were running with sweat, and she could have done with a swim.

The turning to Lyckebo crept up on her, just as it always did. She almost rode past it, and the bike skidded as she braked hard. She pulled her bag off the back and leaned the bike against the barrier, then crept under it and waded off through the tall grass.

'Whiskas!' she called. 'Where's my little boy?'

A couple of seconds later she heard the sound of miaowing in the distance. A little sandy-coloured cat appeared through the grass, its whiskers glistening in the sunlight.

'Oh, Whiskas!'

She dropped her bag in the grass as the cat jumped up into her arms. She sat down among the ants and rolled around with the cat, tickling him on his tummy and stroking his back.

'Look, you've got a tick. Hold on, I'll get it off for you.'

She took a firm grip on the insect that had burrowed in under the cat's chin, and gave it a sharp tug. It didn't break. She smiled happily. She still had the knack.

'So is Grandma home?'

She could see the old woman sitting in the shade

under the oak tree. Her eyes were closed and her hands were folded over her stomach. Annika picked up her bag and went over to her, as the cat wound around her legs, miaowing and wanting to play.

'Are you asleep?'

Her voice was little more than a whisper.

'Oh no, I'm just listening to the forest.'

Annika gave her grandmother a long hug.

'You just get thinner and thinner,' her grandmother said. 'Are you eating properly?'

'Oh, yes,' she said. 'Wait till you see what I've got.'

She let go of her grandmother and hunted through her bag.

She pulled out a box of handmade chocolates from a small factory out in Gärdet in Stockholm. Her grandmother clapped her hands.

'Oh, how kind!' she said. 'But you really shouldn't have.'

Her grandmother opened the box and they each took a chocolate. It was slightly too bitter for Annika's taste, but then she wasn't very fond of chocolate anyway.

'So how are you getting on?' her grandmother asked.

Annika looked down at her lap.

'It's pretty tough,' she said. 'I hope I get to stay on at the paper. Otherwise I don't know what I'll do.'

The old woman looked at her warmly.

'You'll be fine, Annika,' she said. 'You don't need that job. Things will turn out just fine anyway.'

'I'm not so sure,' Annika said, feeling that she was on the verge of crying.

'Come here.'

Her grandmother held out her hand and pulled Annika down onto her lap. Annika sat down carefully and leaned her forehead against the woman's neck.

'I don't know if I can do it,' she said.

'Well, you know what I think you should do,' her grandmother said seriously.

The old woman hugged her granddaughter, rocking her gently. The wind was getting up and the leaves were rustling above them. Annika could see the lake glittering through the trees.

'I'm always here, you know that,' her grandmother said. 'I'm here for you, whatever happens. You can always come back here.'

'I don't want to get you involved,' Annika said.

'Silly girl,' her grandmother said with a smile. 'What sort of talk is that? I don't do anything useful these days, so helping you would be the least I could do.'

Annika kissed her on the cheek.

'Are there any chanterelles yet?'

Her grandmother laughed. 'You won't believe how many! All that rain in the spring, and now this heat. The forest is full of them. Get two bags!'

Annika jumped up.

'I just want to have a quick swim first!'

She pulled off her skirt and blouse on the way down to the jetty. The water was warm and the bottom of the lake was muddier than ever. She swam towards the rocks, pulled herself out and lay there for a while, catching her breath.

The wind pulled at her wet hair, and she looked up at the cirrus clouds floating past a couple of thousand metres above. She slid down into the water again and floated slowly towards the jetty on her back.

The lake was surrounded by thick forest, with not a living creature to be seen, apart from Whiskas, who was waiting for her on the jetty. You could easily get lost in these woods. She had managed it when she was little. A team from the orienteering club had found her a long way away on the far side of the road, crying and half frozen.

She started sweating as soon as she clambered ashore and pulled on her clothes without drying herself.

'I'm borrowing your boots,' she called to her grandmother, who was busy with her knitting.

She tucked one plastic bag into the waist of her skirt, and held another in her hand. Whiskas followed her as she marched into the forest.

Her grandmother was right. There were great clumps of mushrooms growing beside the path. She found ceps, parasol mushrooms and masses of hedgehog mushrooms as well.

Whiskas danced around her feet the whole time, hunting ants and butterflies, jumping at gnats and eating a baby bird. She crossed the road to Granhed and carried on past Johannislund and Björkbacken. She turned off towards Lillsjötorp to say hello to Old Gustav. His lovely little cottage was bathed in sunlight, great walls of pines behind it.

The silence was deafening: there were no sounds of wood-chopping from the woodshed, which probably meant the old man was out in the forest doing the same as her.

The door was locked. She carried on towards the White Hills, where she clambered up an old elk-hunting tower for a rest. An area of cleared woodland spread out beneath her. If she shouted, there would be a great echo.

She closed her eyes and listened to the wind. It was loud, almost hypnotic. She sat for a long while until a snapping sound made her jump.

Carefully she looked over the edge of the platform

A thickset man was cycling down from Skenäs. He was panting for breath and weaving slightly. A dried pine twig had got caught in his back wheel, and he stopped right under the tower to pull the twig out. He sighed deeply and then carried on his way.

Annika blinked in astonishment. It was the Prime Minister.

27

Christer Lundgren stepped into his overnight flat with a feeling of unreality. He could sense disaster like a cloud on the horizon, feeling the heady winds starting to blow around his face. The electric charge in the air made him appreciate the reality of the threat: stormy weather was heading his way. And he was going to get absolutely soaked.

The heat inside the little flat was incredible. The sun had been pouring through the windows all day, making him angry. Why weren't there any blinds?

He put his overnight bag down in the hall and opened the balcony door wide. The air-conditioning unit in the yard rumbled and shrieked.

Wretched bloody hamburger chain, he thought.

He went into the little kitchen and poured himself a large glass of water. The sink smelled awful, of sour milk and apple peel. He rinsed it as best he could.

His meeting with the party chairman and secretary of state had been terrible. He was under no illusions about the position he was in. It was all crystal clear.

Taking the glass of water with him, he sank heavily onto the bed and pulled the phone onto his lap. He took several deep breaths before calling his wife.

'I'm going to have to stay down here for a while,' he told her.

His wife held her fire. 'Next weekend too?'

'You know I don't want to,' he said.

'You promised the children,' she said. He shut his eyes and put a hand over his forehead. He could feel tears prickling behind his eyelids.

'I want you so much I feel ill,' he said.

This worried her.

'What's happened?'

'You wouldn't believe me if I told you,' he said. 'It's a complete nightmare.'

'But, Christer, just tell me what's happened!'

He gulped, then said, 'Listen to me. Take the children and go to Karungi. I'll be there as soon as I can.'

'I'm not going without you,' she said quickly.

His voice hardened. 'You have to. Things are going badly wrong here. You'll be besieged if you stay in town. The best thing would be if you could leave this evening.'

'But Stina isn't expecting us until Saturday!'

'Call her and ask if you can go a bit earlier. Stina's always happy to help.'

His wife waited in silence.

'It's the police,' she said finally. 'It's because of the police calling.'

He could hear the twins laughing in the background.

'Yes,' he said. 'Partly. But that's not all.'

Annika was back in time for the 5.45 news on the radio.

'You've no idea who I saw in the forest. The Prime Minister!'

She emptied the contents of the two bags on the table as the news bulletin began.

'He's decided to lose some weight,' her grandmother said. 'He does a lot of cycling round here.'

They sat on either side of the kitchen table cleaning the mushrooms as the voices chattered on the radio. Nothing much had happened.

'So you're still in touch with Harpsund?' Annika said.

Her grandmother smiled. She had been the house-keeper at the Prime Minister's summer residence for thirty-seven years. The local news came on and she turned up the volume.

Annika cut up the mushrooms and placed them on the already full bowl beside her. She let her hands drop, and her eyes relax. The clock on the wall ticked, the minutes floated past. Her grandmother's kitchen was her ideal of peace and warmth. The iron stove and the white cupboards, the cork tiles, the wax-cloth, the vase of meadow flowers on the window sill. And this was where she learned to live without hot water.

'Are you staying the night?' her grandmother asked.

At that moment the theme tune to the discussion programme *Studio Six* came on. The old woman reached out a hand to turn the radio down, but Annika stopped her.

'Let's just hear what they've got today,' Annika said.

The music faded slightly and the presenter's deep voice said, 'The police have been questioning a man about the rape and murder of a young girl in Kronoberg Park in Stockholm. Initial reports indicate that the man is none other than the Minister for Foreign Trade, Christer Lundgren. We'll have discussion and debate on this story in today's edition of *Studio Six*.'

The music came on again. Annika sat with her hands over her mouth. Good grief, was that really possible?

205

'But whatever is it? You look quite pale,' her grandmother said.

The music faded away and the presenter came on again.

'It's Monday, thirty-first July. Welcome to Studio Six in Radio House in Stockholm,' he said, then went on: 'Well, the Social Democrats are facing one of their biggest ever scandals. The minister has been questioned twice so far: he was interviewed over the phone yesterday, and today he has been at the headquarters of the violent crime unit on Kungsholmen for further questioning. We're going over live to our reporter outside Police Headquarters in Stockholm.'

There was some crackling, then an authoritative male voice said, 'Yes, I'm standing here with the police press spokesman. Can you tell us what's been happening here today?'

Annika turned up the volume and the press spokesman's voice filled the kitchen.

'I can confirm that the police are pursuing several lines of inquiry in their hunt for the killer of Josefin Liljeberg,' he said. 'But I'm afraid I can't give any further details. No one has been officially identified as a suspect, even if our inquiries are leading us in one direction in particular.'

The reporter wasn't listening.

'What's your view about a government minister being suspected of a crime of this nature, in the middle of an election campaign?' he asked.

The press spokesman hesitated. 'Well,' he said, 'I can neither confirm nor deny any aspect of this investigation at present. No one has been officially identified—'

'But the minister has been here for questioning today?'

'The Minister for Foreign Trade, Christer Lundgren,

206

is one of many people who have been questioned, that's correct,' the press spokesman said.

'So you're confirming that he has been questioned?' the reporter said, a note of triumph in his voice.

'I can confirm that we have conducted approximately three hundred sessions of questioning so far in this murder investigation,' the press spokesman said, starting to sound uncomfortable.

'What did the minister have to say in his defence?'

The press spokesman sounded irritated now. And his mobile phone started to ring.

Yeah, right, Annika thought. He won't get much sleep tonight.

'Naturally I cannot comment on what was said during questioning in an ongoing police investigation,' he said.

The live link cut off and the programme presenter came back on.

'Right, we're back in Studio Six in Radio House here in Stockholm,' he said. 'Of course, this is going to be very difficult for the Social Democrats during the election campaign, even if the minister isn't charged with any crime. The mere fact that a minister of state is being linked to an incident of this nature will have dire consequences for the party's credibility. And that's one of the subjects up for discussion in today's *Studio Six*.'

A small fanfare sounded as the presenter took a sip of water and presumably conferred with his control room.

When he returned he had a studio guest with him, an absurd professor of journalism who had only been appointed for political reasons after working as the editor-in-chief of a workers' paper that owned the biggest printworks in Sweden publishing porn magazines.

'Well,' the supposed professor said, 'this is naturally an absolute catastrophe for Social Democracy. Any suspicions of this sort of abuse of power put the party in a very difficult position. Yes, very difficult indeed . . .'

'Of course we don't know if the minister is guilty or not, and we certainly don't want to judge anyone in advance,' the presenter pointed out. 'But what would happen if he were found guilty?'

Annika stood up, her head spinning. So there *was* a minister involved. The fat old woman in the block of flats had been right.

The professor and the presenter of *Studio Six* chattered on, with occasional inserts from two reporters out in the city.

'Is this something to do with your work?' her grandmother wondered.

Annika smiled weakly. 'You could say that. I've written quite a lot about this murder. She was only nineteen, Grandma. Her name was Josefin and she loved cats.'

The programme presenter was sounding serious and confident.

'So far we haven't been able to get hold of the Minister for Foreign Trade for a comment,' he said. 'He's spent the whole afternoon in a crisis meeting with the Prime Minister and party secretary in government offices in Rosenbad. Our reporter is there for us . . .'

Annika's eyes opened wide.

'They've got that wrong!' she said, astonished.

Her grandmother looked at her quizzically.

'The Prime Minister. He can't have been at any crisis meeting this afternoon.'

She quickly packed all her things in her bag, tipped the bowl of clean mushrooms back in the plastic bag and tucked that into her bag as well.

'I've got to get back to Stockholm,' she said. 'Have the rest of the mushrooms!'

'Do you have to go?' her grandmother asked.

Annika hesitated. 'No, but I want to,' she said.

'Just look after yourself,' her grandmother said.

Annika gave her a quick hug and stepped out into the warm evening sunlight. Whiskas scampered along beside her on the path.

'No, you've got to go back. You can't come with me. You've got to stay with Grandma.'

Annika stopped and bent down to stroke the cat before nudging him back down the path.

'You've got to stay there,' she said. 'Off you go, now.'

The cat ran past her up the path, towards the barrier. Annika sighed, got the cat to come back to her, then picked him up and carried him back to the house.

'You'll have to keep the outside door shut until I've gone,' Annika said, and her grandmother laughed.

The wind had picked up again, rolling down the road and giving her a bit of extra speed as the pine trees flickered past. She pedalled as hard uphill as down, and was out of breath when she got off and leaned the bicycle outside her front door.

'I heard you were home.'

Sven slammed his car door and walked towards her from the car park. Annika locked her bike, stood up and smiled weakly at him.

'It's only a flying visit this time,' she said.

Sven smiled as he gave her a hug.

'I've missed you,' he whispered.

Annika hugged him back. He kissed her hard. Annika pulled away.

'What's the matter?'

He let go of her.

'I have to get back to Stockholm.'

The gravel crunched under her feet as she walked towards the door. She could hear his footsteps as he followed her.

'You've only just got here. Don't you get any time off?'

She pulled the door open. The hallway smelled of warm rubbish.

'Well, yes, but there've been some developments in that murder I've been covering.'

'Isn't there anyone else who could do it?'

She leaned against the wall, shut her eyes and thought.

'I want to do it,' she said. 'This is my big chance.'

He was standing in front of her, his hands either side of her head, a thoughtful look on his face.

'To do what? Get away from here? Is that it?'

She looked him in the eye.

'To get somewhere. I've already covered everything at the *Katrineholm Courier*. Forestry supplements, auctions, council meetings, advice on composting. I've got to move on.'

She bobbed down under his outstretched arm. He put his hand on her shoulder.

'I'll drive you up.'

'There's no need. I'll get the train.'

28

The room was empty. Business was always quiet when it was as hot as this. The dirty old men could sit and stare at tits all day long at the beach. Patricia took a quick look at the takings from the door. Only 3,000 kronor. Just six customers all afternoon and evening. Hopeless. She closed the cashbox. Oh well. Things would pick up later on. The heat always seemed to get the tourists' blood up.

She went into the sparsely decorated changing room next to the office and hung up her bag and denim jacket, pulled off her vest and shorts and put on her sequinned bra. Her thong was a bit sticky, she'd have to remember to rinse it out before she went home tomorrow morning. She hurriedly applied some make-up – a lot of make-up. She didn't much care for it. Her shoes were looking a bit scuffed. The sole had almost come off one of the heels. She fastened the straps, took a deep breath and went out into the club again.

The roulette table was grey with cigarette ash on the customers' side, and she noticed another new scorch mark on the green baize. Annoyed, she moved the ash-tray. Smoking wasn't allowed at the table. She took out the brush from the shelf on the croupier's side and cleaned up the ash, sweeping it onto the floor.

'So you're Mrs Mop now?'

Joachim was standing in the door of the office, leaning against the doorpost. Patricia froze.

'It just looked a mess,' she said.

'You shouldn't worry your pretty head about things like that,' Joachim said to her. 'You just need to be beautiful and sexy.'

He stood up and walked slowly towards her, still smiling, his hand out. Patricia gulped. He stroked her shoulder, then her arm. She pulled away cautiously. His smile died.

'What are you worried about?' he wondered. He had a completely different look in his eyes, cold, questioning. Patricia looked down at her sparkling breasts.

'Nothing. What makes you think I'm worried?'

Her voice wasn't quite under control. He let go of her abruptly.

'You've read what they wrote in that rag,' he said.

Patricia looked up at him, eyes innocently wide-open.

'What rag?'

He looked hard at her, and she made an effort not to look away.

'They'll soon have him,' he said.

She blinked.

'Who?'

'That minister. They said so on the radio. That group of blokes who were here that evening. It was one of them. They've been questioning him all day. The Prime Minister's furious, apparently.'

Her eyes narrowed. 'How do you know that?'

He turned and walked off towards the bar.

'They said so on the radio. *Studio Six*.'

He stopped and looked back at her over his shoulder, smiling again.

'Can you think of a better place for them to announce it?

Part Two
AUGUST

Eighteen years, one month and three days

Love is often described so flatly and unambiguously, a monotonous rosy pink. Loving another human being can embrace all the colours of the rainbow, it can grow in strength and intensity, it can be black and green and yellow.

It has been difficult for me to realize this. I was stuck in the bright, crystal-coloured version, and I had trouble seeing any discordant colours.

I know he's doing it for my own good, but it still tears me apart.

His theory is that something happened to me in my childhood which means that I can't let go of my sexual inhibitions. I've thought about this over and over again, but I still can't imagine what this something might have been.

We experiment to find ways for me to get over this, united in our love. I sit on top of him, feeling him deep within me as he slaps me hard on the face with the palm of his hand. I stop, my eyes filling with tears. I ask him why he'd do something like that.

He strokes my cheek, and pushes in hard and deep.

It's to help you, he says, and hits me again, then thrusts in hard until he comes.

We talk about it at length afterwards – how we can

rediscover the divine aspect of our relationship. It's a lack of trust, I realize that. I have to have faith in him. Because how would I manage otherwise?

*We are the most important things
in the world
to each other.*

Wednesday 1 August

29

Annika arrived at the paper just before nine o'clock. Tore Brand was sitting behind the reception desk and greeted her grumpily.

'Bombs and grenades,' he said. 'That's all this paper's interested in.'

He nodded towards that day's flysheet, displayed beside the lift. Annika looked over and it took a few seconds for the information to sink in. She felt the floor sway beneath her. This can't be true, she thought, as she reached out to grab the reception desk and read the words again. 'TERRORIST ATTACK – Ninja Barbies Attack Police', accompanied by a large picture of a burning car.

'Who wrote that article?' she whispered.

'Sensation and scandal, that's all we seem to cover,' Tore Brand said.

She went over and picked up a couple of copies of the paper instead. The front page was dominated by a picture of the Minister for Foreign Trade, Christer Lundgren. He was standing next to the Prime Minister, who had his arm round Lundgren's shoulders. They were both smiling broadly. The picture had been taken when Lundgren was appointed and presented to the media eight months earlier. The headline struck Annika as rather weak: STORMY WEATHER.

The news from the flysheet was at the very top of the page, above the title, with a reference to pages six and seven inside. She leafed through, her hands shaking. She scanned the page to see who had written the article.

Carl Wennergren.

She lowered the paper.

'It's bloody awful, isn't it?' Tore Brand said.

'You're damn right there,' Annika said, heading towards the lifts.

She went to the cafeteria and sat down with a coffee and a large roll. The drink cooled as she read the articles, first the one about the Ninja Barbies, and then the government minister.

They got what they wanted, she thought, staring at the picture of the burning car. The vehicle was on its side, its underside facing the photographer. She noted that Carl Wennergren was also credited with the picture. According to the caption, the car belonged to a chief constable in the Stockholm district. Behind the flames you could make out a detached house built in the sixties. The article gave the Ninja Barbies the opportunity to broadcast their childish, violent message. It didn't include a single word of criticism. Annika started to feel sick. Fuck, she thought. Fuck that fucking bastard.

The article about the minister in stormy weather was better. It treated the accusations from the *Studio Six* programme for what they were: unsubstantiated rumours of guilt. The minister himself hadn't been available for comment, but his press secretary, Karina Björnlund, declared that the allegations had no basis whatsoever in fact.

Annika didn't know what to believe. Christer Lundgren had certainly been questioned, that much had been confirmed by the police's press spokesman on the radio the day before. But a lot of the other information in the programme was undoubtedly false. And what had happened to the suspicions against Joachim?

She threw her roll in the bin without even unwrapping it. She finished the coffee in three large gulps.

Spike was already at his post, phone glued to his ear. He didn't react to the fact that Annika had come in on her day off; that sort of thing was normal behaviour for the summer temps.

'You fucked up badly on that murder,' he said as he hung up.

'The minister, you mean? It doesn't make any sense, though,' Annika said.

'Aha,' Spike said. 'In what way?'

'I thought I'd dig about a bit today, if that's all right?'

'Bloody lucky that we got that scoop about the Ninja Barbies,' he said. 'Otherwise we'd have had to run harder on the minister and the murder. And it would have looked pretty bloody weird if we'd run with two different murderers, two days in a row, don't you think?'

Annika blushed. She didn't have a reply. Spike's eyes were cold and watchful.

'Thanks to Carl we managed to keep our dignity intact,' the head of news said, spinning away from her on his chair, inadvertently showing her the beginnings of a bald patch.

'Okay,' Annika said. 'Is Berit here?'

'She's out on Fårö, trying to track down the speaker of parliament. For her IB scoop,' Spike said without turning round.

Annika went back to her desk and dropped her bag on the floor, her cheeks burning. Presumably she wouldn't

221

be getting a picture byline for quite some time now.

She looked through what the other papers had about the minister and his suspected involvement in the murder. No one else was running very hard with the story.

The morning papers just had short pieces about a government minister, Christer Lundgren, being questioned in relation to the murder of a young woman in Stockholm. And the other evening paper had taken pretty much the same line as the *Evening Post*.

So how could *Studio Six* be so sure of their story? Annika wondered. They have to know more than they're letting on. There's a lot more to come out yet.

The thought made her stomach churn. Why on earth do I feel so guilty? she thought.

The air was dusty and hot in spite of the air-conditioning. She went off to the toilets and rinsed her face in cold water.

I've got to get to the bottom of this, she thought. I've got to work this out. I've missed something, but what?

She leaned her forehead against the mirror and shut her eyes. The glass was cool, spreading clarity through her sinuses and into her brain.

The old woman, she thought. The fat old woman with the dog, Daniella's neighbour.

She wiped her face with a paper towel. She left behind her a smear of sweat and water on the mirror.

The new head editor, Anders Schyman, was worried. He had been aware of the ethical difficulties that went with his new job, but he would have preferred to wait a day or two before being forced into any acrobatic manoeuvres on the moral trapeze. What on earth was this hysterical story Carl Wennergren had uncovered? A feminist combat group that set fire to cars and threatened the police . . . What the fuck? And not a single critical comment, just the police spokesman's predictable comment that they took matters of this nature very seriously and were devoting the necessary resources to track down those responsible.

Schyman sighed and sat down on the orange-flowered sofa in his little alcove. This sofa has to go, he thought. It was so ingrained with cigarette smoke that it stank like an old ashtray. He got up and sat down behind his desk instead. This really wasn't a very nice room. There were no windows, just indirect light from the glass walls facing the newsroom. He could just make out the contours of the multi-storey car park through the windows on the far side of the sports section. With a sigh he stared at the mountain of cardboard boxes that had been delivered from Swedish Television the previous evening.

God, what a lot of crap we accumulate, he thought.

He decided to skip the unpacking for now, and spread the newspaper out in front of him instead. He read through the controversial articles slowly one more time. He may not be legally responsible for the paper's contents, but he knew that from now on he needed to be aware of the mechanisms that shaped the paper's editorial line, as well as its contents.

There was something not quite right about the terrorism article. How on earth could their reporter have been at the right place at exactly the right time, and how come the women spoke to him? 'He got a tip-off,' was all Spike had said. That wasn't good enough. If the group wanted maximum publicity, they would have filmed and documented their actions themselves, then sent them to all the media. But if they did that, their problem would be that they wouldn't have control of how it was used. So they must have had some sort

223

of arrangement, or they'd imposed a set of conditions. Something odd, anyway.

He'd have to look into this with the reporter.

The story about the minister wasn't quite as peculiar. It wasn't impossible for government ministers to be questioned about various crimes. Personally he thought that the radio programme had gone too far when it identified Christer Lundgren as a suspect. As far as he could make out, there was nothing to suggest that. Even so, a paper like the *Evening Post* had to cover the story.

Anders Schyman sighed.

He may as well get used to it.

30

No one answered. Annika rang and rang, but the old woman was pretending not to be at home. She could hear the dog's panting breath through the letterbox, and the woman's heavy steps on the floor.

'I know you're in there,' she called through the letterbox. 'I just want to ask you some quick questions. Please, just open the door!'

The steps fell silent, but the dog carried on panting. She waited another five minutes.

Stupid woman, Annika thought, and rang on Daniella Hermansson's door instead. The young woman opened, her child and a baby's bottle in her arms.

'Oh, hello! It's you!' Daniella Hermansson exclaimed happily. 'Come in! It's a bit of a mess, but you know how it is with small children . . .'

Annika muttered something and stepped into the dark hall. The flat was long and narrow, and had been decorated and polished to within an inch of its life. There was a large mirror and a chest of drawers in front of her, and on top of that a blue glass vase with carved wooden tulips. Annika shuddered as she saw her own reflection. She looked pale in spite of her suntan, her cheeks drawn. She quickly looked away and took off her sandals.

'What a wonderful summer we're having, don't you think?' Daniella chirruped from the kitchen. 'Feel free to look round, by the way.'

Annika dutifully looked into the bedroom and sitting room, and said that the flat was lovely, and that the lease must have cost a fortune.

'It's awful, this business with Christer Lundgren,' Daniella said as the coffee machine spluttered between them on the kitchen table. The child was clutching Annika's leg and dribbling on her skirt, but she tried to ignore him.

'How do you mean?' she asked, taking a bite of one of the low-fat biscuits.

'As if he could be a murderer, it's crazy. He's a bit of a skinflint, but he isn't the violent sort . . .'

Annika's eyes opened wide in surprise. 'You know him?'

Daniella poured weak coffee into some cups from the fifties.

'Of course I do,' she said, offended. 'He's been putting the brakes on plans to renovate the front of the building for over a year now. Milk and sugar?'

Annika blinked in confusion and gulped the coffee.

'Sorry,' she said, 'but I don't quite understand?'

'It isn't really his flat; it belongs to some newspaper, a Social Democrat paper up in Luleå. He's chairman of the board and has been treating the flat like it's his own for the past year or so. He's really mean.'

Daniella refilled Annika's cup.

'So he lives in this building!' Annika said.

'Fourth floor of the western stairwell,' Daniella said. 'One and a half rooms, forty square metres. Balcony. A nice little flat. The price of flats here is something like fourteen thousand kronor per square metre these days.'

Annika finished her second cup and leaned back.

'Bloody hell,' she said. 'Fifty metres from the scene of the murder.'

'More coffee?' Daniella said.

'Mean, you say? In what way?'

'I'm secretary of the residents' committee,' she said. 'Christer's one of the members. Every time we discuss any improvements or renovations, he always opposes them. He flatly refuses to see the service charges go up. I think it's pathetic. He hasn't even bought his flat like the rest of us, he's just sponging off one of the party's papers, and the service charge is the only thing he has to pay. Oh, come here, darling . . .'

Daniella picked up her son. He promptly upset his mother's coffee cup, and the warm liquid ran across the table and into Annika's lap. It wasn't hot enough to burn, just left yet another stain on her skirt.

'Don't worry,' Annika said.

Daniella rushed over with an evil-smelling dishcloth and tried to wipe her skirt, but Annika slipped quickly into the hall and pulled on her sandals.

'Well, bye for now,' she said, and went out into the stairwell.

'I'm really sorry, he didn't mean to . . .'

Annika walked down the stairs to the ground floor, then went past the door and across to the other lift. It wasn't working. She groaned and started walking up the stairs. By the third floor she was shattered and had to stop and catch her breath.

I really ought to start taking vitamin pills, she thought.

She padded up the last flight, breathing deeply and silently through her open mouth, and looked at the eight apartment doors. Hessler. Carlsson. Lethander and Son. HB Lundgren. She stared at the minister's letterbox. His name was handwritten and taped onto the plastic of the actual name-plate. She walked slowly over to it, listening intently. She put her finger to the doorbell, then hesitated. Instead, she opened the letterbox. A warm stream of air flowed out at her from inside the flat.

At that moment a phone started to ring inside. Aghast, she let go of the letterbox, which closed without a sound. She put her ear to the door. The ringing had stopped, so someone must have answered. She could make out an indistinct male voice. Her upper lip started to sweat, and she wiped it with the back of her hand. She looked at the letterbox. She really shouldn't do this.

Mind you, the Social Democrats bugged and burgled flats, she thought. So surely I can eavesdrop a bit . . .

She bent over and opened the letterbox again. The warm air hit her in the face. She turned her head and put her ear to the gap, into the stream of air.

'I've got to attend another session of questioning,' she thought she could hear a male voice say through the rush of air.

Silence. She changed position to be able to hear better.

'I don't know. It's not good.'

Another silence. Sweat was running down her cleavage now. When the voice spoke again it was louder, more agitated.

'What the hell am I supposed to do, then? The girl's dead, for fuck's sake!'

Annika sank to her knees to be more comfortable. She thought she could hear him clearing his throat, then footsteps. Then the voice again, quieter now.

'Yes, yes, I know. I'm not going to say anything. No, I'm not going to confess. What the hell do you take me for?'

The door opposite, Hessler's, opened. Annika's heart leaped, and she jumped clumsily to her feet. She put her finger firmly on the doorbell and glanced at Hessler out of the corner of her eye. He must have been eighty, and he was holding a little white dog on a lead. He glared suspiciously at Annika, and Annika looked up and smiled.

'Isn't it hot?' she said.

The man didn't answer. He walked over to the lift instead.

'I'm afraid it's not working,' Annika said, and rang again.

She stared at the bright spot of light in the door's spyhole. Suddenly it went dark: someone was blocking the light. She looked right at the spyhole and tried to look pleasant. Still the door didn't open. She rang again. The darkness vanished and the spyhole shone brightly again. Nothing happened. She rang a fourth time.

'Hello?' she called quietly through the letterbox. 'My name's Annika Bengtzon, I'm from the *Evening Post*. I'd like to ask you a few questions . . .'

Hessler started to shuffle down the stairs, his dog a few steps ahead of him.

She rang again.

'Go away,' said a voice from inside the flat.

Annika's breathing quickened, and she realized that she really needed a pee.

'It'll only get worse if you don't say anything,' she said, and gulped.

'Rubbish,' the minister said.

She closed her eyes and took a deep breath.

'Could I use your toilet?' she said.

'What?'

She crossed her legs. Daniella's weak coffee was about to burst her bladder.

'Please,' she said. 'I really need the toilet.'

The door opened.

'I've never heard that one before,' the minister said.

'Where is it?' Annika said.

He pointed at a pale green door on the left. She stumbled in and closed the door behind her, breathed out, flushed and washed her hands.

The flat was extremely light and unpleasantly hot. The rooms were all linked, so you could walk from the kitchen into the dining room, then into the living room and back to the hall.

'Okay, you're leaving now,' the minister said from the doorway of the main room.

She looked at the man in front of her with curiosity. He seemed tired and pale, and was wearing a white shirt that he hadn't bothered to button, and crumpled black trousers. His hair was a mess and he hadn't shaved.

Good-looking, Annika thought. She smiled.

'Thank you,' she said. 'Needs must . . .'

The words hung ambiguously between them. He turned and went back into the room.

'Close the door behind you,' he said.

She followed him into the room.

'I don't believe you did it,' she said.

'How did you find me?' he said.

'Research,' she said.

He sat down on the bed without replying. Annika stood in front of him.

'But you did see something, didn't you? That's why they're questioning you, isn't it?'

The minister looked up at her with tired eyes.

'There's hardly anyone who knows where I live,' he said. 'How did you know you'd find me here?'

Annika looked hard at the man.

'You're hiding something, aren't you? What is it that you aren't able to say?'

The minister stood up quickly and walked right up to her.

'You don't know anything,' he said. 'Go, before I throw you out!'

Annika gulped, held up both hands and started to back away to the door.

'Okay, okay,' she said. 'I'm going. Thanks for letting me use your bathroom . . .'

She left quickly, closing the door quietly behind her. She caught up with Hessler on the first floor.

'What a marvellous summer!' she said.

The minister buttoned his shirt. It was just as well to head off to Bergsgatan straight away. He sighed, sat down on the bed and tied his shoes.

They come up with some ridiculous tricks, he thought, with a wry glance at the door through which the reporter had just left. Needing the toilet, for heaven's sake! He stood up, wondering if he ought to take a jacket. He picked out a light linen one just in case.

Anyway, how the hell had she managed to find him here? Not even Karina Björnlund knew where he lived when he was in Stockholm. She always called him on his mobile.

The phone rang – the landline rather than his mobile. He answered at once. There were only a handful of people who had the number.

'How are you?'

His wife, sounding anxious. He sank onto the bed again, and to his own surprise, started to cry.

'But, darling, whatever's the matter!'

She started crying too.

'Are you at Stina's yet?'

'We got here yesterday.'

He blew his nose.

'I can't say anything.'

'Is there anything in it?'

He ran a hand over his forehead.

'How can you even ask?'

'What am I supposed to think?'

Betrayed, scared, suspicious.

'Do you really think I could . . . kill someone?'

She hesitated. 'Not of your own volition,' she said.

'But if . . . ?'

'There's nothing you wouldn't do for the party,' she said in a resigned tone.

31

Q answered. Annika was momentarily delighted. It was short-lived, however.

'I can't say a thing,' he said.

'Is the minister really a suspect?' Annika wondered, leaning back in her chair and putting her feet up on the desk.

He laughed coarsely.

'What an incredibly intelligent question. Did you come up with that all by yourself?'

'There's something odd about him,' Annika said. 'He's scared of something getting out. What's he hiding?'

The laughter faded away and was followed by a short silence.

'Where do you get all your information from?' the detective wondered.

'I listen, watch, observe. He lives very close to the scene of the crime, for instance.'

'So you've worked that out.'

'But is it relevant?'

'All the tenants of sixty-four Sankt Göransgatan have been questioned.'

'It's leasehold.'

'What?'

'They're not tenants, they own their flats.'

233

'Oh, for fuck's sake,' the detective said.

'Do you really think he did it?'

Q sighed. 'It isn't out of the question,' he said.

Annika was lost for words.

'But . . . what about the boyfriend? Joachim?'

'He's got an alibi.'

Annika leaned forward in her chair.

'So it wasn't . . . ? But it looked like—'

'It would be nice if you didn't speculate so much in the bloody press,' the policeman said. 'Sometimes you really mess things up.'

Annika blew up. 'That's rich, coming from you! Who the hell was it who called a press conference at ten p.m. on Saturday night, just because you were so bloody keen to get the press involved? That's a load of crap. And what do you mean, "mess things up"? There's been more than one suspicious death in police custody. So don't start accusing us of abusing our position!'

'I don't have to sit here and listen to crap like this,' the policeman said, and hung up.

'Hello?' Annika shouted into the phone. 'Hello? Fuck!'

She slammed the phone down, which made Spike look over at her in annoyance.

'You're sitting at my desk.'

A woman in a suit, somewhere in her thirties, was looking her up and down critically. Annika looked up, momentarily bewildered.

'What?'

'Aren't you supposed to be off today?'

Annika swung her feet onto the floor, got up and held out her hand.

'You must be Mariana,' she said. 'Nice to meet you. I'm Annika Bengtzon.'

The dragon in the suit had a ridiculously 'refined'

posh surname, and was supposed to be very talented.

'I'd be grateful if you could tidy up before you finish a shift. It isn't nice to be confronted by this sort of thing every time I come back to work.'

'I quite agree,' Annika said. 'I had to clear the bookshelf and the desk of your stuff when I got here on Wednesday.'

She quickly gathered together the notes she had laid out on the desk.

'I'm going to get some food,' she said curtly to the head of news, then picked up her bag and walked out.

By the lifts she bumped into Carl Wennergren. He was laughing at something he had just said with a couple of other summer temps. Annika had been wondering how she'd react when she next saw him. She'd been wondering what to say. Now she no longer had to wonder. She stopped, demonstratively in their way.

'Can I talk to you?' she said abruptly.

Carl Wennergren puffed out his chest and smiled a smile that lit up his suntanned face. His hair was still wet from his morning swim, his fringe hanging over his forehead.

'Sure, darling,' he said. 'What's up?'

Annika walked down half a flight of the stairs. Carl Wennergren waved off his friends and followed her down, the picture of confidence and composure. She stood with her back to the wall on the small landing and stared angrily at her colleague.

'I was made an offer on Monday,' she said in a low voice. 'A group calling themselves the Ninja Barbies wanted to sell me a scoop. For fifty thousand in cash they were going to let me tag along when they carried out some sort of attack on the police.'

She was staring intently at Carl Wennergren.

The young man had stopped smiling, and was blushing

furiously all the way to his ears. He narrowed his lips to a thin strip.

'What do you mean?' he said in a rather strangled voice.

'How come you got that story in today's paper?'

Carl Wennergren tossed his hair back.

'What the hell has that got to do with you?' he said. 'Who put you in charge?'

She looked at him without replying. He turned, as if to go back upstairs. Annika didn't move. After four steps he turned round and came back, coming to a halt just inches from Annika's face.

'I didn't pay a single damn penny,' he snarled. 'What the hell do you think I am?'

'I don't think anything,' she said, and noticed that her voice was shaking. 'I just thought it was all a bit bloody peculiar.'

'They wanted to get their message out,' Carl Wennergren snarled, 'but they weren't selling the scoop. No newspaper would be stupid enough to pay for a terrorist attack against the police; surely even you can work that out?'

'So they let you have it for nothing,' Annika said.

'Exactly.'

Carl Wennergren spun round and went up the stairs, two steps at a time.

'Did they wait till you'd got your camera ready before they set fire to the car?' she called after him.

The reporter vanished into the newsroom without looking back.

Annika carried on down the stairs. Carl Wennergren might be right. There'd be no point in setting fire to cars if no one knew why they were doing it. The Ninja Barbies may just have given him a perfectly ordinary tip-off.

But he hadn't known that they had already made the offer to her, she was sure of that. That really had stopped him in his tracks.

She walked out of the building, pretending not to hear Tore Brand's whining.

It was hotter than ever. The sun was blazing down on the turning circle in front of the building and the tarmac was soft. She went over to the hotdog kiosk on Rålambsvägen and got something to eat, which she proceeded to eat standing up.

The early evening news on television had nothing about Josefin, the minister, or the Ninja Barbies in the opening headlines. Maybe they'd appear later in the broadcast, but no one at the *Evening Post* sat through the programme that long. All activity stopped when the electric guitar of the signature tune to *Studio Six* came on the radio at three minutes past six. Annika was sitting at Berit's desk, staring at the radio.

'The investigation into the murder of nineteen-year-old Josefin Liljeberg is becoming increasingly complex,' the presenter announced over the noise of the guitar. 'The young woman was actually a stripper in an infamous sex club. The Minister for Foreign Trade, Christer Lundgren, has been questioned again today. More debate and discussion of this in today's edition of *Studio Six*.'

Without looking up, Annika could feel people staring at her from over at the newsdesk. She could feel their hostility burning through the back of her blouse.

'It's Wednesday, first August. Welcome to Studio Six in Radio House in Stockholm,' the presenter's voice boomed.

'So, Josefin Liljeberg was a stripper in the infamous sex club that took its name from this very programme, Studio Six. In most of the media, and the *Evening Post* in particular, she has been portrayed as an innocent family girl who dreamed of becoming a journalist and helping children in trouble. But the truth is completely different. This is a recording of the young woman in question.'

And they played a tape-recording. A young woman's voice, trying to sound erotic, announced that anyone who was curious and who had a sense of adventure was very welcome to visit Studio Six, Stockholm's hottest club. She gave the club's opening hours, from 1 p.m. to 5 a.m. You could meet nice young ladies, offer them champagne, watch a show or a private viewing, or watch and buy erotic films.

Annika was having trouble breathing, and hid her face in her hands. She had had no idea that the voice was Josefin's.

The programme ran through the details of the murder. The minister had been summoned to Bergsgatan again for more questioning. They played another recording, of a door slamming, then several reporters shouting questions at Christer Lundgren as he walked into Police Headquarters.

Annika stood up, put her bag on her shoulder and went out the back way. The stares directed at her back were pulling all the air from her lungs. She had to get some fresh air before she died.

32

Patricia had set her clock-radio to go off at 5.58 p.m. That meant she'd have time to pee and get some water before *Studio Six* began.

She had slept deeply and without dreaming, and felt almost drugged as she stumbled back to the mattress. She piled the pillows up against the wall.

She listened in the dark behind her black curtains. Josefin's curtains.

The man on the radio was tearing Josefin to pieces, managing to spoil every crumb of truth and making Josefin out to be a bad person. Patricia was in tears.

It was so unfair. She turned the radio off and went into the kitchen. With trembling hands she made a pot of tea. Just as she was pouring the first cup the doorbell rang. It was the journalist.

'Those bastards!' Annika Bengtzon said, storming into the flat. 'How the fuck can they make her out to be some sort of fucking prostitute? It doesn't make any sense!'

Patricia wiped her tears.

'Would you like a cup of tea? I was just going to have some.'

'Thanks,' Annika said, sinking onto a chair. 'I don't know what we can do. Maybe report them to the Press

Complaints Commission? They can't be allowed to get away with this!'

Patricia found another mug for the reporter. She didn't look well. She was even paler and thinner than last time.

'Would you like a sandwich? I've got some Arctic bread.'

That was Josie's favourite, with Port Salut cheese.

'No thanks, I've been eating all day.'

Annika pushed the mug away and leaned over the table, looking her right in the eye.

'Have I misunderstood everything, Patricia?' she wondered. 'Have I got it wrong in all my articles?'

Patricia gulped and looked down.

'Not as far as I know,' she said.

'Patricia, be honest with me. Have you ever seen that government minister, Christer Lundgren?'

Patricia bit her lip, her tears welling up again.

'I don't know,' she whispered. 'Maybe.'

Annika leaned back in her chair in despair.

'Bloody hell,' she said. 'So it could be true . . . A government minister. Fuck!'

She stood up and started pacing up and down the kitchen.

'It's still absolutely unforgivable to make out that Josefin was a whore. And playing that tape of her voice, that's disgusting.'

'But that wasn't Josie,' Patricia said, blowing her nose.

Annika stopped and stared at her in surprise.

'What? So who the hell was it, then?'

'Sanna, she sits on the door. It's her job to look after the answering machine. Drink your tea before it gets cold.'

The journalist sat down again.

'So the radio guys aren't as clued up as they're making out.'

Patricia didn't answer. She put her hands to her face. Her own life had vanished when Josie's was snuffed out, to be replaced by an uncontrollable reality that seemed to be dragging her down to new depths every day.

'This is all just a terrible dream,' she said, her voice muffled by her hands. She could feel the journalist looking at her.

'Have you had any sort of help?' Annika wondered.

Patricia took her hands away from her face, sighed and picked up her mug.

'How do you mean?'

'A psychologist, counsellor – anyone like that?'

She looked at the journalist, surprised. 'Why should I?'

'Maybe you could use some help from someone?'

Patricia drank some of the now lukewarm tea.

'What could they do? Josie's still going to be dead, isn't she?'

Annika looked hard at her.

'Patricia,' she said, 'please, tell me what you know. It's important to me. Was it Joachim?'

Patricia put her mug down and stared at her lap.

'I don't know,' she said quietly. 'It could have been someone else. One of the bigwigs, maybe . . .' Her voice faded, and a sudden heavy silence filled the kitchen.

'What makes you think that?'

Her eyes filled with tears again.

'I can't tell you,' she said.

'Why not?'

She looked up at the reporter and her tears overflowed, her voice now shrill and aggressive. 'Because he'd know I was the one who talked! Don't you get it? I can't! I won't!'

Patricia jumped up and ran out of the kitchen, threw herself on her mattress and pulled the duvet over her head. A few moments later she heard the journalist's voice from the doorway.

'I'm sorry,' Annika said. 'I really didn't mean to upset you. I'll try to find out if anyone's reported *Studio Six* for the crap they said about Josefin. I'll call you tomorrow, okay?'

Patricia didn't answer, breathing quickly and shallowly under the covers. The air was thick and sweaty, and there was hardly any oxygen under there.

The journalist let herself out and closed the front door gently behind her.

Patricia threw off the duvet. She lay there, looking out through a crack in the black curtains.

It would soon be night-time again.

33

Jansson had arrived, thank goodness! At least he had a brain, unlike Spike.

'You look shattered,' Jansson said.

'Cheers,' Annika said. 'Have you got time for a chat?'

He clicked away from something on his screen.

'Sure. The smoking bubble?'

They went out to the smoking area, and the night-editor lit a cigarette, blowing the smoke upwards.

'Christer Lundgren lives fifty metres from the scene of the murder,' she said. 'Everyone in the building has been questioned.'

Jansson whistled.

'That puts things in a different light. Have you found out anything else?'

She looked down at the floor.

'The boyfriend has an alibi. One of my sources says it could have been some VIP who killed her.'

Jansson carried on smoking and looking at the young temp without saying anything. He couldn't make her out. She was a combination of smart, impulsive and ambitious, but in a way that wasn't altogether healthy.

'Come on, out with it,' he said. 'Who are your sources?'

She pursed her lips. 'You won't say anything, will you?'

He shook his head.

'The victim's flatmate and the detective in charge of the case at violent crime. Neither of them is prepared to talk openly, but they've said quite a lot off the record.'

Jansson was aware his eyebrows had shot up.

'Not bad,' he said. 'How the hell did you manage that?'

She shrugged. 'Just called and kept pestering. I went round to the girls' flat. Her name's Patricia. I'm a bit worried about her.'

Jansson stubbed out his cigarette.

'We've got to go harder with the minister today,' he said. 'He's been questioned three times now. There must be more to that than just the fact that he lives close to the scene of the crime. But that's very interesting; I haven't read anything about where he lives anywhere else. We'll do a separate piece on that. How did you find that out, just out of interest?'

She sighed. 'I was having coffee with one of his neighbours. Then I rang on his door.'

Jansson was taken aback.

'And he answered?'

She blushed.

'I needed the toilet.'

The night-editor leaned back in the plastic chair.

'What on earth did he say?'

She laughed, embarrassed. 'He threw me out.'

Jansson laughed loudly.

'Where's Carl?' Annika wondered.

'He got another tip-off, about those Barbie dolls. They're up to something again.'

Annika stiffened.

244

'How did that actually come about yesterday?' she asked.

'I don't really know,' Jansson said. 'He just turned up with the pictures at nine o'clock or so.'

'Did you know he was bringing them in?'

Jansson shook his head and lit another cigarette.

'Nope,' he said. 'It came as a nice surprise.'

'Do you think it's ethical, to go along on a terrorist attack?' she said.

Jansson sighed and put the cigarette out after just two drags.

'That's a big question,' he said, standing up. 'Can you check with Carl and see if you want to add any extra information to his piece?'

Annika got up as well.

'Sure thing,' she said.

Jansson's phone was ringing madly over on his desk, and he hurried to get it.

'Hi, Berit, how are you getting on? No? Bastard!'

Annika sat down at Berit's desk and wrote her articles. The piece about the government minister living close to the scene of the crime was tricky to get right. She didn't have much to put in it. For a long while she sat and stared at the screen, then she picked up the phone and dialled Christer Lundgren's press secretary.

'Karina Björnlund,' the woman said as she answered.

Annika explained who she was, and said she hoped she wasn't interrupting anything.

'Well, I'm actually in the middle of a dinner party here. Could you call back tomorrow, do you think?'

Annika gasped. 'Are you serious?'

'I just told you, I'm busy.'

'Why is the minister being questioned?'

'I have no idea.'

'Is it because he lives right next to the scene of the murder?'

The press secretary's surprise sounded genuine.

'Does he?'

Annika groaned.

'Thanks for letting me disturb you,' she said sarcastically. 'You've been a great help.'

'Don't mention it,' Karina Björnlund chirped. 'Have a nice evening!'

Jesus Christ! Annika thought.

She called the exchange and asked where Berit was staying, and was given a number in Visby, on the island of Gotland. She was in when Annika called.

'No luck with the hunt?' Annika asked.

Berit sighed. 'The speaker's denying all knowledge of IB whatsoever.'

'What are you trying to find out?'

'He was very influential back in the sixties, one of the people who was most involved. He did his military service at the Information Bureau.'

Annika blinked.

'Is that even possible?'

'Well, the formal description is that he was posted to the defence ministry's security department, but in practice he just carried on with his political activities. How are you getting on?'

Annika hesitated. 'Oh, okay, I suppose. *Studio Six* have announced that she was a stripper.'

'Did you know that?'

Annika closed her eyes.

'Yep.'

'So why didn't you write about it?'

Berit sounded surprised. Annika scratched her ear.

'I gave a description. It didn't really seem relevant,' she said.

'Of course it is! Really, I'm surprised at you!' Berit said.

Annika gulped. 'The picture gets so one-dimensional if you bring up the business of the sex club. She just ends up as a whore. There was so much more, so many more nuances, she was a daughter and a sister and a friend and a schoolgirl—'

'And a dancer in a sex club. Annika, of course it's important,' Berit interrupted.

They fell silent.

'I'm thinking of reporting *Studio Six* to the Broadcasting Commission,' Annika eventually said.

'But why on earth would you do that?' Berit sounded almost angry.

'Patricia didn't know they were going to make that public,' she said.

'Who's Patricia?'

'Josefin's best friend.'

Berit took a deep breath. 'Annika, don't get angry, but I think you're taking this story a bit too personally. Be careful not to get too involved with the people concerned. It can only turn out badly. You have to maintain your professional distance; otherwise you'll be no use to anyone, least of all yourself.'

Annika shut her eyes and felt herself blushing.

A sense of failure began to creep through her brain.

'I know what I'm doing,' she said, slightly too shrilly.

'I'm not altogether sure that you do,' Berit said.

They ended the call quickly. Annika sat with her hands over her face for a long while, feeling bruised and on the verge of tears.

34

'Have you finished the article about the flat?' Jansson yelled from the newsdesk.

She quickly pulled herself together.

'Yes,' she called. 'I'm just putting it in the can . . . now!'

She let go of the keyboard and sent the article rushing through the wires. Jansson gave her the thumbs-up when the text appeared on his screen. She quickly gathered her things from Berit's desk and got ready to go. At that moment Carl Wennergren came galloping in from the lifts.

'Get me a picture byline, because tonight I am immortal!' he proclaimed.

All the men over at the newsdesk looked up as the reporter performed an enthusiastic war-dance on the floor of the newsroom, armed with a notepad and a camera in his hands.

'The Ninja Barbies tried to set fire to the whorehouse where that stripper worked, and guess who's got the exclusive rights to the pictures?'

The men round the newsdesk stood up in unison and went over to slap Carl Wennergren on the back. Annika could see his camera waving like a victory trophy above their heads. She quickly hoisted her bag onto her shoulder and left the newsroom by the back stairs.

The temperature had dropped a few degrees, but the air felt heavier than ever. They were bound to have an enormous thunderstorm soon, Annika thought.

She went past the shuttered hotdog kiosk and the bus-stop, deciding instead to walk to Fridhemsplan, and without really thinking about it she found herself at Kronoberg Park.

All the cordons had been removed, but the mountain of flowers had grown. They were in the wrong place, by the entrance to the cemetery itself, but that didn't matter. The truth about Josefin didn't matter, as long as the myth lived on and could act as a lightning rod for people's emotions.

She turned away and headed down to Hantverkargatan. Blue lights were twinkling in the summer evening.

The Ninja Barbies' arson attack, she thought. Then, a moment later: Bloody hell, Patricia!

She jogged down the hill, past Kungsholmen High School. The three crowns at the top of the tower of the City Hall shone high above in the last of the sunlight. A group of curious onlookers had gathered, and she could see Arne Påhlson from the rival paper standing next to a fire engine. Cautiously she walked closer. One of the narrow lanes of the road had been blocked off, and cars were creeping past on the remaining open lane. Three fire engines, two police cars and an ambulance were parked in front of the anonymous-looking door of Studio Six. The pavement and façade were black with soot; it looked like war had broken out. She stopped behind a group of young men holding cans of beer and excitedly discussing what had happened.

Suddenly the door opened and a policeman in plain

clothes came out. Annika recognized him at once, even though he wasn't wearing his Hawaiian shirt this time. He spoke to someone who was hidden by the door, and Annika pushed forward to look. She saw a thin woman pointing at something in the street.

'Where?' she heard the policeman say.

Patricia stepped onto the pavement. It took a couple of seconds before Annika recognized her. She was heavily made up and had her hair tied in a tight ponytail at the top of her head. She was wearing a glittering red bra and thong. The men standing next to Annika started shouting and whistling. Patricia started, and turned to look at the group. She saw Annika at once. Their eyes met, and Patricia lit up. She raised her hand in greeting. Annika stiffened. Without thinking, she dodged behind the men and moved back. The men pushed forward and she heard a woman shouting. She rushed into a side street and ran down to Bergsgatan. She ran past Police Headquarters and the car park, and turned into Agnegatan. She took the short cut through the court-yard and found herself outside her own front door, trembling and out of breath. The key in her hand was shaking so much that she could hardly open the door.

I'm losing my grip, she thought, and bowed her head as she realized how pathetic she had been.

She was ashamed of Patricia.

Eighteen years, one month,
twenty-five days

When the deepest trust wins out over anxiety, that's when genuine faith can develop. Anything less is a failure, I know that.

He wants me to relive terrible old memories.

Pushes me into the bathroom to masturbate.

Keep going until you come, he says. You mustn't come in, I say.

He opens the door as I'm sitting there with the shower-head pushed up between my thighs, and his face is white with rage.

So you can fuck yourself with that bloody thing until you come, but not with me, he screams.

The hotel corridor. A door locking itself shut. Panic, pulling and tugging, naked and wet. Voices, the pool area, not daring to shout. Lights out, silence, the tiles cold under my feet. Creeping through the plants, treading on a big insect and almost screaming. Hate spiders, hate creepy-crawlies. Crying, freezing, shaking.

A matter of conquering your fears, coming to terms with your demons.

I creep back at regular intervals to check the door.

He unlocks it just before dawn; warm, dry, hot, affectionate.

We are the most important things
in the world
to each other.

Thursday 2 August

35

The Prime Minister caught sight of the press photographers from a distance and let out a deep sigh. The heavily laden journalists had formed an impromptu wall in front of the main government building, Rosenbad. Of course he had been perfectly aware that they would be there, even if he had hoped he was wrong. So far he hadn't made any comment on the predicament Christer Lundgren was in, and had merely referred enquiries to the Minister for Integration, a young woman who was acting head of government during his holiday. But there was no way he could hold that line now. The small allocation of summer days that were supposed to constitute his holiday had been dwindling until they had finally vanished. He sighed again, and yawned. He always did that when he was nervous. People around him thought it made a rather nonchalant impression, which was no bad thing. Like now, when the other men in the car had no idea of the turmoil going on inside him, the knot forming in his stomach. His guts were churning with anxiety, and he realized he would need the toilet pretty soon.

The press corps noticed the car as it turned into Fredsgatan. They ran towards it like a single entity, pulling out their long lenses. The Prime Minister watched them through the dark glass of the windows. There were radio and television reporters, and people from the press waving small tape-recorders.

'They look like action figures,' he said to the security agent in the front seat. 'Like He-Men with ugly clothes and detachable accessories, don't you think?'

The agent agreed. Everyone always agreed with whatever he said. He smiled wearily. Imagine if the press and the opposition could be so cooperative.

The car stopped with a gentle, rocking motion. The security agent was out of the car before the wheels stopped, shielding the Prime Minister with his body at the same time as he held the back door open.

Questions deluged the Prime Minister like a sticky torrent.

'What do you think of the accusations levelled at the Minister for Foreign Trade?'

'How much damage is this doing to the party?'

'Does this change the direction of the election campaign?'

'Do you think Christer Lundgren should resign?'

He shuffled out of the car, standing up in all his bulk, and gave a theatrical sigh. Microphones, tape-recorders, cameras and film all recorded this little puff of air. They could all see that the Prime Minister wasn't terribly concerned by this. He was dressed in a light-blue shirt, open at the neck, crumpled trousers, and he had sandals on his bare feet.

'Well,' the Prime Minister said, stopping in the glare of a television camera. His voice was slow, relaxed, fairly quiet, and carried a faint tone of resignation. 'Christer isn't suspected of anything at all. Of course, this has no bearing on our successful election campaign in any way whatsoever. I sincerely hope that Christer will remain part of the government, both for the sake of the government and for the sake of Sweden and Europe. We need people with passion to drive politics forward in the twenty-first century.'

End of soundbite one, he thought, and started to head to the doorway. The press followed like a parasitical amoeba, exactly according to plan.

'So why have you broken off your holiday?'

'Who's going to be at today's crisis meeting?'

'Do you still have confidence in Christer Lundgren?'

The Prime Minister took a few more steps before stopping to answer, just as he had practised with his media trainer.

Time for the killer quote. When he turned to face the group of reporters, he gave them a wry smile.

'Do I look like a man facing a crisis?' he said, trying to make his eyes twinkle.

Evidently it worked, because several of the amoebas laughed.

He walked up to the door, and the security agent was about to open it.

Time for the finale. He quickly adopted his slightly concerned look.

'Joking aside,' he said, with his hand on one of the heavy brass door handles, 'of course I have every sympathy for what Christer is going through right now. This sort of media witch-hunt is always a severe trial. But I can assure you that for the government, and for the party, these exaggerated allegations have absolutely no significance at all.

'You must have seen today's *Evening Post*, which explains why Christer has been questioned. He just happens to have a flat close to Kronoberg Park. Even government ministers need somewhere to sleep!'

He smiled sadly and nodded to affirm the wisdom of his own words before walking through the security

doors of the government building. As they closed behind him, more questions poured through the gap:

'. . . reason to question him several times?'

'. . . saw anything in particular?'

'. . . comment on the latest revelations about . . .'

He concentrated on walking slowly and nonchalantly
up the steps into the entrance hall for as long as the
journalists could still see him through the glass door.
Bloody hyenas!

'God, it's hot,' he said, pulling open a couple more
buttons of his shirt. 'If I'm going to have to spend the
whole fucking day in here, you'd better make sure
the air-conditioning is working.'

He stepped into a lift and let the doors close before
the security agent got in. Now he really did need the
toilet.

Her shoe-lace snapped and Annika swore. She didn't
have any more at home. With a tired sigh she sat down
on the hall floor, pulled off the trainer and tied the two
ends together, again. Soon there wouldn't be enough
lace left to tie the shoe at all. She really had to remember
to buy some new laces next time she went shopping.

She ran down the stairs carefully, anxious not to put
too much strain on her knees. Her legs felt stiff and
clumsy: she'd neglected her running all summer.

The air in the courtyard was heavy and stagnant. All
the windows were wide open, forming black squares
in the building's shabby façade. Their curtains hung
like tired theatre dressings, not moving at all. Annika
tossed her towel into the shared bathroom on her way
out, then jogged slowly out onto Agnegatan.

The Japanese shopkeeper at the corner of Bergsgatan
had already hung up that day's flysheet for the *Evening
Post*. Carl Wennergren had got the lead again with his

Ninja Barbies. She jogged on the spot for a few seconds as she read the headline: Sex club attack: exclusive pictures, only in the Evening Post.

Her pulse quickened and she started to sweat. The picture showed the door of the club being blown out, the doorway full of flames.

I wonder where Patricia was when it went off, she thought. I wonder how scared she must have been.

From the article it was clear that the club hadn't been badly damaged. To her surprise, she realized that she was relieved.

She turned and ran down Agnegatan, towards Kungsholmsstrand. When she reached the water she turned left and quickened her pace. Soon her lungs were hurting; she really was out of condition. She pounded her feet on the asphalt path harder and harder, not caring that it hurt.

When she saw Karlberg Palace ahead of her on the other side of the water she switched into top gear. Her chest was heaving like a pair of bellows and sweat was running into her eyes. She ran back along Lindhagensgatan and through Rålambshov Park, then up across Kungsholmstorg. By the time she got into the shower she was exhausted almost to the point of collapse. I've got to look after myself, she thought. I've got to get regular exercise; otherwise I'll never make it. Her legs were shaking as she climbed the stairs to her flat.

36

She arrived at the newsroom just before lunch. Berit still hadn't got back, so Annika borrowed her desk again.

Her own contribution to that day's paper consisted of the article about the minister's overnight flat. The headline was striking: WE REVEAL WHY MINISTER QUESTIONED.

She was happy with the opening:

Christer Lundgren lives next to the murder-scene. He has a secret overnight flat just 50 metres from the cemetery.

Not even Lundgren's press secretary knew its location.

'How did you find me?' the minister asked when the Evening Post *visited the one-room flat yesterday.*

There followed a description of the flat, the revelation that everyone in the block had been questioned, and Daniella's quote: *As if he could be a murderer, it's crazy . . . He isn't the violent sort.*

She had left out the bit about him being mean.

Then came several cryptic lines about the fact that the

police were spending more time with the minister than with the other residents. She had kept that bit short, because she didn't know exactly what the police were after.

Mariana, the dragon in the suit with the jumped-up surname, had written a short piece about Josefin working in a sex club called Studio Six.

Berit had a short article about the speaker of parliament denying any knowledge of IB.

An unfamiliar figure was sitting over at the newsdesk, with Spike's phone stuck to his ear. Annika switched on her computer, and looked at him over the screen. Did he know who she was? She knew she was going to have to go over and introduce herself, but hesitated, pushing back her still-damp hair. When he had put the phone down she hurried over. Just as she had taken a deep breath and was about to say something to his back, his phone rang again and he grabbed it. Annika was left standing behind his chair, trying to find something to focus on while she waited. She caught sight of a copy of the rival paper. The front page was dominated by Josefin's graduation picture. The headline was stark and heavy: SEX CLUB STRIPPER. Annika put her hand on the editor's swivel chair and leaned over for a closer look. The piece went on in slightly smaller text: *Murdered Josefin was a sex worker.*

'How the hell did we miss that angle? Perhaps you can explain?'

Annika looked up and met the frosty gaze of the head of news. She ran her tongue over her lips and held out her hand.

'Annika Bengtzon, nice to meet you,' she said in a rather subdued voice.

The head of news looked away, shook her hand

261

quickly and muttered his name, Ingvar Johansson. He picked up the paper and held it in front of Annika.

'You've been dealing with this story, from what I understand. How the hell did we miss the fact that she was a whore?'

Annika felt her pulse racing, and her mouth was bone-dry.

'She wasn't a whore,' she said, her voice trembling. 'She was a dancer at her boyfriend's club.'

'Yes, completely naked.'

'No, she wore a thong. Her boyfriend kept within the law.'

Ingvar Johansson stared at her.

'So why didn't you write anything about that, if you already knew?'

She gulped, her heartbeat thudding in her ears.

'Well, I . . . I got it wrong. I didn't think it was important.'

The phone rang again and the head of news turned away from her. Annika swallowed, feeling close to tears. Fuck. Fuck. Fuck. That's it, then. I'm finished.

She turned and walked back to Berit's desk, as the floor rolled beneath her. It was obvious that she couldn't do anything right on this paper!

Berit's phone was ringing insistently, and she hurried to answer it, quickly clearing her throat.

'Yes, hello, this is Lisbeth,' a mature woman's voice said.

Annika sat down, closed her eyes, and tried to stop herself hyperventilating.

'Who?' she said, momentarily confused.

'Lisbeth, the counsellor.'

The voice sounded reproachful.

Annika sighed inaudibly. 'Oh, of course,' she said. 'The youth centre in Täby. What can I do for you?'

'The youngsters are holding their protest against violence today,' she said. 'They're setting off from here in three coaches at two p.m. They should get to the scene of the murder at about two thirty.'

Annika swallowed and rubbed her forehead.

'Two thirty,' she repeated.

'Yes, I thought you'd want to know,' Lisbeth said.

'Thanks, that's great,' Annika said, and hung up.

She went out to the toilet and splashed her face and wrists with cold water. Gradually her panic subsided.

It's hardly that big a deal, she thought. I really must try to keep things in proportion. So what if everyone thinks I got it wrong?

She tidied her hair, then went to the cafeteria and got a sandwich. Anyway, maybe she got it right, at least as far as press ethics were concerned.

It was worth looking into.

She took the sandwich and a bottle of Fanta Light back to Berit's desk.

The press ombudsman on duty was a woman.

'I'd like to register a complaint,' Annika said.

'I see, of course. Something concerning you yourself?' the ombudsman said.

'No, it's on behalf of a girl who's dead.'

The ombudsman was friendly and patient.

'In that case her relatives would have to register the complaint, unless you're acting on their behalf.'

Annika reflected for a moment.

'This concerns a newspaper and a radio programme – would that be something you would handle?'

'We can look at the newspaper article, but not the radio programme. That's the remit of the Broadcasting Commission.'

Annika groaned. 'But aren't they mostly concerned with political impartiality and factual accuracy?'

'Yes, they do handle matters of that sort, but they also look into questions of ethics and privacy as well. The rules are more or less the same as for the press. What form of complaint is it?'

'Thanks very much for your help,' Annika said quickly, and hung up.

She called the Broadcasting Commission out in Haninge.

'Yes, that's the sort of issue we could look into,' said the section head who took her call.

'Even if I'm the one making the complaint?' Annika said.

'No, we only deal with complaints from members of the public in matters of factual accuracy and impartiality. As far as intrusions into personal privacy are concerned, the complaint has to be made by the individuals whose privacy has been infringed.'

Annika closed her eyes and leaned her head on her hand.

'If that were to happen, what sort of conclusion would you come to?'

The woman considered this.

'Well, the outcome isn't certain,' she said eventually. 'We've had a few cases where the surviving relatives have had their complaints upheld. Could you be more specific?'

Annika took a deep breath.

'It's about a dead woman. She's been called a stripper in a radio programme. Those closest to her hadn't given permission for that information to be made public.'

That wasn't strictly true. Annika hadn't actually spoken to Josefin's parents. But it was true as far as Patricia was concerned, and, in the purely physical sense, they had been living together.

'Ah, yes,' the woman said. It sounded like she was a *Studio Six* listener. She paused.

'This isn't a black-and-white case,' she said eventually. 'The Commission has to receive an official complaint, which would lead to an investigation. But there's also the matter of public interest – that would also have to be considered.'

Annika gave up. She had a feeling she wasn't going to get much further. She thanked the woman and hung up.

Well, at least I'm not barking up the wrong tree entirely, she thought.

37

Annika put her feet up on the desk and settled back to listen to the lunchtime news on Berit's radio. They had five main items: the Middle East, the Prime Minister's comments on the Christer Lundgren affair, and three other stories that Annika forgot the moment she heard them. Her thoughts started to wander as they ran through the situation in the Middle East. When the Prime Minister came on she turned up the volume. The familiar voice sounded a bit rattled.

'Do I look like a man facing a crisis?'

The reporter's voice explained that the Prime Minister looked relaxed and in a good mood when he arrived at Rosenbad that morning. He hadn't seemed at all concerned about the allegations concerning the Minister for Foreign Trade, Christer Lundgren, and was cautiously optimistic about the ongoing election campaign. He had, however, expressed his sympathy for what his colleague was going through.

The Prime Minister's voice again: 'Of course I have every sympathy for what Christer is going through right now. This sort of media witch-hunt is always a severe trial. But I can assure you that for the government, and for the party, these exaggerated allegations have absolutely no significance at all.'

That was the end of the item. A report from the Association of Local Authorities came on instead and Annika turned off the radio. If there was one thing she found utterly boring, it was reports about local councils.

'So have you been shooting your mouth off, then?'

Only just awake, Patricia blinked at the light coming through the gap in the curtains, moved the phone to her other ear and tried to sit up on the mattress.

'Hello,' she said. 'Who—'

'Don't pretend it wasn't you. Tell me the truth!' The shrill voice was on the point of breaking.

Patricia coughed and rubbed her eyes, wishing that the pollen season was over.

'Is that Barbro?' she said tentatively.

'Of course it's Barbro! Who else would it be? One of your sex club friends, perhaps?'

Josefin's mother started yelling down the line, inarticulate and incoherent. Patricia took a deep breath and tried to gather her thoughts. Her words got tangled up, falling over each other, making no sense. Spanish took over, the way it always did when she was stressed.

'*No entiendo*—'

'Do you have any idea what you've done?' Josefin's mother shrieked. 'You've tarnished her memory for ever! How could you?'

Patricia's thoughts cleared: something was wrong.

'What's happened? There must be some misunderstanding . . .'

The voice on the phone sank to a whisper.

'We know what you are. A foreign whore, do you hear? And as if that wasn't bad enough, you had to drag Josefin down into your shit as well!'

Patricia stood up and screamed back into the phone:

'That's not true! None of it! I didn't drag Josefin into anything!'

'Well, one thing's certain,' Barbro Liljeberg Hed snarled. 'You're getting out of my flat, today. Pack up your squalid little life and get back to Africa or wherever the hell you come from.'

'But—'

'I want you out by six o'clock.'

Click. The line went dead. Patricia listened to the silence for a moment. She put the phone down gently and sank back onto the mattress. She pulled her knees up under her chin, wrapped her arms round her legs and rocked slowly back and forth, back and forth.

Where was she going to go?

The phone rang again. She jumped as if she'd been slapped. Without thinking she picked up the phone, tore it from the wall and threw it out into the hall.

'Bloody bitch!' she screamed, and started to cry.

Annika listened to the ringing tone for several minutes. Patricia ought to be at home now, maybe she was asleep, but surely she'd hear the phone ringing?

What if something had happened to her?

Anxiety merged with the shame she had felt the day before: first about Patricia herself, and then at her own betrayal of her.

She took a walk round the newsroom, got a cup of coffee and watched CNN for a while. As she passed the newsdesk she remembered that she hadn't mentioned the demonstration at the scene of the murder.

'You'll have to do it yourself,' Ingvar Johansson said curtly. 'All the other reporters are busy.'

She went over to Picture-Pelle and asked for a photographer at 2.15 p.m.

'It'll be Pettersson,' Pelle said. 'He's on his way in.'

She smiled sweetly, groaning to herself. That clapped-out Golf again.

'I'll be waiting outside,' she said, and went to get her bag.

She took the lift down, left the building and sat on one of the concrete blocks near the garage. The air was stifling, heavy and electric, crackling in her lungs when she breathed. She shut her eyes and listened to the sounds of the city. Maybe they wouldn't be hers for much longer.

When she opened her eyes it took her a second to realize what she was looking at. The young woman who was on her way into the *Evening Post* building looked familiar, but it took her a few moments to place her.

'Patricia!' Annika cried, jogging towards her. 'What on earth are you doing here?'

The woman looked round, startled, and caught sight of Annika. She walked out of the building again, and came close to getting caught in the automatic doors. Tore Brand was shouting something inside, and Patricia started to cry.

'What on earth's happened?'

Annika went up to her and put her arm round the young woman, steering her towards the car park.

'I've got the push,' Patricia said.

Annika breathed out. 'Maybe that's just as well,' she said. 'You'll soon find another job.'

Patricia looked up at her uncomprehendingly.

'Not from the club. From the flat.'

'Josefin's parents?'

Patricia nodded, drying her tears.

'Josie's mother's a bitch,' she said. 'A racist bitch. I ought to do a bit of black magic on her.'

'Where are you going to go?'

The young woman tossed her hair back and shrugged. 'Dunno. Move in with some bloke, probably. There's always a load of sugar-daddies around.'

Maybe it was the residual sense of shame and betrayal, but Annika had made up her mind before she had even formulated the thought. She hunted around at the bottom of her bag.

'Here,' she said, holding out the keys to her flat. 'Thirty-two Hantverkargatan; the top floor of the building in the courtyard. Have you got any money? Go and get the keys copied, Sven's got my spare set.'

'What?' Patricia said.

Annika looked seriously at her.

'It's quite likely that I'm going to get chucked off the paper,' she said. 'I don't know what I'll do then. Have you got your own mattress?'

Patricia nodded.

'I've got a spare bedroom, the housemaid's room just off the kitchen. Put it in there. What about the rest of the furniture in the flat?'

'The bed belongs to Joachim, and Josie bought the table from the free ads.'

'Are you working tonight?'

The young woman nodded again.

'Do you work every day?'

'Almost,' she said quietly.

'Okay, well that's your business. Just don't make a mess, or I'll get annoyed.'

Patricia was looking at her, wide-eyed.

'Why would you trust me? You hardly know me.'

Annika smiled wryly. 'There's nothing worth stealing,' she said.

At that moment Pettersson appeared along Gjörwells-

270

gatan. Annika could tell it was him because the car stalled at the entrance.

'Take the number sixty-two from Rålambsvägen – it goes down Hantverkargatan.'

Patricia smiled with relief. 'I know.'

Annika got up and started to walk towards the photographer's car.

'We're going to get a storm tonight,' Pettersson said through the window.

Patricia waved and glided away. Annika forced herself to smile at Pettersson. So he thought he was some sort of miracle weatherman now, did he?

'Let's not leave the car right next to the park,' she said, settling into the passenger seat.

'Why not?' the photographer asked.

'I'm not sure they're going to be very happy to see us there,' Annika said.

They sat in silence the whole way to the cemetery. The car only stalled a couple of times, and they parked in the Vivo garage on Fleminggatan.

Annika walked slowly up Kronobergsgatan towards the park. They were there in good time: the coaches would only just have left Täby. She sat down in a doorway overlooking the cemetery, while the photographer walked up and down on the other side of the road.

When winter comes I'll look back fondly on these summer days, she thought. When the wind's blowing a storm and the snow is falling, and I have to scrape the windscreen every morning, I'll wish I was back here again. And when I drive into Katrineholm to cover yet another council meeting, and talk to angry old women about the closure of a post office in some godforsaken little village, I'll remember all this. Here and now. Chaos and murder. Heat and blood.

She looked up at the sky. It was bluer than blue. As it faded behind the park it slipped into the colour of steel, sharp and cool.

Maybe Pettersson's right, she thought. Maybe there will be a storm.

38

The first coach pulled into Kronobergsgatan at twenty past two. Annika stayed where she was, watching as the photographer pulled out a long lens and started taking pictures of the youngsters as they got off the coach. The other two buses appeared a couple of minutes later. Annika stood up and brushed off her skirt. She tried to swallow: her mouth was dry. Damn, she'd forgotten to bring anything to drink yet again. She slowly walked over to the crowd, looking out for Martin Larsson-Berg, Lisbeth or Charlotta. She couldn't see any of them.

The youngsters were noisy and were acting up. Several of them were screaming and crying loudly, and some seemed quite aggressive. She stopped on Sankt Göransgatan. This didn't feel right. Even from a distance she could see that some of them looked very tired. Their faces were grey with emotional exhaustion and lack of sleep. She crossed the street towards Pettersson.

'You know what,' she said, 'I think we should give this a miss.'

The photographer lowered his camera and looked at her in surprise.

'What the hell would we do that for?'

Annika nodded towards the coaches. 'Look at them. They're completely hysterical. God knows if it's healthy to encourage this sort of psychosis like they're doing out in Täby. These kids probably haven't been home or had a decent meal since Wednesday.'

'Yeah, but they did call us.'

Annika nodded. 'Yes, they did. Because they obviously think this is important. But we have to take some of the responsibility, and consider whether it's right, if these kids aren't in a position to work it out for themselves.'

The photographer lost patience with her. 'For fuck's sake!' he said. 'I want a permanent contract! I'm not about to bail out of a job just because you've suddenly developed a conscience.'

The group of youngsters had grown into a sea of people. They spread round the cemetery like water round an island. Annika still wasn't sure.

At that moment she saw the other paper's car pull up and park on Sankt Göransgatan, and Arne Påhlson got out.

That decided it.

'Okay, let's go over, then,' she said to Pettersson.

She walked up to the cemetery, the photographer following behind her as she headed towards the ornate railings. Her mouth was bone-dry, and she gulped, her pulse racing. When she was just a couple of metres from the youngsters, they started screaming and shouting.

'There they are. They're here! Vultures, vultures!'

Annika stopped. Pettersson started taking pictures. The attention of the whole crowd was focused on the two journalists now.

'Is Lisbeth here?' Annika asked, but she couldn't make herself heard.

'Fuck off, scum!' shouted a boy who couldn't have been more than thirteen or fourteen.

He walked aggressively towards Annika, and she backed away instinctively. The boy's face was swollen with crying and exhaustion, and his whole body was trembling with adrenalin and rage. Annika stared at him, lost for words.

'We don't want to disturb you at all,' she said. 'We're not trying to intrude—'

A heavily built girl stepped up and shoved Annika on the shoulder. 'Fucking hyenas!' she shrieked in a spray of saliva.

Annika stumbled back, unable to comprehend what was happening. She tried to disarm the girl's fury by being calm and sensible.

'Please,' she said, 'can't we talk to each other like—'

'Hyena!' the girl screamed. 'Scum! Scum!'

The circle of young people tightened around Annika, and she suddenly felt scared. Someone jabbed her in the back, and she lurched forward into the heavily built girl.

'What the fuck are you doing, you cunt?' the girl screamed. 'You having a go at me?'

Annika tried to see where Pettersson was. Where the hell had he gone?

'Pettersson?' she shouted. 'Pettersson, where the fuck are you?'

She heard his voice from over towards the entrance to the car park.

'Bengtzon,' he shouted, panic-stricken. 'They're trying to rip my clothes off!'

Suddenly one voice, threatening and hysterical, could be heard above all the others, cutting through the noise.

'Where are they? Where are they?'

The girl who had grabbed hold of Annika's bag let go of it at once and turned towards the source of the voice.

Annika saw a copy of the *Evening Post* heading towards her, held up above the sea of heads.

The crowd parted, and she saw several more youngsters pulling out copies of the paper.

As the path opened up she caught sight of Charlotta, Josefin's classmate, heading towards her. Annika took another step back at the sight of her.

The girl was on the brink of total collapse. Her eyes were red, her pupils enlarged and black, she had saliva round her mouth, and her movements were jerky and uncoordinated. Her hair was dirty and unkempt, and she was panting for breath.

'You . . . vulture!' she screamed as she rushed towards Annika. 'You bitch!'

Charlotta whacked the paper against the side of Annika's head as hard as she could. Annika put her hands up to her head instinctively as the blows rained down. Other youngsters were aiming at her arms and back, and the screams around her had risen to a collective howl.

Annika felt all reasoned thought vanish. She turned and, shoving one teenager aside, ran for her life. Away, oh God, get me away from here! She heard her steps pounding the street. The greenery on her right rushed past, the ground swayed, the buildings bounced and jerked irregularly. She had a sense that Pettersson was somewhere behind her, followed in turn by the crowd.

The entrance to the car park was pitch black after the sunlight of the park, and she stumbled in the darkness.

'Pettersson?' she shouted. 'Are you there?'

She had reached the car, and as her eyes got used to the darkness she saw the photographer running down the ramp. He had his cameras in one hand, his photographer's tunic hanging from one shoulder. His hair was a complete mess.

'They tried to pull my clothes off,' he said, his voice shaking. 'They were tearing my hair! It was stupid to march up to them like that.'

'Just shut the fuck up!' Annika screamed. 'Get in the damn car and let's get out of here!'

He got the driver's door open, climbed in and unlocked the passenger door. Annika leaped into the car, it must have been a hundred degrees in there. She wound the window down. Astonishingly, the car started first time, and Pettersson roared up the ramp on screeching tyres. Up at street-level again, the light blinded them and Annika shut her eyes for a couple of seconds.

'There they are!'

The shout came through the open window and she turned to see the mob racing towards them like a wall.

'Drive, for fuck's sake!' she yelled, winding the window up.

'It's one way!' the photographer shouted back. 'I've got to go up past the cemetery.'

'No way!' Annika screamed. 'Just drive!'

Pettersson had just pulled out into Kronobergsgatan when the car stalled. Annika locked the door and put her hands over her eyes. Pettersson twisted the key over and over again. The starter motor clicked, but nothing happened. The mob surrounded them, and someone tried to climb on top of the car. The teenagers were banging on the car with their fists, and their screams changed character, becoming a rhythmic chant:

'Burn them! Burn them!'

Annika saw a copy of the *Evening Post* coming towards her, and her article about reactions in Täby was pressed against the window. The picture of the girls with their poems lefts smears of ink on the glass.

'Burn them! Burn them!'

The crumpled paper was placed on the bonnet and

someone set light to it. Annika was screaming at the top of her voice, scared out of her wits.

'Get the fucking car started! Drive, drive!'

More newspapers started to burn, and pictures of the girls and their poems caught fire all around them. The car rocked, and it felt like they were trying to turn it over. The sound of beating fists grew ever louder. Pettersson yelled and the car suddenly burst into life. It jerked forward: the photographer pushed the clutch down and revved the engine. He jammed his hand on the horn and the car slowly crept through the crowd, and the person on the roof jumped off. Annika put her head down, shut her eyes and blocked her ears with her hands. She didn't look up again until the car turned into Fleminggatan.

Pettersson was trying not to cry. He was shaking and could hardly drive. They were heading into the city centre, and pulled in at a petrol station near the Trygg Hansa building.

'We shouldn't have gone up to them,' he sobbed.

'Stop crying,' Annika said. 'What's done is done.'

Her hands were shaking, and she felt shaken and paralysed. The photographer was the same age as her, but she felt that it was somehow her responsibility to sort things out.

'Hey, come on,' she said in a friendlier tone of voice. 'We're okay, aren't we?'

She hunted around in her bag and found an unopened pack of tissues.

'Blow your nose,' she said, 'then I'll treat you to a cup of coffee.'

Pettersson did as he was told, grateful that Annika had taken charge. They went into the petrol station shop, which actually had both coffee and some little marzipan and chocolate cakes.

'God, that was horrible,' Pettersson said quietly, taking a bite of marzipan. 'That's the worst thing I've ever done.'

Annika smiled wryly. 'You've been pretty lucky, then,' she said.

They drank their coffee and ate their cakes in silence.

'You ought to get that car fixed, you know,' Annika said.

He groaned. 'Yeah, tell me about it!'

They got some more coffee.

'So what do we do with this?' he wondered.

'Nothing,' Annika said. 'And I hope no one else does anything with it either.'

'Like who?' Pettersson asked in surprise.

'You don't want to know,' Annika said.

They drove back to the paper, taking the long way round via Gamla Stan and Södermalm. There was no way they were going to drive past Kronoberg Park again.

39

It was almost half past four by the time they got back to the newsroom.

'So how did you get on?' the head of news, Ingvar Johansson, asked.

'Fucking awful,' Annika said. 'They attacked us and tried to set fire to the car with burning newspapers.'

Ingvar Johansson blinked sceptically. 'Yeah, right!'

'God's own truth,' Annika said. 'It was bloody nasty.'

She suddenly felt she had to sit down, and sank onto the newsdesk.

'So you didn't get to talk to any of them? No pictures?' the head of news asked in a disappointed voice.

Annika looked at him, feeling that there was a thick layer of bullet-proof glass between them.

'That's right,' she said. 'It wasn't a story, anyway. They were just letting off steam, winding themselves into a state of mass psychosis. We were lucky, they came very close to overturning the car and setting fire to it.'

Ingvar Johansson was looking at her with wide eyes, then turned away and picked up the phone.

Annika got up and walked over to Berit's desk. She was suddenly aware that her legs were shaking, and she was on the brink of bursting into tears.

God, I'm turning into a right cry-baby, she thought.

She sat down and read news agency stories and some peculiar industry journals until the theme music of *Studio Six* came on the radio at three minutes past six.

Afterwards she would look back on that hour as a surreal nightmare. It would continue to haunt her dreams for the next ten years.

She would remember the feeling when the electric guitar started up, how open-minded and unprepared she was, how naïvely she stood there, waiting to be shot down.

'The evening papers have today plumbed new depths in their relentless search for sensation,' the presenter thundered. 'They expose grieving young people in their pages, they spread false rumours about victims' relatives, and they do the bidding of the police in order to deceive the public. Debate and analysis of this in today's edition of *Studio Six*.'

Annika heard the words without them actually sinking in. She had a vague idea, but simply didn't want it to be true.

The electric guitar faded away and the presenter's voice resumed: 'It's Tuesday, August the second. Welcome to Studio Six in Radio House in Stockholm,' he intoned. 'Today we're looking at the *Evening Post*'s coverage of the murder of stripper Josefin Liljeberg. With us in the studio we have two people who knew Josefin well: we have her best friend, Charlotta, and her former headmaster, Martin Larsson-Berg. And we've also spoken to her boyfriend, Joachim . . .'

Giddiness started to rock all her senses. A suspicion of what was to come began to grow in her mind. She stretched out a hand to turn off the radio, but stopped herself.

Better to hear what they say now than wonder later what they might have said, she thought.

She would regret that decision many times. What she heard fastened like a mantra in her memory.

'If we start with you, Charlotta . . . Can you tell us how the *Evening Post* has treated you?'

Charlotta started howling in the radio studio. The presenter evidently thought it sounded rather effective, because he let it go on for thirty seconds before wondering if she could stop. Which she did, instantly.

'Well,' Charlotta said with a sniff, 'I got a call at home from this reporter, Annika Bengtzon. She wanted to poke about in my misery.'

'In what way?' the presenter said, sounding incredibly sensitive and sympathetic.

'My best friend had just died, and she called in the middle of the night and asked, "How do you feel?"'

'That's awful!' the presenter exclaimed.

Charlotta sniffed. 'Yes, it was one of the worst things that's ever happened to me. How can you go on after something like that?'

'And was it the same for you, Martin Berg-Larsson?'

'Larsson-Berg,' the headmaster said. 'Yes, by and large. I wasn't a close friend of the girl, of course, for obvious reasons, but I'm very close to the family. Her brother was a very talented pupil; he graduated this spring and is going to college in the United States this autumn. We're immensely proud at Tibble High School when our students go on to higher education at international institutions.'

'So how did it feel to get these terrible questions in the middle of the night?'

'Well, naturally, I was shocked. To start with I thought something had happened to my wife, she likes sailing, you see . . .'

'How did you react?'

'It's all a bit hazy . . .'

'Was it the same reporter who bothered Charlotta, this summer temp, Annika Bengtzon?'

'Yes, it was her.'

The presenter rustled a newspaper.

'Let's see what Annika Bengtzon wrote. Take this, for instance.'

The man began to read excerpts from Annika's articles in a gently mocking tone, about Josefin, her dreams and hopes for the future, Charlotta's quotes, and then the orgy of grief in Täby.

'What do you say to that?' he concluded, in a deathly dark tone of voice.

'It's just awful that they wouldn't leave us alone with our grief,' Charlotta squeaked. 'Why don't the mass media ever respect people's privacy when they're in the middle of a crisis? And today, at our demonstration against pointless violence, she forced herself on us again!'

Martin Larsson-Berg cleared his throat. 'Well,' he said, 'you have to understand the mass media as well. We had a very fine set-up in place to deal with the crisis out in Täby, and of course we wanted to set an example for—'

The presenter interrupted him. 'But the *Evening Post* and Annika Bengtzon didn't stop there. The paper has been actively attempting to whitewash the suspected government minister, Christer Lundgren. In her capacity as the parrot of the Social Democratic Party, Annika Bengtzon has tried to pin the blame for Josefin's murder on the person who was closer to her than anyone, her boyfriend Joachim. Our reporter went to meet him.'

They played a recording. Annika was glued to her seat. She was cold with sweat all over, and she had a sense of complete and utter unreality. The newsroom was full of people, but no one was paying any attention to her. She didn't exist. She was already dead.

'I loved Josefin; she was the most important thing in my life,' a male voice said. He sounded young and vulnerable.

'How did it feel when the *Evening Post* identified you as Josefin's killer?' the reporter asked cautiously.

The man sighed. 'Well, I can't really describe it. What can I say? Reading that you're supposed to have . . . No, you just can't take it in.' And he actually sniffed, as if on cue.

'Have you thought about suing the paper?'

Another sigh. 'No, it wouldn't be worth it, everyone knows that. Corporations like that pay whatever it takes to crush ordinary people. I'd never get justice against that rag. Besides, it would stir up too many memories.'

The presenter came back on, and now he had another reporter with him in the studio who was evidently there as some sort of expert commentator.

'Well, this is definitely a problem, isn't it?' the presenter said.

'Yes, that's absolutely right,' the commentator said keenly. 'A young man is identified as a murderer by a summer temp who has decided to play at being an investigative reporter, and then the lie is established as a truth. It's very difficult to get any justice in cases like this. It costs a lot of money to bring a case against a newspaper, but we should point out to anyone who feels that they have been exploited or libelled by the media that they can get legal aid to help convict journalists who overstep the mark and spread lies.'

'Could this be something for Joachim to look into?'

'Yes, it might very well be. We can only hope that

he wants to pursue this all the way through the courts. It would be very interesting to see this become a test case.'

The presenter rustled his papers.

'But why would a young summer temp do something like this?'

'Well, part of the explanation is that she is prepared to do whatever it takes to keep her position at one of the evening papers. The evening press survives on sales of loose copies, and the juicier the headlines and flysheets, the more papers they sell and the more money they earn. Journalists who stoop to this level usually earn a very good salary from their sordid business, I'm afraid.'

'So the juicier the headline, the bigger the journalist's salary?'

'Yes, that's not an unfair summary of the situation.'

'But do you really think it's that simple, that she was trying to advertise her services to the highest bidder?'

'No, I'm afraid there could well be more dubious motivations in this case.'

'Such as?'

The commentator cleared his throat. 'It's like this,' he said. 'There are ten thousand lobbyists in Stockholm. These lobbyists are only after one thing: to get the media and those in positions of power to do what their employers want. Influencing the media is known as "planting" stories. These people trick or bribe a journalist by planting news stories, and then the journalist runs off and does the lobbyists' work for them.'

'Do you think that's what happened in this case?'

'Yes, I'm quite convinced that's exactly what happened here,' the commentator said solemnly. 'It's quite obvious to anyone with any sort of knowledge of the industry that Annika Bengtzon's articles about Christer Lundgren are the result of planted information.'

'How can you be so sure?' the presenter said, sounding impressed.

'I'd like to play you a piece of evidence, a sequence that I recorded outside Rosenbad this morning,' the commentator said triumphantly.

The Prime Minister's voice filled the airwaves.

'Of course I have every sympathy for what Christer is going through right now. This sort of media witch-hunt is always a severe trial. But I can assure you that for the government, and for the party, these exaggerated allegations have absolutely no significance at all. You must have seen today's *Evening Post*, which explains why Christer has been questioned. He just happens to have a flat close to Kronoberg Park. Even government ministers need somewhere to sleep!'

Then back to the studio again.

'Yes, we heard that with our own ears,' the commentator said. 'The Prime Minister made a direct reference to the newspaper and clearly hoped that the rest of the media would follow its lead.'

'How much responsibility does the government have here?'

'Well, of course they can be criticized for exploiting such a young and inexperienced journalist. Summer temps are unfortunately rather easier to manipulate than more practised hands.'

The presenter's voice once more: 'Naturally, we asked the editor-in-chief of the *Evening Post* to participate in this discussion, but were told that he wasn't available . . .'

Annika got up to go to the toilet, the floor swaying beneath her. The feeling only intensified as she got out into the corridor, and she had to lean against the wall.

I'm falling apart, she thought. This isn't working. I'm not going to make it. I'm going to be sick on the floor.

She threw up in the hand-basin of the handicapped toilet, blocking the plughole when she tried to rinse it away. She looked in the mirror and was surprised to see that she was still intact. She looked the same as usual, she was still breathing, her heart was still beating.

I'll never be able to show my face out there again, she thought. I'm finished now, for ever. I'll never get another job. They won't even want me at the *Katrineholm Courier* now, I'll get the sack.

She started to cry.

Hell, where am I going to live? If I can't pay the rent, where am I going to go?

She sank onto the floor, crying into her skirt.

Lyckebo, she thought suddenly, and stopped crying. I'll go to Grandma's. No one will find me there. Grandma moves into her flat in Hälleforsnäs in October each year, but I could stay on out there.

She blew her nose on some toilet paper and dried her tears.

Yes, that's what she would do. Grandma had said she'd always be there for Annika, she wouldn't let her down. She was in the union, she'd get unemployment benefit for at least a year, then she'd just have to see. She could move abroad, a lot of people did that. Pick oranges in Israel or grapes in France. Or why not New Zealand?

She stood up. There were loads of ways out of this.

'Don't limit your options,' she said out loud to herself.

She'd made up her mind. She would never set foot in a newsroom again, and especially not this one. She'd take her bag and her box of notes and give up journalism for ever. She unlocked the toilet door with a fresh sense of determination.

The floor still wasn't quite steady. She stayed close to the wall to make sure she didn't fall.

Back at Berit's desk she quickly gathered her things together in her bag.

'Ah, there you are! Would you mind coming into my office for a few minutes?'

It was the voice of the new head editor, Anders Schyman, and she turned round in surprise.

'Who, me?' she said.

'Yes, you. I'm in the aquarium with the awful curtains. Come when you've got a minute.'

'I've got time now,' she said.

She felt the furtive glances of the rest of the newsroom as she walked into the boss's office.

Oh well, she thought. At least things can't get any worse.

40

It wasn't a nice room. The shabby curtains really were awful, and the air felt stale and enclosed.

'Where's that smell coming from? Haven't you emptied the ashtray?'

'I don't smoke. It's the sofa. Don't sit on it – it gets into your clothes.'

She stayed standing in the middle of the floor, while he sat on the edge of the desk.

'I've called *Studio Six*,' he said. 'I've never heard such a personal attack before, and they didn't give us the right of reply. I've already faxed a complaint to the Broadcasting Commission. The editor-in-chief may well have been unavailable, but I've been here all day. Did they try to contact you?'

She didn't answer, just shook her head.

'I know that so-called expert commentator. He worked for a while on my magazine programme until I got rid of him.

'He's impossible to work with. He plotted and gossiped behind other people's backs until the programme was on the brink of collapse. As luck would have it, he wasn't employed directly on the programme, but used to invoice us from his own company. Once I'd made up my mind, he was gone that same day.'

Annika was staring at the floor.

'And as for planted stories,' Anders Schyman said, pulling a fax out of the mess that had already accumulated on his desk. 'We've received an anonymous tip-off that one of the right-wing party leaders has also been questioned about Josefin's murder.'

He held the fax out to Annika, and she took it, still numb to the world.

'Where's it from?' she said.

'My question exactly,' the head editor said. 'You see the sender's number up in the top corner? It's the number of the Social Democrats' advertising agency.'

'God, that's so blatant,' Annika said.

'Yes, isn't it?'

Silence. Annika took a deep breath.

'I haven't been the target of any planted stories,' she said.

Anders Schyman looked at her intently, waiting for her to go on.

'I haven't spoken to anyone about our coverage of this story, apart from Berit and Anne Snapphane.'

'Not the news editors?'

Annika shook her head.

'Not much, anyway,' she said quietly.

'So you've been looking after our coverage entirely on your own?'

He sounded rather sceptical, and she squirmed.

'Well, almost,' she said, feeling tears welling up. 'There's no one else to share the blame.'

'No, no,' Anders Schyman said quickly. 'That's not what I meant. I think our coverage has been fine, really pretty good. The only thing we missed was the fact that she worked at a sex club. And you knew about that anyway, didn't you?'

She nodded.

'We should have written about that earlier. But doing what our rivals and *Studio Six* have done – making out that the girl was a prostitute – is much worse. By the way, how did you find out about the minister's over-night flat?'

Annika sighed. 'I was having coffee with one of his neighbours.'

'Brilliant!' Anders Schyman said. 'And what really happened with those teenagers out in Täby?'

Annika's eyes flashed.

'That bit's completely fucking unbelievable! They asked us to go, first out to Täby, and then to the demonstration in the park today.'

'Yes, I heard that got a bit out of hand.'

Annika dropped her bag on the floor and held out her hands.

'They're grieving, so anything they say and do can't be questioned. They're having a hard time, which means that you can't really approach them at all. Anything that's the slightest bit unpleasant or controversial in this bloody country can never even be named. We think death and violence and suffering will just disappear if we bury it and never talk about it again. But that's wrong! That's so wrong! It only makes things worse. Those kids out there today were crazy! They were trying to set fire to us!'

'Okay, you're exaggerating a bit now,' Anders Schyman said gently.

'Like hell I am!' Annika exclaimed. 'Those pathetic little social workers have got a monopoly on suffering and grief and sympathy. Crisis team, my arse! All they've done is wind those kids up beyond any semblance of sanity. Most of them had never even spoken to Josefin, I'd put money on that! What the hell are they doing, having a week-long orgy of grief? Schyman, it was like they were in some kind of trance, they had no idea what they were doing. They identified us as evil, as targets for revenge, as sacrifices. So don't try to tell me I'm exaggerating!'

Her face was red with fury and anger, and she was breathing hard and fast. The head editor was watching her with interest.

'Do you know, I think you're probably right,' he said.

'Of course I bloody am!' she said.

He smiled. 'It's a good thing you don't swear this much in your writing,' he said.

'What a bloody stupid thing to say,' she said. 'Of course I fucking don't.'

Anders Schyman started to laugh. Annika walked over to him.

'This isn't funny,' she said. 'This is serious. Those kids at the cemetery were a lynch-mob. I don't know if they'd really have hurt us, but they certainly threatened to. We really ought to report them to the police. Pettersson's car has scorch marks in the paint, not that it makes much difference to a heap of junk like that, but anyway . . . We ought to make some sort of statement that people can't behave however they want to, even if they think they can use grief as an alibi.'

'There are actually a lot of crisis groups that do fantastic work,' the head editor said seriously. 'Tarring them all with the same brush is just as bad as suggesting that the evening papers only ever want to wallow in other people's pain.'

Annika didn't answer, and he looked at her for a while in silence.

'You've been working a lot lately, haven't you?' he said.

She went on the defensive at once.

'I'm not over-reacting because I've been working too much,' she said tersely.

The head editor stood up.

'I wasn't thinking of that,' he said. 'Is this your regular shift?'

She looked down.

'No, I start again on Saturday.'

'Take the weekend off,' he said. 'Go away somewhere and relax, you need to after going through something like this.'

She turned and left the room without another word. On the way out of the newsroom she heard Johansson yell: 'Fuck, we've got a brilliant paper here! The speaker of parliament confesses: I was in charge of IB; the Prime Minister comments on the murder suspect; and the Ninja Barbies have been arrested, and we've got exclusive pictures!'

She hurried into the lift.

It wasn't until she was standing in the courtyard that she realized that she didn't have any keys. And the door could only be opened with a key, there was no coded lock. She almost started to cry again.

'Fuck!' she said, yanking at the door. To her surprise it glided open. A little piece of light-green cardboard floated down to the ground. Annika bent down and picked it up. She recognized the pattern: it came from a box of Clinique skin cream.

Patricia, Annika thought. She worked out that I wouldn't be able to get in, so she wedged this in the lock.

She went up the stairs, they seemed endless. There was an envelope taped to the outside of her door, and the keys inside rattled as she pulled it off.

Thanks so much for everything. Here are your keys. I got some copies cut. I'm off to the club, back early tomorrow morning. PS. I've done some shopping, hope you don't mind.

Annika unlocked the door. A fresh smell of detergent hit her, and the curtains were waving dramatically in the draught. She pulled the door shut behind her and all the curtains fell still. She walked slowly through the rooms, looking round.

Patricia had cleaned the whole flat apart from Annika's bedroom. That was just as messy as usual. The fridge was full of different cheeses, olives, hummus, strawberries, and on the worktop there were plums, grapes and avocados.

I'll never be able to eat all this before it goes off, Annika thought. Then it hit her: There are two of us here now.

She nudged open the door to the little maid's room. Patricia's mattress lay neatly in one corner, made up with flowery linen. Beside it was a sports bag full of clothes. On one wall hung Josefin's pink dress.

I want to stay, she thought. I don't want to go back to Hälleforsnäs. I don't want to spend the rest of my life in Lyckebo.

That night she dreamed of the three men from the *Studio Six* radio programme for the first time – the presenter, the reporter and the commentator. They were standing in silence, dark and faceless beside her bed. She could feel their cold, watchful antagonism like cramp in her stomach.

'How can you say it was my fault?' she shouted.

The men came closer.

'I've really thought about this! Maybe I got things wrong, but at least I tried!'

The men tried to shoot her. The noise of their guns thundered through her head.

'I'm not Josefin! No!'

They bent over her in unison, and as their ice-cold breath reached her consciousness she woke up to the sound of her own screams.

It was pitch black in the room. It was raining torrentially outside. The thunder and lightning came at precisely the same time. The bedroom window was banging in the wind, and the room felt cool.

She staggered up to close the window, the wind making it hard to fasten. In the silence after the rain she felt a trickle down her leg. She had got her period. The box of tampons was empty, but she had a few sanitary towels in her bag.

As the storm passed overhead she lay and cried, curled up into a little ball, for a very long time.

Eighteen years, six months and fourteen days

He feels so insulted, and whatever I say has little effect. I know he's right, of course. No one can ever love me like he does. There's nothing he wouldn't do for me, but somehow I still care more for superficial things than for him.

My despair is growing, my inadequacy is blossoming: poisonous, ice-cold, blue. It's destructive, never being good enough. I want to watch television when he wants to make love, and he dislocates my shoulder. Emptiness that takes over, black and damp, shapeless, impenetrable. He says I'm letting him down, and I can find no way out.

We have to work together, find our way back to our little heaven. Love is eternal, fundamental. I've never doubted that. But who says it's ever simple? If perfection was granted to everyone, why would anyone want to fight for it?

I can't give up now.

We are the most important thing
that has happened
to each other.

Friday 3 August

41

Anders Schyman got completely soaked over the short distance to his car. The rain was pouring down with furious force, trying to make up for all those boiling-hot days in one single, torrential downpour. The head editor swore and tried to wriggle out of his jacket as he sat wedged behind the steering wheel. The back and shoulders of his shirt were wet through as well.

'Oh, it'll soon dry,' he said to himself.

His efforts to get his jacket off had made the windows steam up, so he set the heater on full.

His wife was waving from the kitchen window, and he wiped the side window and blew her a kiss, then sighed and headed towards the city. He could hardly see the road, even though the windscreen wipers were going at top speed. And he kept having to wipe the condensation from the windows to be able to see anything at all.

Traffic was moving relatively smoothly on the main road from Saltsjöbaden, but as soon as he hit the suburb of Nacka everything ground to a halt. An accident on the Värmdö motorway was causing mile-long tailbacks of motionless traffic. He groaned out loud. Traffic fumes were rising like fog through the rain. In the end he switched off the engine and set the air-conditioning to recycle the air inside the car.

He was having trouble getting to grips with the *Evening Post*. He'd been reading it scrupulously for four months now, since he first received the offer to take over day-to-day responsibility for its content. A lot of it was pretty obvious, of course, such as the way the paper was always balancing on the edge of what was morally and ethically defensible. That's what a tabloid was supposed to do. Sometimes they crossed the line, but not very often, when it came down to it. He had studied reports and judgements from the Press Complaints Commission and the press ombudsman, and naturally the evening papers featured heavily in the statistics. They had far more complaints made against them than the other papers, which was entirely understandable. Their purpose was to be provocative and encourage debate. Even so, only a handful of rulings went against them each year. He was surprised to discover that the list of libellous articles was usually topped by the local press, small papers around the country that often seemed to have trouble working out where the boundaries were.

He had come to the conclusion that the *Evening Post* was a responsible media organization, and that its articles, flysheets and headlines were well judged, and were based on continuity, openness and discussion.

But he had already discovered that reality was light-years away from this idealized vision.

The *Evening Post* often didn't have a fucking clue what it was doing. Sending that young temp out to deal with bodies and lynch-mobs, for instance, and expecting her to somehow be able to make clear and responsible decisions. He had spoken to the head of news and the night-editor the previous evening, and neither of them had actually discussed the paper's coverage of the murder of Josefin Liljeberg with her. He regarded this as a prime example of editorial incompetence and irresponsibility.

Then there was the peculiar story of the feminist terrorist group. No one in a position of any authority appeared to know where the story had come from. A temp waltzed into the newsroom with sensational pictures, and everyone was ecstatic and published them without a moment's thought.

It couldn't go on like this. If you're going to balance successfully on the boundary of what was morally and ethically defensible, you had to know where that boundary lay. Disaster was only a short step away, and he had already felt its sour breath. That radio programme the previous evening, *Studio Six*, was only the first sign. The *Evening Post* was on the way to becoming a real target. If any blood was actually shed, the vultures would soon gather. Others in the media would start to tear the paper to shreds. And then it wouldn't matter what the paper published, because it would all be seen as inaccurate and unreliable. If they didn't get their act together soon, they were heading for disaster – in terms of sales, journalism and finances.

He sighed. The traffic started to move again in the lane next to him. He started the car, letting it run in neutral with the handbrake on.

There was no doubt that the paper employed a large number of very knowledgeable and capable people. The problems lay with the management team: there was no real sense of context, no notion of who was responsible for what. Every journalist on the paper had to know exactly what their job was, and what was expected of them. Their targets had to be made clearer.

This had made him realize yet another of his responsibilities in the newsroom. He would have to be the one who steered them all away from disaster. He would have to shine a spotlight on what the dangers were, through discussions, seminars, daily meetings and new routines.

The cars to his left were sweeping past faster and faster, but he still wasn't moving. He swore and tried to look behind him, but couldn't see a thing. In the end he put his indicator on and pulled out regardless. The driver he forced to brake blew his horn.

'Oh, get a life,' he muttered at the rear-view mirror.

And the traffic stopped again. The lane next to him, the one he had been stuck in, began to move and was soon going nicely.

He leaned his head on the wheel and let out a loud groan.

Annika peered carefully inside the maid's room. Patricia was asleep. She closed the door quietly, put some coffee on without making a noise, and went out for the morning paper. She tossed it onto the table, and by coincidence it fell open at the review of yesterday's radio programmes. Annika's eyes were drawn to the article, and she read the reviewer's verdict with a growing sense of nausea.

> *The liveliest and most engaging news programme these days is without doubt* Studio Six *on P3. Yesterday it dealt with the endless dumbing down of the evening papers, and their relentless exploitation of people in grief. Sadly, this debate has never been more called for . . .*

Annika grabbed the paper and screwed it into a ball, then rammed it into the bin. Then she went into the living room and phoned to cancel her subscription.

She tried to eat half an avocado, but the green flesh seemed to swell in her mouth, making her feel sick. She tried a few strawberries, but they had the same effect. Coffee and orange juice went down okay, but she threw out the rest of the avocado and a few more strawberries so Patricia would think she'd eaten something. Then she wrote a note saying that she was going down to Hälleforsnäs for the weekend. She wondered to herself whether she would ever be coming back. If not, Patricia could take over the flat. After all, she'd need it.

When she opened the door to the courtyard the rain hit her like a wall. She stood there for a moment staring out at it. She could hardly see the building facing the street behind the curtain of rain.

Perfect, she thought. There won't be anyone about. No one will see me. Mum won't have to feel ashamed of me.

She walked out into the downpour and was soaked before she'd even got to the bins. She threw away the half-full bag containing the paper, strawberries and avocado, then walked slowly towards the underground.

You reach a point where you just can't get any wetter, she thought. She remembered that from some film she'd seen.

At the Central Station she discovered she was going to have to wait almost two hours for the next train to Flen. She sat down on one of the benches in the large, well-lit hall. The sound of passengers, trains, the electronic voices from the loudspeakers, everything merged into a cacophony of urban chaos.

Annika closed her eyes and let the sounds flow through her brain. They made her want to cry. After a while she felt cold, and went into the toilet, where she stood next to the hand-dryer until the other women started to get annoyed.

At least they've got no idea who I am, she thought. They don't know that I'm the failure from the radio. Thank goodness I never got that picture byline.

The train was a small, local one that was soon packed. She ended up opposite a fat bloke who was wet with rain and sweat. He took out a copy of that day's *Evening Post* and Annika tried not to look at it.

Berit had managed to get the speaker of parliament to admit his involvement in the IB affair.

I did my military service with Elmér, he said on the front page.

Oh well, she thought. None of my business any more.

At Flen she had to wait another hour for the bus to Hälleforsnäs. The rain was still bucketing down, and a big pool of water had gathered on the road in front of the bus-stop. She sat in the station waiting room facing the wall, trying to avoid any form of contact with other people.

It was afternoon by the time the bus pulled up at the bottom of her road. The deserted supermarket car park was covered in puddles. No one saw her get off the bus. She felt tired and shaky as she headed to her flat on legs that ached from her run the day before.

Her flat was gloomy and smelled of dust. Without turning on any lights she pulled off all her wet clothes and crept into bed. She was asleep in minutes.

'It's only a matter of time,' the Prime Minister said.

The press officer protested. 'We can't be sure of that. No one ever knows when they'll decide to chase another story instead.'

The press officer knew what he was talking about. He had been one of Sweden's toughest and most experienced political reporters. Nowadays his role was to direct media coverage to the advantage of the Social Democrats. Together with a couple of election strategists from the US, he was one of the most influential figures in the governing party's election campaign. The Prime Minister knew he voted for the opposition.

'I have to confess, I'm worried,' the Prime Minister said. 'I don't think we should just leave this to chance.'

The thickset man stood up and walked restlessly over to the window. The rain hung like a wet curtain outside, blocking the view over Riddarfjärden. The press officer intruded on his thoughts.

'You shouldn't stand there worrying in full view of the outside world,' he said. 'Pictures like that make excellent illustrations of a government in crisis.'

The Prime Minister backed anxiously away from the window. His bad mood was getting worse and he turned sharply to face the Minister for Foreign Trade.

'How the hell could you be so bloody stupid?' he shouted.

Christer Lundgren didn't react, just carried on staring at the leaden sky from his seat in the corner. The Prime Minister walked towards him.

'We can't just march in and start changing the rules for publicly funded organizations. You knew that perfectly well, for Christ's sake!'

The minister looked up at his boss.

'No, that's just it. Not the rules for the police, nor for anyone else.'

The Prime Minister's eyes narrowed behind his glasses.

'Do you have any idea of the position you've got us into? Have you even the slightest notion of the consequences of what you've done?'

Christer Lundgren jumped to his feet, standing right in front of the Prime Minister.

'Yes, I know exactly what I've done,' he exclaimed. 'I've rescued this fucking party, that's what!'

The press officer interrupted them. 'We can't undo any of this,' he said calmly. 'We have to find a way of making the best of things. Going in and amending the records retrospectively is out of the question. We simply can't do that. But I don't actually think that any journalist would ever manage to find the receipts.'

He walked slowly round the other two men.

'The most important thing is that we cooperate with the police without them finding out too much.'

He put a hand on the Minister for Foreign Trade's shoulder.

'Christer,' he said, 'this is all down to you now.'

The minister shrugged off the hand.

'I'm under suspicion of murder,' he said quietly.

'Yes, it's ironic, isn't it?' the press officer said. 'Death is already squatting on your government desk. That's what this whole business is about, isn't it?'

42

It was already evening when she woke up. Sven was sitting on the edge of the bed looking at her.

'Welcome home,' he said with a smile.

She smiled back. She was thirsty and had a slight headache.

'You make it sound like I've been gone for ages,' she said.

'It feels like it,' he said.

She threw the duvet aside and stood up, feeling dizzy and a bit sick.

'I don't feel very well,' she said.

She stumbled out to the bathroom and took a headache pill, and opened the bathroom window to get some air. The rain had eased a bit, but it hadn't stopped. Sven came and stood in the doorway.

'Do you want to go and get a pizza?' he said.

She swallowed.

'I'm not really hungry,' she said.

'You've got to eat,' he said. 'You've got way too skinny.'

'I've had a lot to do,' she said, and walked past him into the hall. He followed her into the kitchen.

'I heard they gave you a rough time on the radio,' he said.

She poured herself a glass of water from the tap.

'Oh, did you? Don't tell me you've started listening to news programmes?'

'No, Ingela heard it.'

She paused with the glass halfway to her lips.

'What, that sperm-bucket?' she said, astonished. 'Since when did you start socializing with her?'

He got angry.

'That's a really cruel thing to call her. It really upsets her.'

Annika smiled. 'You were the one who came up with it.'

He smirked. 'Well, yes,' he said, laughing.

Annika gulped down the water. He went over to her and hugged her from behind.

'I'm freezing. I've got to put some clothes on,' she said, pulling free.

Sven kissed her.

'Okay. I'll order the pizzas,' he said.

Annika went into the bedroom and opened her wardrobe. The clothes she had left here felt old and tired. She heard Sven calling the local pizzeria and order two Quattros. Even though he knew she didn't like mussels.

'You're staying for a while this time, aren't you?' he called once he'd hung up.

She was still looking through her clothes.

'What makes you think that? My job doesn't finish until the fourteenth of August. I've still got a week and a half to go.'

He leaned against the door frame.

'Yes, but are they really going to want you to stay now that you've been exposed like that?'

Her cheeks started to burn and she hunted through her clothes with renewed vigour.

308

'The evening papers don't really care what they say on a pretentious programme on P3.'

He came up to her and hugged her again.

'I don't care what they say about you,' he whispered. 'You're still the best in my eyes, even if everyone else thinks you're useless.'

She pulled on a pair of jeans that were now too big for her and an old T-shirt.

Sven shook his head unhappily.

'Do you have to look so scruffy?' he said. 'Can't you wear a dress?'

She shut the wardrobe door.

'How long until the pizzas are ready?'

'I'm serious,' he said. 'Put something else on.'

Annika stopped and took several deep breaths.

'Come on,' she pleaded. 'I'm hungry. The pizzas will be getting cold.'

Eighteen years, ten months and six days

I long to get back to when it was all light and easy. When day merged into the shadows of night like a spirit: pure, clean, soft. Time like a vacuum, weightless. Intoxication, the first touch, the wind, the light, the sense of complete fulfilment. I want that moment back more than anything else.

His darkness obscures the horizon. It isn't easy to navigate in the dark. It's a vicious circle. I conjure up the darkness in him, and the darkness veils our love with fog. My steps become hesitant, I lose my footing. His patience is starting to grow thin.

I pay the price.

But we are the most important things
in the world
to each other.

Monday 6 August

43

The pan of water boiled over and she poured it onto the coffee, spilling it and burning herself.

'Shit!' she yelled, as tears sprang to her eyes.

'Did you hurt yourself?'

Patricia was standing in the doorway to the maid's room, in pants and a T-shirt, hair mussed up, still sleepy. Annika felt an instant pang of conscience.

'Oh, sorry, I didn't mean to wake you, I'm really sorry . . .'

'What happened?'

Annika turned away and wiped up the rest of the water.

'My job's looking pretty dodgy, that's all,' she said. 'Do you want some coffee, or are you going back to bed?'

Patricia rubbed her eyes.

'I'm off tonight,' she said. 'Coffee would be good.'

She pulled on a pair of shorts and disappeared out of the front door to go to the toilet. Annika quickly blew her nose and dried her eyes. She took some slices of bread out of the freezer and put them in the toaster, then got out the cheese, marmalade and butter. She heard Patricia come back in and close the front door.

'What on earth happened to you?'

Patricia was staring at Annika's legs. Annika looked down at them.

'I got chased by a lynch-mob on Thursday,' she said. 'They even tried to set fire to the car we were driving off in.'

Patricia stared.

'Bloody hell, sounds like a James Bond film!'

Annika laughed, as the toaster pinged and launched the two slices into the air. They each caught one, and Patricia burst out laughing as well.

They sat and ate breakfast on either side of the kitchen table. Annika missed the morning paper. She stared out of the window, as the rain tapped on the tin window ledge.

'How were things out in the country, then?' Patricia asked.

Annika sighed. 'As you'd expect in weather like this. I stayed with Sven, my boyfriend, then went out to see Grandma. She lives in a cottage that belongs to the Harpsund estate. She's got it as long as she wants, because she was the housekeeper there for thirty-seven years.'

'What's Harpsund?' Patricia asked.

Annika poured coffee.

'An old manor-house between Flen and Hälleforsnäs,' she said. 'An old bloke called Hjalmar Wicander left it to the state when he died in 1952. The condition was that the Prime Minister would use it to relax in, and to entertain guests.'

'Huh?'

'A bit like a cross between a summer cottage and a party venue,' Annika said with a smile. 'Harpsund is really popular with our prime ministers, this current one more than most. He comes from round there and still has family in the area.

'I met him out there one Midsummer's Eve a couple of years ago.'

Patricia's eyes widened.

'Have you been there?'

'I spent a lot of time there with Grandma when I was little.'

They carried on eating in silence.

'Are you going to work today?' Patricia asked.

Annika nodded.

'Your job's really stressful, isn't it?' Patricia said. 'And dangerous, if people keep trying to set fire to you.'

Annika smiled wryly. 'Well, you had an arson attack as well!'

'Yes, but that wasn't personal,' Patricia said.

Annika sighed. 'Stressful or not, I just wish I could keep hold of it.'

'Why do you have to leave?'

'My contract was only for the summer. It ends next week. They only offer a couple of temps a permanent job.'

'So why can't that be you, then? You've written loads, haven't you?'

Annika shook her head.

'They've got a recruitment meeting with the union tomorrow, that's when we find out who's staying. What are you going to do today?'

Patricia had a faraway look in her eye as she stared out of the window.

'I'm going to think about Josefin,' she said. 'I'm going to talk to the spirits and try to find her on the other side. And when I find her, I'm going to ask her who did it.'

44

Anne Snapphane was back at her desk when Annika walked into the newsroom.

'So you're still alive, then,' Annika said.

'Hardly,' her colleague said. 'It's been an awful weekend. The bosses have been going mad. Whatever the head of news has planned during the day gets chucked out by the night-editor. I've written five pieces that have been canned.'

Annika settled into her chair. The dragon in the suit had left a minefield of empty coffee cups, printouts and used paper handkerchiefs behind her.

'I couldn't make up my mind if I should come in today,' Annika said. 'Now I know why.'

Anne Snapphane started laughing. Annika swept everything off the top of the desk into the bin, including five pads of paper, two books and three china mugs with 'Mariana' painted on them.

'Eat shit, you stuck-up bitch.'

Anne Snapphane was laughing so hard she almost fell off her chair.

'It wasn't that funny, was it?' Annika said.

Anne sat up again, dried her eyes and tried to stop herself laughing again.

'No, not really,' she said with a giggle. 'Mind you, I've

got other reasons to be cheerful. Such as the fact that I'm getting out of here.'

Annika stared at her, wide-eyed.

'You've got a job? Where?'

'A production company down in South Hammarby Harbour. I'm going to be a researcher for a daytime women's chat-show on one of the cable channels. I start on the twelfth of September. It might be awful. But what the hell, I'm really looking forward to it!'

'But you might be able to stay on here?'

'Don't know if I'd want to, I'm so knackered. And the television job's a permanent contract.'

'Well, congratulations!' Annika said, going round the desk and giving her friend a hug. 'God, that's really great for you!'

'Right, you couple of dykes, have either of you got time to do some work?'

Spike was back at the newsdesk.

'Go fuck yourself, you sex-obsessed old arsehole,' Anne Snapphane shouted back.

'You're mad,' Annika said quietly.

'Who cares? I'm leaving anyway,' Anne Snapphane said, standing up.

Anne got the job, a story about a kitten that was being looked after by the police in Norrköping. It had spent two weeks in the police station, and now it was going to be put down.

'We need a picture of the fucking cat under arrest,' Anne Snapphane said. 'Imagine the headline: DEATH ROW KITTY.'

Spike glanced at Annika.

'There's nothing for you, you're on standby for the time being.'

Annika gulped. She got it. The freezer door slammed shut on her, leaving her in the cold.

'Okay,' she said. 'I'll be reading the papers.'

She went over to the archive shelves and pulled out copies of the *Evening Post* from Friday onwards. She hadn't read a newspaper or looked at the news all weekend. She was never going to listen to the radio again unless she really had to.

She started off by carefully reading Berit's article. The speaker of parliament was now openly admitting that he exploited his contact with Birger Elmér to avoid doing an extra month of national service in 1966.

It had been an election year, and the speaker had been deputy chairman of the Social Democratic Youth Movement, and that month of national service would have been extremely inconvenient for the party. So Elmér arranged for him to be posted to the Information Bureau instead. This meant he could carry on with his political work as usual, at the same time as fulfilling his duty to the state.

According to the call-up papers Berit had dug out, the speaker had been allocated to the security section of the Ministry of Defence, which could well have meant IB. In 1966 he was thirty-three years old, and he was never called up again after that.

Annika lowered the paper. How had Berit got the speaker to admit this? He'd spent decades denying any involvement in IB, and suddenly he was laying all his cards on the table. Very odd.

The next two-page spread had spectacular pictures of the arrest of the Ninja Barbies, all taken by Carl Wennergren. The article revealed that the terrorist group had decided to mount an attack on a judge who lived out in Djursholm. The reason was that the judge had recently found a suspected paedophile not guilty due to lack of evidence. The police had received a tip-off about the attack and had deployed special forces. Residents

318

in the area had been evacuated and a discreet exclusion zone had been set up. Some of the police had taken up position in Stockhagen sports centre next to the judge's house, and the rest were hidden in the garden.

The Ninja Barbies had been completely overwhelmed by the police counter-attack, and had surrendered once two of the women were shot in the leg.

The article unsettled Annika. The uncritical parroting of the Ninja Barbies' manifesto that had formed the core of the previous articles was completely absent this time, replaced by uniform praise for the heroic actions of the police. If any articles in the *Evening Post* deserved to be analysed and dissected, then it was these, she thought.

'Soon we'll be drowning in the tears of everyone wanting to give the kitten a home,' Anne Snapphane said.

Annika smiled.

'What's it called?'

'Harry, according to its collar. Have you had lunch?'

The minister was driving into a small town called Mellösa. He braked and looked left through the rain. The turning ought to be around here somewhere.

A big yellow building loomed through the greyness down by the water, and he slowed even more. This didn't seem quite right. The car behind sounded its horn.

'Okay, calm down, for fuck's sake!' the minister shouted, hitting the brakes. The Volvo behind slammed its brakes on, swerved, and drove past him with inches to spare.

His hire-car spluttered and died, the fan came on, and the windscreen wipers whined. He realized how much his hands were shaking.

What the hell am I doing? he thought. I can't risk killing someone just because . . .

The irony of this ambiguous thought hit him, and he started the car again and drove slowly on. Two hundred metres further on he saw the sign: HARPSUND 5.

He turned left and crossed the railway. The road twisted and turned past the church, school and several farms in a landscape from another age. Large farmhouses with glassed-in verandas and conifer hedges slid past in the gloom.

Round here the landowners have been exploiting the working class for a thousand years, he thought.

A few minutes later he passed the heavy gates marking the entrance to the Prime Minister's summer residence. At the end of the grand, well-kept drive he could just make out the main house.

He parked to the right of the main doorway and sat in the car for a while, looking at the house. It had two floors, and the hipped manor-house roof typical of the area. It was built sometime in the 1910s, a pastiche of earlier styles. He sighed, pulled out his umbrella, opened the door and ran to the house.

'Welcome to Harpsund. The Prime Minister called to say you were coming. I've prepared some lunch for you.'

The housekeeper took his dripping umbrella and wet jacket.

'Thanks, but I got something to eat on the way. I'd really just like to go to my room.'

The woman looked disappointed.

'Of course. This way.'

She led him up to the first floor and stopped at a room with a view of the lake.

'Just ring if there's anything you need.'

The housekeeper closed the door silently behind her and he pulled off his shoes, and then his shirt. The Prime Minister was quite right. They'd never find him here.

320

He sat down on the bed and put the phone on his lap, then took three deep breaths.

Then he dialled the number to Karungi.

'It's over,' he said when she answered.

There was a long pause while he listened.

'No, darling,' he said. 'Don't cry. No, I'm not going to prison. No, I promise.'

He stared out of the window and hoped he wasn't lying.

45

The afternoon was sluggish. She hadn't been given a story to work on. She understood what that meant, it was hardly subtle. She was no longer covering Josefin's murder, or the story about the government minister.

At one point, when she was particularly bored, she phoned the violent crime unit and asked to speak to Q. He was actually there.

'They were pretty hard on you on the radio last week,' he said.

'They were wrong,' she said. 'I was right. They were just making something out of nothing.'

'I'm not sure I agree with you,' he said calmly. 'You can be bloody pushy.'

'Rubbish,' she said, annoyed. 'I can be restrained when I want to!'

He laughed out loud.

'Restraint isn't the first thing I think of when you phone me,' he said. 'But you can deal with this sort of thing. You're tough. You can't be too sensitive in your job.'

To her own surprise she realized he was right.

'Listen,' she said, 'about this business with the Ninja Barbies.'

'What?' He was suddenly serious.

'Were they carrying much cash?'

She heard him take a deep breath.

'Why the hell do you want to know that?'

She shrugged and smiled to herself.

'Just wondered . . .'

There was silence as he thought hard.

'Do you know something?' he said quietly.

'Maybe,' she said.

'Okay, give it to me, baby,' he said.

She laughed. 'Like I'm going to do that!'

They sat in silence.

'Not on them, no,' he said.

Annika's pulse quickened.

'But in the car? At home? In the cellar?'

'At home. Just one of them.'

'Fifty thousand or so?' Annika said innocently.

He sighed. 'It would be nice if you just told me what you know,' he said.

'I could say the same about you,' she said.

'Forty-eight thousand and five hundred kronor,' he said.

Confirmation of her suspicions bubbled through her brain. So he actually did it, the bastard!

'Now maybe you'd like to tell me where the money came from?' he said gently.

Annika didn't answer.

When the theme tune of *Studio Six* started Annika turned off the radio and went down to the canteen. She had just got a plate of rabbit food from the salad bar when one of the staff called out her name.

'There's a phone-call for you,' she said.

It was Anne Snapphane.

'You should be listening to this,' she said quietly.

Annika closed her eyes and felt her heart sink.

323

'I can't handle another character assassination,' she said.

'No, no,' Anne said. 'It's not about you. It's the minister.'

Annika took a deep breath.

'*Qué?*'

'It looks like he really did do it after all.'

Annika hung up and headed for the exit with her plate of salad. She heard someone shout behind her: 'Hey! You can't just walk off with that!'

'So call the police!' Annika shouted back as she pushed the door open and left.

The newsroom was completely silent.

The voice of the *Studio Six* presenter echoed from various speakers around the room, as all the journalists sat crouched over, trying to absorb the news.

Annika sat down gingerly behind her desk.

'What is it?' she whispered to Anne Snapphane.

Anne leaned over her desk.

'They've found an expenses claim,' she said quietly. 'The minister was at the sex club the night Josefin was murdered. She added something to his bill half an hour before she died.'

The colour drained from Annika's face.

'Bloody hell!'

'It all fits. Christer Lundgren was part of a meeting with some German Social Democrats and union leaders here in Stockholm on Friday the twenty-seventh of July. He gave a speech about trade and cross-border cooperation. Then he took the Germans on a serious pub crawl.'

'What a slimeball,' Annika said.

'And that's not all. *Studio Six* have evidently found the invoice. The names of the Germans are on the back.'

Annika sighed. 'So has he resigned?'

'Do you think he's going to?' Anne Snapphane said.

'Don't you recognize the story?' Annika said. 'A Social Democrat in a sex club, all paid for by the tax-payer?'

A man from the proofreaders' corner shushed them. Annika turned on her radio and turned up the volume, and the presenter's voice boomed out.

'In the Foreign Ministry archive our reporter found the fateful invoice from the sex club. But by then the police were already on the trail of the minister . . .'

The man's voice was full of scarcely contained triumph. He took a deep breath, and then said, slowly and deliberately: 'Because there was . . . actually . . . a witness.'

A pre-recorded insert began to play, and it sounded like the reporter was inside a large, empty room, as the echo bounced off the walls. Annika shivered.

'I'm standing inside the door of the block where Christer Lundgren, the Minister for Foreign Trade, has his secret overnight flat in Stockholm,' the reporter whispered excitedly. 'Until just a few days ago no one knew of its existence, not even his press secretary, Karina Björnlund. But there was one thing the minister hadn't taken into account: his neighbours.'

This was followed by the sound of steps going up a staircase.

'I'm on my way up to see the woman who has become the key to the investigation into the murder of stripper Josefin Liljeberg,' the reporter said breathlessly.

The lift must have been on strike again, Annika thought.

'Her name is Elna Svensson, and it was her early-morning routine and razor-sharp observations that caught the minister.'

A doorbell rang, and Annika recognized it. Yes, he

was definitely inside number 64 Sankt Göransgatan. A door opened.

'He was coming in through the front door just as Jesper and I were on our way out,' Elna Svensson said.

Annika knew the whining voice at once: it was the fat woman with the dog.

'Jesper likes to play in the park before I have my morning coffee. Coffee and a bun, that's my breakfast . . .'

'And on the morning in question you met the Minister for Foreign Trade, Christer Lundgren, on your way out?'

'That's what I just said!'

'And he was coming in?'

'He came in, and he looked a little the worse for wear. He almost trod on Jesper, and he didn't even apologize.'

The worse for wear? Annika thought, jotting the phrase down in her notebook.

'And what time would this have been?'

'I get up at five every morning. It was soon after that.'

'Did you see anything unusual up in the park?'

The woman sounded nervous now.

'Absolutely not. Nothing at all. And Jesper didn't either. He did his business and then we came home.'

The presenter's voice came back on, this time joined by the commentator. They discussed whether the minister ought to resign, what the impact on the election campaign would be, the future of Social Democracy, the development of democracy generally. No subject was too big for *Studio Six* on a night like this.

'God, that's annoying,' Anne Snapphane said.

'What is?' Annika said.

'That it had to be them who found that bloody receipt. Why didn't I go over to the Foreign Ministry and ask to see it?'

'The real question is how they knew that it was there to be asked for,' Annika said.

'Of course, we tried to reach Christer Lundgren to get his reaction,' the presenter said, 'but the minister has gone to ground. No one knows where he is, not even his press secretary, Karina Björnlund. She also claims to have had no knowledge of his visit to the sex club.'

Karina Björnlund's nasal voice came over the radio.

'I have no idea where he was that evening,' she said. 'He told me he was having an unofficial meeting with several foreign visitors. I thought it was all very peculiar.'

'Could he have meant the German union leaders?' the reporter said in an insinuating manner.

'I couldn't really say,' she said.

'And where is he now?'

'I've actually been trying to reach him all day,' she said. 'I think it's very remiss of him to leave me to take responsibility for all of this mess.'

Anne Snapphane raised her eyebrows.

'Karina Björnlund is no Einstein, is she?' she said.

Annika shrugged.

'The Prime Minister declined to comment on our new revelations,' the presenter said. 'He has announced that there will be a press conference at eleven o'clock tomorrow morning.'

'Do you think that's when Lundgren will resign, then?' Anne Snapphane said.

Annika frowned. 'That depends,' she said thoughtfully. 'If the Social Democrats want an end to this, they'll drop him like a hot potato. They can make him a county governor or bank director or something else dull up in bastard Lappland.'

Anne Snapphane wagged a finger at her.

'Careful, my little metropolitan sophisticate – you're talking about my home territory there.'

'Provincialist!' Annika said. 'But on the other hand, that would mean that the government was admitting it had a murderer as a minister, even if he hasn't been charged. If every Social Democrat is as pure as the driven snow, then the minister ought to be allowed to stay, if they're being logical about it.'

'In spite of the receipt from the sex club?'

'You can bet they'll have a damn good excuse for that. It was probably the chauffeur's fault,' Annika said with a smile.

The pseuds on the radio started solemnly summarizing the programme. Annika was forced to admit to herself that their revelations were sensational, the result of some good work.

'A minister in a Social Democratic government invites seven German union bosses to a sex club,' the presenter said. 'A busty blonde stripper adds an item to his bill at half past four in the morning. The minister signs for it, and carefully writes the names of his German guests on the back of the receipt.

'Half an hour later he gets home to his flat, the worse for wear. He almost stands on his neighbour's dog without being aware of it. Later on that morning the stripper is found murdered fifty metres from his flat. She died sometime between five and seven o'clock. The minister has been called in by police for questioning several times, and is now in hiding somewhere . . .'

The last word was left hanging in the air as the theme music began. Annika turned the radio off.

46

The head honchos gathered round the newsdesk: Spike and Jansson, Ingvar Johansson, Picture-Pelle and the sports editor, Anders Schyman and the editor-in-chief. They had their backs to the rest of the newsroom.

'God, what a symbolic sight,' Annika said. 'They have absolutely no idea they're destroying this paper with that impenetrable backward-facing wall of theirs.'

'Well, it doesn't matter what they decide, we won't be involved,' Anne Snapphane said. 'They'll get their blue-eyed boy to look after this little morsel.'

She was absolutely right: the group shifted collectively towards Carl Wennergren's desk.

'Does Jansson work all the time?' Annika asked.

'Three ex-wives and five kids to pay off,' Anne Snapphane said.

Annika slowly ate her way through the wilting salad. Maybe that's how you end up in this profession, she thought. Maybe it's just as well to get out before I end up in the blue cock parade, just another sensation-fatigued old hypocrite with a brain that can only think in 72-point Arial.

'You can keep an eye on Cold Calls,' Spike said to her as he walked past.

A week and a half left, Annika thought, clenching her teeth as she took the plate into the little kitchen.

'Oh well, I could probably do with a quiet evening,' she said as she sat down again.

'Ha!' Anne Snapphane said. 'That's what you think! Look at the weather. All the nutters are at home thinking up things they can phone in as tip-offs. And especially to us.'

And of course Anne was right.

'I think immigration stinks,' a voice said. It reeked of testosterone and the southern suburbs.

'Really?' Annika said. 'In what way?'

'They're taking over. Why can't they sort their own problems out in Bongo Bongo Land instead of bringing all their shit over here?'

Annika leaned back in her chair and sighed quietly.

'Could you be more precise?' she said.

'First they kill each other at home and rape all the women. Then they come over here and strangle our girls. Like that dead girl in the park. I bet you it was one of them who killed her.'

So there was at least one person who didn't listen to *Studio Six*.

'Hmm,' Annika said. 'I'm not sure the police share your suspicions.'

'You see? That's the worst thing! The cops are protecting the bastards!'

'So what do you think should be done?' Annika said meekly.

'Throw them all out. Ship them back to the jungle, for fuck's sake. They're no better than monkeys anyway.'

Annika smiled. 'Well, I'm having a little trouble agreeing with you, because I happen to be black.'

The man on the line went completely quiet. Anne

Snapphane stopped typing and looked up at her in surprise. Annika was having trouble keeping a straight face.

'I want to talk to someone else,' the racist said when he had gathered his thoughts.

'I'm afraid there's no one else available,' Annika said.

'What sort of nutter have you got there?' Anne said.

'Of course there is,' the man said. 'I can hear some bird in the background.'

'Oh, yes,' Annika said. 'She's Korean. Hang on, I'll transfer you.'

'Oh, fuck it,' the man said and hung up.

'God, there are some real cretins out there,' Annika said.

'Korean. Thanks for that,' Anne Snapphane said. 'I don't think I'll ever be that pretty.'

She pulled at her limp blonde hair and took a firm grip of her spare tyre.

'Oh, you're not fat,' Annika said, standing up to get some coffee.

'Better thin and rich than fat and poor,' Anne said.

The phone rang again and Annika answered it standing up.

'This is anonymous, right?'

The voice was that of a nervous young girl.

'Of course,' Annika said. 'What's it about?'

'Well, it's that bloke off the telly, that presenter bloke . . .' She named one of Sweden's most popular and respected television journalists.

'What about him?' Annika said.

'He likes dressing up in women's clothes, and he messes around with young girls.'

Annika groaned, then remembered that she'd heard this one before.

'People can dress how they like in this country,' she said.

'He goes to weird clubs as well.'

'And we've got freedom of speech, and religious freedom, and freedom of association,' Annika said, feeling herself getting angry.

The girl on the phone lost her thread. 'So, you don't want to write about this, then?'

'Has this man done anything illegal?'

'Nooo . . .'

'You said he "messes around", do you mean that he's raped anyone?'

'No, not at all, they were happy enough . . .'

'Has he paid for sex with public funds?'

The girl got confused. 'What does that mean?'

Annika groaned. 'Has he paid for prostitutes with taxpayers' money?'

'I don't know . . .'

Annika thanked her for the tip-off and ended the call.

'You're right,' she said to Anne. 'It's nutters' night.'

The hotline rang a third time and Annika grabbed it.

'Hello, my name's Roger Sundström and I live in Piteå,' a man said. 'Are you busy, or have you got a few minutes to talk?'

Annika sat down on her chair out of sheer astonishment. A polite nutter!

'I've got time,' she said. 'What's this about?'

'Well,' the man said in a broad Norrland accent, 'it's about that government minister, Christer Lundgren. They said on that radio programme, *Studio Six*, that he went to a sex club in Stockholm, but that can't be right.'

Annika perked up; there was something in the man's voice that made her take him seriously. She found a pen under her keyboard.

'So tell me,' she said, 'what makes you say that?'

'Well,' the man said, 'the whole family went to Mallorca on holiday. Stupid really, it was hotter in Sweden than it was in Spain, but we didn't know that when . . . Well, we were on our way home to Piteå, and we'd booked to fly with Transwede from Arlanda, because it's a bit cheaper . . .'

A child laughed in the background, and Annika could hear a woman singing.

'Go on,' she said.

'And that's when we saw him, the minister,' Roger Sundström said. 'He was at the airport at the same time as us.'

'When was this?' Annika asked.

'Friday the twenty-seventh of July, at five past eight in the evening.'

'How can you be so precise?'

'It's on the ticket.'

Of course!

'But what makes you think the minister wasn't at the sex club? The receipt mentioned on *Studio Six* wasn't signed for until five the next morning. And a neighbour saw him coming home.'

'But he wasn't even in Stockholm then.'

'How do you know that?'

'He was on the flight. We saw him at the check-in desk. He had one of those little briefcases with him, and a small suitcase.'

Annika felt the hairs on the back of her neck stand up. This could be important. Even so, she was still suspicious.

'Why did you look so carefully at the minister? Why did you even recognize him?'

The children in the background started singing. Roger Sundström gave an embarrassed laugh.

'Well,' he said, 'I tried to talk to him, but he looked terribly stressed. I don't think he even noticed me.'

'Stressed?' Annika said. 'In what way?'

'He was sweating badly, and his hands were shaking.'

'It was very hot that day, I was sweating badly as well,' Annika said.

'Yes, but he didn't look the same as usual,' Roger Sundström replied patiently. 'His eyes were sort of, well, staring.'

Annika felt her excitement sink. Roger Sundström was a nutter after all.

'What do you mean, staring?'

The man made an effort to think.

'He was so tense, and he's usually so confident and relaxed.'

'You know him?' Annika said, surprised.

'Christer's married to my cousin, Anna-Lena,' Roger Sundström said. 'They live somewhere in Luleå, they've got twins the same age as our Kajsa. We don't see them very often, the last time was probably Grandad's funeral, but Christer doesn't normally look like that. Not even at funerals . . .'

He fell silent, aware that Annika had no reason to believe him.

Annika had no idea what to think, but decided to assume that the man was telling the truth for the time being. At least he believed in what he was saying.

'Did you see him on board the plane as well?'

Roger Sundström hesitated.

'It was a pretty big plane, and it was almost full. I don't think I saw him.'

'Could he have flown back to Stockholm later that evening?'

The man on the phone sounded like he was beginning

to have doubts himself. 'I don't know. I suppose he could have. I don't know when the last plane goes.'

Annika shut her eyes and thought about what they had said on *Studio Six* about the 10,000 lobbyists in Stockholm. Maybe they had an outpost in Piteå.

'There's one thing I'd like to ask you, Roger,' she said. 'And I want you to be completely honest with me. It's really important.'

'Okay, what is it?'

Annika sensed the suspicion and anxiety in his voice.

'Did someone ask you to make this call?'

He didn't understand. 'How do you mean?'

'Did anyone tell you to call this number?'

He thought again.

'Well,' he said, 'I talked to Britt-Inger beforehand. She thought I ought to ring.'

'Britt-Inger?'

'My wife.'

'And why did Britt-Inger think you should call?'

'Well, because they got it wrong on *Studio Six*,' Roger Sundström said, starting to sound annoyed. 'I called them first, of course, but they didn't want to talk to me. They told me I must be mistaken, but I know what I saw. Britt-Inger saw him as well.'

Annika was thinking furiously.

'And no one else asked you to call?'

'No.'

'You're absolutely sure?'

'Now, listen—'

'Okay,' Annika said quickly. 'Look, what you've told me is extremely interesting. It puts *Studio Six*'s revelations in a completely different light. I'll see if I can use or publish your information somehow. Thanks very much for—'

Roger Sundström had already hung up.

47

As soon as she had put the tip-off phone down, her own phone started to ring.

'You've got to help us. We're at our wits' end!'

It was Daniella Hermansson.

'What's happened?'

'They won't leave Elna alone. She's in with me now. There are fifteen reporters with television cameras and aerials and all sorts outside the door. They keep ringing and shouting and want to get in. I don't know what we're going to do.'

She sounded extremely upset. Her son was screaming in the background. Annika adopted her calmest voice.

'You don't have to let anyone in at all, unless you want to. Neither you nor Elna Svensson is obliged to talk to any reporters. Are they calling your number as well?'

'All the time.'

'As soon as we finish talking, leave the phone off the hook, then they'll just get the engaged tone. If you feel that they're invading your privacy or threatening you somehow, you should call the police.'

'The police? Oh no, I couldn't do that.'

'Do you want me to call them?' Annika said.

'Could you? Oh, thank you . . .'

'Hold on, and I'll call them from another phone,' Annika said.

She picked up the hotline phone and dialled the number of the police control room.

'Hello, I'm calling from sixty-four Sankt Görans-gatan,' she said. 'The press have invaded our stairwell, and they're terrifying our elderly neighbours. The reporters are shouting and yelling, ringing on all the doors and intimidating people. I've got five terrified pensioners in my flat right now. It's the right-hand stairwell, second floor.'

She switched phones.

'They're on their way.'

Daniella let out a sigh of relief.

'Thank you *so* much. How can I ever thank you? It's really kind of you, I won't . . .'

Annika wasn't listening.

'Why did Elna Svensson talk to the reporter from *Studio Six*?'

'She says she hasn't spoken to any reporters at all.'

'She must have done, I heard her on the radio. Some-time today or yesterday?'

Daniella put the phone down to talk to someone else in the room.

'Elna says she definitely didn't.'

Annika thought for a moment.

'Daniella,' she said, 'is Elna senile?'

The answer was instant and unambiguous.

'Absolutely not, she's bright as a button. No reporters, she's one hundred per cent sure.'

'Well, she spoke to someone, unless both I and that flock of journalists are all hallucinating.'

'A policeman,' Daniella said. 'She spoke to a police-man this morning. He said he wanted to ask her a few extra questions.'

'Did he record what she said?'

'Did he record what you said?' Daniella asked the woman.

There was a long sequence of muttering.

'Yes,' Daniella said down the phone. 'For evidence. He said it was vital to have everything documented properly.'

They're shameless, Annika thought.

'And she's sure about the time, and the day? When she bumped into the minister, I mean?'

'Yes, absolutely sure.'

'How come?'

'Can I tell her?' Daniella asked her neighbour.

More muttering. Back on the phone she said: 'No, I can't tell you why, but she's sure. Hang on, something's happening out there. I'm just going to take a look—'

She put the phone down. Annika could hear her walking away. She was peering through the spyhole in the door. The steps returned.

'The police are here now, they're clearing the stairwell. Thanks for helping out.'

'Oh, don't mention it . . .'

Annika hung up, her head spinning. The tip-off line rang again.

'You'll have to take that one,' she said to Anne Snapphane, getting up and going off to the canteen. She got a bottle of water and sat by the window, staring out at the rain. It was a damp, grey evening. Not even the lamps of the Russian Embassy compound had any effect on the gloom.

I wonder when Josefin's funeral is? she thought. It'll probably be a while yet. The pathologists and police will want the chance to cut her into little pieces first so they don't have to dig her up again.

She thought about the government minister, wondering which window he might be staring out of right now.

Talk about landing yourself in the shit, she thought. How could anyone be stupid enough to claim expenses from the Foreign Ministry for a night in a sex club?

Mind you, he was supposed to be mean.

As she finished her water, her thoughts went back to Josefin again. The dead girl had been completely forgotten. From the moment she was revealed to be a stripper, she had been nothing but a piece of meat, a plaything for more influential people. Annika thought of the girl's parents.

I wonder how Mum would react if it was me, she thought. Would she cry for the local paper?

Probably not; her mother didn't like journalists. You should keep things to yourself and not give a shit about what anyone else does, that was her motto. She had never said so in so many words, but she had never been very happy with Annika's choice of career. She had agreed with Sven when he said she should never have taken up the offer of a trainee post.

'It's a really tough job,' Sven had said. 'Going after people and proving they did stuff, that wouldn't suit you at all. You're far too nice . . .'

Annoyed, she got up and went back to her desk.

'Okay, I've had enough of this crap,' she said to Anne Snapphane. She picked up her bag and left.

Patricia jumped when the outside door opened. Annika appeared as a dark silhouette against the harsh light of the stairwell.

'Were you asleep?' Annika said, turning the light on.

Patricia blinked against the sudden brightness.

'I was letting the energies flow,' she said.

'And now I've spoiled everything?' Annika said with a sheepish smile.

Patricia smiled back.

'They're always here.'

Annika hung up her coat in the hall, her light jacket was soaked. Patricia sat up on the sofa.

'Josefin had a jacket just like that,' she said, sounding amazed. 'Exactly the same.'

Annika looked at her with surprise.

'It's a few years old now. H&M, I think.'

Patricia nodded. 'That's where Josie got hers. It's still hanging in the hall at Dalagatan. "I'm always going to wear this jacket," she used to say. She often said things like that, huge exaggerations. "I'm always going to do this", "I'm never, ever doing that", "This is the absolute biggest whatever". "You're the very best friend I've ever had". And then there was "until I die". Until I die . . .'

Patricia started to cry, and Annika sat down beside her on the sofa.

'Did you listen to *Studio Six*?'

Patricia nodded.

'What do you think? Could it have been the government minister?'

Patricia looked down at her hands through her tears.

'It could have been one of the bigwigs. They left just after Josie. They had smart bank cards, government cards. And there were the Germans. You know what they're like. Hiding away in Asunción after the war. Dad used to talk about them.'

Annika sat in silence as Patricia cried.

'Anyone who means anything to me dies,' she said.

'Oh, but—' Annika said.

'First Dad, then Josie . . .'

'Well, that can't be "everyone"? What about your mum?'

Patricia pulled out a handkerchief and blew her nose.

'She doesn't talk to me any more. She thinks I'm a slut. She's got the whole family on her side.'

Annika stood up and fetched two glasses of water from the kitchen. She handed one to Patricia.

'So why do you work there, then?'

'Joachim thinks I'm good behind the bar,' she said defensively. 'And I earn a lot of money. I save ten thousand every month. When I've got enough I'm going to open my own shop. I already know what it's going to be called. Crystal. I've learned from Joachim, so I looked it up. The name's available. I'm going to sell tarot cards and do horoscopes, help people onto the right track—'

'You've seen pictures of the minister now,' Annika interrupted. 'Was he at the club with the other men?'

Patricia shrugged. 'They're all pretty much the same, they sort of blur together.'

Annika recognized the phrase, she'd heard it some-where before. She looked hard at the young woman on the sofa. Presumably she avoided looking at the men at all.

'Have the police asked you about this?'

'Course they have. They've asked everything a million times.'

'Like what, for instance?'

Patricia got up, irritated.

'Everything, loads of stuff. I'm tired now. Good-night.'

She closed the door to the maid's room carefully behind her.

Eighteen years, eleven months and five days

We don't know where we're going. The truth that was hidden behind the clouds has drifted off into space. I can't see it any more; I can't even sense its presence.

He cries about the emptiness. My senses are shut off, cold. I can't be touched: numb, sterile.

Resignation is pretty close to failure. Desire that is either too strong or too weak, love that is either too demanding or too feeble.

I can't back out now.

We are, in spite of everything,
the most important thing in the world
to each other.

Tuesday 7 August

48

'She's got to go,' the first one said.

'How are we going to get rid of her?' the second one said.

'Shoot her?' said the third.

The men from *Studio Six* were sitting round her kitchen table. She wasn't going to be staying on at the paper; that much was obvious.

'You haven't asked me yet,' Annika cried.

They carried on muttering at the table, and Annika could no longer make out what they were saying.

'Listen!' she said. 'Maybe I don't want to go with you! I don't want to go to Harpsund!'

'Do you want breakfast?'

Annika opened her eyes and stared at Patricia.

'What?'

Patricia put her hand over her mouth.

'Oh, sorry, you were asleep. I thought . . . you were talking. It must have been a dream.'

Annika closed her eyes and ran a hand through her hair.

'It was a really weird dream,' she said.

'About Harpsund?'

Annika stood up, pulled on her dressing-gown and

padded down to the toilet. When she got back Patricia was pouring coffee.

'Aren't you sleeping well at the moment?' Patricia said.

Annika sat down with a sigh.

'Today's the day,' she said.

'I reckon they'll keep you on,' Patricia said with a smile.

Annika reflected.

'Maybe,' she said. 'I'm a member of the Journalists' Union, so I'll have the union behind me. Even if the bosses have been influenced by *Studio Six*, the union would object.'

She took a bite of a bread roll, and her face relaxed.

'Yes, that's what'll happen,' she said. 'It's entirely likely they'll want to get rid of me, because they're losing their grip right now, frankly. But the union takes a more sympathetic view of cases like this, so they'll fight my corner.'

'There you are, then,' Patricia said, and this time Annika smiled back at her.

The rain had stopped. Even so, his first breath filled his lungs with damp air. The fog was so thick he could hardly see the hire-car.

He walked out onto the crunching gravel and let the door close behind him. All sound was muffled, as if everything was wrapped in cotton-wool. He pushed his hands through the veils of fog. They danced around him.

He walked round to the back of the house. There was no sign of the lake and its little rowing boats just a few hundred metres away. He assumed the fog would lift later that morning, so if he was going to get any fresh air, it had to be now.

A car drove past out on the road, but he couldn't see any trace of it.

Talk about the perfect hiding place, he thought.

He sat down on a bench, and the damp came through his trousers at once. He ignored it.

A sense of failure was burning in his lungs. He drew several deep, misty breaths. The view of the lake was about as clear as his own future.

The Prime Minister hadn't been willing to discuss what he was going to do afterwards. Right now all their energy was devoted to rescuing the election campaign. Nothing could be allowed to threaten that. The Prime Minister was going to abandon him today, execute him in public, and invent some excuse for his departure that he would feed to the press corps. The amoebas, as he called them, were in control of the election campaign, and that was the most important thing right now.

Apart from the truth, he thought.

The thought had the same effect on his future as if the sun had suddenly broken through all the clouds and lifted the fog in an instant.

It was as simple as that!

He laughed out loud.

He could do whatever the hell he wanted.

As long as no one found them.

His laughter died instantly, swallowed up by the fog.

'He's resigned,' Anne Snapphane cried. 'We've just had a newsflash from the agency.'

Annika dropped her bag on the floor.

'And?' she said.

'"The Prime Minister announced the resignation of the Minister for Foreign Trade at a press conference at Rosenbad",' she read on the screen. '"The Prime

347

Minister expressed his regret at Christer Lundgren's decision, but understood the reasons for it."'

'Which were?' Annika said, sitting down and turning on her computer.

'To spend more time with his family,' Anne Snapphane said.

'There's something fishy about this,' Annika said.

'Oh,' Anne said, 'you see ghosts everywhere.'

'So what's the alternative? That he really did kill her?'

'Well, everything's certainly pointing to that right now,' Anne Snapphane said.

Annika didn't reply. She was looking down the list of items on the news agency website. They were already up to 'minister's resignation: 5'. They hadn't been able to reach Christer Lundgren himself for a comment. The Prime Minister once again stressed that the minister hadn't been formally identified as a suspect in any criminal activity, and that the police were questioning him as a matter of routine.

'So why did he resign, then?' Annika muttered.

The expenses claim from *Studio Six* was currently being examined by an internal government investigation.

She let go of the mouse, leaned back and looked out over the newsroom.

'Where are all the führers, then?' she asked.

'Recruitment meeting,' Anne said.

Annika's stomach lurched.

'I'm going to get some coffee,' she said quickly, and got up.

Shit, I'm nervous, she thought.

She picked up a copy of the paper, and burst out laughing when she got to pages six and seven.

The cat was tiny, and was sitting on a dark-green

348

plastic bunk in a holding cell. It had huge eyes, and looked rather confused, possibly as a result of the flash. The tip of its tail was neatly positioned on top of its paws.

DEATH ROW KITTY, shrieked the huge headline.

'It's a good job the media take an interest in the really important stories sometimes,' Annika said when she could speak again.

'We've had a huge response already,' Anne said. 'My task today is to make sure it gets a good home.'

She waved a thick bundle of phone memos.

'The receptionists are already sifting out anyone who doesn't live in the area,' she said. 'What do you think of Arkösund? Do you think it looks like a seaside cat?'

Anne Snapphane leaned forward, peered at the picture for a few seconds and answered her own question.

'I don't know,' she said. 'I don't think he likes herring. I think he likes mice and birds. What about Haversby? That sounds like a real rat-hole, doesn't it?'

Annika stood up, restless.

Why wasn't Christer Lundgren taking part in his own press conference? How come the Prime Minister made the announcement and not him? Didn't he want to resign? Or were the election strategists worried that he'd go off-message?

It could be any or none of those, Annika reasoned. Either way, it gave the impression that they had something to hide.

She went over to the noticeboard, and saw that the recruitment meeting was due to start at ten o'clock. So they ought to be finished soon. She felt she needed to go to the toilet. Again.

When she came out she saw Bertil Strand talking to Picture-Pelle over by the picture desk. She knew the photographer was one of the union representatives, and took part in recruitment meetings. Without realizing she was doing it, she jogged over to him.

'Well, what did you decide?' she said breathlessly.

Bertil Strand turned round slowly.

'It was unanimous,' he said. 'We think you should leave at once. The callous way you treat people has damaged the credibility of the paper.'

Annika didn't understand. 'But,' she said, 'don't I get to stay?'

His eyes narrowed and his voice was cold. 'We think you should be dismissed forthwith.'

The room swayed, the blood drained from her face, and she took hold of the picture desk.

'Dismissed?' she said.

Bertil Strand turned away and she let go of the desk. Oh God, sacked, bloody hell. Where's the door? She had to throw up. The newsroom shimmered and swayed, the walls rippling away from her.

Anger rose up in her, blood red and sharp.

49

Fucking hell, she thought. That's enough of this crap! I'm not the one who's behaved badly. It's not my fault the paper's heading for disaster. And they had the nerve to blame her, her own union reps!

'How dare you!' she said to Bertil Strand.

The man's back stiffened.

'People like me pay for your expensive committee dinners,' she said. 'You're supposed to help us. How the fuck can you treat someone like this?'

He turned to face her again.

'You aren't a full member of this branch of the union,' he said curtly.

'No, because I'm not on a permanent contract. But I pay exactly the same membership fee as everyone else. How come I don't get the same rights? And how the hell can your committee decree that one of your own members should get the sack? Are you mad?'

'You shouldn't say things you might regret,' the photographer said, looking over her head.

She took a short step towards him, and he backed away nervously.

'You're the one who ought to watch what you're saying,' she said in a low voice. 'Yes, I've made mistakes, but nothing as big as the one you're making right now.'

From the corner of her eye she saw Anders Schyman walking towards his glass aquarium with a cup of coffee. She fixed her eyes on the back of his head and went after him. Computers, people, shelves, plants all flew past as detached fragments until she was standing in front of him.

'You're firing me?' she said, far too shrilly.

The head editor guided her into his office and pulled the curtains. She sank onto the tobacco-engrained sofa and stared at him.

'Of course we aren't,' he said.

'The union want me out of here,' she said, her voice shaking.

Don't start crying now, she thought.

Anders Schyman sighed and nodded, sitting beside her on the sofa.

'I can't work out how the union reps think,' he said. 'A lot of them seem to be on the committee just to make themselves feel important. They don't give a damn about their members; they just want to feel influential.'

She looked at him suspiciously.

'Why are you telling me this?'

He looked at her calmly. 'Because that's what's happening in this instance.'

She blinked.

'I'm afraid there's no vacancy for you at the moment,' Anders Schyman said. 'We can't employ everyone who shows talent. There's only one vacancy this autumn.'

'And that's gone to Carl Wennergren?' Annika said.

'Yes,' the editor said, staring at the floor.

Annika laughed. 'Congratulations! This paper really does get the people it deserves!' she said, standing up.

'Sit down,' Schyman said.

'Why?' Annika said. 'There's no reason to stay in this

building another damn second. I'm leaving today, just like the union want.'

'You've still got a week and a half left,' the head editor said. 'Stick it out.'

She laughed again. 'And eat shit?'

'In small doses and under the right circumstances that can be character-building,' Anders Schyman said with a smile.

She made a face.

'I've got time owing.'

'Yes, you have. But I want you to stick it out to the end.'

She went over to the door, then stopped.

'Just tell me one thing,' she said. 'Would this paper ever pay for a tip-off from a terrorist group?'

'What do you mean?' he said, standing up.

'Exactly what I say: money to tag along on a terrorist attack?'

He folded his arms and looked at her hard.

'Do you know something?'

'I never reveal my sources,' she said.

'But you are actually employed on this paper,' he said. 'And I'm your boss.'

She pulled her ID card out of its holder and laid it on his desk.

'Not any more,' she said.

'I want to know why you asked,' he said.

'I want an answer,' she said.

He looked at her without speaking for several seconds.

'Of course not,' he said. 'That would never happen. Not in a million years.'

'If the paper had done so since you started work here, then you'd know about it?'

His eyes darkened.

'I assume that I would,' he said.

'And you can guarantee that it hasn't happened?'

He nodded slowly.

'Okay,' she said breezily. 'That's fine. Well, it's been nice knowing you.'

She held out her hand in an arrogant gesture.

He didn't take it.

'What are you going to do now?'

Annika looked at the editor with derision.

'And what's that got to do with you?'

'I'm interested,' he answered nonchalantly.

'I'm going to the Caucasus,' she said. 'Flying out tomorrow.'

Anders Schyman blinked.

'I don't think that's a very good idea,' he said. 'There's a civil war going on there.'

'Oh, don't worry about me,' Annika said. 'I'll be staying with the guerrillas, so I'll be fine. The government troops haven't got any weapons. The global community has made sure the slaughter's entirely one-sided. Good luck with getting this paper back on its feet again. You've got one hell of a job ahead of you. The bosses have no idea what they're doing.'

She put her hand on the door, then paused.

'You really have to get rid of that sofa,' she said. 'It stinks.'

She left the door wide open. Anders Schyman watched her cruise across the newsroom. She went over to her desk, her movements jerky and angry. She didn't say a word to anyone on her way out.

50

Anne Snapphane wasn't at her desk.

Just as well, Annika thought. All I want is to get out of here without going to pieces. I'm not going to give them the satisfaction of seeing that.

She gathered her belongings together, and managed to grab a few packs of pens, a pair of scissors and a stapler. Good. They owed her that much, the bastards.

She left the newsroom without looking back. In the lift she felt a sudden surge of anger. She had trouble breathing, and stared at her face in the mirror. The same blue-tinged pallor as usual.

Fucking lights, she thought. And this is summer. Imagine what you'd look like in this lift in the middle of winter.

I'm never going to find out, she thought a second later. This is the last time I'll be in here.

The lift stopped with its familiar jolt. She pushed the heavy door open and headed towards the fog outside. Tore Brand must have gone off on holiday, because there was a woman she didn't recognize sitting behind the glass of the reception desk.

The front doors slid shut behind her. Well, that was that.

She stood for a while facing the turning circle in front of the building, breathing in the damp air. It felt raw and unpleasant.

She recalled what she had said to Schyman up in his office.

Where did that bit about the Caucasus come from? she wondered. Mind you, maybe it wasn't such a stupid idea to go abroad, on some last-minute holiday.

A figure emerged from the veils of fog drifting over the road. Carl Wennergren. He was carrying two heavy bags full of bottles. Naturally, he was going to celebrate his luck!

'Congratulations,' Annika said sourly as he passed her.

He stopped and put the bags down.

'Yes, it feels really great,' he said with a broad smile. 'Six months, the longest temp position I could have got. Then I start looking again.'

'It must feel good,' Annika said. 'Getting in here, all as a result of your own effort. And your own money.'

The man smiled nervously. 'What do you mean?'

'Daddy's little rich boy,' Annika said. 'Did you already have the money in the bank, or did you have to sell off part of your investment portfolio?'

His smile vanished instantly. He turned away and clenched his teeth.

'So you got the push, then?' he said brightly.

Her voice sounded shrill when she replied.

'I'd rather live on cat food than buy myself a job from a group of terrorists!'

He looked her up and down scornfully.

'*Bon appétit*,' he said. 'You're actually a bit scrawny. It probably tastes better with a bit of seasoning.'

He picked up his bags and turned to go into the building. Annika could see they were full of bottles of Moët & Chandon.

'And not only did you buy yourself a scoop and a six-month contract,' Annika said, 'you also shafted your sources.'

He stopped and looked round.

'You're talking crap,' he said, but she could see anxiety in his eyes.

She walked closer to him.

'How the fuck could the police know that the Ninja Barbies were going to be at that precise place at that precise time? How the hell did they know which houses to evacuate? How come they were under cover in exactly the right places?'

'How the hell should I know?' Carl said, running his tongue over his lips.

She took another step closer to him, snarling right in his face.

'You sold out your own sources,' she said. 'You worked with the police so you could get pictures of the arrest, didn't you?'

He raised his eyebrows, leaned his head back and looked at her scornfully.

'And . . . ?' he said.

She lost her grip and started yelling. 'Christ, what a fucking heap of shit you are! Fuck you!'

He turned and started walking towards the door.

'You're not right in the head,' he shouted over his shoulder. 'You're fucking nuts! Fucking bitch!'

He disappeared through the glass doors. Annika could feel tears welling up.

Bastard! He strolls in with champagne, and they throw me onto the street.

'Bengtzon, do you want a lift?'

She spun round. Jansson was sitting in a rusty old Volvo at the entry to the garage.

'What are you doing here at this time?' she called.

'Recruitment meeting,' he said, switching off the engine. She went over to the car as the night-editor climbed out of it.

'God, you look tired,' she said.

'Yes, I was working last night,' he said. 'But I really wanted to be at this meeting. I wanted to lobby in your favour.'

She looked at him sceptically. 'Why?'

He lit a cigarette.

'I think you're the best temp we've had this summer. I thought you should have got the six-month contract. So did Anders Schyman.'

Annika raised her eyebrows. 'Really? So why didn't I get it?'

'The editor-in-chief didn't agree. If you ask me, the man's an idiot. He's terrified of any sort of disagreement, and the union was against you.'

'Yes, I worked that out,' she said.

They stood in silence as Jansson smoked.

'So you're leaving now?'

Annika nodded.

'Maybe you can come back another time,' Jansson said.

Annika laughed. 'I wouldn't bet on that.'

The night-editor laughed too.

'Can I give you a lift anywhere?'

She looked at the exhaustion in his face and shook her head.

'I'll walk,' she said. 'I want to enjoy this beautiful weather.'

They both looked up at the fog and laughed.

*   *   *

Her clothes reeked of cigarette smoke, so she pulled them off and left them in a heap on the floor out in the hall. She pulled on her dressing-gown and sat down on the sofa in the living room.

Patricia was out somewhere, which was just as well. She reached for the phone book.

'You can't leave the Journalists' Union just like that, you know,' an operator at the union told her reproachfully.

'Really?' Annika said. 'So what do I have to do?'

'First of all you have to write to your local group and ask to leave, then you have to write to us here. Then you have to confirm your resignation six months later, both locally and to us.'

'You're joking!' Annika said.

'The six months are counted from the first day of the following month. Which means that the earliest you can leave the union is the first of March next year.'

'And I have to pay the full membership fee until then?'

'Yes, unless you stop working as a journalist.'

'Ah, well, you see, that's exactly what I'm going to do,' Annika said. 'As of now.'

'So you're leaving your current position?'

She sighed. 'No, I've got a permanent contract with the *Katrineholm Courier*.'

'Then you can't leave.'

I'm going to strangle this stupid bitch with the phone-wire, Annika thought.

'Listen,' she said, 'I'm leaving the union, now! Today. For ever. Whatever I do or don't do is none of your damn business. I'm not paying another penny to your rotten union. Take me off your database, right now.'

The woman on the other end was angry and insulted.

'I certainly can't do that,' she said. 'And anyway, it isn't our union, it's yours.'

Annika gave up, and started laughing.

'God, you're just unbelievable,' she said. 'If you won't let me leave at once, I'll pay for the privilege. Send me a paying-in slip.'

'We don't work like that.'

Annika swallowed and closed her eyes. It felt like her brain was about to explode.

'Okay,' she said. 'Fine. And I want to give up my right to unemployment support from you as well! Go to hell!'

She put the phone down and leafed through the phone book again. She called the General Workers' Union on Sveavägen.

'I'd like to join your unemployment programme,' she said.

'Great! Sure, I'll send the papers.'

As easy as that.

She went out into the kitchen and made a sandwich. She ate half, then threw the rest away. Then she found a pad of paper and settled down. She closed her eyes and took a deep breath, then wrote two letters. She had to go and buy envelopes and stamps from the Japanese newsagent on the corner.

51

It was already evening by the time Patricia walked into the hall and almost tripped on the pile of clothes.

'Hello?' she called out. 'Have you been at the pub?'

Annika poked her head out from the kitchen.

'What do you mean?'

'Your clothes smell of pub.'

'I got the sack.'

Patricia hung up her jacket and went into the kitchen.

'It's started raining again,' she said, pushing her hair from her face.

'I know,' Annika said. 'I just got in.'

'Have you eaten?'

Annika shook her head. 'I'm not hungry.'

'You've got to eat,' Patricia said encouragingly.

'Otherwise what? Bad karma?'

Patricia smiled. 'Karma means your sins from a past life catching up with you in this one. This is called hunger. People die from it, you know.'

She went over to the stove, cracked some eggs and started cooking. Annika looked out of the window as the rain rattled down, making the grey evening even more dismal.

'It'll soon be autumn,' Annika said.

'There you go, mushroom omelette,' Patricia said, sitting down opposite her.

To her own surprise, Annika ate the whole lot.

'So what do you mean, "got the sack"?' Patricia said.

Annika looked down at her empty plate.

'They didn't extend my contract. The union wanted me gone right away.'

'They're idiots,' Patricia said, so firmly that Annika couldn't help laughing.

'Yes,' she said, 'they are. I left the union.'

Patricia cleared the table and washed up.

'So what are you going to do now?'

Annika swallowed. 'I don't know,' she said. 'I've resigned from the *Katrineholm Courier* and told the housing office that I'll be moving out of my flat in Hälleforsnäs. I posted the letters this afternoon.'

Patricia stared at her, wide-eyed.

'But what are you going to do for money?'

Annika shrugged. 'I have to wait a month before I get any unemployment benefit, but I've got some savings.'

'Where are you going to live?'

Annika held out her hands.

'Here, at least for the time being,' she said. 'It's due to be pulled down, but that could be a year away. After that, well, I'll just have to see.'

'We always need people at the club,' Patricia said.

Annika laughed mirthlessly.

'Yes, I've got all the right qualifications,' she said. 'I've got tits, and I've played a bit of roulette in my time.'

Patricia stared at her.

'You play roulette?'

Annika sniffed.

'I used to work part-time at the town hotel in

Katrineholm when I was a student. I can spin the wheel eleven times and can sometimes even get the ball to land on thirty-four if I start from zero.'

She started to cry.

'But we need someone for the roulette table,' Patricia said.

'I'm going away for a bit,' Annika said.

'Where?'

She shrugged. 'I can't remember the name of the place. It's in Turkey, somewhere on the Mediterranean.'

'That sounds nice,' Patricia said.

They sat in silence for a while. Annika tore off a piece of kitchen roll.

'You need to work out what you're going to do,' Patricia said.

'Thanks, I know,' Annika said, blowing her nose.

'Hang on, I'll get the cards,' Patricia said.

She got up and went over to her room. Annika heard her unzip her sports bag. A few seconds later Patricia appeared in the doorway holding a dark-brown wooden box in her hands.

'What's that?' Annika said, crumpling the sheet of kitchen roll into a little ball.

Patricia put the box down on the kitchen table and opened it. Inside was a piece of black cloth, which she carefully unwrapped.

'Tarot is an ancient form of knowledge,' she said, laying a pack of cards on the table. 'It's based on a set of cards with different esoteric images. Each image possesses the energy of what it represents. It's a tool for finding your way towards greater consciousness.'

'I'm sorry,' Annika said, 'but I don't believe in things like that.'

Patricia sat down.

'You don't have to believe,' she said. 'You just have

363

to listen, to be open, and able to look into your own kingdom.'

Annika couldn't help smiling.

'Okay, you're sounding a bit weird now.'

'Don't laugh, this is serious,' Patricia said sternly. 'Look, seventy-eight cards, the Major Arcana, the Minor Arcana, and the court cards. They each represent different insights and perspectives.'

Annika shook her head and stood up.

'No, don't go,' Patricia said, taking hold of Annika's wrist. 'Let me do a reading for you!'

Annika hesitated, then sat back down with a sigh.

'Okay,' she said. 'What do I have to do?'

'Here,' Patricia said, placing the pack of cards in her hand. 'Shuffle them, then cut the pack.'

Annika shuffled the cards, cut them, then handed them back to Patricia.

'No, you've got to cut them three times, then shuffle and cut them another two times.'

Annika looked sceptical. 'Why?'

'Because of the energies. Come on!'

Annika sighed silently and shuffled and cut, shuffled and cut.

'Good,' Patricia said. 'Now, don't put them back together. Pick a pile with your left hand and shuffle those cards again.'

Annika raised her eyebrows.

'Good,' Patricia said. 'Now, concentrate on the question you want answered. Are you facing a big change in your life, for instance?'

'You know I am!' Annika said, getting annoyed.

'Okay, then I'll deal a Celtic cross . . .'

Patricia lay the cards on the table. She put two in the centre, on top of each other, and the others heading away from them in the shape of a cross.

'Nice pictures,' Annika said. 'Weird designs, though.'

'This pack was designed by Frieda Harris, from sketches by Aleister Crowley,' Patricia said. 'It took her five years. The symbols have their origins in the Hermetic Order of the Golden Dawn.'

'Good grief,' Annika said sceptically. 'And these are going to tell me my future?'

Patricia nodded seriously and pointed at one card lying beneath another.

'This one,' she said, 'is your central card. This is your situation today. The Tower, the sixteenth card of the Major Arcana. You see that it's on the point of collapse. This is your life, Annika. Everything you know, all your security, is on the verge of collapse, and you already know it.'

Annika looked closely at Patricia.

'What else?'

Patricia moved her finger and pointed at the card lying over the Tower.

'The five of Coins is crossing your central card, blocking or obstructing it. It means Mercury in Taurus, anxiety and fear.'

'And?' Annika said.

Patricia gave her a serious look.

'You're afraid of change, but you don't need to be,' she said.

'Okay; what else?'

'Your conscious attitude to your situation is what you might expect. Judgement, which stands for self-criticism and reflection. You think you've failed and are giving yourself a hard time. But your unconscious attitude is much more interesting. See here, the Prince of Swords. He's a master of creative ideas, always trying to break free from narrow-minded idiots.'

Annika leaned back in her chair as Patricia went on.

'You're coming from the seven of Coins, restriction and failure, and are heading towards the eight of Swords, involvement.'

Annika sighed. 'Sounds nasty.'

'This is you. The Moon. That's odd. The last time I did a reading on myself I got the Moon too. It stands for the female sex, the final test. I'm sorry, it isn't a good card.'

Annika didn't say anything. Patricia studied the rest of the cards in silence.

'This is what you're most afraid of,' Patricia said. 'The Hanged Man. Rigidity. Fear that your will is going to be broken.'

'So what happens?' Annika said, no longer sounding quite as sceptical.

Patricia pointed hesitantly at the tenth card.

'That's the result. Don't worry, it shouldn't be taken literally.'

Annika leaned forward. The card was a picture of a skeleton holding a scythe.

'Death,' she said.

'It doesn't necessarily mean physical death. It can also mean radical change. Old relationships dissolving. Can you see, Death has two faces? One tears things down and destroys, and the other frees you from your shackles.'

Annika stood up suddenly.

'I don't give a shit about your stupid cards,' she said, going into her room and slamming the door.

Part Three
SEPTEMBER

Nineteen years, two months and eighteen days

I think I'm good at living. I like to think that my life is actually quite bright. My breath is so light, my legs so smooth, my mind so open. I think it's easy for me to be happy. I think I love life. I have a suspicion that there's something just out of reach, quite close to me, unobtainable.

How simple things can be. How little we actually need.

Sun. Wind. Direction. Context. Involvement. Love.
Freedom.
Freedom . . .

But he says
he will never
let me go.

Monday 3 September

52

The landscape only appeared a minute or so before the plane hit the ground. The clouds were hanging on the treetops, spreading a fine haze of rain.

I hope the weather's been this bloody awful the whole time, Annika thought. It would serve the bastards right.

The plane taxied to a stop at Terminal 2 at Arlanda, the same one they'd left from. Annika had been seriously disappointed. Terminal 2 was like a little appendix to the main departure hall, and it had hardly any duty-free shops. The smaller airlines were based there, domestic and foreign, charter and scheduled flights alike, no glamour at all.

There was little sign of life as she went through customs.

Oh well, I suppose that's something, she thought as she sailed through the green channel.

Of course her bags were the last to appear. The airport bus was packed, and she had to stand all the way in to the City Terminal in the centre of Stockholm. By the time she stepped out onto Klarabergsviadukten it was raining properly. Her bags sucked up the moisture like sponges, the contents getting soaked. She swore through her teeth and got on the number 52 bus at Bolindersplan.

Everything was silent and white up in the flat, the curtains hanging limply in the morning light. She put her bags down on a mat in the hall and sank onto the sofa, dizzy with tiredness. The plane should have left Antalya at four o'clock the previous afternoon, but for reasons that were never properly explained they had to sit in the Turkish hangar for eight hours, then inside the cabin for another five before the plane finally took off.

She leaned back in the sofa, shut her eyes and let the feeling come back. She had been suppressing it through all those hot days in Turkey, concentrating instead on absorbing the Asiatic light, the sounds and smells. She had eaten properly, salads and kebabs, and had drunk wine with lunch. But now she felt her stomach clench and her throat contract again. When she tried to visualize the future she couldn't see anything. A blank. White. Empty. Shapeless.

I have to forget, she thought. This is where everything starts afresh.

She dozed off, slumped on the sofa, then woke up ten minutes later because her wet clothes were making her feel cold. She quickly undressed and ran down to the bathroom in the next building.

When she came up again she crept into the kitchen and looked into Patricia's room. It was empty. She was taken aback, and surprised. On the way into Stockholm she had wound herself up about Patricia being there, imagining that she'd rather be alone. She was wrong. The absence of that mane of dark hair on the pillow gave her a terrible sense of loss, and she didn't like it.

Restless, she wandered through the flat, in and out of the rooms, and made coffee that she didn't drink. She tipped her wet clothes out in a heap on the living-room floor, hanging them over chairs and doors to dry. The room smelled of damp, and she opened a window.

What now? she thought.

What am I going to live off?

What am I going to do with my life?

She sank into the sofa again, her tiredness growing into a lump of anxiety in her chest, making it hard to breathe. The curtain in front of the open window billowed into the room, then sank back down again. Annika noticed that the floor by the window was getting wet, and got up to wipe it.

It's down for demolition anyway, she suddenly thought. It doesn't matter. There's no point. No one cares if the floor gets ruined. Why bother?

The parallels with her own situation sent a wave of sentimental self-pity through her. She slumped back in the sofa, pulled her knees up under her chin, and rocked back and forth, crying. Her arms stiffened round her legs, aching with cramp.

It's all over, she thought. What am I going to do? Who can help me now?

And suddenly the answer was crystal clear.

Grandma.

She dialled the number, shut her eyes and prayed that her grandmother would be in her flat and not out at Lyckebo.

'Sofia Hällström,' the old woman said as she picked up the phone.

'Oh, Grandma!'

Annika was in tears.

'But, little one, whatever's the matter?'

The woman sounded worried, and Annika forced herself to stop crying.

'I feel so lonely and awful,' she said.

Her grandmother sighed. 'That's what life is like,'

she said. 'It can be a real struggle sometimes. The main thing is never to give up, you hear?'

'But what's the point?' Annika said, tears running down her face.

'Loneliness is hard.' The old woman's voice sounded tired. 'Human beings can't survive without their flock. You've been forced out of the group you wanted to belong to, so it feels like you're out on your own right now. There's nothing strange about that, Annika. It would be more remarkable if you felt okay. Just let yourself feel bad, and take care of yourself.'

Annika wiped her face with the back of her hand.

'I just want to die,' she said.

'I can understand that,' her grandmother said. 'But you're not going to. You're going to survive, so that you can bury me when the time comes.'

'What on earth do you mean?' Annika exclaimed. 'Are you ill? You can't die!'

The woman laughed. 'No, I'm not ill, but we all have to die. Just look after yourself and don't do anything in too much of a hurry now, darling. Take it easy and let the pain come. You can run from it for a while, but it will always catch up with you in the end. Let it wash over you, and make sure you feel it. You're not dying. You're going to survive, and when you emerge on the other side you'll be stronger. Older and wiser.'

Annika smiled. 'Like you, Grandma.'

The woman laughed. 'Make yourself some hot chocolate, Annika. Curl up on the sofa and watch something silly on television, that's what I do when life feels hard. Put a blanket over your legs and keep yourself nice and warm. Everything will turn out just fine, you'll see.'

'Thanks, Grandma,' Annika whispered.

They were silent for a few moments, and Annika realized how selfish she was being.

'How are things with you?' she asked quickly.

Her grandmother sighed. 'Well, it rained every single day while you were away. I've only come into town to get some shopping and do a bit of washing, so it's a stroke of luck I was here.'

There is a God, Annika thought.

'I spoke to Ingegerd, they've been having a busy time of it up at Harpsund,' her grandmother said in a different voice, the one she used for gossip.

Annika smiled. 'How's the Prime Minister's diet going?'

'It isn't going at all; it's on hold for the foreseeable future. But they've had other people there who eat even less.'

Whatever gossip her grandmother had gleaned from the new housekeeper at Harpsund didn't really interest Annika, but she asked politely, 'Really, who?'

'That minister who resigned, Christer Lundgren. He came the day before it was announced, and stayed a whole week. The journalists were all looking for him, but no one found him.'

'You see?' Annika laughed. 'You're still at the centre of things!'

They both laughed, and the lump in Annika's chest gradually dissolved and disappeared.

'Thanks, Grandma,' she said quietly.

'Come out and see me if things get too much. Whiskas misses you.'

'I doubt it,' Annika said, 'not the way you spoil him! Give him a kiss from me!'

The warm glow lived on after they had hung up, but even so she started to cry again. Sad, but no longer despairing. And somehow lighter this time.

When the phone rang, the shrill signal made her jump.

'So, you're home at last? God, you've been gone ages. How was it?'

Annika wiped her face with the back of her hand.

'Good, it was really good. Turkey's wonderful.'

'I'm sure it is,' Anne Snapphane said. 'Maybe I should go. What's the health system like?'

Annika couldn't help laughing, it bubbled out before she could stop it. Anne Snapphane was still happy to call her, despite everything that had happened.

'They've got special clinics for hypochondriacs,' Annika said. 'Magnetic X-ray for breakfast, Prozac with coffee, and antibiotics for lunch.'

'Sounds good. What about the radon levels round there? And anyway, where did you end up?'

Annika laughed again. 'In a half-built tourist ghetto twenty kilometres outside Alanya,' she said. 'Loads of Germans. I went up to Istanbul and stayed with a woman I met on the bus, I spent a week working in her hotel. Then I went on to Ankara. Much more modern . . .'

She could feel her body relaxing as she spoke.

'Where did you stay there?'

'I got there late at night, and the bus station was a bit chaotic. I jumped in the first taxi I could find and said "Hotel International". As luck would have it, there's one called that. The staff were lovely.'

'And you got to stay in a suite even though you were only paying for a single room?' Anne Snapphane said.

Annika was astonished. 'How did you know that?'

Anne laughed. 'You always land on your feet, haven't you noticed?'

They both laughed, in amiable companionship. The silence that followed was warm and fuzzy.

'Are you off work now?' Annika wondered.

'Yep, I finished yesterday. The television job doesn't

376

start until the twelfth, when they kick off their autumn season. What are you going to do now?'

Annika sighed, and the lump started to take shape again.

'Don't know, haven't got that far. I can always go back to Istanbul and work in the hotel again; they need waitresses and kitchen staff.'

'Come with me up to Piteå,' Anne said. 'I was thinking of flying up this afternoon.'

Annika laughed again. 'No thanks, I've just spent the last twenty-four hours on an assortment of airport benches.'

'Well, at least you're in practice. Come on, have you ever been any further north than Karlstad?'

'But I haven't even unpacked,' Annika said.

'So much the better,' Anne said. 'My parents live in a huge house out in Pitholm; there's plenty of room. You can come back home tomorrow if you want.'

Annika looked at her damp clothes draped around the room and made up her mind.

'What plane are we catching?'

When they hung up Annika rushed into her bedroom and pulled out her old reporter's bag. She threw in a couple of pairs of pants, a T-shirt, and grabbed her toilet-bag from the living-room floor.

Before she left to meet Anne Snapphane at Kungsholmstorg she fetched a cloth to wipe the rain from the living-room floor.

53

Annika looked around, disappointed.

'Where are the mountains?' she said.

'Don't be so fucking metropolitan,' Anne Snapphane said. 'This is the coast. The Norrland Riviera. Come on, the airport taxi's over there.'

They crossed the acres of tarmac surrounding Kallax Airport. Annika looked around at the scenery: mostly pine forests, and very flat.

The sky was almost clear, and the sun was shining. It was cold, at least to someone who had only just got back from Turkey. A Viggen air-force plane thundered past overhead.

'The F21 airbase,' Anne Snapphane said, tossing her bags in the boot of the taxi. 'Kallax is a military airfield as well. I learned to parachute here.'

Annika put her bag on her lap. Two men in suits squeezed into the taxi as well, then they set off for Piteå.

Little villages flew past, a few meadows with crooked barns, but the E4 was mostly lined with forest. The leaves were starting to glow with autumn colour even though it was only the beginning of September.

'When does winter arrive?' Annika asked.

'I took my driving test on the seventh of October one

year, and two days later we had a snowstorm. I drove straight into a ditch,' Anne said.

They stopped at the Norrfjärden junction to let one of the men out.

Twenty minutes later Annika and Anne got out at the bus station in Piteå.

'It looks like Katrineholm,' Annika said. 'Social Democrats in charge of local government, I suppose?'

'You're in Norrbotten now, darling,' Anne Snapphane said. 'What do you think?'

They left Anne's bags in a locker in the waiting room.

'Dad's picking us up in an hour. Shall we get some coffee?'

They went into Ekberg's café on the main street, and Annika asked for a prawn sandwich. Her appetite had come back.

'This was a good idea,' she said.

'Haven't you missed it?' Anne wondered.

Annika looked up, surprised. 'What?'

'Life. News. The government minister.'

Annika took a large mouthful of her sandwich.

'I don't give a damn about journalism,' she said tersely.

'Don't you want to know what's been going on?'

Annika shook her head and carried on eating.

'Okay,' Anne said. 'Why is your name spelt with a "Z"?'

Annika shrugged. 'Don't really know. My grandfather's grandfather on my father's side, Gottfried, arrived in Hälleforsnäs in the 1850s. Lasse Celsing, who owned the ironworks, had installed a new crusher and my great-great-grandfather was employed to look after it. One of my cousins has tried to look into our family history, but didn't get very far. He never got any further back than Gottfried. No one knows where he came from. He could have been German, or possibly Czech. Either way, he registered under the name of Bengtzon.'

Anne Snapphane took a large bite of her potato-cake.

'How very dull. What about your mum?'

'She comes from the oldest family of foundry-managers in Hälleforsnäs. Basically, I've got a blast furnace stamped on my forehead. How about you? How can you be called Snapphane and come from Norrland?'

Anne groaned and licked her spoon.

'I told you, this is the coast. Everyone up here, apart from the Sami, comes from somewhere else. Sailors and navvies and Walloons and all sorts. According to family legend, Snapphane was first used as an insult to a dishonest Danish ancestor of ours. He was hanged for theft on the gallows outside Norrfjärden sometime in the eighteenth century. And to set an example to others, his kids were called Snapphane as well. And they didn't turn out too well either. Just be grateful you've got a blast furnace stamped on your forehead. Our family crest is a fucking gallows.'

Annika smiled and ate the last of the sandwich.

'Good story,' she said.

'There probably isn't a word of truth in it,' Anne said. 'Shall we go?'

Anne's father was called Hans, he drove a Volvo, and he seemed genuinely pleased to meet one of Anne's friends from Stockholm.

'There's a lot to see up here,' he said enthusiastically as the car headed off down Sundsgatan. 'There's Storfors, and the Elias Cave, Bölebyn tannery, the agricultural museum in Gran, and Altersbruk, an old ironworks with a pond and a mill . . .'

'Oh, Dad!' Anne Snapphane said, slightly embarrassed. 'Annika's here to visit me. You sound like a tourist guide!'

Hans Snapphane didn't seem offended.

'Just say if you want to go anywhere and I'll drive you,' he said cheerily, looking at Annika in the rear-view mirror.

Annika nodded, then turned to look out of the window. A narrow canal flashed past and then they were out of the town centre.

Piteå. This was where he lived, the bloke who had called the tip-off line the day *Studio Six* had revealed that Christer Lundgren had been to a sex club. Married to the minister's cousin, if she remembered right?

Instinctively she reached for her bag and dug around at the bottom. Yes! Her notepad was still there, and she leafed through to the end.

'Roger Sundström,' she read. 'From Piteå. Do you know anyone with that name?'

Anne's father turned left at a roundabout and thought out loud.

'Sundström . . . Roger Sundström. What's his line of business?'

'I don't know,' Annika said, looking through her notes. 'Ah, his wife's called Britt-Inger.'

'Everyone's wife is called Britt-Inger up here,' Hans Snapphane said. 'Sorry, but I can't help you.'

'Why do you ask?' Anne said.

'A Roger Sundström phoned in with an odd tip-off about the Minister for Foreign Trade the evening before he resigned.'

'I know someone who isn't remotely interested in journalism any more,' Anne Snapphane said sweetly.

Annika put her notepad back in her bag and put it on the floor.

'Me too,' she said.

Anne Snapphane's parents' home lay on Oli-Jansgatan on Pitholm. It was a large, modern house.

'You girls can have the upstairs,' Anne's father said. 'I'll get dinner started. Britt-Inger's working this evening.'

Annika looked questioningly at Anne.

'Mum,' she said. 'He wasn't joking.'

The upstairs was open and light. To the right, over by the window, stood a desk with a computer, printer and scanner. To the right were two guestrooms, one each.

While Hans was busy cooking they looked through Anne's old record collection, stored under the stereo in the living room.

'Bloody hell, have you got this!' Annika said in delight, pulling out Jim Steinman's solo album *Bad for Good*.

'It's pretty rare,' Anne Snapphane said.

'I don't know anyone apart from me who's ever heard of this record,' Annika said.

'It's amazing,' Anne said. 'You know he reused chunks of it on *Meatloaf* and *Streets of Fire*?'

'Old Jim stuff is just brilliant,' Annika said.

'Close to divine,' Anne said.

They sat in silence for a few minutes, contemplating Jim Steinman's greatness.

'Have you got his Bonnie Tyler records?' Annika wondered.

'Of course. Which one? *Secret Dreams and Forbidden Fire*?'

Anne put the needle on the record and they both sang along. Hans came in and carefully turned down the volume.

'This is a residential area,' he said. 'Have you ever eaten Pitepalt dumplings?'

'Nope,' Annika said.

They tasted pretty good, not too different from ordinary potato dumplings.

'Do you fancy the cinema?' Anne Snapphane asked as the dishwasher got going.

'There's a cinema?' Annika said, surprised.

Anne looked enquiringly at her father.

'Have we still got a cinema?'

Her father shrugged apologetically from behind his paper.

'Sorry,' he said, 'don't know.'

'Can I borrow the phone book?' Annika asked.

'Next to the computer,' Hans Snapphane said.

There were two Roger Sundströms, one whose wife was called Britt-Inger. They lived on Solandersgatan.

'Djupviken,' Anne said. 'On the other side of town.'

'Shall we go for a walk?' Annika said.

54

The sun had started to go down behind the pulp factory. They crossed Strömnäs and skirted round the Nolia district behind the community centre. The Sundström family's house was a single-storey building with a cellar. Yellow brick, built in the sixties. Annika could hear children singing.

'Do whatever you like,' Anne said. 'I'm just along for the ride.'

Annika rang the doorbell and Roger Sundström answered. He was both suspicious and surprised when Annika explained who she was.

'I haven't been able to stop thinking about what you said,' Annika told him. 'I just happened to be up here visiting my old friend Anne, and I just thought I'd call by.'

The children, a boy and a girl, rushed into the hall and hid behind their father's legs, curious to see who was at the door.

'Okay, time to get your pyjamas on,' the man said, shepherding the children into a room off to the left.

'Can we do some more singing after that, Daddy?'

'Okay, but brush your teeth first.'

'May we come in?' Annika asked.

The man hesitated for a moment, then showed them

into the living room. Leather corner sofa, glass coffee table, china figurines on the bookcase.

'Britt-Inger's doing an evening course,' he said.

'What a nice house,' Anne Snapphane said, in a considerably stronger Norrland accent than usual.

'So what do you actually want?' Roger Sundström said, sinking into a plush armchair.

Annika perched on the edge of the sofa.

'I'm sorry to intrude like this,' she said, 'but I'm just wondering if my memory is right. You flew from Arlanda with Transwede?'

The man scratched his stubble.

'Yes,' he said. 'Yes, with Transwede. Would you like some coffee?'

The question was hesitant, as if he knew he ought to make the offer.

'No thanks,' Anne said. 'We won't be long.'

'So you would have flown from Terminal Two, is that right?' Annika said. 'The small hall?'

'Which one?' the man said.

'Not the big domestic hall, but the one a bit further away?'

Roger Sundström nodded thoughtfully.

'That's right,' he said. 'We had to get the transfer bus, dragging all our luggage with us – we had to go through customs in Stockholm.'

Annika nodded. 'Exactly! So it was there, in the small hall, that you and Britt-Inger saw the minister?'

Roger Sundström thought for a moment.

'Yes,' he said, 'it must have been. Because it was at the check-in.'

Annika swallowed. 'I realize that this sounds a bit odd,' she said, 'but do you remember which gate you flew from?'

The man raised his eyebrows.

'Gate?' he repeated.

'Which exit you left through?'

He shook his head. 'Not a clue, sorry.'

Annika sighed silently. 'Oh well, it was a long shot.'

'Mind you,' the man said, 'the kids took a ride on the suitcases in the terminal, it looked hilarious. I think Britt-Inger recorded them doing it. You might be able to tell which gate it was from the video.'

Annika opened her eyes wide.

'Seriously?' she said.

'Let's see . . .' the man said, going over to the bookcase. He opened the door to the drinks cabinet and started rooting through the mini-video cassettes inside.

'Mallorca, here it is,' he said, slotting the tape into a converter and turning on the video machine. The picture flickered into life, two children playing in a pool. The sun was high in the sky; there were only very small shadows. Two hairy legs, presumably Roger's, appeared in shot from the left. The date in the corner of the screen said: 24 July, 2.27 p.m.

'Is the clock accurate?' Annika asked.

'I think so,' Roger said. 'I'll fast-forward a bit.'

A sleeping blonde woman on a plane, her chin resting on her chest. The date had jumped to 27 July, 4.53 p.m.

'My wife,' the man explained.

And then a suntanned, smiling Roger steering a baggage trolley laden with luggage and the two children: 27 July, 7.43 p.m. The boy was holding on to the handle of the trolley, and his sister was perched on top of the bags. They were both waving to their mother behind the camera. Then the picture wobbled, and did a sweep of the departure hall.

'There!' Annika said. 'Did you see? Sixty-four!'

'What?' Roger said.

'Rewind,' Annika said. 'Can you pause it?'

Roger pressed the remote.

'Bloody hell,' Anne said. 'How did you catch that?'

'I was there today, and I was thinking about this then,' Annika said. 'Keep going, maybe there's more.'

A mass of people suddenly crowded in front of the camera. Someone jogged it, and Roger appeared in shot again.

'Christer!' he cried on screen, waving his hand.

The Roger on screen stood on tiptoe, looking over to his left, then turned to his wife and spoke into the living room.

'Did you see? There's Anna-Lisa's Christer! He's on the same plane.'

'Well, go and say hello!' a disembodied woman's voice said.

Roger Sundström turned round, and on the screen Annika saw how the sea of people suddenly parted, and at the far end, albeit out of focus, she could see Christer Lundgren rushing towards a gate. It was the former Minister for Foreign Trade, there was no doubt about that.

'Do you see?' Annika exclaimed. 'He's holding a ticket! He was definitely getting on a plane!'

The Roger on screen lost the minister in the crowd, looked in another direction, called out 'Christer!', and then the screen went dark. The picture started to break up, then the tape started to rewind. Annika felt a surge of adrenalin rush through her body.

'It's not surprising you didn't see him on the plane,' she said. 'Christer Lundgren didn't leave from gate sixty-four. He was heading for gate sixty-five!'

'So where was that going?' Anne asked, bewildered.

'We're going to find out,' Annika said. 'Thank you so much for letting us disturb your evening, Roger.'

She shook his hand and hurried out.

'What did I tell you?' she said jubilantly when they got down to Ankarskatavägen. 'The bastard, the sodding bastard. He was somewhere else that night, and he can't tell anyone where!'

She performed a little war-dance on the road.

'We know where he was,' Anne Snapphane said calmly. 'At the sex club.'

'No!' Annika said. 'He was flying somewhere, somewhere absolutely secret.'

'Pah,' Anne said. 'You're talking nonsense.'

Annika did a little pirouette.

'It's so damn secret that he'd rather be accused of murder and have to resign.'

'Rather than what?'

Annika stopped.

'Rather than tell the truth,' she said.

Nineteen years, four months
and seven days

I have to decide what's important. I have to reach a conclusion about who I am. Do I exist, apart from through him? Do I breathe, apart from through his mouth? Do I think, apart from with his world view?

I've tried talking to him about it. His logic is simple and clear.

Do I exist, he says, apart from through you? Do I live without you? he asks. Can I love, without your love?

Then he gives the answer.

No.

He needs me. He can't live without me. Never leave me, he says. We are the most important thing in the world to each other.

He says
he will never
let me go.

I've been alone for so long.

Tuesday 4 September

55

Patricia had been asleep for several hours when she was woken by an indefinable sense of unease.

She sat up on the mattress, pushed the hair from her face, caught sight of the man and screamed.

'Who are you?' the young man by the door said. He was squatting down, looking at her as if he'd been sitting there for a while.

Patricia pulled the covers up to her chin and backed against the wall.

'Who are you?' she said.

'My name's Sven,' he said. 'Where's Annika?'

Patricia gulped, trying to get everything to fit together.

'I . . . she . . . I don't know.'

'Wasn't she supposed to get back from her holiday yesterday?'

Patricia cleared her throat. 'Yes, I think so. Her clothes were spread out to dry when I got home.'

'Home?'

She looked down.

'Annika said I could stay here for a while. I was living with a friend who . . . I didn't see her yesterday. I don't know where she is. She didn't sleep here last night.'

The words hung in the air, and Patricia was struck by a disorientating sense of déjà vu.

'So where do you think she is now?'

She'd heard the question before, and the room started to spin. She answered much as she had the last time round.

'I don't know. Maybe she's out shopping, maybe she's gone to see you . . .'

The young man looked at her hard.

'And you've no idea when she's coming back?'

She shook her head, feeling tears pricking her eyes.

Sven stood up.

'Okay, we've cleared up who I am, and what I want. So who the hell are you?'

Patricia swallowed. 'My name's Patricia. I got to know Annika when she worked at the *Evening Post*. She said I could stay here for a while.'

The man studied her carefully, and she clutched the duvet closer to her chin.

'So you're a journalist too? What do you write about? Have you known her long?'

Patricia was starting to feel extremely uneasy. She'd answered so many questions, had to explain so many things that were nothing to do with her. The man took several steps towards her, stopping only when he was looming over her.

'Annika hasn't been herself lately,' he said. 'She got it into her head that she could get some sort of big career in the city, but that was never going to happen. Are you the one who's dragged her into all this?'

The words flashed into Patricia's head, and she screamed right at him: 'I haven't dragged anyone into anything! Never! How can you say it's all my fault?'

She glared up at him, and he took a step back.

'Annika's going to be moving back to Hälleforsnäs

soon,' he said. 'I hope you've got somewhere else to go. I'm going to be staying for a couple of days. Tell her I'll be back this evening.'

Patricia heard him walk through the flat and shut the front door as he left. She let out a long whimpering sound, rolled onto her side and curled up into a little ball. She clasped her hands tightly round her and began to cry, until she drifted off to sleep again.

Hans Snapphane was drinking coffee and reading the local paper when Annika padded into the kitchen.

'There are boiled eggs on the stove,' he said.

Annika fished out a hard-boiled egg, ran it under the cold tap, then sat down.

'I presume my daughter's still asleep?'

Annika nodded with a smile.

'She been working too hard for too long,' she said.

Hans Snapphane sighed and folded his paper.

'It's good that she got away from there. That job was no good for her. This new job in television sounds much better – the hours are more humane, and there are more women in senior positions.'

Annika glanced over at him. He was pretty smart.

'Could I borrow the phone to make a couple of calls?' Annika asked as he stood up with his briefcase.

'Of course, but maybe lay off the Jim Steinman for a while? Britt-Inger's working late again tonight.'

He waved from the car.

Annika forced herself to finish the egg, then ran upstairs lightly. She dialled the Civil Aviation Administration's information centre at Arlanda.

'Yes, hello, I was wondering if I could check when a particular flight left?'

'Of course,' the man at the other end said. 'Which flight?'

'Ah, well, it's a bit tricky,' Annika explained. 'All I really know is which gate it left from.'

'That's okay, as long as it was in the last couple of days.'

Annika was stumped.

'I'm afraid it wasn't. Is there no way of finding out?'

'Do you know the time of the flight? I can see flights one day back and six days ahead.'

Annika's heart sank.

'This was five weeks ago,' she said.

'And you only know the gate number? That's makes it pretty difficult. We can't see that far back.'

'But you must have timetables?' she said. 'I know roughly when the plane left.'

'I'm afraid you'll have to approach the airline direct. Can I ask what it's about? Is it for insurance purposes?'

'No, not at all,' she said.

There was silence on the line.

'Well,' the man at the Civil Aviation Administration said, 'I'm afraid you'll have to go direct to the airline in question.'

She sighed. 'I don't know which airline it was,' she said gloomily. 'Which ones fly from Terminal Two?'

The man listed them: 'Maersk Air, a Danish company flying out of Jutland, Alitalia, Delta Air from the US, Estonian Air, Austrian Airlines and Finnair.'

Annika was writing the names down.

'And they all fly from any of the gates?'

'Not quite,' the man said. 'Foreign flights usually leave from gates sixty-five to sixty-eight, and seventy to seventy-three, which are on the ground floor and use buses to get passengers to their planes.'

'Sorry?' Annika said. 'Gate sixty-five is for foreign flights?'

'Yes, it's beyond passport control and the security checks.'

'And gate sixty-four, what sort is that one?'

'Mostly domestic,' the man said. 'The gates are arranged in pairs. Although it's possible to alter them by changing the layout of the doors . . .'

'Thanks very much for your help,' Annika said quickly and hung up.

A foreign flight . . . So Christer Lundgren travelled abroad on the evening of Friday, 27 July, and was back soon after five o'clock the next morning.

'Well, he didn't go to the States,' Annika said out loud to herself, crossing out Delta Airlines.

Denmark, Finland, Estonia and Austria were all possible. The distances were short enough to make a return trip possible. Italy was more doubtful.

But how could he have got home in the middle of the night? she wondered. It must have been a bloody important meeting, which meant it must have lasted a while.

She counted on her fingers.

If he left at 8 p.m., wherever he was going he wouldn't have got there and cleared customs before 9.30 p.m. Then he'd probably have gone on by car or taxi, unless the meeting took place at the airport.

Let's say that the meeting started at 10 p.m., she reasoned. Maybe he could have been finished by 11 p.m. Back to the airport, check in . . . He couldn't have arrived back in Sweden before midnight.

There weren't that many scheduled flights at that time of day, not with those airlines. So, what exactly was Maersk Air?

She sighed.

He could have come home by a different means, she thought, by car or boat. Which would rule out Austria and Italy.

She looked down at her notebook. That left Denmark, Finland and Estonia. She found a number for Finnair's ticket office in the phone book. It was a free call, an 020 number, and she ended up talking to the airline's customer services department in Helsinki.

'No,' said a friendly man who had an accent just like Moomintroll in the cartoon series, 'I can't check that sort of information on my computer. You don't have a flight number? If you have, I could check back . . .'

Annika closed her eyes, rubbing her forehead.

'Where do you fly to from Stockholm?'

The man checked.

'Helsinki, of course,' he said. 'Oslo, Copenhagen, Vienna, Berlin and London.'

A dead end. She couldn't find out where the plane was going this way, it was impossible.

'One last question,' she said. 'When does your last flight to Stockholm leave?'

'From Helsinki? At nine forty-five p.m. It gets into Stockholm at nine forty. You're an hour behind us, of course.'

She thanked him and hung up.

He must have got back to Sweden some other way, certainly not by any scheduled flight. A private plane, she thought. He could have chartered a plane.

Expensive, though, she thought, remembering the fuss about the cost of the Prime Minister's private flights. Chartered flights had to be paid for, and she doubted Christer Lundgren would have footed the bill. It would be against his religion.

She looked up, out through Hans Snapphane's office window. Off to the right she could just make out one of the commonest sort of house in Piteå, a red, wooden, single-storey building from the seventies. In front of her, on the other side of the street, was a larger white brick building with dark, stained gables. Beyond that she could see a small patch of forest.

There has to be a receipt, an expenses claim somewhere, she thought. Regardless of how he got back to Sweden, the Minister for Foreign Trade must have invoiced a government department or some other state-funded body.

It struck her that she didn't even know which department foreign trade came under.

She went into Anne's room and woke her up.

'I have to get back to Stockholm,' Annika said. 'I've got a lot to do.'

56

She went straight from the City Terminal to the Foreign Ministry building on Gustav Adolfs torg. The pale pink building was surrounded by dark, shiny cars, important-looking men with watchful expressions, and pensioners with cameras. The crowd made her nervous, and she walked uncertainly towards the main entrance. A large black car with a stylized crown on the number-plate stood in the way. As she walked round it a plump little guard in an olive-green uniform blocked her path.

'And where are you going?'

'In,' Annika said.

'There's enough press in there already,' the guard said.

Fuck, Annika thought.

'But I'm going to see the registrar,' she said.

'You'll have to wait,' the man said, crossing his hands in front of his crotch.

Annika stood her ground. 'Why?'

The guard looked less sure of himself.

'There's a state visit. The South African President is here.'

'Shit,' Annika said, realizing how out of the loop she was.

'Come back after three p.m.,' he said.

Annika turned on her heel and headed off across Norrbro. She looked at her watch: over an hour to wait. It had stopped raining and she decided to take a quick walk to Södermalm. She'd done a lot of running in Turkey and had noticed the difference regular exercise made to her mood. So she walked quickly through Gamla Stan towards the steps leading up to Mosebacke torg. With her bag strapped across her chest she ran up and down the steep steps until her pulse was racing and she was running with sweat. She stopped at the top of a narrow street, Klevgränd, and looked out over Stockholm, at the little alleys leading away from the water at Skeppsbron, at the gleaming white hull of the clipper, *af Chapman*, and at the pale-blue roller-coaster over at the funfair, Gröna lund, standing out against the greenery of Djurgården behind it like a tangled ball of wool.

I have to find some way of staying here, she thought.

At five minutes to three all the cars in front of the Foreign Ministry had gone.

'I'd like to know the procedures for when government ministers travel abroad,' Annika politely asked the woman behind the desk. She felt a drop of sweat running down her nose and quickly wiped it away.

The woman raised her eyebrows slightly.

'I see,' she said. 'And you are?'

Annika smiled. 'I don't have to provide ID. You don't even have the right to ask. But you are, however, obliged to answer my questions.'

The woman stiffened.

'What happens when a government minister is planning a foreign trip?' Annika asked sweetly.

The woman's voice was frosty. 'The minister's PA books the trip through the agency currently being used by the government according to agreed protocols. Nyman and Schultz have the contract at the moment.'

'Do ministers have their own travel budgets?'

The woman sighed quietly. 'Yes, of course.'

'In that case I would like to make a request to consult a document in the public domain. An expenses claim signed for by the Minister for Foreign Trade, Christer Lundgren, on the twenty-eighth of July this year.'

The Foreign Ministry woman could hardly conceal the note of triumph in her voice. 'No, that isn't possible,' she said.

'Oh?' Annika said. 'Why not?'

'The Minister for Foreign Trade comes under the Ministry of Enterprise, Energy and Communications, not the Foreign Ministry. That's been the case since the current Prime Minister took office,' she said. 'The Prime Minister moved the promotion of exports from the Foreign Ministry to the Ministry of Enterprise, and in return the Foreign Ministry assumed responsibility for asylum and immigration.'

Annika blinked.

'So the Minister for Foreign Trade doesn't claim expenses from this department at all?'

'No, not at all,' the woman said.

'Nothing for entertainment, nor any other expenses claims?'

'Not a single one.'

Annika was at a loss. The presenter of *Studio Six* had said they'd found the invoice from the sex club at the Foreign Ministry, she was absolutely sure of that. The entire programme was still echoing through her head, whether or not she wanted it to.

'Where's the Ministry of Enterprise?'

She walked up past the Museum of Mediterranean Antiquities to number 8, Fredsgatan.

'I'd like to look at a claim for travel expenses and one for entertainment from the twenty-eighth of July this year,' Annika said. 'Will it take long?'

The registrar was a friendly, efficient-looking woman.

'No, it should be pretty quick. Come back in an hour and we'll have it ready for you. But don't be any later than that, because we'll be closed . . .'

She turned onto Drottninggatan, the pedestrian street running through the heart of Stockholm, and looked around her. It was drizzling, and dark clouds behind the parliament building suggested there was more rain to come. She wandered aimlessly, looking at the street performers, the posters and cheap clothes. It was all out of her reach, she had no money left at all. That impulsive trip to Piteå had swallowed her last few notes.

Anne Snapphane had been rather cross when she announced she wanted to come back to Stockholm.

'Can't you just let that damn minister go?' she had said. 'Let him rot in peace!'

Annika had been embarrassed, but had insisted.

'I've got to go,' she had said. 'I want to know what happened.'

She walked up towards Klarabergsgatan, and went into some terrible American coffee-house in the square where she ordered iced water. They wanted ten kronor for a glass of tap water. Annika swallowed the urge to make a smart remark and dug out the money. It was starting to rain more heavily now, and it would be worth ten kronor just to stay dry.

She sat at the counter and looked around. The place was full of fashionable types with mugs of cappuccino and small cups of espresso. Annika took a sip of water and crunched on an ice-cube.

So far she had avoided thinking about it, but she

couldn't avoid it any longer. She had forfeited a month's worth of unemployment benefit because she had left the *Katrineholm Courier* voluntarily, and there was no more money coming from the *Evening Post*.

I don't really have that many outgoings, she thought, and jotted them down.

The rent on the flat was only 2,970 kronor a month, and now there were two of them. Food didn't have to cost much, she could live on pasta. She didn't need a monthly travel card, she could make do with single bus tickets, walking and sneaking onto the underground without paying. The telephone was an essential, so she had to prioritize that. Clothes and make-up were no real sacrifice, at least not for a while.

I still need to make some money, she thought.

'Is this seat taken?'

A boy with multicoloured hair and mascara was standing in front of her.

'No, go ahead,' Annika muttered.

She took the opportunity to go to the bathroom. After all, it was free.

She was back at Fredsgatan within fifty minutes. The registrar disappeared at once to fetch some papers, and looked worried when she came back.

'I haven't found any travel claims for that date, but here's the receipt for entertainment.'

Annika was given a copy of the receipt for the visit to Studio Six. It ran to all of 55,600 kronor, and was described as payment for 'entertainment and refreshments'.

'Bloody hell,' Annika said.

'It's probably going to be tricky getting that one past the auditors,' the registrar said without looking up.

'Have many people asked to see this?' Annika asked.

The woman hesitated. 'Not many, actually,' she said, looking up. 'We were expecting considerably more, but so far there have only been a handful.'

'But there's no claim for travel expenses?'

The woman shook her head. 'I checked one week further back, and a week forward as well.'

Annika thought for a few moments, looking at the receipt and the spidery signature.

'Could he have made a claim through another department?'

'The Minister for Foreign Trade? It's unlikely. It would have ended up with us anyway.'

'Any other government office? He must travel a lot, lobbying for different organizations and companies?'

The registrar sighed. 'Yes, naturally,' she said. 'There may be some companies that pay, I don't really know.'

Annika persisted. 'But if he was travelling on government business and the claim wasn't presented here, where else could it have gone?'

The woman's phone rang, and Annika could see her getting stressed.

'I'm sorry, I really don't know,' she said. 'Keep the copy, you're welcome to it.'

Annika thanked her and left as the woman answered the call.

57

It was quiet and peaceful in the flat. She went straight to the maid's room and peered in. Patricia was lying asleep, rolled up like a little ball. She shut the door carefully, and it closed with a little click.

'Annika?'

She opened the door slightly.

'Annika!'

To her surprise, Patricia sounded scared and upset, and she went in.

'What is it?' Annika said with a smile.

Patricia rushed up and wrapped her arms round Annika's neck, in floods of tears.

'Goodness, whatever's the matter?' Annika said, alarmed. 'Has something happened?'

Patricia's hair had caught on Annika's eyelashes and she tried to push it away so she could see.

'You didn't come home,' Patricia said. 'You didn't sleep at home, and your boyfriend came and asked for you. I thought . . . something had happened to you.'

Annika laughed, stroking the young woman's hair.

'You daft thing,' she said. 'What could happen to me?'

Patricia let go of Annika, dried her eyes and nose on her T-shirt.

'Don't know,' she whispered.

'I'm not Josefin,' Annika said with a smile. 'You don't have to worry about me.'

She could see the other woman's confusion and couldn't help laughing.

'Come on, Patricia! You're worse than my mum! Would you like some coffee?'

Patricia nodded, and Annika went out into the kitchen.

'A sandwich?'

'Yes, please,' Patricia said.

Annika prepared a snack as Patricia pulled on some tracksuit bottoms. The atmosphere round the table was a little subdued.

'Sorry,' Patricia said, spreading some marmalade.

'Oh,' Annika said, 'don't worry about it. You're just a bit jumpy, but that's hardly surprising.'

They ate in silence.

'Are you going to move out?' Patricia asked quietly after a while.

'Not at the moment,' Annika said. 'Why?'

Patricia shrugged. 'Just wondered . . .'

Annika poured more coffee.

'Has there been much in the papers about Josefin while I've been away?' she said, blowing on her cup.

Patricia shook her head. 'Hardly anything. The police say that their inquiries are pointing in one direction, but that they won't be arresting anyone. Not yet, at least.'

'And everyone thinks that means the minister is guilty?' Annika said.

'Pretty much,' Patricia said.

'Has there been much about him?'

'Even less. It's like he died the moment he resigned.'

Annika sighed. 'You don't kick a man when he's down.'

'What?' Patricia said.

'That's the thinking. You don't keep digging when someone has faced up to the consequences of their mistakes and resigned. What else have they written since I've been gone?'

'They're saying on the news that a lot of voters are ignoring the election,' Patricia said. 'A lot of people are saying they aren't going to vote at all. People really don't like politicians at the moment. They're saying the Social Democrats might not manage to hold on.'

Annika nodded; that made sense. Having a minister under suspicion of murder must be a nightmare for them.

Patricia wiped her hands on a sheet of kitchen roll and started to clear the table.

'Have you spoken to the police recently?' Annika asked.

Patricia stiffened. 'No.'

'Do they know you're living here?'

The young woman stood up and went over to the sink.

'I don't think so,' she said.

Annika got up.

'Maybe you ought to tell them. They might need to ask you about something.'

'Don't tell me what to do,' Patricia said abruptly.

She turned her back and filled a saucepan with water for the washing-up.

Annika sat down at the table again, looking at the young woman's tensed back.

Okay, be like that, she thought, and went into her own room.

Rain was beating hysterically against the window ledge. God, it just won't stop, Annika thought, sinking onto

408

her bed. She lay on top of the covers without turning on the lights.

The room was gloomy and shadowless. She stared at the old council wallpaper, grey, slightly yellowing.

It had to fit together somehow, she thought. Something happened immediately before 27 July that made the Minister for Foreign Trade take a flight from Terminal 2 at Arlanda, so wound up and stressed that he didn't even notice that some of his relatives were calling to him. The Social Democrats must have been in a real panic.

Although it could have been a private matter, Annika suddenly realized. Maybe he wasn't on duty for the government, or the party. Maybe he had a lover somewhere.

Could it really be that simple?

Then she remembered her grandmother.

Harpsund, she thought. If Christer Lundgren had messed things up in his private life, the Prime Minister would never have let him use his summer residence as a hiding place. It had to be political.

She stretched out on her back, put her hands behind her head and took several deep breaths with her eyes closed. Patricia was busy in the kitchen, she could hear plates clattering.

Structure, she thought. Work out what happened. Take it right from the start. Get rid of any wishful thinking, be logical. Weigh things up. What is it that has actually happened?

A minister resigns from the government following suspicions of involvement in a murder. And not just any murder: a sexual attack in a cemetery. Suppose the man is innocent? What if he was somewhere else entirely the morning the woman was raped and murdered? Suppose he has a watertight alibi?

Then why the hell doesn't he come clean? His life is in ruins, his political career is finished, he's a social pariah.

There's only one explanation, Annika thought. My first instinct was right: the alibi is even worse.

Okay, even worse, but who for? For himself? Unlikely, that could hardly be possible. Which leaves just one option: worse for the party.

So, she had reached one conclusion.

What about the rest of it, then? What could be worse for the party than having a minister suspected of murder in the middle of an election campaign?

She shifted uncomfortably on her bed, lay on her side and looked out into the room. She heard Patricia open the front door and go down the stairs. She was probably heading for the shower.

The idea drifted into her head like a soft breeze.

Only the loss of power could be worse. Christer Lundgren did something that night that would lead to the Social Democrats losing power if it ever came out. It had to be something utterly fundamental, something massive. What sort of thing could bring a government down?

Annika sat bolt upright on the bed. She could remember the words, replaying them in her head. She hurried into the living room and sat down on the sofa with the phone on her lap. She closed her eyes and took several deep breaths.

Anne Snapphane was still talking to her, even though she'd lost her job. Maybe Berit Hamrin would still regard her as a colleague as well, even though they were no longer working together. If she didn't try, she'd never know.

With a sense of determination she dialled the *Evening Post*'s reception desk. When she asked to speak to Berit she tried to make her voice sound lighter than usual, in the hope that the receptionist wouldn't recognize her.

'Annika, great to hear from you!' Berit said merrily. 'How are things with you, then?'

Annika's pulse began to calm down.

'Fine, thanks. I spent a couple of weeks in Turkey, it was really fascinating.'

'Were you doing something about the Kurds?'

Berit assumed she was still a journalist.

'No, just holiday. Listen, there's something I've been wondering about the Information Bureau, the whole IB thing. Have you got time to meet for a chat?'

If Berit was surprised, she didn't show it.

'Of course, when?'

'Are you busy this evening?'

They agreed to meet at the grotty pizza parlour in half an hour.

Patricia came back in, in her tracksuit and with a towel wrapped round her hair.

'I'm heading out for a while,' Annika said, standing up.

'I forgot to give you a message,' Patricia said. 'Sven said that he'll be staying for a couple of days.'

Annika went over to the coat-rack.

'Are you working tonight?' she said as she pulled on her coat.

'Yes, why?'

58

The rain was tipping down, making the restaurant's filthy windows glisten in the darkness. Berit was already there. Annika's umbrella had blown inside out, and she stumbled through the door, soaked to the skin.

'Good to see you,' Berit said with a smile. 'You're looking well.'

Annika laughed and shrugged off her wet coat.

'Leaving the *Evening Post* has done wonders for my health. How are things up there?'

Berit sighed. 'Pretty messy. Anders Schyman's trying to sort things out, but the rest of the management team are presenting serious opposition.'

Annika shook her wet hair and pushed it back.

'In what way?'

'Schyman wants to establish new routines, have regular progress meetings and seminars about the direction of the paper.'

Annika opened her eyes wide.

'That would explain it,' she said. 'Let me guess: the others are saying that he's trying to turn the *Evening Post* into a new version of Swedish Television?'

Berit nodded and smiled. 'Exactly. You picked up quite a bit about how that paper works during your few weeks there, didn't you?'

A waiter came to take their order: coffee and a bottle of water. He walked away sullenly, annoyed the order was so small.

'So how badly is the election campaign going for the Social Democrats?' Annika wondered.

'Appallingly,' Berit said. 'They've dropped from fifty-four per cent in the polls back in the spring to less than thirty-five per cent now.'

'Is that because of the IB affair or the business with the sex club?'

'Probably a combination of both,' Berit said.

Their drinks arrived with an unnecessary amount of clattering.

'Do you remember our talk about the IB archives?' Annika said once the waiter had gone.

'Of course,' Berit said. 'Why?'

'You said you thought the original archives still existed somewhere. What makes you so sure?' Annika said, taking a sip of her water.

Berit thought for a moment before replying.

'Several reasons,' she said finally. 'There were registers of political affiliations before and during the war, but they were made illegal after the war ended. Long after that the Defence Minister, Sven Andersson, said that the register from the war years had "disappeared". In actual fact, it was in the Ministry of Defence archive the whole time, filed as a security document. It was finally made public a few years ago.'

'So the Social Democrats have lied about archives disappearing before,' Annika said.

'Exactly. And a year or so later Sven Andersson said that the IB archives were destroyed as long ago as 1969. The latest suggestion is that they were burned shortly before the story broke in 1973. But the destruction of the archives was itself never documented – not the domestic list, and not the foreign files.'

'You mean they used to keep records of when things were destroyed?' Annika said.

Berit sipped her coffee and pulled a face.

'Ugh, this has been stewing for a while. Yes, the Information Bureau was a typical piece of Swedish bureaucracy. There are masses of IB papers stored in the security archives of the Ministry of Defence. Everything was documented, including reports of when records were destroyed. And there's nothing like that relating to the archives of political affiliations, which suggests that they still exist somewhere.'

'Anything else?' Annika said.

Berit thought for a moment.

'They've always claimed that the domestic and foreign archives were destroyed at the same time, and that there are no copies. But now we know that's a lie.'

Annika looked hard at Berit.

'How did you persuade the speaker of parliament to admit his involvement with IB in the paper?'

Berit rubbed her forehead and sighed. 'I had a good argument,' she said.

'Can you tell me?'

Berit sat in silence for a while, stirring two sugar-lumps into her coffee.

'The speaker always maintained that he never knew Birger Elmér,' she said quietly. 'He claimed they had never even met. But I know that's wrong.'

She fell silent. Annika waited.

'In the spring of 1966,' Berit finally continued, 'the speaker, Ingvar Carlsson and Birger Elmér, all met in the speaker's flat out in Nacka. The speaker's wife was there as well. They had dinner together. Conversation turned to the fact that the speaker and his wife had no children. Birger Elmér suggested that they consider

414

adopting, which they later went on to do. I repeated this to the speaker, and that's when he decided to talk . . .'

Annika was staring at Berit.

'How the hell could you know that?'

Berit looked at her tiredly.

'I can't tell you, you know that,' she said.

Annika leaned back in her chair. It was mind-blowing. Bloody hell! Berit must have a source right at the very top of the party.

They sat without talking for several minutes, listening to the rain outside.

'Where were the archives kept before they disappeared?' Annika eventually said.

Berit sighed. 'The domestic archive was kept at twenty-four Grevgatan, and the foreign archive at fifty-six Valhallavägen. Why do you ask?'

Annika had pulled out her notebook and was writing down the addresses.

'Maybe it wasn't the Social Democrats themselves who made the archives vanish,' she said.

'What do you mean?' Berit said.

Annika didn't reply, and Berit folded her arms.

'Hardly anyone knew that the archives even existed, much less where they were kept.'

Annika leaned forward.

'The copy of the foreign archive was found in the post room at the Ministry of Defence, wasn't it?'

'Yes,' Berit said. 'The parcel arrived at the ministry's print and distribution centre, where it was registered, logged and classified. It wasn't deemed confidential.'

'What date did it arrive?'

'The seventeenth of July.'

'Where did it come from?' Annika wondered.

'The log doesn't reveal that,' Berit said. 'The sender

was anonymous. It could have come from any dusty old government office.'

'But why would a government office want to stay anonymous like that?' Annika said, surprised.

Berit shrugged. 'Maybe they found the documents at the back of a cupboard and didn't want to admit to sitting on them all these years.'

Annika groaned. Another dead end.

They sat in silence for a while, looking at the other customers. At the back of the room a group of men in overalls were eating. A couple of noisy women were drinking beer.

'So where were the documents when you read them?' Annika wondered.

'They'd only just arrived at the ministry,' Berit said.

Annika smiled. 'You've got friends all over the place,' she said.

Berit smiled back. 'It's very important to be nice to receptionists, secretaries, registrars and archivists.'

Annika emptied her glass.

'And there was no indication of where the documents might have come from?'

'No. They arrived in two big bags, sacks almost.'

Annika raised her eyebrows. 'Sacks? What, like potato sacks?'

Berit sighed. 'I didn't really think about what they were in, I was concentrating on what was in the documents themselves. It was one of the best tip-offs I'd had in my entire career.'

Annika smiled. 'I can understand that. What did the bags look like?'

Berit looked at her for a few seconds.

'Now that you mention it,' she said, 'they had some sort of printed text on them.'

'You didn't see what it said?' Annika asked.

Berit shut her eyes and rubbed them, stroked her forehead and ran her tongue over her lips.

'What is it?' Annika said.

'It might have been a diplomatic bag,' she said.

Annika didn't follow. 'What the hell's a diplomatic bag?'

'In the Vienna Convention there's a paragraph about inviolable communications between a state and its diplomats abroad, I think it's article twenty-seven. That means that diplomatic mail is sent in special diplomatic bags that are immune from any sort of interference. Government couriers usually take the bags through customs. It could have been that sort of bag.'

Annika felt her hair stand on end.

'How would any of those end up at the Ministry of Defence like that, though?'

Berit shook her head. 'A Swedish diplomatic bag should never end up there. They're supposed to go between the Foreign Ministry and our missions abroad, and nowhere else.'

'But these were foreign bags?'

Berit shook her head. 'Hmm,' she said, 'I must be getting confused. Swedish diplomatic bags are blue with yellow text – the word "diplomatic". This one was grey with red lettering. I didn't really think about what it said, because I was really only interested in getting an idea of how comprehensive the archive was, and whether it contained any of the original documents or appendices. Which it didn't, of course . . .'

They sat without talking for a while, and Annika looked at her former colleague.

'How do you know all this? Articles and conventions . . .'

Berit smiled at her. 'Over the years you get to write about most things. Some of it sticks.'

417

Annika looked out through the window.

'So this could have been a diplomatic bag from another country?'

'Or a potato sack,' Berit said.

'Do you see what this points to?' Annika said.

'What?' Berit said, curiously.

'I'll tell you when I know for sure,' Annika said. 'Thanks for coming!'

She gave Berit a quick hug, opened her umbrella and rushed out into the pouring rain.

Nineteen years, four months and thirty days

He senses the abyss like a flash in the darkness, balancing on the edge without being aware of its depth. It takes expression in desperate demands and clenched lips. He licks and sucks until my clitoris is big as a plum, claiming that my screams are pleasure rather than pain. The swelling lasts for days, and it feels sore when I move.

I am fumbling. The darkness is so immense. Angst hangs like grey mist inside me. Tears form just below the surface, always there, unreliable, increasingly difficult to control. Reality is shrinking, diminished by pressure and cold.

My single source of heat simultaneously spreads icy rawness.

And he says
he will never
let me go.

Wednesday 5 September

59

'For fuck's sake, you can't live like this. No hot water, not even a bloody toilet. When are you coming home?'

Sven was sitting in the kitchen, wearing just his pants, eating breakfast.

'Put some clothes on,' Annika said, tying her dressing-gown. 'Patricia's asleep in there.'

She went over to the stove and poured some coffee.

'Exactly,' Sven said. 'What the fuck is she doing here?'

'She needed somewhere to stay. I had a spare room.'

'And that stove,' Sven said. 'It's lethal. You're going to set fire to the whole building.'

Annika sighed silently. 'It's a gas stove, and it's no more dangerous than an electric one.'

'Crap,' Sven said crossly.

Annika didn't respond, just drank her coffee in silence.

'Listen,' Sven said in a more conciliatory tone, 'stop all this and just come home. You've given it a go, and you can see it hasn't worked. You're no hot-shot journalist; this city doesn't suit you.'

He got up and stood behind her chair, and started to massage her shoulders.

'But I still love you,' he whispered, leaning over and

nibbling her earlobe. His hands slid down her neck and took a firm hold of her breasts.

Annika stood up and tipped her coffee away.

'I'm not coming home yet,' she said quietly.

Sven looked at her curiously.

'What about your job?' he said. 'You're supposed to start back at the *Courier* after the election.'

She took a deep breath and gulped.

'I've got to get going,' she said. 'I've got loads to do today.'

She hurried out of the kitchen and got dressed. Sven stood in the doorway and watched her as she pulled on a pair of jeans and a T-shirt.

'What do you spend your days doing?' he wondered.

'Finding things out,' Annika said.

'So you're not seeing anyone else?'

Annika let her arms drop to her sides in a gesture of despair.

'Oh, please!' she said. 'Even if you think I'm worthless as a journalist, there are still people who think I'm pretty okay—'

He interrupted her by giving her a hug.

'I don't think you're worthless,' he said. 'Quite the opposite. I get really pissed off when I hear them talking shit about you on the radio. I know how great you are.'

They kissed, long and hard. Sven started to pull down the zip on her jeans.

'No,' Annika said, pushing him away from her. 'I've got to go if I'm going to—'

He stopped her with a kiss and laid her down on the bed.

The archive of the broadsheet morning paper was next to the entrance to the *Evening Post*. Annika hurried through the door without looking up at the other doorway. She didn't want to meet anyone she knew, and slid past reception and in amongst the shelves of newspapers. Three older men had taken up position at the microfiche readers and the main table, so she put her bag on the smaller table.

Issue nine of *People in Focus* from 1973 had been published at the start of May. She picked out the issues of the morning paper published in April that year and started to leaf through them. It was a long shot, she had to admit. She pulled out the page of her notebook and put it in front of her.

Domestic archive, 24 Grevgatan.

Foreign archive, 56 Valhallavägen.

The pages of the newspaper were yellow and torn in places. The text was tiny and difficult to read; it couldn't be more than seven-point. The editing was messy and inconsistent. The fashion adverts made her want to laugh: people really did look mad in the early seventies.

But the content of the articles felt surprisingly familiar. Millions threatened by famine in Africa, young people having trouble adapting to the employment market. Lasse Hallström had made a new film for television entitled *Shall We Go to Your Place or My Place or You to Yours and Me to Mine?*

Evidently the ice hockey world championships were taking place, and Olof Palme had given a speech in Kungälv. That year's wars were being fought in Vietnam and Cambodia, and the Watergate scandal was unfolding in Washington. She sighed. Not a word about what she was looking for.

She tried another bundle, giving up 16–30 April in favour of 1–15 April.

Monday, 2 April was similar to all the others. Cambodian guerrillas had mounted an attack on government forces in Phnom Penh. A Danish lawyer called Mogens Glistrup had had a lot of success with his one-man political party, the Progress Party. The former US Attorney General John Mitchell had agreed to testify in Senate hearings. And then, at the bottom of page seventeen, alongside a piece on 'Northern Lights Visible in Stockholm', there it was: Mysterious office break-in.

Annika felt her pulse quicken, racing until it seemed to fill the whole room.

According to the short paragraph, an office at 24 Grevgatan had been broken into and searched sometime over the weekend, probably on Sunday night. The strange thing was that nothing was missing. The office equipment was still there, but all the cupboards and drawers had been ransacked.

I know what was stolen, she thought. Bloody hell, I know exactly what went missing!

She found the next piece in the second section of the paper, at the top left of page thirty-four. An office at 56 Valhallavägen had been damaged during the weekend. It was a short piece, squeezed between a picture of Crown Prince Carl Gustaf with two salmon he had caught in the Mörrumsån river and an article suggesting that Gullfiber AB in Billesholm was going to close down.

Evidently no one on the paper had seen any connection between the two break-ins. Perhaps the police hadn't either.

She copied the two articles and put the bundles of papers back on their shelf.

I'm on the right track, she thought.

Then she took the number 62 bus down to Hantverkargatan.

426

60

Sven had gone out and Patricia was still asleep. She sat down in the living room beside the phone with her note-pad.

What are the Minister for Foreign Trade's responsibilities? she wrote, and sighed.

Trade and exports, she thought. Promoting trade with other countries. So what publicly funded bodies would be able to pay for the trips necessary to do that?

Swedish Trade Council, she wrote.

So what does Sweden actually export? Cars. Wood. Paper. Iron-ore. Electricity. Nuclear power technology, maybe?

Nuclear Power Inspectorate, she wrote.

What else? Drugs.

National Board of Health and Welfare, she wrote.

Electronics. Weapons.

Weapons? Yes, weapons exports would be the responsibility of the Minister for Foreign Trade.

Instruments of War Inspectorate, she wrote, and looked at the list. These were just the ones she could think of off the top of her head, there must be loads more organizations that she wasn't aware of.

Well, no point putting it off, she thought, and dialled the Swedish Trade Council.

427

The public relations manager wasn't in the office today, and a woman took her call instead.

'We're not a publicly funded body. So you can't get any documents from us,' she said curtly.

'Are you absolutely sure of that?' Annika said. 'Do you think your PR manager could call me back?'

She gave her name and number.

'I'll pass on your message, but the answer will be the same,' the woman said sourly.

Bitch, Annika thought.

Next she looked up the number for the Nuclear Power Inspectorate, noting that it was based at 90 Klarabergs-viadukten. The office was closed until 12.30. There was no Instruments of War Inspectorate listed in the phone book, so she called Directory Inquiries.

'They've changed their name to the Inspectorate for Strategic Products,' the woman at Telia said.

The registrar at the National Board of Health and Welfare was at lunch. Annika sighed, put down her pen and leaned back in the sofa.

Maybe she ought to get something to eat as well.

Number 90, Klarabergsviadukten was a relatively newly built glass-fronted building on the Kungsholmen side of the bridge. Annika stopped at the door and read the list of companies based there: the Amu Group, the National Environmental Protection Board, the Nuclear Power Inspectorate, and the Inspectorate for Strategic Products, ISP.

Great, two birds with one stone, Annika thought.

She pressed the button for the Nuclear Power Inspectorate but got no answer. So she tried the renamed weapons inspectorate.

'Building A, fifth floor,' said a slightly doubtful-sounding voice over the speaker.

She got out of the lift on the fifth floor and found herself in a hall of mirrors, surrounded by copies of herself: the walls were lined with polished steel. There was only one door, the ISP's. She rang the bell.

'Who did you want to see?'

The blonde woman who opened the door was friendly but cautious.

Annika looked around. The organization seemed fairly small. There were corridors heading off in both directions. There was no reception desk: the woman who opened the door evidently worked in the room closest to the entrance.

'My name's Annika Bengtzon,' Annika said nervously. 'I'd like to look at some public papers.'

The blonde woman looked worried.

'About ninety per cent of our documents are classified as secret,' she said apologetically. 'But you're welcome to leave a request, and we'll check if we can let you have those files.'

Annika sighed quietly. Naturally. She could have worked that out for herself.

'Do you have a registrar?' she wondered.

'Of course,' the woman said, pointing down the corridor. 'She's down there, the door at the end.'

'I don't suppose you have an archive?' Annika said, getting ready to leave.

'Oh yes, it's all here,' the woman said.

Annika stopped.

'So you'd have any travel expense claims from five or six weeks ago?'

'Yes, but not in the archive. I'm in charge of travel expenses. I keep them in my office until the end of each financial year. I'm also in charge of booking trips; there are more than you'd think. The ISP takes part in a lot of international meetings and summits.'

Annika looked more closely at the woman.

'Are travel expenses classified as confidential?'

'No,' the woman said. 'They're in the ten per cent we're allowed to make accessible.'

'How often would a government minister take part in these meetings abroad?'

'In so far as any minister ever participates in the work of the Inspectorate, the Foreign Ministry usually handles their expenses.'

'But if the Minister for Foreign Trade were to go?'

'Even then it would be covered by the Foreign Ministry.'

'But he actually comes under the Ministry of Enterprise, Energy and Communications.'

'Oh. In that case, expenses claims would be handled there.'

'All of them?' Annika wondered.

The woman was suddenly defensive.

'Well, maybe not every time,' she said.

Annika swallowed. 'I was wondering if you'd received an expenses claim from Christer Lundgren for the twenty-seventh and twenty-eighth of July this year.'

The woman looked at Annika thoughtfully.

'Yes,' she said, 'we did, actually.'

Annika blinked.

'Fantastic! Could I see it?'

The woman wet her lips.

'I should probably check with my boss first,' she said, backing towards her room.

'Why?' Annika said. 'You said that expenses claims are in the public domain.'

'Yes, but this one was a bit special.'

Annika could feel her heartbeat thudding in her ears.

'In what way?'

The woman hesitated. 'Okay,' she said. 'When an

expenses claim comes in from a minister, particularly when you're not expecting it, it comes as a bit of a surprise. It's unusual, to put it mildly.'

'So what did you do?' Annika said.

The woman sighed. 'I took it to my boss. He called someone in the Ministry and got clearance for it. I paid it out a week or so ago.'

Annika swallowed again. Her mouth was completely dry.

'Can I have a copy of the invoices and tickets?'

'I really do have to ask my boss first,' the woman said, and she disappeared inside her office.

A moment later she emerged and hurried off down the corridor. Thirty seconds later she was back, and handed over several photocopied pages to Annika.

'There you are,' she said, smiling.

Annika's fingers were trembling as she took the documents.

'So where did he go?' she asked, looking over the pages.

'He flew to Tallinn with Estonian Air on the evening of the twenty-seventh and chartered a private plane back that night, landing at the old Barkarby airfield. The private plane was Estonian. Would you like the total converted into Swedish kronor?'

'Thanks, but I don't think so,' Annika said.

She was staring at the photocopies of credit card receipts. They'd been handed in on 30 July. The minister had hired the plane using a government Eurocard. She had been expecting to see the same spidery signature she had seen on the receipt from Studio Six, but this one was rounded and rather childish.

'Thanks ever so much,' Annika said, and smiled at the woman. 'You've got no idea how much this means.'

'You're very welcome,' the woman said.

61

Her feet were drumming against the tarmac of the pavement, but somehow didn't seem to be touching the ground. She was walking on little cushions of air, lifted upwards by bursts of laughter.

The miserable old skinflint, of course he couldn't resist putting in his claim for expenses as soon as he could!

She floated home towards Hantverkargatan. She had been right! The minister had been on a trip, and was absolutely determined not to reveal it, no matter what the consequences were.

Bastard, Annika thought. He's done for now.

The telephone was ringing as she opened the front door and she raced over to catch it.

'Hello, yes, I'm the public relations manager at the Swedish Trade Council,' said a man with very pronounced vowels. 'I understand that you're interested in seeing some of our files.'

Annika sank onto the sofa, still wearing her coat and carrying her bag.

'I was told that the Council isn't a publicly funded body, so that wouldn't be possible,' Annika said.

'Well, if you put your request in writing, we'll register it and decide whether or not the documents can be released. Although obviously some of our files are confidential.'

Well, you've changed your tune, Annika thought.

'Thanks so much for calling back,' Annika said tiredly.

The woman she had spoken to before had been completely wrong, but she couldn't be bothered to get annoyed at the complete lack of joined-up thinking.

A lot of people still didn't know that the principle of openness was enshrined in the section of the constitution dealing with freedom of the press. Any document held by any state-funded organization had to be disclosed if someone asked for it, as long as it hadn't been declared confidential.

If we all kept an eye on what was going on, Annika thought, maybe things would get done properly.

She stood up and took off her coat and bag, then called the Cherry group of companies to see if she could get any work in one of their casinos.

'We haven't got any vacancies,' the head of personnel said. 'Try again next spring.'

Reality struck her like a blow to the head. She put the phone down and gulped. So what was she going to do now?

Restless, she got up to get some water in the kitchen, and looked in on Patricia.

The young woman was sleeping soundly with her mouth open. Annika stood and watched her for a few minutes.

Patricia knows a lot more than she's telling me, she thought. It's ridiculous that the police don't know where she's living.

She closed the door quietly and went back to the phone. Q was in.

'Of course I remember you,' he said. 'You're the one

who was fishing around the Josefin Liljeberg case.'

'Yes, I was working as a journalist then,' Annika said. 'I'm not doing that any more.'

'I see,' the detective said, intrigued. 'So why are you calling me?'

'I know where Patricia is.'

'Who?'

She was momentarily speechless.

'Josefin's flatmate.'

'Oh. So where is she?'

'At mine. We're sharing the flat.'

'That sounds familiar,' the detective said. 'Watch out.'

'Don't be ridiculous,' Annika snapped. 'I'm interested in hearing how the investigation's going.'

He laughed. 'Really?'

'I know the minister was in Tallinn that night,' she said. 'Why doesn't he want anyone to know about that?'

The detective had stopped laughing.

'Bloody hell, you're a demon at digging stuff up,' he said. 'How did you find that out?'

'I suppose you've known all along?'

'Of course. We know lots of things we don't leak to the press.'

'Do you know what he was doing there?'

The detective hesitated. 'No, we don't,' he said. 'That was outside the scope of the investigation.'

'But you must have wondered?' Annika said.

'No, not really,' the detective said. 'Some political meeting, I suppose.'

'On a Friday night?'

They fell silent.

'I'm not interested in what the minister was doing,' the detective said. 'My only concern is finding the culprit.'

'And that isn't Christer Lundgren?'

'No.'

'The case is finished, isn't it, from your point of view?' Annika said.

Q sighed. 'Thanks for letting me know about Patricia,' he said. 'Not that we've missed her, but you never know.'

'Can't you tell me anything about the investigation?' Annika pleaded.

'You already know everything I could tell you. Well, I've got work to do . . .'

They hung up. Annika slumped back in the sofa and shut her eyes. She had a lot to think about.

'Have you got a minute?'

Anders Schyman looked up. Berit Hamrin's head was poking round the door.

'Of course,' the head editor said, clicking to save the document on his screen. 'Come in.'

Berit closed the door carefully behind her and sat down on the new leather sofa.

'So how's it going?' she asked.

'Okay,' Schyman said. 'This is one hell of a sluggish ship.'

Berit smiled. 'It can't really handle handbrake turns,' she said. 'Just so you know, I think you're doing the right thing. What you're trying to achieve in terms of fact checking and greater awareness is vital to our survival.'

The man sighed. 'I'm glad someone agrees with me,' he said. 'Sometimes it doesn't feel like it.'

Berit rubbed her hands together.

'Well,' she said, 'I've been thinking about the state of the crime section at the moment. We've got a vacancy there, now that Sjölander has gone over to politics. Is he going to be replaced?'

Schyman turned to the bookcase and pulled out a file. He leafed through it thoughtfully.

'No,' he said eventually. 'Management have decided that Sjölander should stay where he is, so crime will have to manage with you and the other two. The editor-in-chief thinks we should lie low on crime for a while. He's still a bit shaken up by the pasting we took on *Studio Six*.'

Berit bit her lip. 'I think he's making a mistake,' she said carefully. 'I don't think we get out of this crisis by slowing down. I think we ought to speed up. Fight our corner, and really focus on well-researched articles. And that just isn't possible with staffing levels the way they are.'

Anders Schyman nodded. 'Actually, I agree with you,' he said. 'But the way things are at the moment, I can't get anything like that pushed through. For a start, as you suggest, it would require quite some reorganization, and a new appointment.'

'I've got a suggestion,' Berit said, and the head editor smiled.

'I thought you might have,' he said.

Berit became animated.

'Annika Bengtzon is an extremely perceptive young woman. She sees things from a different angle, she thinks differently. Sometimes she goes over the top, but that can be worked on. I think we ought to try to find her a job.'

The head editor held his hands out.

'I'm sorry,' he said, 'but right now she's finished as a crime journalist. The editor-in-chief has palpitations if he so much as hears her name.

'I argued hard for her when Carl Wennergren was appointed, it almost cost me my job. Jansson agreed with me, but the rest of the management team wanted us to throw her out there and then.'

436

'Which you did,' Berit said pointedly.

Schyman shrugged. 'Yes,' he said. 'But it didn't kill her. I spoke to her before she left, she was angry, but sounded fairly together.'

Berit stood up.

'I met Annika yesterday evening,' she said. 'She's on to something. She's digging about in something connected to the IB affair, but I couldn't work out exactly what.'

'She's welcome to offer us material as a freelancer,' Anders Schyman said.

Berit smiled. 'I'll tell her that if I see her.'

Patricia knocked on the door to Annika's room.

'Sorry,' Patricia said, 'but we haven't got any food in, and it's your turn to do the shopping.'

Annika put her book down and looked up.

'Um . . .' she said. 'I haven't got any money.'

Patricia folded her arms.

'Well, you'd better get a job, then,' she said.

Annika stood up and they went into the kitchen. The fridge was empty, apart from a tin of sardines.

'Fuck,' Annika said. 'I called Cherry, but they haven't got any jobs until next spring.'

'Have you tried looking in the paper?' Patricia said.

'Not yet.'

'Maybe you could get something as a journalist.'

'I'm not a journalist any more,' Annika said curtly, pouring herself a glass of water and sitting down at the table.

'Okay, so take a job at the club then,' Patricia said, sitting down opposite her. 'We need a croupier.'

'Come on, I can't take a job in a sex club,' Annika said, taking a sip of water.

Patricia raised her eyebrows and looked at Annika with derision.

'So you think you're better than me and Josefin? Isn't it good enough for you?'

Annika could feel herself blushing.

'I didn't mean it like that.'

Patricia leaned forward.

'We're not whores. We aren't even naked. I wear a red bikini, it's really smart. You've got big tits; you can wear Josefin's. It's blue.'

Annika felt herself blush even more.

'Are you serious?' she said.

Patricia snorted. 'It's hardly that big a deal. But I'd have to talk to Joachim, I don't decide anything. Do you want me to talk to him?'

Annika hesitated.

It would give me an opportunity to see where she worked, she thought. And I'd get to know her boyfriend and boss. And I'd have to wear her bra and pants . . .

This last thought sent a shiver through her crotch, which made her feel both excited and ashamed.

She nodded.

'Okay,' Patricia said. 'If you're asleep when I get home I'll leave you a note.

And with that she went off to work.

Annika sat at the kitchen table for a long time after she'd gone.

Nineteen years, five months and two days

Insight never comes cheap. Experience is never wasted. When the time comes to pay, the price always seems too high, way too costly. But still we stand there with our credit cards, getting our emotional happiness in debt for years to come.

And gradually, once we've got our account under control and the repayments are behind us, we always think it was worth the trouble. That's my consolation today, because today I made up my mind. I know what I have to do. I've pulled out my credit card and cashed in my soul.

It almost happened yesterday. I can hardly remember the reason; there was something he couldn't find, something he said I must have thrown away. Naturally, it wasn't true, and of course he knew that too.

I know what I have to do. My back's up against the wall.

I have to confront him, and I know it's going to cost me.

Because he says
he will never
let me go.

Thursday 6 September

62

The folded note was on the table, and contained just two letters: *OK*.

Annika shuddered and gulped, then quickly threw the note away. Sven came into the kitchen, naked, with mussed-up hair. Annika couldn't help smiling.

'You look like a little boy,' she said.

He gave her a kiss.

'Are there any good running tracks round here?'

'Nothing official, but there's a path that runs all the way round Kungsholmen. That's not bad for running.'

'Last one back's a sissy,' Sven said, rushing into the hall to find his running gear.

They ran together the whole way. Sven won, of course, but Annika wasn't far behind. Then they made love in the shower in the neighbouring house, quietly and intently so as not to let everyone know what they were doing.

Back in the flat again Annika made coffee.

'Training starts again next week,' Sven said.

Annika poured two mugs for them and sat down opposite him.

'I'm going to stay up here a bit longer,' she said.

Sven shuffled on his chair.

'There's something I've been thinking,' he said. 'Isn't

it a bit daft that we each have flats in Hälleforsnäs? We could rent a four-room apartment together, or even buy a house.'

Annika got up and opened the fridge. It was just as empty as it had been the previous evening.

'Would you mind getting some shopping?' she said. 'There's a supermarket down in the square.'

'Didn't you hear what I said?' Sven said.

She sat down with a sigh. 'Yes,' she said, 'but I don't think you heard what I said. I'm thinking of staying up here.'

The man stared into his coffee.

'For how long?'

Annika took several deep breaths.

'I don't know,' she said. 'A few weeks, at least.'

'What about your job?'

'I'm on leave.'

Sven leaned over the table and put his hand over hers.

'I miss you,' he said.

She gave his fingers a quick squeeze, then got up and gathered together the empty cans from the draining board: she could get the deposit money back on them.

'If you're not going to go shopping, I'll go,' she said.

He stood up.

'You're not listening to me, damn it,' he said. 'I want us to move in together. I want us to get married. I want us to have kids.'

Annika's arms dropped and she stared down at the collection of cans.

'Sven,' she said, 'I'm not ready for that.'

He held out his arms.

'What are you waiting for? I've told you, it's what I want.'

She looked up at him, struggling to keep calm.

444

'I'm just saying that I want to finish a project up here first. I'm busy with something, and it could take a while.'

He took a step towards her.

'And I'm saying that I want you to come home. Now. Today.'

She put the last Coke can in the bag, the drops in the bottom dripping onto the floor.

'Okay, now you're the one who's not listening,' she said, and walked out of the kitchen. She pulled her coat on and went down to the supermarket on Kungsholmstorg. She didn't actually like going to that one, it was cluttered and messy and pretentious. They had umpteen different varieties of garlic but no bath plugs. The staff looked on in disapproval as she walked in with her bags of empty cans and plastic bottles. She ignored them: the money she got back on them would pay for a sliced loaf and a box of eggs.

The flat was silent and empty when she got back.

She found a bottle of cooking oil and a tin of mushrooms in the cupboard and fried them up together with three eggs to make a decent-sized omelette. She stared at the house opposite as she ate it, then went and lay down on her bed and stared at the ceiling.

63

Patricia opened the door of Studio Six with both a key and a code.

'You'll be given your own,' she said over her shoulder.

Annika gulped, her heart pounding. She was regretting her decision with every fibre of her being.

The darkness inside the door had a red tint to it, and there was a spiral staircase leading down towards the light.

'Take care,' Patricia said. 'We've had guests who've almost killed themselves on these stairs.'

Annika kept a nervous grip on the handrail and she slowly stepped down into the underworld.

The porn swamp, she thought. This is what it looks like. Shame and expectation; curiosity and disgust.

Immediately in front of her in the hallway was the roulette table, and she felt an odd rush of calm and self-confidence. There were several black leather armchairs, a round table, and a small counter with a phone and a till.

'So, this is the entrance,' Patricia said. 'Sanna looks after things out here.'

Annika looked round the walls, white plaster, a bit grimy. The floor was wooden, covered with cheap imitation oriental rugs from IKEA. A dull red lamp hung from the ceiling, its light hardly penetrating the lampshade.

Behind the counter were two discreet doors.

'That's the changing room and the office,' Patricia said, gesturing towards the doors. 'We'll start by getting changed. I've washed Josie's bikini for you.'

Annika took a deep breath and suppressed a feeling of morbid excitement. Patricia went in and turned on the light, and cold, blue-white light filled the room.

'This is my locker,' Patricia said. 'You can have number fourteen.'

Annika pushed her bag into the locker.

'There's no lock,' she said, and thanked God she had emptied her bag of anything that might give her away.

'Joachim says we don't need any locks,' Patricia said. 'Here you are; I think it'll fit.'

She was holding out a bra covered in sky-blue sequins, and an extremely narrow thong. Annika took them, somehow imagining that the material was burning hot. She turned away and undressed.

'There's a dance-floor, the bar and an area for private shows,' Patricia said, pulling a plastic bag of make-up out of her locker. 'I'm in charge of the bar, so I hardly do any posing. Josie did mostly dancing, Joachim wouldn't let her pose. It made him so jealous.'

Patricia fastened her red sequined bra at the back, and Annika watched as she rolled up her socks and pushed them into the cups.

'Joachim thinks they're too small,' she explained, shutting the door of her locker. 'Here, put these shoes on.'

Annika had trouble putting her bra on, she very rarely wore one.

'Does everyone wear a bikini?' she wondered.

'No,' Patricia said as she started to apply her make-up. 'Most of the girls are completely naked, apart from the dancers. They have to wear a thong, because you aren't allowed to perform naked in Sweden.'

Annika gulped, bent over and fastened her vertiginous stiletto sandals.

'What sort of men come here?'

Patricia was brushing her eyelashes.

'All sorts,' she said. 'Well, they've all got money, I suppose. I usually check their ties, mostly just for fun. They're lawyers, car salesmen, directors, policemen, estate agents, guys who work for laundry companies, advertising agencies, media companies . . .'

Annika stiffened. Bloody hell, what if someone she knew came in? She ran her tongue over her lips.

'Do you get many celebrities?'

Patricia passed her the bag of make-up.

'Here you are,' she said. 'Slap loads on. Yeah, we get some celebrities. One bloke from telly is a regular. He always comes dressed in women's clothing, and pays for two girls to go into one of the private rooms with him. So far he's spent over four hundred and sixty thousand kronor in forty-nine visits.'

Annika raised her eyebrows, remembering the tip-offs on Cold Calls.

'How can he afford it?'

'You don't imagine he pays for it himself?'

Patricia picked up a ring of keys from the make-up table.

'Joachim will be in later. Hurry up, I'll show you round and explain the prices before the girls arrive. You'll have to discuss exactly how you're going to run the roulette table with Joachim.'

She was standing expectantly by the door. Annika

hurriedly applied a thick layer of dark-green eye-shadow, rouge and eyeliner.

'It costs six hundred kronor to get in,' Patricia said, patting the counter. 'Guests can also pay for a private room when they arrive if they like. That costs twelve thousand kronor, and they don't have to pay to get in. Then he gets to choose which girl he wants from the bar.'

Annika was taken aback.

'You mean . . . this is a brothel?'

Patricia laughed. 'Of course not. The girls are allowed to touch the client, massage him and so on, but they never touch his dick. The guys have to take care of themselves while the girls pose at least two metres away from them.'

'Why the hell would anyone pay twelve thousand kronor just to have a wank?' Annika said, with genuine astonishment.

Patricia shrugged. 'Don't ask me,' she said. 'I don't care. Anyway, I'm too busy behind the bar. This is the office.'

Patricia unlocked the door with one of her keys. The room was the same size as the changing room, and contained the usual office furniture, a photocopier and a safe.

'We can leave it unlocked,' Patricia said. 'I've got to fill in the bar accounts for August. Joachim's only got the books here until Saturday.'

They went into the main stripping room, and Annika gasped. The walls and ceiling were painted black, and the floor was wall-to-wall dark red carpet.

The furniture was all black and chrome, and reeked of cheap eighties design. Along the left-hand side of the room was a long bar-counter, and to the right was a row of black-painted doors leading to the private rooms. In front of them was a small stage with a shiny chrome pole running from floor to ceiling, lending the stage the air of a fire station. The room was windowless, and the low false ceiling was held up by black-painted concrete pillars that only enhanced the sense of being in a bunker.

'What was this place originally?' Annika wondered. 'An old garage?'

'I think so,' Patricia said, going behind the bar. 'Carwash and repairs. Joachim turned the old inspection pit into a jacuzzi.'

She lined up several bottles on the counter.

'Okay,' she said. 'Non-alcoholic champagne, sixteen hundred kronor. The girls get to keep twenty-five per cent of the first two bottles they sell, and fifty of the third.'

Annika blinked her stiff eyelashes.

'Unbelievable,' she said.

Patricia looked over at the stage.

'Josie was great at getting sales,' she said. 'She was the most beautiful girl here. She used to drink champagne with the clients all night long, but she never went into the private rooms. But they paid anyway, because she was so pretty.'

Patricia's eyes were wet with emotion, and she quickly put the champagne bottles away.

'Josefin must have been rich,' Annika said.

'Hardly,' Patricia said. 'Joachim looked after the money; he said it was paying off the cost of her breast enlargement. That's why she was working here. And she was only here at weekends, because she used to have school during the week.'

'Does Joachim take money from the other girls as well?'

'No, of course he doesn't. All the girls are here for

the money. They earn a lot, up to ten thousand a night, tax-free.'

Annika's eyes narrowed.

'What do the tax office say about that?'

Patricia sighed. 'No idea. Joachim and Sanna look after the finances.'

'But if you write down the takings from the bar in the accounts, then they become taxable?'

Patricia was getting annoyed. 'Well, there are different sets of books, you must know that! Right, shall we go out to the roulette table?'

Annika paused. 'What about me? What sort of money do I get?'

Patricia frowned and walked out into the entrance hall.

'I don't know what Joachim's thinking of doing,' she said.

Annika turned her back on the terrible, dark room. She was teetering on her sandals, the heels sank into the carpet, stirring up clouds of dark-red synthetic fibre.

The roulette table had seen better days. The green baize was scorched by cigarettes and ash. The gaming area, so familiar with its numbers and squares, finally shifted Annika's insecurity.

'This needs a good brush,' she said, inspecting the table.

While Patricia dug out a brush Annika ran her hand along the gilded edge of the table. It would probably be okay, it wasn't so bad. She wasn't in the sex room itself, and the entrance hall wasn't so very different from the hall of the Town Hotel in Katrineholm.

Patricia showed her where everything was kept, and Annika brushed the table and took out the chips.

'Why are there different colours?' Patricia asked.

'So you can tell the players apart,' Annika said,

451

stacking the chips against the edge of the wheel, twenty in each pile. 'Where's the ball?'

'There are two, one large one and one small,' Patricia said, pulling out a cardboard box. 'I don't know which is the right one.'

Annika smiled and weighed the balls in her hand. The gesture felt familiar, and made her feel more confident.

'They spin at different rates,' she said. 'I usually prefer the heavier one.'

She gently spun the wheel anticlockwise, then picked up the larger ball between her thumb and forefinger, held it to the side of the wheel and sent it spinning clockwise. Patricia gasped.

'How did you do that?' she said.

'It's all in the wrist,' Annika said. 'The ball has to go round at least seven times, otherwise the spin is invalid. I usually get an average of about eleven.'

The ball slowed down and eventually stopped on number nineteen. Annika leaned over the wheel.

'And when I release the ball next time, I have to do it from the number I picked it up from,' she said.

'Why?' Patricia asked.

'So you can't cheat.'

'So how do you work out who's won what?'

Annika briefly explained what straight up, split, street, corner, six line and the other bets meant, and what various combinations stood for, and how every type of bet resulted in different payouts.

Patricia clutched her head. 'How do you work out how much it is, then?'

'That comes quite quickly,' Annika said. 'To start with it helps if you're good at mental arithmetic, but you soon pick up the different combinations.'

She showed how she shared out the winnings: twenty chips in each column, halve it, running your fingers down the edges so the rest of the heap follows. Patricia stared at the speed of Annika's fingers in fascination.

'God, that looks smart,' she said. 'Maybe roulette could be something for me after all.'

Annika laughed and set the ball off again.

Just then the other girls arrived.

64

Sanna, the hostess, was standing stark naked at her counter when the men started to arrive. She smiled and flirted with them, telling them how turned on they were going to be. Annika recognized her voice from the message on the answering machine.

Once Sanna had persuaded the men to pay, the customers turned to look at Annika. The way they looked at her hit her like bullets, making her feel as though the bra was shrinking and revealing more and more of her breasts. She looked down, staring at the burns on the baize and forcing herself not to cover herself up with her hands. No one was interested in playing roulette.

'You've got to flirt,' Sanna said when a group of Italian businessmen had just gone into the main room. 'Try to be a bit sexy, for fuck's sake.'

Annika swallowed in embarrassment.

'I'm not very good at that,' she said in far too high a voice.

'You'd better learn. There's no point having you standing there if you don't bring in any money.'

Annika's eyes flashed. 'The table's here anyway,' she said. 'Surely it doesn't make any difference to you if I stand here? Unless you're charging for oxygen, of course.'

Deep male laughter on the stairs silenced them.

'I think we've got two wildcats in the same cage,' said the man who was slowly coming down the stairs.

Annika knew at once that this was Joachim: long fair hair, expensive and slightly unusual clothes, a heavy gold necklace hanging against his chest. He was the sort of man for whom Josefin would have had her breasts enlarged.

She went over and introduced herself.

'Annika,' she said. 'It's good to be here.'

Sanna pursed her lips.

Joachim looked her up and down slowly, nodding approvingly when he got to her breasts.

'You'd be good on stage,' he said. 'If you like, we could give you a show-number later on tonight.'

No one cares about my surname, Annika thought, trying to smile naturally.

'Thanks,' she said, 'but I think I'd better get to grips with the roulette first.'

'You know,' he said, 'Sanna's right. You have to bring in some decent money, otherwise there's no point in you being here.'

Annika's smile died. 'I'll try,' she said, looking at the floor.

'Maybe you should sit at the bar with the other girls for a few evenings first, find out how it all works.'

The man was standing slightly too close to her. Annika could feel the electricity of his presence. He was good-looking, she had to give him that. She closed her eyes for a moment before looking up and meeting his gaze.

'Thanks,' she said, 'that's a good idea. But I want to see if I can persuade a few customers to stop on their way out.'

Just then two mildly drunk insurance salesmen

stumbled out of the main room. They were sweating and their clothes were dishevelled. Annika went up to them, sticking her breasts in their faces, and put her arms round them.

'Hello, boys,' she said, 'you've been lucky in love, but an evening isn't complete until you've had some luck at the table as well, is it?'

She smiled as playfully as she could, her knees trembling. Joachim had his thigh against her backside, and she wanted to scream.

'What the hell . . . ?' one of the men said.

Annika took a step forward and escaped Joachim's thigh, wrapping her arm round the other man.

'What about you? You seem like a lucky guy, a real gentleman. Come and play with me!'

The man grinned. 'What do we win, then? Do we win you?'

Annika managed to laugh. 'Who knows?' she said. 'Maybe you'll win so much money you can buy any girl you like!'

'Okay,' the man said, pulling out his wallet. His friend did the same, albeit reluctantly.

He put a hundred-kronor note on the table.

Annika smiled nervously. This man had just paid several thousand to drink some fizz and stare at some naked tits, and she was supposed to make all this effort for a pathetic hundred kronor?

'That won't even send the ball round,' she said coyly. 'We play big here, darling. High stakes, big wins. A thousand for twenty chips.'

The man hesitated, and Annika ran her hand over the table.

'A six line pays out five thousand kronor, and a split sixteen thousand, eight hundred – almost seventeen thousand kronor, in just fifteen seconds. You could win back all the money you've spent here tonight.'

The men's eyes lit up simultaneously. And it was actually true.

The each bought a thousand kronor's worth of chips with their bank cards, and placed them as split bets, a combined total of 1,200 kronor.

Annika set the ball spinning, hard and fast. It circled almost thirteen times before it started to drop.

'No more bets,' she said, her old routine coming back to her.

The ball landed on number 3. With a practised hand she swept the table clean and stacked up the chips.

'New bets,' she said, glancing at the look of disappointment on the men's faces.

They were more cautious this time, betting only six lines and switching numbers, to 9 and 18. A new spin, no more bets, number 16. One of the men won ten chips.

'There you are,' Annika said, pushing the small pile of chips towards him. Five kronor. 'Isn't that just what I said, you're a lucky guy!'

The man's face lit up, and Annika could see she'd got him. Between them the men lost another 3,000 kronor until they eventually settled their final bills with Sanna and slunk out. Annika noted that Sanna wrote 'food and drink' on the receipts.

Joachim had been sitting behind the counter watching her.

'You know how to do this, don't you?' he said as he walked towards her. 'Where did you learn to run a casino?'

'The Town Hotel in . . . Piteå,' she said with a smile, and gulped.

'Do you know Peter Holmberg?' he said, smiling back.

Annika felt her own smile wobble slightly. Shit, she thought, he's going to find me out before I've even got going.

'No,' she said, 'but do you know Roger Sundström, lives on Solandersgatan? Or Hans on Oli-Jansgatan out in Pitholm?'

Joachim dropped the subject.

'You're charging too much for chips,' he said. 'That's not allowed. You're playing too high.'

'I can adjust the prices to fit the player. No one knows what anyone else has paid for their chips, there's no sign on the chips themselves. I'm following all the rules.'

'You run the risk of breaking the bank,' Joachim said.

Annika stopped smiling.

'There's only one way for a player to win at roulette,' she said. 'That's winning big at the start, and then stopping at once. No one does that once they've started to win. It's a piece of piss, being a croupier. You just have to keep hold of the players until they've lost everything they've won.'

Joachim smiled easily.

'I think we're going to get along just fine, you and me,' he said, running his hand down her arm.

Then he went into the office. Annika turned away, with Sanna's harsh stare scorching her back.

They're together, she realized: Joachim and Sanna are a couple.

The sound of high-heeled shoes on the spiral staircase made Annika look up. She couldn't believe her eyes. The oh-so-serious television presenter was entering Studio Six wearing a micro-skirt, nylon stockings and a transparent blouse that showed his bra.

'Hello, girls!' he said in a high voice.

'Good evening, madam,' Sanna said, smiling

458

flirtatiously. 'What delights can we tempt you with tonight?'

The man named several of the girls, and Annika realized she was staring at him. She used to watch his programme, raw, entertaining debates with politicians and celebrities. She knew he had a family.

The man glided into the strippers' room with Sanna, and Annika sighed tiredly. The sandals were hurting her feet. She was thinking about taking them off, no one would notice the difference behind the table, but at that moment the Italian businessmen came out again. They looked unhappy. Annika went over and spoke to them in English. That didn't work. She switched to French, which failed as well. Finally Spanish worked.

They played until they had lost 13,000 kronor. Sanna looked more and more angry the more the men lost.

She doesn't like me, Annika thought. She knows I'm Patricia's friend, she sees me as an extension of Josefin, which probably isn't so strange, really.

She glanced down at her tiny bikini with all its sky-blue sequins. Josefin's work-clothes.

'I have to go to the toilet,' she muttered.

The evening crawled past, sliding into night. Down in the old porn garage no time existed except night, no season but darkness. Annika sat for a few minutes in the changing room under the blue strip-light, her eyes closed as she tried to suppress the urge to cry.

What am I doing here? she wondered. Am I just going to slip into this *demi-monde* until it feels like I belong here? Will I end up thinking I can earn even more by posing in the private rooms, and will I actually go through with it? And what I'm doing with the chips – changing the price to suit different customers – is illegal. I could even end up in prison if I get caught.

She applied some more make-up, to cover the paleness of her fading suntan.

Patricia came into the changing room and gave her an encouraging smile.

'I hear it's going well.'

Annika nodded. 'Yeah, not bad.'

Patricia looked proud.

'I knew you were smart.'

Annika shut her eyes, thinking: I mustn't listen. I mustn't allow myself to feel flattered. I can't find validation here. This sex club is not going to become my social context, the place where I finally fit in. I deserve better than this. Patricia deserves better.

She put on some more lipstick and went out.

65

In the early hours of the morning Sanna disappeared into one of the private rooms with an older man.

'He's a regular,' the hostess whispered before she went. 'There are hardly any customers left, just make sure they pay before they leave. Their bills are on the counter.'

Annika stood in front of the roulette table, confused as to what to do. If she was trying to encourage them to play roulette, how was she going to take payment from anyone else as they left?

She decided to abandon the roulette table, and a moment later the television celebrity came out into the hallway.

'Where's Sanna?' he said, and this time Annika recognized the voice he used in his programmes.

'She's busy at the moment,' Annika smiled. 'Can I help you?'

The man handed her a credit card, and Annika moistened her lips in anticipation. She went over to the counter and looked through the various bills. Sure enough, his was there: 9,600 kronor.

She put the card in the machine and prepared the receipt. She knew Sanna would be getting a percentage of the fee, because the bill had her code on it. The man signed the payment slip.

'Oh, darling, are you leaving already?' a girl piped up from the door.

She was stark naked, her pubes were completely shaved and her hair was tied in Pippi Longstocking pigtails. She had also painted on some freckles to complete the illusion.

'Oh, my little baby,' the man said, and gave her a hug.

'Just one moment,' Annika said, and slipped into the office. The room was empty. She put the signed payment slip on the photocopier, closed her eyes and said a silent prayer.

Please don't make a huge racket, please don't take an age to warm up, please let there be enough paper . . .

The strip of light under the glass swept silently and quickly over the receipt, and a sheet of paper slid through the machine and out of the side. She breathed out, but what the hell was she going to do with it now?

She quickly rolled the copy into a hard little tube, folded it in half and slid it into the front of her thong, scratching herself in the process.

'Here you are,' Annika said, walking back to the counter.

The man was sucking on one of Pippi's nipples. When the girl caught sight of Annika she pushed him off her.

'Sorry, I didn't mean . . .' she said anxiously.

Annika suddenly realized that the other girls saw her as a figure of authority, possibly because Josefin had been. She decided to make the most of it.

'Just don't let it happen again,' she said sternly, and gave the man his receipt.

He left, and the girl hurried into the changing room. Annika waited a few seconds, listening to the noises from inside the club.

The low muzak from the stage was filtering out

462

through the doorway, and she shivered. It wasn't very warm in here.

She slid into the changing room, pulled out the photocopy and slipped it into the toe of her shoe. She quickly went out and stood leaning on the roulette table. She stayed there until Sanna's hour in the private room was over.

'Did it go okay?' the hostess asked.

'No problem,' Annika said, pointing at the receipt.

Sanna looked at the total with a satisfied smile, and gave Annika a mischievous look.

'Do you pay your TV licence?' she asked.

The question was rhetorical, and she fanned herself with the receipt, laughed, and went into the office.

Annika smiled towards the closed door.

Patricia was making tea.

Annika was sitting on the sofa in the living room, staring into the turquoise-grey gloom of the room. She was so tired; her body was aching all over. Her feet had huge blisters from those terrible sandals.

'How do you stick it?' she said quietly.

'What?' Patricia said from the kitchen.

'Oh, nothing,' Annika said inaudibly.

She had an underlying feeling of disgust in her gut, and when she closed her eyes all she could see was the image of the skinny, naked Pippi Longstocking.

'Here you are,' Patricia said as she put the tray down next to the phone on the little table.

Annika sighed deeply. 'I don't know how I'm going to manage another night,' she said. 'How do you do it?'

Patricia smiled and poured the tea. She handed Annika a cup and settled back on the sofa.

'Everyone always exploits you,' she said. 'This is no worse than anything else.'

463

Annika took a sip of the tea and burned her mouth.

'You're wrong,' she said. 'This is worse than most other options. The girls at the club, you included, have crossed all manner of invisible boundaries in order to end up where you are.'

Patricia stirred the slice of lemon round in her cup.

'Maybe,' she said. 'Do you feel sorry for me?'

Annika reflected.

'No,' she said, 'not really. You know exactly what you're doing. You crossed those boundaries of your own free will. Doing that takes a certain sort of strength; it suggests a degree of flexibility. You're no shrinking violet, and that's a big advantage.'

Patricia looked hard at Annika.

'What about you, then?' she said. 'What boundaries have you crossed?'

Annika smiled wryly, and didn't answer.

Patricia put her cup down on the floor, sighed almost imperceptibly, and looked down at her hands.

'That morning,' she said, 'that last morning. Josefin and Joachim were fighting like cat and dog. They were really screaming at each other, in the office to start with, then up on the stairs. Josefin rushed out and he went after her.'

Annika sat in silence, aware that Patricia was sharing an important confidence. Patricia sat quietly for a moment before going on.

'Josie wanted to finish at the club; she wanted to take some time off before she started her course. She'd got into university, to do journalism in the school of media and communication. Joachim didn't want her to go. He kept trying to trap her, to tie her to the club and get her to give up her education. Josie told him she was going to leave anyway, that she'd earned enough money to pay for her breast enlargements ten times over. She told him they were finished, that their relationship was over. It was a really bad fight.'

Patricia fell silent again, and the sounds of the city waking up began to seep through the windows. The night-bus that stopped outside the passageway onto Hantverkargatan, the endless sirens, the autumn wind whispering of cold and rain.

'They used to have sex in the cemetery,' she whispered. 'Joachim got a kick out of it, but Josie thought it was really creepy. They used to climb over at the back; the railings aren't so high there. I always thought it was awful. Imagine, among all those graves . . .'

Annika said nothing, and they sat in silence for several minutes. It started to rain, first a few drops, then more seriously.

'I know what you're thinking,' Patricia said.

'What?' Annika said quietly.

'You're wondering why she stayed with him. Why she didn't just leave.'

Annika gave a deep sigh. 'I think I know why,' she said. 'To begin with she was in love and he was nice, then he started making little demands, simple little things that Josefin thought were sweet. He had opinions about who she should see, what she should do, how she should talk. Everything was fine to start with, until the bubble round them burst and Josefin wanted to engage with the outside world again – study, go to the cinema, talk to her friends on the phone. Then Joachim got angry, demanded that she stop all that and do what he wanted, and when she refused he hit her. Afterwards he was sorry, crying and telling her that he loved her.'

Patricia nodded in surprise. 'How do you know all that?'

Annika smiled sadly. 'There are plenty of books about domestic abuse,' she said. 'The evening papers often run

465

series of articles about that sort of violence. It usually follows a pattern, and I don't suppose Josefin was much different. She always thought it would get better, if only she could change and become the person he wanted her to be. Some days it probably went pretty well, and she must have thought they were working things out. But his need to control her just got bigger, and I imagine his jealousy got worse and worse. He criticized her more often, even in front of other people, and she felt her self-confidence draining away.'

Patricia nodded. 'It was like watching her slowly being brainwashed,' she said. 'He made Josie unsure of herself, made her think she wouldn't be able to handle her course. She was a useless, fat whore, and no one apart from him would ever love her. Josie cried more and more, until in the end she seemed to be in tears almost the whole time. She didn't dare leave him, he'd promised he would kill her if she ever tried.'

'Did he rape her?' Annika asked. 'Sexual violence is very common. Some men get excited if the woman is terrified . . . What is it?'

Patricia had covered her ears with her hands, screwing her eyes shut and clenching her jaw. She burst into a fit of tears.

'Patricia, whatever's the matter?'

Annika took the young woman in her arms and gently rocked her. Her tears fell as hard as the rain outside, an uncontrollable torrent, forced out by unbearable pressure.

'That was worst of all,' Patricia whispered when she had finally cried herself dry. 'When he used to rape her. Her screaming was so awful.'

Nineteen years, six months
and thirteen days

I see him coming through the fog of memory, the pattern repeats, the chorus kicks in. He works himself into the usual fury, starting by stamping about, ranting and swearing, then he hits me and starts yelling. I get all the usual signs, my field of vision shrinks, my shoulders slump, my elbows are stuck to my side, hands to my head. I lose focus, sound takes over, paralysis is near. A corner to sink into, a soundless plea for mercy.

His voice echoes in my head, and I can't hear my own. Terror is chanting within me, that nameless fear, that inarticulate horror. Maybe I try to scream, I don't know, his roars come and go, and I am transfigured, warmth spreads around me, redness arrives. No, I don't recognize any pain. The pressure is red and hot. The chanting stops with the worst of the blows, jumping like an old vinyl record, then resumes half a key higher. Terror, terror, fear and love. Don't hurt me! Oh please, just love me!

*Because he says
he will never
let me go.*

Friday 7 September

66

Annika still felt sick with tiredness when the alarm clock started ringing. She turned it off with a groan. Her legs ached, heavy as lead. The rain was still beating against the tin window ledge, an abstract rhythm that rose and fell in strength.

She settled into the sofa in the living room and made two phone-calls. She was in luck. Both the men she was calling were in. She arranged to meet the first in an hour's time, and the second one the next day. Then she crept into bed again and fought against sleep for half an hour. When she finally got up she felt even more tired. She smelled of sweat, sharp and pungent, but she didn't have the energy to shower. She rolled some deodorant under her arms and put on a thick sweater.

He had already arrived, and was sitting at a table by the window, staring out at the rain. In front of him were a cup of coffee and a glass of water.

'So do you recognize me?' Annika said, holding out her hand.

The man stood up and gave her a crooked smile.

'Of course,' he said. 'After all, we've bumped into each other before, quite literally.'

Annika blushed. They shook hands and sat down.

'So exactly what is it you want?' Q asked.

'Studio Six uses double-entry bookkeeping, and Joachim has a second set of books to fool the tax office. The real books, the ones with the actual takings in them, are only brought to the club very occasionally.'

Annika drank the detective's water in a single go. Q raised his eyebrows.

'Be my guest,' he said. 'I wasn't really thirsty.'

'The books are there now, until Saturday.'

'And how do you know that?' the detective asked quietly.

'I've taken a job as the croupier there. I'm not a journalist any more. I've resigned my job and left the union. The girls at the club are paid cash in hand. No tax, no national insurance.'

'Who told you that?'

'Patricia. She has no responsibility for, or influence over, the finances, but she enters the figures from the bar. And I saw it for myself this morning.'

The detective got up and went over to the counter. He got another cup of coffee and two glasses of water and brought them back to the table.

'You look like you could do with some caffeine,' he said.

Annika took a sip. The coffee was lukewarm.

'Why are you telling me this?' Q wondered.

She didn't reply.

'Do you see what you're doing?' he said.

She drank some water.

'What?'

'You're cooperating with the police,' he said. 'I thought doing something like that was beneath your dignity.'

'I don't have to worry about protecting my sources any more,' Annika said curtly. 'I'm no longer a representative of the mass media, so I can say what I like to the police.'

He looked at her in amusement. 'I see,' he said. 'But leopards don't change their spots so easily. If I know you at all, somewhere inside your head you're thinking how to turn this conversation into an article.'

She jerked. 'Bullshit. You don't know me at all.'

'Yes I do. I know the journalist in you.'

'She's dead.'

'Bullshit,' he countered. 'She's just wounded and tired. She's taking a rest, and will be back in the fight soon enough.'

'Never,' she said.

'So you're going to be a croupier at shitty dives for the rest of your life? What a shame.'

'I thought you said I was a real nuisance?'

He grinned. 'Well, you are, you're worse that a spot on the arse. And that's good, we need that. We need to feel we're alive.'

She was looking at him suspiciously.

'You're winding me up,' she said.

He sighed. 'Well, maybe just a little,' he said.

'You can get him on the bookkeeping,' she said. 'I don't know what's in there, but there ought to be enough to shut down the club. I'm committing a crime as well, by the way, using the roulette table for illegal gambling. Joachim seems to think that's okay.'

'You'll get caught,' Q said, 'sooner or later.'

'I was thinking of going again tonight, then no more after that. I earned eight thousand kronor last night. One more night will see me through until I can get unemployment benefit.'

'That's what everyone says,' Q told her.

Annika fell silent. She could feel her shame burning on her face. She realized he was right as she stared down at her hands.

473

'Well, I've said enough,' she said. 'Now I just want to listen.'

The detective got up and came back with a cheese sandwich.

'This is absolutely off the record,' he said. 'If you ever write about it I'll see you roasted slowly over hot coals.'

'"Unlawful threat",' Annika said.

He smiled quickly, then was serious again.

'You were right,' he said. 'We do regard the murder of Josefin Liljeberg as finished, at least as a police matter.'

'So why haven't you arrested him?' Annika said, a little too loudly.

Q leaned over the marble tabletop.

'Don't you think we would if we could?' he said quietly. 'Joachim's got a watertight alibi. Six men swear he was at a smart bar, the Sture Company, until five o'clock, then he went home with the other lads in a hired limousine for a private party. They all give the same story.'

'Maybe, but they're lying!' Annika said.

The detective took a bite of his sandwich.

'Of course they are,' he said, swallowing. 'The problem is proving that they're lying. One of the waiters at the Sture Company confirms that Joachim was there, but he can't say exactly when. And he can't tell us what time he left either. The limousine driver confirms that he drove a group of drunk young men from Stureplan to Birkastan, and Joachim has the receipt. The driver can neither confirm nor deny that Joachim was in the car because he couldn't see who was right at the back. Either way, Joachim certainly wasn't at the front, and he didn't pay. The girl who owns the flat on Rörstrandsgatan says Joachim fell asleep on her sofa sometime after six o'clock. She's probably telling the truth.'

'Joachim was at the club just before five,' Annika said

eagerly. 'He was having a fight with Josefin, Patricia heard them.'

Q sighed. 'Yes, we know. It's Patricia's word against the seven blokes. And if this case were ever to get to court and we somehow managed to break their story, we'd have to charge all of them with perjury. And that would be pretty impossible.'

They sat in silence for a few minutes. Annika drank the last of her cold coffee. The detective finished his sandwich.

'One of them might talk,' Annika said.

'Sure,' Q said. 'The problem is that most of them were too drunk to remember anything at all. They've had the story served up to them as the truth, so now they probably actually believe it. I should think maybe one, or at most two of them, actually know that they're lying. They're Joachim's best friends. And they've both suddenly got a lot of money to splash around. They're not going to squeal.'

Annika felt tired, almost ill.

'So what really happened?' she asked in a flat voice.

'Exactly what you think,' Q said. 'He strangled her in the cemetery.'

'And raped her?'

'No, not there, and not then. We found traces of sperm inside her, and the DNA test proved it was Joachim's. They'd probably had sex within the past few hours, and it was still there.'

Annika shut her eyes and searched her memory.

'But you said it was a sexually motivated killing to start with,' she said. 'You said there were traces of sexual violence.'

The detective rubbed his forehead.

'That was mostly old injuries,' he said. 'Mostly to the opening of the anus. He used to rape her anally.'

Annika felt like she was going to be sick.

'Bloody hell . . .' she said.

They sat in silence again.

'What about the other woman who was murdered in Kronoberg Park?' Annika suddenly asked. 'Eva – that was her name. That was never cleared up, was it?'

Q sighed. 'That's right, but the same thing applies there. We regard the case as closed. It was her former husband. We picked him up two or three years later, but had to let him go. We never got him convicted. He's dead now.'

'So is Joachim going to get away with it?' Annika said.

Q was putting his jacket on.

'Not if your information is correct,' he said. 'There isn't time to organize a raid tonight, but we'll be going in tomorrow. Make sure you're not there.'

He stood up, and stopped by her chair.

'There's one thing we're still wondering about,' he said.

'What?' Annika said.

'How she got the injury to her hand.'

Annika sat slouched on her chair as he left the café.

67

Time dragged by in the club. Patricia looked at Annika in concern.

'You look really knackered. Are you coming down with something?'

'I think I might be,' she said. 'I'm freezing, and I feel sick.'

They sat down on the wooden bench in the changing room, and the harsh lighting made the blisters on Annika's feet shine bright red.

'How much money have you taken tonight?' Patricia said.

Annika felt like crying.

'Not enough,' she said, staring down at her sky-blue bikini.

She was having more and more difficulty suppressing the urge to throw up. It was Friday, and there were even more girls wandering around the club completely naked. They were sitting on the men's laps, grinding their crotches against ironed creases and silk ties. They enticed the men into private rooms and smothered them in massage lotion: big bottles from the chemist, cheap and unperfumed.

'It has to be unperfumed,' Patricia had explained. 'They have to go home to their wives afterwards.'

Annika was nervous and worried. What if she'd got everything wrong?

She didn't dare ask Patricia anything else about the bookkeeping, and Patricia didn't bring it up again. What if the police came tonight after all? What if Joachim had already moved the books?

She brushed her hair from her face with trembling hands.

'Would you like a sandwich? Or some coffee?' Patricia asked anxiously.

Annika forced herself to smile. 'No thanks, I'll be fine in a minute or two.'

Joachim was sitting in the office next door. Thank goodness she had been busy with clients when he arrived.

How does someone end up like that? she thought. What has to be wrong with you to make you kill the person you love? How could you kill another person and then just carry on with your life as though nothing had happened?

'I'd better get out there again,' Patricia said. 'Coming?'

Annika leaned over and put fresh plasters on her blisters.

'Sure,' she said.

The music was louder now. Two girls were up on stage. One was writhing around the pole, thrusting against it and licking it, and the other had pulled a man out of the audience. He was smearing shaving foam over the girl's breasts, and she was moaning, head thrown back, in a semblance of ecstasy.

Annika followed Patricia behind the bar and poured herself a Coke.

'Don't you get fed up, having to look at that all night long?' Annika whispered in Patricia's ear.

'Another bottle of champagne on the bald one's bill,' one of the naked girls said to Patricia, who turned away to mark it up.

Annika went out, back to her table. She shivered, it was cold out there.

Sanna wasn't there. She settled onto the bar stool she had dragged behind the roulette table.

'How's business?'

Joachim was standing in the door of the office, smiling, arms folded.

Annika leaped to the floor at once.

'Okay, but not as good as last night.'

He came over to the table without letting his smile drop, and without looking away from her.

'I think you've got a great future ahead of you here,' he said, coming round the table to stand beside her.

Annika licked her lips and tried to smile.

'Thanks,' she said, and fluttered her eyelashes.

'So how come you ended up here?' he said, his voice a touch cooler.

Lie, she thought, but keep it as close to the truth as possible.

'I needed to make some money fast,' she said, looking up at him. 'I got fired from my last job – they thought I was a troublemaker. A . . . a customer complained about me and the boss got jittery.'

Joachim laughed, stroked her shoulder and let his hand linger on her breast.

'What sort of work was it?'

She swallowed, fighting an urge to pull away from him.

'Supermarket,' she said. 'The meat counter at Vivo on Fridhemsplan. Slicing sausage all day long. Not exactly fun, day after day.'

He laughed loudly, and removed his hand.

'I'm not surprised you got out,' he said. 'Who did you work with?'

Her heart stopped. Did he know someone there?

'Sorry?' she said with a smile. 'You've got friends in the sausage world?'

He burst out laughing. 'You really should consider going on stage,' he said when he'd calmed down, taking another step closer. 'You'd look great under the spotlights. Haven't you ever dreamed of being a star?'

He thrust both hands into her hair, caressing her neck. To her horror, it made her crotch tingle.

'What, a star like Josefin?'

The question slipped out of her mouth before she had time to think. He reacted as though she'd slapped him, letting go of her and stepping back.

'What the fuck? What do you know about her?'

Fuck, how stupid could she possibly be? she thought, cursing her big mouth.

'She worked here, didn't she?' she said, unable to suppress a shiver.

'Did you know her, or what?'

Annika smiled nervously. 'No, not at all, I never met her. But Patricia told me she worked here . . .'

He stepped closer again and put his face right up to hers.

'Things didn't turn out well for Josefin,' he said tightly. 'We have a lot of powerful clients, you see. She thought she could trick them out of their money. Watch out for that. Never try to trick anyone here, not the clients, and not me.'

Joachim turned on his heel and went up the spiral staircase.

Annika grabbed the roulette wheel, ready to faint.

Nineteen years, seven months
and fifteen days

I'm driven by a desire to understand. I know I'm look-ing for explanations and connections that may not even exist. What do I know about the way love works?

He isn't really mean. Just isolated, small and fragile, damaged by his childhood. There's no reason why his sense of powerlessness should always express itself the way it does. When he grows up maybe he'll drop the violence. My own pathetic lack of faith makes me horribly ashamed. I've been far too quick to judge him. I take my own development for granted, and ignore his completely.

Even so, I feel a great chill in my chest.

Because he says
he will never
let me go.

Saturday 8 September

68

It felt odd to be going up in the lift again. She remembered the last time she had been in there, when she had been convinced it was the last time ever.

Nothing lasts for ever, she thought. Everything is cyclical.

The newsroom was light, quiet and completely empty, just the way she liked it. Ingvar Johansson had his back to the door and was talking on the phone. He didn't see her.

Anders Schyman was sitting behind his desk in the aquarium.

'Come in,' he said, gesturing towards the dark red leather sofa that had replaced its stinking predecessor. Annika shut the door behind her, glancing out at the newsroom behind the tired curtains. It felt odd that it all looked just the same as when she left, almost as if she'd never been there.

'You look well,' he said.

Rubbish, Annika thought.

'I can't imagine I was ever this tired before,' she said, sitting down on the sofa. The seat was firm, the leather cold.

'How was the Caucasus?' he wondered.

She didn't follow, and bit her lip.

'Isn't that where you were going?' Schyman said.

'There were no last-minute deals,' Annika said. 'I went to Turkey instead.'

The head editor smiled. 'That was lucky,' he said. 'They're heading for war down there. The army's mobilizing, apparently.'

Annika nodded. 'The government forces have got hold of some weapons at last.'

The sat in silence for a few moments.

'So what is it that you're working on?' Schyman asked.

Annika took a deep breath.

'I haven't written it yet,' she said. 'I haven't got a computer at home. I thought I'd tell you about it instead and you can see what you think.'

'Go ahead,' the head editor said.

Annika pulled the photocopies out of her bag.

'It's about the murder of Josefin Liljeberg and the minister suspected of killing her,' she said.

Anders Schyman waited without saying anything.

'The minister didn't kill her,' she said. 'The police regard the case as finished. It was her boyfriend, Joachim, the owner of the sex club. They can't arrest him, because he's got six witnesses to confirm his alibi. They can't all be convicted of perjury, but the police are sure they're lying.'

Annika fell silent and looked at her papers.

'So no one will ever be charged with her murder?' Schyman said slowly.

'Nope,' Annika said. 'It'll remain unsolved unless one of the six men talks. It'll be beyond the statute of limitations in twenty-five years.'

She stood up and laid two receipts on Schyman's desk.

'Look at these,' she said. 'This one's the bill from

486

Studio Six, from the night of twenty-seventh to the twenty-eighth of July this year. Seven people enjoyed "entertainment and refreshments" worth fifty-five thousand, six hundred kronor. It's under Josefin's name, you can see that from this code, and it was paid for with a Diners Club card issued to Christer Lundgren. Look at the signature.'

Anders Schyman picked up the photocopy and studied it.

'It's illegible,' he said.

'Yep,' Annika said. 'Now look at this one.'

She handed him the expenses claim from Tallinn.

'Christer Lundgren,' Schyman read, then looked up at Annika's face. 'These were written by different people.'

Annika nodded and moistened her lips. Her mouth was completely dry and she wished she had a glass of water.

'The Minister for Foreign Trade was never at the sex club,' she said. 'I think the Studio Six bill was signed for by his undersecretary in the department.'

Anders Schyman picked up the first receipt again and held it close to his glasses.

'Yes,' he said. 'That would make sense.'

'Christer Lundgren was in Tallinn that night,' Annika said. 'He flew out with Estonian Air at eight o'clock on the evening of July twenty-seventh; you can see that from the expenses claim. He met someone there, and flew back on a private plane in the early hours of the next morning.'

The head editor looked at the other photocopy.

'Bloody hell,' he said. 'What was he doing there?'

Annika breathed in.

'The meeting was top secret,' she said. 'It was to do with weapons exports. He didn't want to make the expenses claim through his own department where it might be found. He sent it to the Inspectorate for Strategic Products.'

Anders Schyman looked up at her. 'The body that monitors Swedish weapons exports?'

Annika nodded.

'Are you sure?'

She pointed at the verification stamp without speaking.

'Good grief,' the head editor said. 'Why?'

'I can only think of one explanation,' Annika said. 'There was something dodgy about this deal.'

Anders Schyman frowned. 'That doesn't make sense,' he said. 'Why would the government get involved with anything like a dodgy weapons deal?'

Annika straightened her back and gulped.

'I don't think they had any choice,' she said quietly.

Schyman leaned back in his chair.

'This is starting to get a bit tenuous,' he said.

'I know,' Annika said stubbornly, 'but the facts remain: Christer Lundgren went to Tallinn that night to do something so controversial that he'd rather be suspected of murder and have to resign than tell anyone what he was really doing. That much is absolute fact. And what could possibly be worse than that?'

She had stood up and was gesticulating wildly now. Anders Schyman was looking at her thoughtfully.

'I assume you have a theory,' he said.

'IB,' she said. 'The lost archives of the Information Bureau – the originals that would ruin the Social Democrats for the foreseeable future if they ever came out.'

Schyman leaned over his desk.

'They were destroyed.'

'I don't think so,' Annika said. 'A copy of the foreign archive arrived at the Defence Ministry on July seventeenth this year. It was a warning to the government:

488

do as we say, or the rest will come out. In their original form.'

'But,' Schyman said, 'how on earth could that have happened?'

Annika sat on the corner of the desk and sighed.

'The Social Democrats were spying on Communists for the whole of the post-war period, storing whatever information they could find about them. Do you suppose the lads over there just sat and twiddled their thumbs while that was going on?'

She pointed over her shoulder, towards the Russian Embassy complex.

'Hardly,' she continued. 'They were perfectly aware of what the Swedes were up to.'

She stood up and dug her notebook out of her bag.

'In the spring of 1973 Elmér and his cronies knew that Guillou and Bratt were on their trail,' she said. 'The Social Democrats started to panic. And the Russians would have been aware of that. They realized the Swedes would try to remove any trace of their spying. So what did they do?'

She held out the text she had copied from the newspaper articles published on 2 April 1973.

'The Russians stole the archives,' she said. 'The senior KGB officer posted to the embassy in Stockholm made sure everything was taken out of the country, probably in large diplomatic bags.'

Schyman took her notepad and read in silence.

'And who was the senior KGB officer in Stockholm in the early 1970s? Well, he just happens to be the man who is currently President of that benighted country in the Caucasus. He even speaks Swedish. And that President has a massive problem: he has no weapons to fight the guerrillas with, and the global community has decreed that he isn't allowed to buy any.'

489

The head editor was staring at the photocopies again.

Annika sat down on the sofa and presented her conclusion: 'So what does the President do? He digs out his old files from twenty-four Grevgatan and fifty-six Valhallavägen. If the Swedish government won't supply him with arms, he'll make sure they're out of power for decades. First the government refuses to listen. Maybe they think he hasn't actually got the archives, which is why that warning was sent to the Ministry of Defence. A selection of papers from the foreign section of the archive, not enough to bring down the government, but enough to be a problem in the middle of an election campaign. So the Prime Minister decides to send one of his ministers to meet representatives of the President. They meet halfway, in Estonia. The deal is agreed, and the weapons are shipped at once via a third country, probably Singapore. And the army mobilizes.'

Annika rubbed her forehead.

'It all goes according to plan,' she said. 'There's just one problem. The same night that the meeting in Tallinn takes place, a young woman is killed outside the minister's front door. Through a bizarre set of circumstances it turns out that the minister's undersecretary took a group of German union bosses to the sex club where the woman worked, and paid the bill with the minister's card. The minister is in the shit. And he can't do anything. He can't tell anyone where he's been, or what he's done . . .'

The ensuing silence was deafening. Annika could see Anders Schyman's brain whirring at high speed. He was looking between the photocopies and the notebook, making his own notes, running a hand through his hair.

'Bloody hell,' he said. 'This is incredible . . . So what does he have to say?'

490

Annika swallowed in a desperate attempt to moisten her throat. It didn't really work.

'I've only spoken to his wife, Anna-Lena. Christer Lundgren refuses to come to the phone. Then I tried to go through his press secretary, Karina Björnlund. I laid out the whole scenario for her, exactly as I thought it had unfolded. She said she'd try to get a comment from him, but she never called back . . .'

They sat in silence again, until the head editor cleared his throat.

'How many people have you told about this?' he asked.

'No one,' Annika said quickly. 'Only you.'

'And Karina Björnlund. Anyone else?'

Annika shut her eyes and thought.

'No,' she said. 'Just you and Karina Björnlund.'

She felt her muscles tense. Here came the counter-argument.

'This is absolutely fascinating,' Anders Schyman said. 'But it isn't publishable.'

'Why not?' Annika snapped.

'Too many loose threads,' Schyman said. 'Your reasoning is logical, even highly credible, but it can't be proved.'

'But I've got copies of the receipts!' Annika said.

'Yes, you have, but that isn't enough. You know that.'

Annika didn't reply.

'The fact that the minister was in Tallinn is new, but it doesn't give him an alibi for the murder. He was home by five, when the girl was killed. Remember, the neighbour who met him at the door?'

Annika nodded. Schyman went on: 'Christer Lundgren has resigned, and you don't kick—'

'You don't kick a man when he's down, I know,'

Annika said. 'But we can publish the facts: the break-ins at the addresses where the archives were kept, the travel expenses, the receipt from the sex club . . .'

The head editor sighed. 'To what purpose? To prove that the government is smuggling arms? Imagine the implications for freedom of the press that would inevitably follow something like that.'

Annika was staring at the floor.

'This story is dead, Annika,' Anders Schyman said.

'What about the claim for the trip to Tallinn?' she said quietly. 'Isn't that something?'

Schyman sighed. 'Maybe,' he said, 'if circumstances were different. Unfortunately the editor-in-chief is now allergic to this whole story. He says no the moment you so much as mention the murder or the minister. And, frankly, the fact that a minister travels to a meeting in a neighbouring country is hardly controversial enough for me to want to risk my job over it.

'We've got nothing to prove who he met, or why. Any trade minister probably travels abroad three hundred times a year anyway.'

'So why did he make the claim through the Inspectorate for Strategic Products?' Annika wondered quietly.

'That is odd, but it's hardly a story in itself. The department must send out hundreds of invoices and expenses claims every day, and this one isn't particularly controversial. There's hardly anything wrong with the minister responsible for foreign trade travelling abroad.'

Annika felt her heart sink. Deep down she knew Anders Schyman was right. Now she just wanted to die, for the floor to open up and swallow her.

The head editor stood up and looked out at the newsroom.

'We could do with you here,' he said.

Annika started. 'What?'

Schyman sighed. 'We could do with someone of your calibre on the crime team. At the moment there are only three of them: Berit Hamrin, Nils Langeby and Eva-Britt Qvist. Berit could do with someone competent alongside her.'

'I've never met the other two,' Annika said quietly.

Schyman turned to face Annika.

'What are you doing at the moment? Have you found another job?'

She shook her head.

The head editor came and sat next to her on the sofa.

'I'm very sorry we can't publish what you've come up with,' he said. 'You've done a brilliant job to find out all of this, but the story is simply too incredible for us to be able to tell it.'

Annika didn't answer, just sat staring at her hands. They were cold and damp. Schyman looked at her without speaking for a few seconds.

'The worst thing is that you're probably right,' he said.

'I've got something else,' Annika said. 'I can't write it myself, but you can give it to Berit.'

She picked up her bag and took out the copy of the television presenter's receipt. It was a copy of a copy: she had used the photocopier in the post office on Hantverkargatan.

'He hired two girls and spent almost an hour with them in a private room. On the way out he bought three films involving animals. But this is the real story: he paid with his Swedish Television bank card.'

Schyman whistled. 'Bloody hell,' he said. 'This one's nice and straightforward: TV star in brothel on licence-payers' money.'

Annika smiled weakly.

'Glad I had something for you,' she said sarcastically.

'Why don't you write it yourself?' Schyman asked.

'You don't want to know,' Annika said.

'But surely you'd like something in return. Does anything come to mind?'

Annika looked out at the deserted newsroom, bathed in weak autumn sun.

'A job,' she whispered.

Schyman returned to his desk and looked through a file.

'Sub-editor in Jansson's night team, from November,' he said. 'To cover maternity leave. How does that sound?'

Annika blinked away a tear without Schyman noticing.

'It sounds good – sold!' she said.

'It's a six-month post, and the terms will need to be negotiated,' the head editor said. 'The hours are horrible, ten p.m. to six a.m., four nights on, four nights off. You'll have to wait for a formal offer, but this time I'm not backing down. This job is yours. Shall we shake on it?'

He stood up and offered her his hand. She got up and shook it, embarrassed that hers was so cold and clammy.

'Good to have you back,' Schyman said with a smile.

'There's just one more thing,' Annika said. 'You remember that *Studio Six* said they'd found the receipt from the sex club at the Foreign Ministry?'

Schyman blinked, thought for a moment, then shook his head. 'I don't remember.'

'I'm one hundred per cent sure,' Annika said. 'But it wasn't there; it was in the Ministry of Enterprise, Energy and Communications. What do you think that means?'

Schyman looked at her thoughtfully.

'Probably exactly what you think it means,' he said. 'They didn't find it themselves.'

Annika smiled. 'Exactly.'

'Some lobbyist let them have it,' Schyman said. 'It was planted.'

'Ironic, isn't it?' Annika said as she walked out.

69

The rain clouds seemed to be hanging just above the treetops, and the wind was raw. She turned up her collar and walked down towards Fridhemsplan. She felt a great, warm calmness inside: she was being allowed to join in again. Sub-editing wasn't the best thing she could think of, but it still felt like a triumph. She would sit on the edge of the night desk and go through other reporters' articles, correcting typos and bad grammar, shortening text if necessary, adding a sentence if need be. She would come up with captions and small fact boxes, suggest headlines and rewrite unclear text.

She had no illusions about why Schyman had offered her the job. No one on the paper wanted it, and they would have to get someone in from outside. Even though it made an important contribution to the finished news-paper, it was regarded as a terrible job. No byline, no glamour, no chance of heading off to Café Opera after work to show off. No fun at all.

But they've never run a roulette table in a brothel, Annika thought.

The wind freshened as she emerged onto the ramp of the Western Bridge. She was walking slowly, taking deep breaths, holding the air in. She shut her eyes to the dampness, letting her hair blow however it wanted.

November, she thought. Almost two months till then. Freedom to think and recharge her batteries. Time to clean out her flat in Hälleforsnäs and insulate the windows on Hantverkargatan. Time to go to the Museum of Modern Art, to go to the theatre. To visit Grandma, to cuddle Whiskas.

All of a sudden she realized how much she missed her cat. She couldn't have him in the city; he'd have to stay with Grandma.

And she had to finish with Sven.

There, she'd thought it. She'd been putting off thinking about it all summer. She shivered in the wind and pulled her coat more tightly round her. Summer was definitely over; it was time to dig out the autumn wardrobe.

She walked along the Drottningholm road, kicking the wet leaves that had started to gather on the pavement. She didn't look up until she was right next to the park.

The vegetation of Kronoberg Park seemed like a pulsating, rotting mass.

Slowly she walked up to the cemetery. The damp air made the railings glisten. The air was still, the wind unable to reach the ground here. The sounds of the city faded away, absorbed by the dying greenery.

Annika stopped by the entrance and put her hand on the padlock, closing her eyes. Suddenly she remembered the heat of the summer, and how dizzy she had felt that day when Josefin lay stretched out between the graves, the sun playing over the granite, the rumble of the underground trains far below.

So meaningless, she thought. What had Josefin Liljeberg's life been for? Why was she born, why did she learn to read, count, write, why did she worry about her beautiful body changing? What was the point, if she was only going to die?

There had to be some meaning, Annika thought. There has to be an underlying reason for everything. Otherwise how could we bear it?

'Hello, you! What are you doing here?'

Annika groaned to herself.

'Hi, Daniella,' she said. 'How are things?'

'Great, thanks,' Daniella Hermansson chirruped. 'We've been in the park, but it got too cold. We've got a nursery place from next Monday. It feels a bit nervy, but I'm sure we'll be fine.'

Her son was scowling from his pushchair.

'Would you like to come up for coffee? It would be good to have a nice, girly chat.'

Annika remembered Daniella's piss-poor coffee with horror.

'Another time, perhaps,' she said with a smile. 'I'm just on my way home.'

Daniella looked around, then took a step closer to Annika.

'You're with the press,' she said in a stage whisper. 'Did they ever catch that bloke?'

'The one who killed Josefin? No, they didn't. Not for murder, anyway.'

Daniella sighed. 'It's awful, that he's still out there.'

'The police know who he is,' Annika said. 'They're going to get him anyway, for something else. He won't be free for much longer.'

Daniella Hermansson breathed a sigh of relief.

'That's good to know. Well, none of us ever believed it could have been Christer.'

'Not even your neighbour, the lady with the dog?'

Daniella giggled in a nervous and rather practised way.

'Well,' she said, 'don't tell anyone, but Elna had already seen the body by then, at five o'clock that morning.'

Annika felt herself stiffen, and made an effort to look friendly.

'Really?' she said. 'How come?'

'Her dog – you've seen him, Jesper? Lovely little thing! Anyway, the dog ran into the cemetery and bit the girl, and poor Elna didn't know what to do. She daren't call the police, she thought they'd put Jesper in prison. Have you ever heard anything so silly?'

Daniella laughed brightly. Annika swallowed.

'No,' she said, 'I haven't.'

The child started to howl, tired of his mother's chatter.

'Okay, little fellow, let's get you home and you can have a banana, that'll be nice, won't it?'

The woman skipped off homewards down Kronobergsgatan. Annika stood and watched her go.

Everything has its explanation, she thought.

Slowly she headed in the opposite direction, towards the fire station. No sooner had she turned the corner than she saw the police cars blocking the whole road. She stopped.

They're early, she thought. I hope they find the books.

She took a different route home.

Nineteen years, eleven months
and one day

Roughness against bare skin, air heavy with dust, air used up: my life shrunk to the size of a coffin. The lid touching my head, my knees and elbows scratch the sides.

Deep hole, dark grave, smell of earth.

Panic.

He says I've misunderstood everything, that I've got it all out of proportion. It's not that life is too small, it's that I'm too big.

His love is endless. He loves me in spite of everything. No one could give me what he does. He has just one condition.

He says
he will never
let me go.

Sunday 9 September

70

Her decision matured overnight. She was going to finish with Sven. There was another life, she'd finally found a way out.

The situation filled her with a sense of sadness and loss. She and Sven had been an item for so long. She'd never slept with anyone else. She shed a few tears in the shower.

The rain had stopped, and the sun was pale and cold. She made coffee and rang the station to check the times. The next train to Flen left in an hour and ten minutes.

She opened the living-room window, sat on the sofa and watched the curtains gently breathing. She was allowed to stay. She was allowed to live her own life.

Annika had got up, put on her coat and was on her way out when she heard the sound of keys on the other side of the door. She stiffened, but relaxed when she saw it was Patricia.

'Hi,' Annika said. 'Where've you been?'

Patricia closed the door carefully behind her, holding on to the handle for a few seconds before looking up.

'How could you?' she said breathlessly.

Her face was flushed, her eyes red from crying. Annika was horrified, realizing immediately what had happened.

'You were at the club,' she said. 'They got you in the raid!'

'You shafted me, you shut down the club. How could you?'

Patricia walked towards her, her mouth twisted, fists clenched. Annika stood where she was and tried to exude calm.

'I haven't shut down any club,' she said.

Patricia took another step closer and gave her a shove, throwing her keys on the floor, and Annika took a couple of involuntary steps back.

'I did it to help you!' Patricia yelled. 'You needed money, I got you a job. Why did you do this to me?'

Annika held her hands in front of her as she backed into the living room.

'Patricia, I didn't mean you any harm, you must know that? I want nothing but good for you! I want to help you. I want you to get away from that club, from the degradation—'

'Don't you see what's going to happen?' Patricia shouted. 'He's going to blame me! He's fucked all the other girls there, they're all his! I was Josefin's; he's got no loyalty to me. He's going to drag me into the shit. Oh, God!'

The young woman started to howl with anguish and Annika took hold of her shoulders and shook her.

'That's not true!' she said. 'The other girls will tell the truth. Go to the police and tell them what really happened, they'll believe you.'

Patricia tossed her head back and laughed, loud and shrill.

'You're so naïve, Annika,' she said, with tears running down her face. 'You always think the truth will win in the end. Ha! Grow up! It never does!'

She pulled herself away and rushed into her bedroom,

threw her things in her sports bag and started dragging
the mattress behind her. It got caught in the doorway.
Patricia yanked at it, swearing under her breath.

'You don't have to leave,' Annika said.

The mattress came loose and Patricia almost fell over.
She was shaking with emotion as she pulled the lump of
foam behind her.

'I'm staying,' Annika said. 'I've got a job at the
Evening Post again. You can stay as long as you want.'

Patricia had reached the front door. She stiffened.

'What did you say?' she said. 'You got a job?'

Annika smiled nervously.

'I found out a load of stuff and told the head editor,
and he's given me a job again.'

Patricia let go of the mattress, turned and walked up
to Annika. Her dark eyes were burning like fire.

'Fuck you!' she snarled. 'Fuck anyone who shafts
their friends!'

'But it didn't have anything to do with you,' Annika
tried to explain, 'or with the club—'

'And you told the police, you fucking bitch! How the
fuck could you have known that the accounts would be
there, then? You shafted me, your friend, for a fucking job!' Patricia had lost control completely and was
screaming at Annika now.

'What a revolting piece of fucking shit you are! Fuck
you!'

Annika backed away, hearing her own words echo in
her head. Bloody hell, Patricia's right. What have I done,
what have I done?

The young woman ran back to her mattress, grabbed
it and left the flat without bothering to close the door.

Annika rushed over to the window and saw Patricia
run off, dragging her mattress behind her over the
gravel. Slowly she walked through to the little maid's

505

room. A glass lay on its side on the floor, and Josefin's pink dress was still hanging on the wall.

Annika felt tears welling up.

'I'm so sorry,' she whispered. 'I didn't mean this to happen.'

She was numb all the way to Flen. She watched the farmland fly past, unable to feel anything, unable to eat anything. The sound of the rails beneath the train turned into chants in her head: Studio Six, her fault, Patri-cia, her fault, be-trayal, her fault, her fault, her fault . . .

She put her hands over her ears and closed her eyes.

The bus was already at the bus-stop outside the station, which was something, she supposed. It set off for Hälleforsnäs a few minutes later, passing through Mellösa and stopping at a DIY store in Flenmo.

This could be the last time I'm coming home when I come back here, she thought.

She got out at the supermarket as usual, and watched the bus as it disappeared down the road. She didn't feel like going home, couldn't face her soon-to-be-abandoned flat yet. After some hesitation she decided to go to her mother's.

It would be an exaggeration to say that her mother was pleased to see her.

'Come in,' she said. 'I've just made coffee.'

Annika sat down at the kitchen table, still feeling numb and ashamed.

'I've found a house,' her mother said, putting out another cup.

Annika pretended not to hear, and looked out at the old ironworks through the window.

'Carport and pool,' her mother went on, louder this time. 'White bricks. It's big – seven rooms. There's room for you and Sven as well.'

'I don't want to live in Eskilstuna,' Annika said without looking away from the ironworks.

'It's in Svista, outside the town. Hugelstaborg. It's a nice area. Good people.'

Annika blinked and looked away from the window, then closed her eyes in irritation.

'What do you want seven rooms for?'

Her mother stopped fussing about, evidently hurt.

'I only want room for you, for you and Sven and Birgitta. And the grandchildren, of course.'

Annika stood up, and her mother blinked innocently.

'You're probably going to have to rely on Birgitta, then,' Annika said. 'I'm not going to be having any kids for a long time yet.'

She went over to the sink, took a glass out of the cupboard above and filled it from the tap. Her mother was watching her, gently reproachful.

'And is Sven allowed to have an opinion about this, then?'

Annika spun round. 'What's that supposed to mean?'

Her mother tilted her chin. 'Some people think you bully him. Just moving to Stockholm like that, without asking him.'

Annika's face was white with rage. 'What would you know about that?' she said.

Her mother fumbled for a packet of cigarettes, clicking her lighter several times before it worked. She took a deep drag and coughed hard.

'You know nothing about me and Sven,' Annika said once the woman had finished coughing. 'Do you mean to say I should have turned down this chance for his sake, is that it? Do my career and income have to depend on his bloody goodwill? Is that really what you think? Well?'

507

Her mother had tears in her eyes when she finally got her breath back.

'Goodness, I really must stop smoking these horrid things.'

She tried to smile, but Annika didn't smile back.

'Of course I think you should make an effort with your job. You're so talented. But it's hard up there, everybody knows that. No one's blaming you for failing.'

Annika turned and filled her glass again. Her mother came over and stroked her arm rather clumsily.

'Annika,' she said, 'don't be so angry with me.'

'I'm not angry with you,' Annika said in a subdued voice, without turning round.

Her mother hesitated. 'It seems like it, sometimes,' she said.

Annika turned round and looked at her mother with tired eyes.

'I just don't understand why you insist on thinking you should move to some flashy house in Eskilstuna. You don't have the money! Where would you work? Or are you thinking of commuting to the supermarket here?'

Now it was her mother's turn to look away.

'There are lots of jobs in Eskilstuna,' she said, affronted. 'Good, honest cashiers don't grow on trees, you know.'

'So why don't you start with that, then? Start by looking for a job! It doesn't make sense to start with the luxury villa, surely you can see that?'

The woman took several deep drags on her cigarette.

'You don't respect me,' she said.

'Of course I do!' Annika said, holding her arms out. 'Good grief, you're my mother! I just think you should keep your feet on the ground. If you want to live in a detached house, why not buy one here in Hälleforsnäs! They hardly cost anything! I saw another For Sale sign in Flen today – have you called to see how much they want for that one?'

'Finns,' her mother said contemptuously.

'Now you're just being stupid,' Annika said.

'What about you, then?' her mother said. 'You don't want to live here either. You only want to live in Stockholm.'

Annika held her arms out again.

'That's not because there's anything wrong with Hälleforsnäs! I love this place. But the job I want just isn't here.'

Her mother put her cigarette out on the sink. Her cheeks were glowing, and she had red circles round her eyes. Her voice was shaking.

'I don't want to live in an old hovel in this shithole, surely you can understand that! I'd rather stay here, in this flat.'

'Okay, why don't you?' Annika said, picking up her bag and walking out.

71

She picked up her bicycle and went off to see Sven.

There was no point in putting it off any longer. He lived in the old stable that had belonged to the ironworks. It had once been a smart, impressive building, but now it just sat, miserable and rundown, at the bottom of Tattarbacken.

He was home, sitting and drinking a few beers as he watched the football on television.

'Darling,' he said, getting up to give her a hug. 'You've no idea how glad I am that you're home.'

She tried to wriggle discreetly out of his arms, her heart thudding, her legs trembling.

'I'm here to pack, Sven,' she said, her voice shaking.

He smiled. 'Yes, I want us to move in together as well.'

She gulped and gasped for air, on the brink of bursting into tears.

'Sven,' she said, 'I've got a job in Stockholm. At the *Evening Post*. They want me back. I start in November.'

She was clutching the strap of her bag nervously. She still had her outdoor shoes on.

Sven shook his head. 'But that's never going to work,' he said. 'You can't commute every day; surely even you can see that?'

She closed her eyes as her tears brimmed over.

'I'm going to move,' she said. 'For good. I've given up the flat and my job at the *Courier*.'

As she said this she began to back instinctively towards the door.

'What the fuck are you saying?'

Sven came towards her.

'I'm so sorry,' she sobbed. 'I never wanted to hurt you. I really did love you.'

'You're leaving me?' he said breathlessly, grabbing her by the arms.

She leaned her head back and shut her eyes, tears running down her face and neck.

'This is how it has to be,' she said breathlessly. 'You deserve someone who loves you more. I can't do it any more.'

He started to shake her, slowly at first, then more violently.

'What the fuck do you mean?' he shouted. 'Are you trying to say you're dumping me? *Me?*'

Annika wept, her head hit the door behind her as she tried to hold him away from her.

'Sven,' she said, 'Sven, listen to me—'

'Why the fuck should I listen to you?' he screamed. 'You've been lying to me all fucking summer! You said you wanted to give living in Stockholm a try, but you never had any intention of coming home, did you? Christ, you really pulled a fast one on me!'

Annika stopped crying at once and looked him right in the eye.

'You're absolutely right,' she said. 'All I want is to be free of you.'

He let go of her, staring at her incredulously.

She turned and kicked the door open, then just ran.

Nineteen years, eleven months and twenty-five days

Yesterday the tears never came, the terrified panic when the attack is over. The heat was too much, it grew and grew until the red became black. They say he saved my life. Mouth-to-mouth brought back the spirit that his hands had released. I can't talk yet. The damage may be permanent. He says I got a piece of meat caught in my throat, and I can see in the eyes of the doctors that they don't believe him. But no one asks.

He cries on my blanket. He's been holding my hand for hours. He prays and prays.

If I do as he asks I will be removing the last barrier. I will be erasing what remains of my personality, there will be nothing left. He will have reached his goal. Nothing will stop him from taking the final step. And he won't be able to call back my spirit.

He says
he will kill me
if I leave.

Monday 10 September

72

The lake sparkled like an icy sapphire in the morning sun. Annika was slowly walking down to the water with Whiskas at her heels. The cat leaped and danced round her feet, completely giddy with joy. She laughed and picked him up. The animal rubbed against her chin, licking her neck and purring like a little machine.

'You're the soppiest cat in the world, do you know that?' Annika said, scratching him behind the ears.

She put him down on the jetty and looked out across the lake. The wind, light and mild, rippled the glittering surface. Annika squinted, looking at the rocks emerge from the water on the far shore and disappear under their blanket of pine trees. In the far distance, where the lake stopped and the denser forest began, was where Old Gustav lived. She really ought to look in on him one day; it was ages since she last saw him.

The future lay ahead of her like an unpainted watercolour. She could choose what colours and patterns to paint, how strong they should be, how deep.

Warm and satisfying, she thought. Light and easy.

The cat curled up in her lap and fell asleep. She shut her eyes, her fingers stroking the cat's soft fur. She was filled with an intense feeling of happiness. This is what life should be like, she thought.

Her grandmother called something from the cottage and Annika straightened her back and listened. Whiskas pricked his ears and jumped down from the jetty. The old woman was forming her hands into a megaphone.

'Breakfast!'

Annika jogged back up to the cottage. The cat thought they were having a race and rushed off like an idiot. When she got to the steps he jumped out of his hiding place and attacked her feet. Annika picked up the wriggling animal, burrowed her nose into his fur and blew on his stomach.

'Now you're just being silly, aren't you!' she said.

Her grandmother had laid out sour milk, wild raspberries, rye bread and cheese. The smell of coffee hung in the air. Annika realized how hungry she was.

'No, down you go,' she said to the cat, who was trying to jump onto her lap.

'He's going to miss you,' her grandmother said.

Annika sighed. 'I'll come and visit often,' she said.

Her grandmother poured the coffee into delicate cups.

'I want you to know that I think you're doing the right thing,' she said. 'You need to focus on your work. Taking responsibility by making your own living gives you self-belief and satisfaction, I've always thought that. You shouldn't be with a man who holds you back.'

They ate in silence, the sun shining onto the kitchen table, making the wax-cloth soft and warm.

'Are there many mushrooms?'

Her grandmother laughed. 'I wondered how long it would be before you asked. There are masses of them this year.'

Annika jumped up.

'I'll go and pick some for lunch.'

She dug out two plastic bags from the bottom drawer

and hurried into the forest, with Whiskas bounding after her.

Within the gloom of the forest she had to blink several times before she could make out the pattern of the moss. She could hardly believe her eyes. The ground was completely covered with brown mushrooms, growing in clumps of hundreds, maybe thousands at a time.

She filled her two bags, taking less than an hour. Whiskas caught two wood mice while she was busy.

'Who's going to clean all of those?' her grandmother said, looking horrified at the thought.

Annika laughed and tipped the first bag onto the table.

'It's not so bad,' she said, but as usual it took longer to clean the mushrooms than it did to pick them.

They ate fried bread and two mountains of mushrooms for lunch.

'I'm out of bread and butter now,' her grandmother said once the washing-up was done.

'I'll cycle in and get some,' Annika said.

The old woman smiled. 'That's kind of you.'

Annika brushed her hair and fetched her bag.

'Right, now you stay with Grandma,' she said to the cat.

Whiskas ignored her and bounded off ahead of her towards the barrier by the road.

'No,' Annika said, picking him up and carrying him back to the cottage. 'I'm going to be riding on the road, and you could get run over. You have to stay here.'

The cat wriggled free and ran off into the forest. Annika sighed.

'Can you shut him in when he comes back?' she said to her grandmother. 'I don't want him running around on the road.'

She strolled off towards her bike. The sun was shining low in the sky, clear and sharp. She saw the chrome of the bicycle in the distance, twinkling as it stood beside the barrier.

Only when she got closer did she realize something was wrong. She took hold of the handlebar and leaned the bike away from her to get a better look. Both tyres had been cut to shreds, as had the saddle. She stared at it, unable to work out what had happened.

'That's just the start, you fucking whore.'

She gasped and looked up. Sven was standing in the ditch a couple of metres away. She knew what was coming.

'I've trashed the whole of your fucking flat,' he said. 'And I've cut up all your slut clothes.'

He staggered, with a snort. Annika could see he was drunk. Slowly she went round the barrier without taking her eyes off him.

'You're angry, Sven,' she said. 'You're drunk. You're not yourself. Think about what you're saying.'

He started to cry, flailing with his arms.

'You're a SLUT and now you're going to DIE!'

She dropped her bag and ran. Her vision narrowed, everything went white. She raced as fast as she could, a branch hit her face, cutting her cheek, she fell, stood up again; sound, where was all the sound? Oh God, run, run. Feet thudding against soil; shit, shit, where is he? Oh God, help me!

She ran without seeing anything, in through the trees, over the road, into the ditch, vanishing into the under-growth. She stumbled over a tree-root and fell headfirst to the ground. Ants crawled onto her face. She shut her eyes and waited to die, but it didn't happen. Instead came sound, the wind in the trees, her own breathing, silence.

He isn't following me, she thought. Then: I've got to find someone else. I've got to get help.

She got to her feet, soundless and hesitant. She brushed off the dirt and ants, listening intently. Where was he?

Not here, not yet. She looked around and realized she wasn't far from Old Gustav.

Crouching slightly, she set off, running cautiously towards Lillsjötorp. Mushrooms squashed beneath her feet. Tree-trunks flew past, brown and unyielding, scratching her hands. She jumped a stream by the abandoned sawmill.

There it was, the red cottage through the trees, Old Gustav's house. She straightened up and ran as fast as she could towards it.

'Gustav!' she screamed. 'Gustav, are you home?'

She rushed onto the veranda and tugged at the door. Locked. She looked around, over to the woodshed where the old man spent most of his time. There was someone there, but it wasn't Gustav.

'I knew you'd come here, you whore!'

Sven rushed towards her, holding something in his hand.

She leaped over the railing of the veranda, landing in Gustav's rose-bed, among the thorns and the heady scent of the flowers.

'Annika, I just want to talk to you! Stop!'

She stumbled back into the forest again, across the stream, round the marsh, but never escaping the sound of panting behind her. Her feet pounded the moss, she flew over rocks and fallen branches, tunnel vision, breathlessness, the world around her reduced to dancing fragments.

I'm running, she thought, I'm not dead. I'm running, I'm alive, it isn't over yet. I've still got a chance. Running isn't so bad, running is the solution. I'm good at running.

She tried to think of it as a tough training session, forcing her adrenalin into line, concentrating on breathing. Breathe, breathe! Her vision returned, the cacophony in her head faded, thoughts began to form.

He can run faster than me, she thought. But he's drunk and I know this forest better than him. He can run better than me on firm ground. I have to stick to the woods.

And she turned north, away from the road. Up there were two lakes, Gorgsjön and Holmsjön, and if she ran round them she'd be able to head east, onto the Sörmland Trail, which would lead her into town behind the ironworks.

Her legs were starting to feel numb. She'd only just eaten half a kilo of mushrooms. She forced her legs to work faster, steeling herself against the pain. She could no longer hear any panting behind her and took a quick glance over her shoulder. Trees and green, sky and rocks.

He can take one of the forest trails and cut me off, she suddenly thought, and stopped instantly.

Her pulse was racing, hard and fast. She listened to the sounds of the forest. Nothing, just the wind.

Where were the forest trails?

Something rustled behind her and she looked back, feeling panic rising again.

Oh God, where's the trail? There's a trail here, where is it?

She tried to breathe deeply, forcing herself to think. What did the trail look like?

It was a loggers' track, they had used it to take the timber out, it had started to regrow, the new growth should be almost two metres high by now.

Head for the new growth, she thought.

At that moment her cat leaped out and rubbed against her legs, and she almost tripped.

'Whiskas, you silly boy, go home!'

She pushed him away with her foot, trying to get him to go.

'Back to Lyckebo! Go on, back to Grandma!'

The cat miaowed and dodged into a thicket.

She headed east, and suddenly the forest became low and tangled. Yes, this was the trail. She waited a few seconds at its edge before setting off. Breathing carefully, she made steady progress. She passed Gorgnäs, but there was no one home. Then Mastrop, no one there. She continued east, heading towards the hikers' trail.

73

He was standing at the last bend before she reached the Sörmland trail. She saw him just three seconds before she reached him and turned sharply north, towards the ironworks pond. Something flashed in his hand, and, realizing what it was, she was terrified. She ran, screaming and stumbling, until she reached the water. She waded out, gasping at the cold, then swam as fast as she could, clambering up the beach on the far side, coughing and spluttering, heading for the buildings. A fence, then more fence, she ran to the left, scrambled up a tree and over the fence, in among the ironworks buildings.

'You can't get away, you fucking slut!'

She looked round, couldn't see him, rushed past a white building, tore open a sun-bleached blue metal door, into the darkness. Blinded, she stumbled into a heap of clinker, spat out a mouthful of ash, went further in, further away, sobbing. The darkness lifted and the shadows around her took shape; a blast furnace, abandoned smelting moulds. Rows of grimy little windows up by the roof, soot, rust. The door she had come through was a rectangle of light in the distance, and the man's silhouette gradually grew larger. She saw the knife glinting in his hand and recognized it: his hunting knife.

She turned and ran, the floor plates rattling as she crossed them, past the holding furnace. Stairs, heading up, darkness, more stairs, she stumbled and hit her knee, light returned, a platform, windows, winches. She hit her head on a pipe.

'There's nowhere else to go now.'

He was breathing hard, his eyes shining with alcohol and hatred.

'Sven,' she sobbed, backing towards the scrap chute. 'Sven, don't do this. You don't really want—'

'You fucking whore!' he said.

At that moment there was a faint miaow from the staircase. Annika peered into the shadows, searching the soot and clinker. The cat – her cat – he'd followed her the whole way!

'Whiskas!' she cried.

Sven took a step nearer and she backed away. The cat came closer, miaowing and purring, trotting along, rubbing against the rusty machinery, playing with a piece of coke.

'Fucking cat,' Sven said hoarsely.

She recognized that voice. It meant he was on the verge of tears.

'You can't leave me like this. What am I going to do without you?'

He was racked with sobs. Annika couldn't reply. Her throat felt tight, incapable of speech. She could see the edge of the knife glinting in a beam of sunlight, aimlessly waving around as Sven began to sob harder.

'Annika, for fuck's sake, I love you!' he cried.

She sensed rather than saw the cat approaching him, stretching up on its back legs to rub its head against his knee. She followed the course of the glinting blade as it swept down towards the cat.

'NO!'

The scream deep as a canyon, no conscious thought. The cat's body flew through the air in a wide arc over the coke intake, leaving a bright red trail of splattered blood after it.

'You bastard!'

She suddenly felt as powerful as fire and iron, like the furnace building she was standing in; glowing with unstoppable fury. Her vision turned red, images reached her mind in slow motion. She bent down and reached for a pipe, rusty and black, far below on the ground, the distance impossible to measure. She grasped it with both hands, strong as iron, and swung it with a force she didn't know she had.

The pipe hit him on the temple. As her sight gradually returned, she watched as it came into contact with his skull, shattering it like an eggshell, his eyes rolling back to show the whites, something squirting from the hole, his arms flying out, the knife sailing through the air like a falling star, his body lurching to the left, tumbling, his legs off the ground, dancing, flailing.

The next blow hit him in the chest, she heard his ribs crack. His whole body left the ground, strafed by iron and fire and rolling slowly over the edge, into the shaft leading into the furnace.

'You fucking bastard!' Annika said.

She tipped him into the blast furnace with one final shove. The last thing she saw was his feet tumbling over the edge.

She dropped the pipe on the floor, and it rattled noisily in the sudden silence.

'Whiskas . . .' she said softly.

He was lying behind the intake belt. His back legs were twitching, his eyes looked into hers. He tried to miaow. She hesitated before picking him up, not wanting to cause him more pain. She sat down and took him in her arms. She rocked him gently as his breathing slowed and came to a rest. His eyes left hers, now glazed and vacant.

Annika wept, rocking the broken little body in her arms. The sounds she made were long howls of anguish and pain. She sat there until her tears were exhausted, as the sun began to go down behind the factory.

The cement floor was hard and cold. She was shaking with cold. Her clothes had almost dried, her legs were numb, and she staggered to her feet, clutching the cat in her arms.

She went cautiously over to the stairs, the dust dancing in the air. It was a long way down and she fumbled towards the light, the shining rectangle. Outside the day was as clear as it had been earlier, just colder, the shadows longer. She stood there for a while, then headed towards the factory gate.

The eight people who still worked at the ironworks were about to go home. Two of them were already in their cars. The others were chatting about something as the foreman locked the gate.

The man who caught sight of her shouted and pointed at her. She was covered in blood from her head to her waist, and she was cradling the cat's body in her arms.

'What the hell's happened?'

The foreman was the first to reach her.

'He's in there,' Annika said flatly. 'In one of the blast furnaces.'

'Where are you hurt? Do you need an ambulance?'

Annika didn't reply, just walked towards the gate.

'Come on, we'll help you.'

The men gathered round her, the two who had already started their cars switched them off again and got out.

The foreman unlocked the gate and led Annika into his office.

'Has there been an accident? Here, in the factory?'

Annika didn't answer. She was sitting holding the cat tightly in her arms.

'Go and check the forty-five-tonner in the old plant,' the foreman said quietly. Three of the men went off.

The foreman sat down beside her, taking a good look at the shocked woman. She was covered in blood, but didn't seem to be injured.

'What's that you're holding?' he said.

'Whiskas,' Annika said. 'He's my cat.'

She leaned over and stroked his soft fur with her cheek, blowing gently into one ear. He was so ticklish, always used to scratch his ear with his back leg when she did that.

'Do you want me to take it?'

She didn't answer, just turned away from the foreman and hugged the cat's body harder. The man sighed and went out.

'Keep an eye on her,' he said to one of the men in the doorway.

She had no idea how long she had been sitting there when another man put his hand on her shoulder. God, what a stereotype, she thought.

'How are you, miss?'

She didn't reply.

'I'm the chief inspector of police in Eskilstuna,' he said. 'There's a dead man in one of the blast furnaces. Do you know anything about that?'

She didn't react. The policeman sat down next to her. He looked at her carefully for several minutes.

'It looks like you've been through something very nasty indeed,' he said eventually. 'Is that your cat?'

She nodded.

'What's her name?'

'His. Whiskas.'

So at least she could talk.

'And what happened to Whiskas?'

She started to cry again. The policeman waited quietly at her side until she stopped.

'He killed him, with his hunting knife,' she said in the end. 'I couldn't do anything to stop him.'

'Who did?'

She didn't answer.

'The men here think that the dead body over there is Sven Matsson, the ice-hockey player. Is that correct?'

She hesitated, then looked up at him and nodded.

'He shouldn't have attacked my cat,' she said. 'He really shouldn't have done anything to Whiskas. Do you understand?'

The policeman nodded. 'Of course,' he said. 'And who are you?'

She sighed and took a deep breath.

'Annika Sofia Bengtzon,' she said.

He took his notebook out of his pocket.

'What's your date of birth?'

She looked into his eyes.

'I'm twenty-four years, five months and twenty days old,' she said.

'Bloody hell,' he said. 'That's very precise!'

'I keep count in my diary,' she said, and bowed her head over her dead cat.

Epilogue

'Yes, hello, this is Karina Björnlund. I hope I'm not disturbing you?'

The Prime Minister sighed silently.

'No, not at all. What can I do for you?'

'Quite a lot, actually. As you'll understand, this has been a very difficult period for me. In the middle of the election campaign and everything . . .' She tailed off, and the Prime Minister waited for her to go on.

'Well, of course I only spent eight months in the job,' she said, 'so my leaving package isn't very generous.'

Yes, he couldn't dispute that.

'So I was wondering if I could possibly carry on working for the government. I've learned a lot and I've got a lot to contribute.'

The Prime Minister smiled. 'I'm sure you have, Karina. Working at the eye of the hurricane changes us all. I'm sure you'll find a good job before long. No one could possibly doubt your abilities and experience.'

'Nor what I've learned.'

'Absolutely. But you know that government ministers like to choose their own press secretaries themselves. I can't promise anything.'

She giggled. 'Of course you can. Everyone knows you

make the decisions. No one disagrees with anything you say. If they did, they'd be history.'

That's actually true, he thought with amusement. Maybe she wasn't that stupid after all.

'Karina, I understand what you're saying. Okay? You want to stay on, and I'm saying no. Can we agree on that?'

The woman was silent for a few seconds.

'Well, if there was nothing else?' the Prime Minister said, ready to hang up.

'You really haven't got it at all, have you?' Karina Björnlund said quietly.

'Sorry?' He was starting to sound ever so slightly irritated now.

'Perhaps I didn't make myself clear,' Karina Björnlund said. 'This isn't some damn negotiation. I'm telling you that I've learned things during these eight months that are impossible to put a value on. And I'm telling you that I've got a lot to offer, and that I want to carry on working for the government.'

The Prime Minister breathed quietly down the phone, his brain not quite joining the dots. How the hell . . . ? What the fuck had she found out?

'I suggest that you listen very bloody carefully,' the woman said, 'because I'm only saying this once. After this I never want to talk about it again. But I'm not the one who can make that decision.'

His mouth had gone completely dry.

'You're not even a Social Democrat,' he said.

'And what fucking difference does that make?' she said.

Evening Post

Two Surprises in New Government

So the Prime Minister has finally presented his new government. The whole process has been shrouded in secrecy – there wasn't a single leak before the new Cabinet was unveiled at Rosenbad yesterday.

'Ministers are under severe pressure this time,' a source told the *Evening Post*. 'Anyone caught talking to the press in advance is out.'

Among the usual suspects there are two surprises. The new Minister for Foreign Trade, following Christer Lundgren, who was recently appointed head of Swedish Steel in Luleå, is the former head of social services in Katrineholm. He has no previous experience of national politics, but is believed to be a good friend of the Prime Minister.

The second surprise is, if anything, even more astonishing. Karina Björnlund, who is Christer Lundgren's former press secretary, has been appointed as the new Minister for Culture.

'The mass media have become far too commercialized,' the new Culture Minister said in her first statement. 'I want to set up a committee to look into the concentration of media ownership, to make sure that we retain a variety of media voices and avoid ending up with monopolies. The media have too much power, in my opinion.'

The question is, however: how many of their policies will Karina Björnlund and the rest of the new government be able to push through?

This autumn's election saw the worst performance by the Social Democrats in modern times. They will need the support of at least two other parties if they are to stand any chance of getting their policies through parliament and onto the statute book.

Memo from:
The United Provincial Newspapers' Association
Date: 10 November
Subject: General

STUDIO SIX AWARDED THIS YEAR'S PRIZE FOR JOURNALISM

STOCKHOLM (UPNA):

Studio Six, the daily news programme featuring debate and analysis, and broadcast live from Radio House in Stockholm, has been awarded this year's prize for radio journalism.

Studio Six has been awarded the prize for its coverage of the involvement of former Minister for Foreign Trade Christer Lundgren in the murder of a stripper in July this year.

'This is a victory for investigative reporting,' the programme's presenter told UPNA. 'This award shows that it pays to invest in scrupulous editorial practices and talented staff.'

The prize will be presented on 20 November.

Copyright: UPNA

TT Agency Newsflash

Date: 24 February

Subject: Domestic

PORN MAGNATE JAILED

STOCKHOLM (TT): A twenty-nine-year-old man who used to run the sex club Studio Six in Stockholm was sentenced on Tuesday to five and a half years in prison. The man was found guilty of dishonesty to creditors, false accounting and tax fraud, tax crime and obstructing tax control at Stockholm Magistrates' Court.

A twenty-two-year-old woman who is suspected of running the business with the man is still wanted for questioning by the police. The woman, originally from South America, is the subject of an arrest warrant.

Copyright: TT

Swedish Weapons Used in Civil War in Caucasus

In September last year conflict broke out again in a small mountainous republic in the Caucasus. During the past six months more than ten thousand people have been killed in fighting between guerrillas and government forces.

The Swedish Peace and Arbitration Association claims that the government troops are using weapons manufactured by Swedish Weapon Ltd. The accusations were made in an article in today's *Evening Post*.

The government refutes the accuracy of the claim. The Prime Minister's press spokesman made the following statement: 'We are extremely sceptical about the veracity of this information. This republic is subject to a weapons embargo and we are unable to understand how Swedish weapons could have found their way there. The Swedish Government has not and will not be granting export licences for any shipments to the area for the foreseeable future.'

Eskilstuna Courier

23 June

Woman Found Guilty of Manslaughter

ESKILSTUNA: A twenty-five-year-old woman has been found guilty of manslaughter at Eskilstuna Magistrates' Court, for causing the death of ice hockey player Sven Matsson in Hälleforsnäs last year. A probationary sentence was passed.

The prosecution had initially pursued a charge of murder, but the court agreed with the defence case. According to the judge's statement, the victim's abuse of the woman over many years had influenced the decision to apply the lesser charge of manslaughter. The act was also deemed to have been committed at least in part for reasons of self-defence.

'The details of the abuse described over many years in the woman's diary undoubtedly contributed to the outcome of this case,' the woman's lawyer said.

The woman herself did not wish to comment on the sentence.

'She has made a whole new life for herself since this tragic event,' her lawyer said. 'She now lives in Stockholm, and was yesterday offered a permanent contract of employment, on the same day sentence was passed.'

(EC)

THE END

Liza Marklund on *Exposed*

I spent the summer of 1994 working for the *Expressen* evening paper in Stockholm. Most people in Sweden probably remember the heatwave, and the fact that the national football team almost went all the way in the World Cup in America. My memories are dominated by completely different things. It was the sixth summer I had spent at *Expressen*, and it ended up being my last.

I had been on maternity leave following the birth of my third child, and when I returned I was one of very few permanent members of staff working during the heatwave. As a result, I ended up covering the story when it emerged that the head of the Swedish Confederation of Professional Employees, Björn Rosengren, had visited a sex club, Tabu, three years earlier.

The story began that spring when *Dagens Nyheter*, one of the two big Stockholm broadsheets, published a long article on the club itself. A few days later this was followed up by an exclusive on the front page. During the course of his research the reporter, Peter Bratt, had uncovered a bill for 55,600 kronor, signed for by the head of the professional workers' union, Björn Rosengren, and paid for using a union bank card. And now Rosengren had come forward to explain what had happened.

It was very embarrassing that he had been to a sex club, and extremely unfortunate that the union had paid, but everything had been sorted out in the end.

Björn Rosengren explained that on the evening of 3 September 1991 he had eaten dinner at Café Opera with an American businessman in the ventilation industry. After the meal the American wanted to go on somewhere, so they jumped into a taxi, and the driver had dropped them off at a nightclub called Tabu.

Björn Rosengren and the American ordered champagne. Three quarters of an hour after they arrived at the club, a naked woman came over to them, and that was when Björn Rosengren realized what sort of place it was, and he paid the bill and left.

It wasn't until the following day that he realized that the club had cheated him. The bill should have been for 600 kronor, not 55,600. With the help of a lawyer, also named Björn Rosengren (what a coincidence!), he eventually negotiated the amount down to 'below 10,000 kronor', and paid with his own money.

No more was written about the story in the press. It looked like it was done and dusted.

Then several weeks later the other big evening paper, *Aftonbladet*, published an entirely different version of events during the night of 3 September 1991. They printed a photograph of a young, blonde Swedish woman with her back to the camera, a tie hanging down her back.

She said that she had been at Café Opera with a female American friend. After a while an American man came over and joined them, then a few minutes later Björn Rosengren came over as well. He was happy and drunk and gave her his tie. When the bar closed at three o'clock the four of them got into a huge white limousine and went on to the Tabu sex club. Björn Rosengren

538

fell down the stairs into the club, then vanished into one of the private rooms with a naked Asian girl. The women and the American man found the whole thing embarrassing and were driven home by the chauffeur, who then returned to pick up Björn.

The article was written by the reporter Bengt Michanek.

At *Expressen* our reaction was one of complete panic. We were way behind on the story, and I was given the job of trying to catch up and find something new. I went into my office and thought for a while. Either the young woman was lying, or Björn Rosengren was. It was as simple as that.

So who was in a position to confirm what had actually happened?

The staff at Café Opera obviously had no idea what had happened after they closed. Maybe the guy at the hotdog kiosk in Östermalm would remember a big white limo, but three years later? That was pretty unlikely, and he wouldn't have known where they were going. The naked Asian girl would probably remember, but where was she? And how credible a witness was she?

Which left one person who must have been sober: the driver of the limo. And there ought to be some sort of receipt for payment of the trip. I started making some phone-calls, asking questions, trying to feel my way forward. To my surprise I got lucky almost straight away.

Björn Rosengren turned out to be a big customer of the limo company Freys Hyrverk. He spent up to quarter of a million kronor on limos each year, even though the union provided him with a car.

And I found out something else interesting: only three weeks after the now infamous night at Tabu, Freys Hyrverk went bust. I got hold of the official receiver at his summer cottage down in Skåne and was told that there were no suspicions of tax evasion or anything else illegal concerning the bankruptcy, which meant that all documentation surrounding the case was in the public domain. They were gathering dust in a massive storage facility in South Hammarby Harbour.

I went out there the next day and discovered twenty-six metres of shelving full of old invoices and other documents. After an hour or so I found it: the order form and receipt from Freys Hyrverk showing that a customer called Rosengren had booked a limo from Café Opera on 4 September 1991 at 3.22 in the morning.

After that everything happened pretty quickly.

Björn Rosengren had clearly not been telling the truth about that night at Tabu, but that wasn't why he had to resign.

The board of the Confederation of Professional Employees had no idea that he had a contract with Freys. They didn't know that their chairman, his family, and people at the top of the Social Democratic Party hierarchy had been travelling around for years in limos paid for by the union's members. And that was the straw that broke the camel's back.

On 19 July 1994, Björn Rosengren resigned as chair of the Confederation of Professional Employees. The press conference where he announced his decision was well-attended, all the main media were there. I saw the union's head of information go round greeting people: he smiled rather sadly as he shook hands with Peter Bratt from *Dagens Nyheter* and Bengt Michanek from *Aftonbladet*, and then he reached me.

When I said my name his face darkened, contorted with rage. He yanked his hand back and shouted:

'HAVE YOU ANY IDEA WHAT YOU'VE DONE?!'

I took a couple of steps back and tried to say something,

but before I found the right words he had turned round and was marching off through the room, fuming.

Afterwards I thought a lot about this.

Why was the head of information so angry with me in particular? Bratt had written that Rosengren had been in a sex club. Michanek had written that he had disappeared into a private room with a naked Asian girl. All I had written was that the man had taken a few car journeys.

In the end I reached the conclusion that it was easiest to blame me. I was twenty years younger than the others, and I was also female.

But the worst was yet to come.

Once Björn Rosengren had resigned there was a campaign to distort the truth about the media's coverage of the case. There was a rumour that Bengt Michanek and I had been the victims of 'planted' stories – that we had been tricked or bribed to write our articles. The rumour became more and more widespread until it ended up becoming the established truth.

Worst of all, as usual, was the radio programme *Studio Ett* (Studio One).

I was in Gothenburg, covering the murder of a young woman in a cemetery, when one of the programme's presenters called me to get me to answer for what I'd done. Then they set loose a whole group of liars who made up stories on the radio.

At that point, Bengt Michanek and I did something that reporters on rival papers never usually do: we met and laid all our cards on the table.

And this is what really happened:

As early as the morning of 4 September, the day after the visit to the Tabu sex club, *Aftonbladet*'s editors already knew the whole story.

The girl with the tie was going out with someone who

541

worked on the paper, and she told him everything when she got home that morning.

An article was written, about the union boss going to a sex club, and it was considered for publication for several days, but in the end the decision was taken not to publish. The reason was that the story was thought to be too sordid and too private. Björn Rosengren had been drunk and not in full control of his faculties, and there was no public interest in exposing his personal misery.

Three years later, when it came out that he had paid for the whole thing with union money, the story looked completely different. The only problem was that the girl with the tie had moved to the USA and no one knew where she was. It took a couple of weeks to track her down, which was why the article was so slow appearing.

As far as my own articles were concerned, I didn't speak to a single person about what I was doing or what I was thinking of writing. Not even my news editors knew who I was calling or what I was working on.

No one influenced what I wrote, not even my bosses at the paper. It was all the result of my own initiative, entirely my own work.

Together, Bengt Michanek and I wrote a long article for our union paper, *Journalisten*, where we explained exactly what had really happened. And after that the lies did actually stop.

Everything turned out okay in the end, but afterwards I thought a lot about the forces that had been set in motion during and after Björn Rosengren's visit to Tabu. It was abundantly clear that men were prepared to do whatever it took to protect their power and influence.

I was able to withstand the pressure heaped upon me because I had been working for ten years and knew exactly what I was doing. But what would have happened if I had written those articles during my first summer at the paper? How would I have handled the attacks and lies?

These events and thoughts formed the basis for this book, *Exposed*.

When it was first published in Sweden, in 1999, a branch of the Confederation of Professional Employees, the Swedish National Union of Local Government Officers, named me Author of the Year.

It's funny the way things turn out.

Liza Marklund
Stockholm, April 2011

Author's Acknowledgements

This is fiction. The *Evening Post* newspaper does not exist, but it bears traces of many different actual media organizations.

The novel's depiction of Swedish government departments, their areas of responsibility and geographic locations is largely based upon the situation that existed before 1999.

All the characters are entirely the product of the author's imagination. Any similarities to real people are purely coincidental. However, a number of political figures appear under their real names. These names are taken from historical records of the Social Democratic Party's espionage on the population of Sweden. The details of this activity depicted in the novel are based on previously published facts. The conclusion of the IB affair and its repercussions as shown in the novel are, however, entirely fictional.

My sources for information about the IB affair are: *Folket i Bild Kulturfront* (People in Focus) no. 9, 1973, by Jan Guillou and Peter Bratt; *Kommunistjägarna* (The Communist Hunters) by Jonas Gummesson and Thomas Kanger (Ordfront förlag); *Aftonbladet*, supplement 3/12 1990, 'Sanningen om den Svenska neutraliteten' (The

Truth About Swedish Neutrality), by Jonas Gummesson and Thomas Kanger; item on TV4 News broadcast during the 1998 election campaign.

Information about and interpretation of tarot cards is taken from Gerd Ziegler's book *Tarot, själens spegel* (Tarot, the Mirror of the Soul) (Vattumannen förlag).

Details concerning the management of a sex club are taken from Isabella Johansson's biography *En strippas bekännelse* (Confessions of a Stripper).

I would also like to thank the following, who have been kind enough to answer my occasionally bizarre questions: Jonas Gummesson, head of domestic news for TV4, for source material, proofreading and information about Swedish espionage, both domestic and foreign; Dr Robert Grundin of the Department of Forensic Medicine in Stockholm, for an introduction to the work of the department; Sven-Olov Grund, head of the technical unit of Stockholm Police, for his patient explanations of the department's work; Claes Cassel, press spokesman for the Stockholm Police, for a guided tour of police headquarters; Kaj Hällström, a pattern-maker at Hälleforsnäs foundry, for a tour of the site and for advice on the terminology of forging and blast furnaces; Eva Wintzel, a district prosecutor in Stockholm, for legal advice and analysis; Kersti Rosén, press ombudsman, and Eva Tetzell, section head of the Broadcasting Commission, for advice and analysis of questions of media ethics; Birgitta Wiklund, head of information at the Ministry of Defence information department, for explanations of public access and postal routines within the ministry; Nils-Gunnar Hellgren, departmental secretary in the Foreign Ministry's courier office, for background and regulations governing diplomatic couriers and bags; Peter Rösch, winner of the Round Gotland race, for sailing terminology; Olov Karlsson, head editor of TV Norrbotten, for detailed information about Piteå; Maria Hällström and Catarina Nitz for details about Södermanland; Lotta Snickare, head of management training at FöreningsSparbanken, for ongoing creative discussions; Emma Buckley, my fantastic editor at Transworld; my agent Niclas Salomonsson and his staff at Salomonsson Agency.

And, last but not least, Tove Alsterdal, dramatist, who reads everything first of all: a genius sounding-board, reader and critic.

Any mistakes or errors that have crept in are entirely my own.

Liza Marklund

Name: Eva Elisabeth Marklund (which only the bank statement calls her. To the rest of the world, she's Liza).

Family: Husband and three children.

Home: A house in the suburbs of Stockholm, and a town-house in southern Spain.

Born: In the small village of Pålmark in northern Sweden, in the vast forests just below the Arctic Circle.

Drives: A 2001 Chrysler Sebring LX (a convertible, much more suitable for Spain than Pålmark).

Five Interesting Facts About Liza

1. She once walked from Tel Aviv to London. It took all of one summer, but she made it. Sometimes she hitchhiked as well, sometimes she sneaked on board trains. When her money ran out she took various odd jobs, including working in an Italian circus. Sadly she had to give that up when it turned out she was allergic to tigers.

2. Liza used to live in Hollywood. Not because she wanted to be a film star, but because that was where her

first husband was from. In the early 1980s she had a two-room apartment on Citrus Avenue, a narrow side-street just a couple of blocks from Mann's Chinese Theatre (the cinema on Hollywood Boulevard with all the stars' hand and footprints). She moved back to Sweden to study journalism in Kalix.

3. She was once arrested for vagrancy in Athens. Together with fifty other young people from all corners of the world she was locked in a garage full of motorbikes. But Liza was released after just quarter of an hour: she had asked to meet the head of police, commended him on his work, and passed on greetings from her father, the head of police in Stockholm. This was a blatant lie: Liza's father runs a tractor-repair workshop in Pålmark.

4. Liza's eldest daughter is an actress and model. Annika, who lends her name to the heroine of Liza's novels, was the seductress in the film adaptation of Mikael Niemi's bestseller *Popular Music from Vittula*. Mikael and Liza have also been good friends from the time when they both lived in Luleå in the mid-1980s. Mikael was one of Liza's tutors when she studied journalism in Kalix.

5. Liza got married in Leningrad in 1986. She married a Russian computer programmer to help him get out of the Soviet Union. The sham marriage worked; he was able to escape, taking his brother and parents with him. Today the whole family is living and working in the USA.

Liza's Favourites

Book: *History* by Elsa Morante

Film: *Happiness* by Todd Solondz

Modern music: Rammstein (German hard rock)

Classical music: Mozart's 25th Symphony in G-minor. And his Requiem, of course.

Idols: Nelson Mandela, Madeleine Albright and Amelia Adamo (the Swedish media queen).

Liza's Top Holiday Destinations

1. North Korea. The most isolated country in the world, and the last iron curtain. Liza has seen it from the outside, looking into North Korea from the South, at the Bridge of No Return on the 38th parallel.

2. Masai Mara, Kenya. Her family co-owns a safari camp in the Entumoto valley.

3. Rarotonga, the main island in Cook archipelago in the South Pacific. The coolest paradise on the planet.

4. Los Angeles. Going 'home' is always brilliant.

5. Andalucia in southern Spain. The best climate in Europe, dramatic scenery, fantastic food and excellent wine. Not too far away, and cheap to fly to!

Turn the page for a sneak preview
of Liza Marklund's gripping,
multi-award-winning thriller,
THE BOMBER – coming soon

'*The Bomber* is a classic international thriller:
sharply written, briskly paced, politically
intriguing, and psychologically astute.
It's no accident that Liza Marklund is
one of the most popular crime
writers of our time.'
PATRICIA CORNWELL

Prologue

The woman who was soon to die stepped cautiously out of the door and glanced quickly around. The hallway and stairwell behind her were dark, she hadn't bothered to switch on the lights on her way down. She paused before stepping down onto the pavement, as if she felt she were being watched. She took a few quick breaths and for a few seconds her white breath hung around her like a halo. She adjusted the strap of the handbag on her shoulder and took a firmer grasp of the handle of her briefcase. She hunched her shoulders and set off quickly and quietly towards Götgatan. It was bitterly cold, the sharp wind cutting at her thin nylon tights. She skirted round a patch of ice, balancing for a moment on the kerb of the pavement. Then she hurried away from the street-lamp and into the darkness. The cold and the shadows were muffling the sounds of the night: the hum of a ventilation unit, the cries of a group of drunk youngsters, a siren in the distance.

The woman walked fast, purposefully. She radiated confidence and expensive perfume. When her mobile phone suddenly rang she was thrown off her stride. She stopped abruptly, glancing quickly around her. Then she bent down, leaning the briefcase against her right leg, and started searching through her handbag. Her movements were suddenly irritated, insecure. She pulled out the phone and put it to her ear. In spite of the darkness and shadows there was no mistaking her reaction. Irritation was replaced by surprise, then anger, and finally fear.

When the conversation was finished the woman stood for a few seconds with the phone in her hand. She lowered her head, clearly thinking hard. A police-car drove slowly past her, the woman looked up at it, watchful, following it with her eyes as it went away. She made no attempt to stop it.

She had clearly reached a decision. She turned on her heel and started to retrace her steps, going past the wooden door she had come out of and carrying on to the junction. As she waited for a night-bus to pass she looked up, her eyes following the line of the street to the square, Vintertullstorget, and beyond to the Sickla Canal. High above loomed the main Olympic arena, Victoria Stadium, where the summer games were due to start in seven months' time.

The bus went past, the woman crossed the broad sweep of Ringvägen and started to walk down Katarina Bangata. Though her face was expressionless, her fast pace let on that she was freezing. She crossed the pedestrian bridge over Hammarby Canal to reach the media village of the Olympic Park. With quick, slightly jerky movements she hurried on towards the Olympic Stadium. She decided to take the path beside the water although it was further, and colder. The wind from the Baltic was ice-cold, but she didn't want to be seen. The darkness was dense, and she stumbled a few times.

She turned off by the post office and pharmacy towards the training area and jogged the last hundred metres towards the stadium. When she reached the main entrance she was out of breath and angry. She pulled the door open and stepped into the darkness.

'Say what you want to say, and be quick about it,' she said, looking coolly at the figure emerging from the shadows.

She saw the raised hammer but didn't have time to feel any fear.

The first blow hit her left eye.

Saturday 18 December

The sound reached her in the middle of a bizarre sexual dream. She was lying on a bed of glass on a spaceship, Thomas was on top of her. Three presenters from the radio programme *Studio Six* were standing alongside them, watching expressionlessly. She was desperate for a pee.

'You can't go to the toilet now, we're on our way into space,' Thomas said, and, looking through the big panoramic window, she saw he was right.

The second ring tore the cosmos to shreds, leaving her sweaty and thirsty in the darkness. The ceiling loomed above her in the gloom.

'Answer the bloody thing before it wakes the whole house,' Thomas grumbled from the mess of pillows.

She twisted her head to see the time: 03.22. The excitement of the dream vanished in a single breath. Her arm, heavy as lead, reached for the phone on the floor. It was Jansson, the night-editor.

'The Victoria Stadium's gone up. Burning like fuck. Our reporter's out there for the night edition, but we need you for the next edition. How soon can you get there?'

She took several breaths, letting the information sink in, feeling adrenalin rolling like a wave through her body and up into her brain. The Olympic Stadium, she thought. Fire, chaos. Bloody hell. South of the city centre. Should she take the southern bypass or the Skanstull bridge?

'How are things looking in town, are the roads okay?'

Her voice sounded rougher than she would have liked.

'The southern bypass is blocked. The exit by the stadium has collapsed, but that's all we know. The Södermalm tunnel is shut off, so you'll have to go above ground.'

'Who's doing pictures?'

'Henriksson's on his way, and the freelancers are already there.'

Jansson hung up without waiting for a reply. Annika listened to the dead crackle on the line for a few seconds before letting the phone fall to the floor.

'So what is it this time?'

She sighed silently before replying.

'Some sort of explosion at the Olympic Stadium. I've got to go. It'll probably take all day.'

She paused before adding:

'And all evening.'

He muttered something inaudible.

Carefully she extricated herself from Ellen's slightly damp pyjamas. She breathed in her daughter's scent, her skin sweet, her mouth sour, her thumb firmly lodged between her lips, then she kissed the child's soft hair. The girl stretched happily, then rolled up into a ball, three years old and utterly content, even in her sleep. She dialled for a taxi with a heavy hand, climbing out of the numbing warmth of the bed and sitting on the floor.

'A car to Hantverkargatan 32 please. Bengtzon. It's urgent. To the Olympic Stadium. Yes, I know it's on fire.'

**Read the complete book –
available December 2011**

THE BOMBER
LIZA MARKLUND

SEVEN DAYS. THREE KILLINGS. ONE WOMAN WHO KNOWS TOO MUCH...

Crime reporter **Annika Bengtzon** is woken by a phonecall in the early hours of a wintry morning. An explosion has ripped apart the Olympic Stadium. And a victim has been blown to pieces.

As Annika delves into the details of the bombing and the background of the victim, there is a second explosion.

When her police source reveals they are hot on the heels of the bomber, Annika is guaranteed an exclusive with her name on it. But it soon becomes clear that she has uncovered too much, as she finds herself the target of a deranged serial killer...

'Edge-of-your-seat suspense'
Harlan Coben

'Nail-biting action and excitement'
Daily Express

The number one international bestseller
AVAILABLE DECEMBER 2011

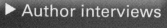